The Tent
of
Fine Linen

Also by Corinne Brixton

THROUGH MARTHA'S EYES
ALTARS OF STONE
published by Matador

All profits to Tearfund
Registered Charity No.265464 (England & Wales)

The Tent

of

Fine Linen

Book Two of
The Line of Shem Trilogy

Corinne Brixton

Matador
9 Priory Business Park,
Wistow Road, Kibworth Beauchamp,
Leicestershire. LE8 0RX
Tel: 0116 279 2299
Email: books@troubador.co.uk
Web: www.troubador.co.uk/matador
Twitter: @matadorbooks

ISBN 978 1838594 558

British Library Cataloguing in Publication Data.
A catalogue record for this book is available from the British Library.

Printed and bound by CPI Group (UK) Ltd, Croydon, CR0 4YY
Typeset in 11pt Aldine401 BT by Troubador Publishing Ltd, Leicester, UK

Matador is an imprint of Troubador Publishing Ltd

To the glory of the One
who is the ultimate
High Priest, Redeemer and King.

'In The Tent of Fine Linen, Corinne Brixton has once again capitalised impressively on the biblical stories' powerful appeal. Using the ingenious narrative device of re-telling the biblical story from Moses to David through the eyes of 'minor' characters (Ithamar, Naomi and Abigail), she has combined careful research with literary imagination and verve. I was struck by her ability to "join the dots" of the biblical narrative intelligently, and I enjoyed her characterisation, and her use of conversation and point of view, to bring events to life. There is real insight in her understanding of how Israel nurtured its memory of its origins and identity through families. The style is nicely tinged with a certain biblical "otherness". Above all, this is an invitation into a closer engagement with Scripture. There is much to enjoy and learn from here!'

Prof. Gordon McConville, *Professor of Old Testament Theology, University of Gloucestershire;*
author of "Exploring the Old Testament" and "Deuteronomy" (Apollos Old Testament Commentary)

'Corinne Brixton is a wise and experienced guide to the Christian life. This is a book which I hope will introduce many to the riches of the Bible, and help them to understand it better.'

Rt. Revd. Graham Tomlin, *Bishop of Kensington and President of St Mellitus College;*
author of "The Seven Deadly Sins and How to Overcome Them" and "Looking Through The Cross"

'This novel takes some of the most dramatic stories from the Old Testament and brings them to life, giving the reader a more detailed understanding of Scripture. Corinne Brixton's painstaking research has been seamlessly woven into the narrative to make a compelling read. It's a great story, plus skilfully demonstrates the working of God in the lives of ordinary men and women to bring about His loving designs.'

Revd. Clive Gardner, *Team Vicar of St Mark's, Wimbledon*

Acknowledgements

I could not have written this book without the careful study of the Biblical text that has been previously accomplished by others, who have published their scholarly findings in commentaries and other books. Many of their insights have been incorporated into the writing of *The Tent of Fine Linen,* and I am indebted to them for sharing their learning. The main sources of information are listed in the Bibliography at the end. Thanks also go to: the members of *Writers Inc,* who have helped me to hone my writing skills; Clive Gardner and Angie Blanche, who read and commented on the manuscript as it was evolving; Geoff Burnes, Sue Dowler and Cairine Hart, for their excellent proof-reading; Peter Warne, for using his extraordinary artistic gifts to create the cover design.

In addition to all those mentioned above, I will always and most chiefly be grateful to and in awe of the God who has revealed Himself in Scripture and in the lives of flawed men and women down through history.

Foreword

The Line of Shem trilogy does not seek simply to retell stories that Scripture has already made memorable. It has a two-fold aim. Firstly, to provide background to and commentary on some of those stories, set in a world far removed from our own culture and time and involving many customs and details with which modern readers may be unfamiliar. Secondly, to build up, over the course of the three books, an overview of the main characters and events of the Old Testament. It will do this by taking ten 'bit-part players' from pivotal stories across the fifteen hundred years or so of Old Testament history.

Generally, story-telling in Scripture differs in a number of ways from modern styles. One particular difference is that the Bible is fairly scant when it comes to the internal feelings and thoughts of those involved. *The Line of Shem* has, therefore, deliberately chosen characters peripheral to the main stories to lessen the risk of any unintended misrepresentation of the 'main players' in Scripture. In *Altars of Stone,* we met three characters in the book of Genesis. In *The Tent of Fine Linen,* we meet three more characters: Ithamar, one of the sons of Aaron; Naomi, the mother-in-law of Ruth; and Abigail, one of the wives of David. The events described start in the book of Exodus and go through to the start of the first book of Kings. Each chapter starts with a quote from the original story in Scripture.

The Biblical accounts on which this book is based have been taken as history. This is, after all, what much of the Old Testament claims to be (the text generally making it clear when it is not). Its events are set in a real geographical setting, with plenty of historical details that relate to the times and places in which those stories are set.[1] As one writer has helpfully pointed out, 'the Old Testament has consistently been shown to be a reliable guide in those areas where it can actually be tested. The accounts of personalities and conflicts are often corroborated by sources outside the Bible.'[2] The traditional view of the emergence of the nation of Israel through the Exodus has therefore been maintained.[3]

Every effort has been made to be as accurate as possible in the historical details included. However, various assumptions have had to be made at times. Notes at the end of each chapter have therefore been included to indicate, as far as possible, where and why any assumptions or choices have been made. This will hopefully enable the reader to distinguish more easily between what comes directly from Scripture and what is artistic licence or conjecture. The notes also contain, where appropriate, historical or archaeological details. It is not necessary to read the notes to enjoy the book, but hopefully they will enrich the experience and enlighten the reader.

A few additional comments are also worth making. Firstly, the personal name of God, *Yahweh* (which translates the Hebrew YHWH), has been used throughout. In most modern Bible translations, YHWH is rendered *the LORD*, reflecting the Jewish practice of reverencing the name of God by not speaking it. It is not clear when this became common practice among the Jews, but certainly there is nothing within the Scriptures themselves to imply that this was the practice during Old Testament times. Therefore, the characters in the stories use the actual, revealed name of God, although *the LORD* is used in the Bible references at the beginning of each chapter.

Secondly, in the maps that have been included, any scales are in miles for the convenience of the reader. The language employed throughout the book has attempted to avoid anachronisms.

Thirdly, it is worth remembering that just because the Bible records something, it doesn't mean it approves of it, even if there is no specific comment to that effect within the text itself. Certainly there are within the Old Testament a number of stories that modern readers may find deeply troubling. Sometimes this is because we *are* meant to be troubled by the behaviour described, as it runs contrary to the revealed will of God. At other times, it may be our modern perspectives that need to be challenged. As always, the whole of Scripture must be our guide. As the commentator Dale Ralph Davis helpfully states:

> *'The Bible is our authority, the whole Bible. But it is strange, isn't it, that we who pride ourselves on holding to the full authority of Scripture have our own way of negating its authority? That is, we simply ignore a good bit of it, especially those sticky parts of the Old Testament that embarrass our enlightened sensibilities.'* [4]

Fourthly—and most importantly—there is, of course, only one place where these stories are told with complete reliability and without error: the Word of God. Any thoughts, words or actions beyond the Biblical narratives are a work of imagination. Hopefully, however, this book will leave readers with what has been gained in the writing of it: a deeper love for the Scriptures and for the God who inspired them to be written down.

Notes

1. *See, for example, Kenneth Kitchen's extensively-researched book, On the Reliability of the Old Testament (Grand Rapids: Eerdmans, 2003).*
2. *Chris Sinkinson, Time Travel to the Old Testament (Nottingham: IVP, 2013), p. 29. He also adds, 'Of course, the further back we go, the less evidence remains, but there is still enough to remind us that we are dealing with some form of history, even in its earliest writings.'*
3. *The following quote concerning different theories about the emergence of*

Israel as a nation may be of help: '...each proposal depends on a subjective manipulation of the text to suit the theory. The traditional view, that the Israelites who came from Egypt under the leadership of Moses were the descendants of Abraham and that under the command of Joshua they engaged the Canaanite population, is not only reasonable; it lets the Hebrew authors say what they want to say. After all, the ancient writers were much nearer to the original events than we are and in a much better position to know what happened. There is no doubt the Israelite authors who wrote these accounts perceived what they wrote to be factually based and not merely fiction.' Daniel I. Block, Judges, Ruth (New American Commentary), (Holman Reference, 1999), p30.

4. *Dale Ralph Davis, Judges (Christian Focus, 2010), p58.*

Ithamar

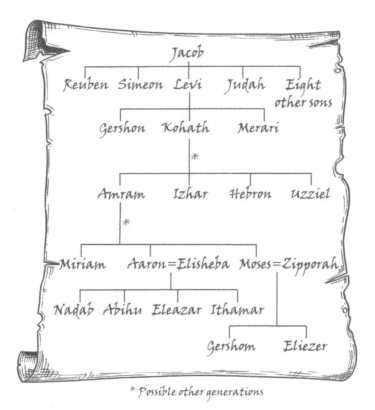

* Possible other generations

I

The Israelites groaned in their slavery and cried out, and their cry for help because of their slavery went up to God. God heard their groaning and he remembered his covenant with Abraham, with Isaac and with Jacob. So God looked on the Israelites and was concerned about them. (Exodus 2:23-25)

Mud and *misery*. The two words summed up Ithamar's life. His years were little more than a score and ten and yet he felt far older. His whole body often ached after a day of hauling heavy buckets under the harsh and pitiless Egyptian sun. He emptied his latest load of wet dirt into a large shallow pit dug into the baked earth, and stood for several moments, catching his breath. A deep, ever-present weariness pervaded both his bones and his being. *Would his days amount to no more than this? A life spent by the Egyptians as they wished and for their gain?*

'Don't stand idle for too long,' whispered a voice behind him. 'Khamet is watching you.'

Ithamar glanced across at the taskmaster who was seated, rod in hand, far enough away to be out of earshot but close enough to scrutinise their movements. The Egyptian rose to his feet, slowly and deliberately. His white linen shenti, which fell from the girdle around his waist to his knees, was devoid of any mud. He fixed Ithamar with a disdainful gaze, as if to make clear that his inaction had been noted.

Ithamar turned his back on him and bent over, grunting and thrusting a tired arm down into the brown mud left in the bottom of his bucket and scraping out the remnants into the pit. His eyes met those of his brother Eleazar, three years his senior, who was by now also laboriously emptying out his own bucket. 'They forget the debt

3

they owe us,' muttered Ithamar. Four hundred years had been more than enough for the Egyptians to turn sojourners into slaves.

'You are right,' replied Eleazar, as they both straightened up and began their walk back towards the irrigation canal fed by the waters of the Nile. 'But even if the Egyptians have forgotten Joseph, Yahweh has not forgotten us.'

Ithamar didn't respond, so they walked in silence. The scorching sandy earth beneath their feet didn't bother him. His feet were toughened by years of walking barefoot and his mud-caked soles felt little. *Yahweh has not forgotten us.* Eleazar shared the confidence of their father, Aaron, but Ithamar wasn't so sure. He knew the stories of their ancestors—of Jacob, Isaac and Abraham—and yet it was the Egyptians' gods that seemed to stalk and rule the land. *Amun-Ra and Osiris are nothing,* his father had said. And yet the strange deities seemed to loom large, like vast and brooding shadows, whilst Yahweh seemed hidden and deaf to their groaning.

'I wish we were working in the fields instead,' grumbled Ithamar eventually.

'I do not imagine it is any less gruelling. Taskmasters are everywhere.'

Ithamar had to grudgingly agree. Eleazar might not be the eldest of his brothers, but was usually the one who spoke the most sense. 'At least I'd look less like a pig in its filth.' He then glanced over at Eleazar. His loin cloth—their only clothing out in the brickfields— was grubby and far from white, and even his beard and hair were matted with the sweat and mud that covered much of them. He knew his own appearance would be no different. Their eyes met, and for a moment they shared a rare laugh. After a few more paces, they came to a halt.

'You took your time,' said a fellow Israelite standing near the canal and beside the patch of damp ground from which the mud was being dug. But his tone was not harsh.

'We were quick enough, Shimron,' said Eleazar as he set his bucket down, 'given the sun is overhead—and it is the hottest time of year.'

'The day's quota is not lessened because of the heat,' replied the older man with a sigh. 'But at least the longer days match the slower pace and give us some chance of meeting the number.'

'We will try to be quicker next time,' said Eleazar, 'though for your sake, not the Egyptians'.'

As they began refilling their buckets, Shimron headed back to the pits. He was the foreman whom the Egyptians had appointed over their team, responsible for ensuring that two thousand bricks were made each day. However much Ithamar might have wished for an easier lot, he had no desire to change places with Shimron. He was nearer to Khamet's rod and the first to feel it on his back if the hefty quota was not reached. And they had all heard stories of foremen whose severe beatings had proven fatal.

As they trudged back, Ithamar could see Abihu, one of his other two brothers, tramping around in a nearby pit, mixing and kneading mud, water and chopped straw with his feet. The eldest, Nadab, was kneeling a little way off, pouring thick, fermented mixture into brick-moulds. Others of their people stacked or hauled the finished bricks, dried and baked for several days by the hot sun. Although Egyptians also worked on building the storage cities for which their bricks were destined, Pharaoh required of his own people only a month of their labour each year as tax. Theirs was not the unremitting hard toil of foreign slaves.

'What *does* Abihu think he is doing?' whispered Eleazar, as they emptied out their loads again. Ithamar looked up and squinted. His brother had not only ceased treading the mud, but had stepped out onto the slightly raised ground around it and was gazing off to their left. 'He will feel Khamet's displeasure—again—if he is not careful.'

But when Ithamar glanced in the direction of Abihu's gaze, he could see what his brother was staring at. Others further off had ceased work, and were talking together in small knots or running about. *What on earth was happening?* His thoughts were abruptly interrupted by a sharp *thwack* accompanied by a yelp.

'You lazy!' screamed Khamet, bringing his rod swiftly down on Abihu's back for a second time. 'You work harder! You all excrement of the gods!' He then cursed Abihu loudly in his own tongue.

Ithamar's grasp of Egyptian was nowhere near as good as that of his father, but he was almost sure Khamet had shrieked, among other things, *May Horus rain down scorpions upon your buttocks and manhood. Or something similar.*

Khamet's head turned in the direction of the disruption—and he finally seemed to realise that something was happening. He hesitated, but then barked at them, 'You work!' before turning on the spot and striding off.

But they didn't. And when Shimron ran towards Nadab, the three brothers hurried to join them. 'Thutmose is dead!' announced their foreman breathlessly.

'How?' asked Abihu.

Shimron shrugged. 'No-one is speaking of any bloodshed. He had, after all, seen fifty-six years of life.'

'Many Egyptians see far fewer,' said Eleazar.

Thutmose was the only pharaoh Ithamar had ever known; his father had known three, all bearing that same name. But there was no need to ask the identity of the new king. Amenhotep was not his father's firstborn, but the death of his brother had left him heir to the throne, and he would be the second pharaoh to bear that name.

'Amenhotep is—what—eighteen, nineteen?' Ithamar asked, looking around at the others.

Shimron cast his eyes to the sky as he pondered. 'He has reigned alongside his father for two years now. I do not believe he has reached his twentieth year.'

'And will he be any different from his father?' asked Eleazar.

'By which you mean,' said Shimron, '*will he treat us any better*?' He paused. 'Nothing I have heard of him suggests our lives will be any easier.'

When Abihu grimaced as his mother embraced him that evening outside their house, Aaron looked steadily at him. 'Have you earned yourself a beating again, my son?'

6

'It was hardly my fault,' protested Abihu with what little vigour he had left. 'Half of those making bricks had stopped working when they heard about Pharaoh.'

Nadab came to his defence. 'His only fault was to be the one standing closest to Khamet!'

'Let me look at it,' fussed Elisheba.

'It is nothing, Mother,' replied Abihu. 'I've known worse.'

Aaron shook his head and sighed. 'You are as impetuous as our father Levi, and your older brother is not much better! You two are as much of a pair as Simeon and Levi.' He pulled up a wooden stool and sat down. At eighty, it was many years since he had been required to labour in the brick-fields for their overlords, but there were still the family herds to be cared for, fish to be caught from the rivers of Egypt, and their vegetables to be tended. And it had been a long day.

The brothers all took the small cakes of dates offered by their mother. As Ithamar chewed the sweet fruit, dried—like the bricks— by the Egyptian sun, he studied his father for a moment. The last rays of the same sun, stealing through gaps between the Israelite houses, picked out small creases on his leathery skin. *As dried and almost as wrinkled as the dates*, he thought to himself. His face was, however, still a noble one, and his body as able as that of many Egyptians half his age.

'And what are our brothers saying about our new pharaoh?' continued Aaron.

'That he will be no better than Thutmose,' replied Eleazar.

'We should rise up and fight for our freedom,' exclaimed Abihu suddenly. 'Now—whilst the country mourns and before Amenhotep strengthens his power.'

'Speak like that and you will get more than a beating,' said Aaron sharply.

'But he is right,' insisted Nadab. 'We are a great people and the Egyptians fear us! We have numbers—'

'And they have chariots!' replied Eleazar. 'Chariots pulled by horses, and bronze spears and swords aplenty!'

'Your brother is right,' said Aaron, looking directly at his eldest sons. 'But we also have the one true God, Yahweh—'

'And yet He does nothing to help us,' interrupted Nadab. 'Maybe He has forgotten us.'

'He has not,' replied his father simply. 'He has neither forgotten nor forsaken us. We continue to multiply despite the heavy yoke the Egyptians lay upon us.' He paused. 'And we have seen the hand of Yahweh in our own family.'

'For all the good it brought,' muttered Abihu under his breath.

Aaron did not hear the remark—or chose to ignore it.

Ithamar collapsed onto the small stool outside the family's mudbrick house. He let out a long sigh as he sat motionless for a moment, his eyes closed. He felt a kiss on his forehead and a cup of water put into his hands.

'You survived another day,' said a sweet voice.

He nodded. 'Just… At least they don't expect us to make bricks at night.' Three years had passed since Amenhotep had taken the throne. His reign had, if anything, been harsher than that of his father. *It is as if he needs to prove his prowess*, Eleazar had commented. The only good thing to come from those years was Keziah. Whereas his three older brothers had married Levite women, a wife from among his mother's tribe of Judah had been chosen for Ithamar. And Ithamar was more than content with his father's choice. He opened his eyes, smiling weakly in the fading sunlight. 'But you will never guess the latest claims of our young pharaoh,' he said, before taking a long draught from the cup.

'Then you will have to tell me,' replied Keziah with a smile, rubbing his aching shoulders gently.

'He proclaims that he singlehandedly killed seven princes in battle at Kadesh.'

'You think it is an empty boast?'

'Even before he became pharaoh he claimed to be able to shoot an arrow through copper as thick as your palm is wide,' replied Ithamar with a raised eyebrow. 'Not to mention having the strength to row faster and further than two hundred men!' He paused. 'It is certainly true, however, that the seven princes are dead. Amenhotep mounted their bodies, upside down, on the prow of his ship, and then on the walls of Thebes on his return.'

Keziah screwed her face up in disgust. 'And the Egyptians think that we are the vulgar ones, a lesser breed.'

Ithamar finished the contents of the cup and handed it back to her, looking around. The settlement in which they lived was noisy and crowded, as it always was when the men were finally allowed to return from their labouring in the last light of the day. Two of their goats picked at the small amount of grass around the house. 'Where is my father?'

The expression on Keziah's face puzzled Ithamar. 'You will have to ask your mother,' she replied simply. 'She is inside with Miriam.' His father's older sister had been widowed some years earlier and was often in their house, as was her firstborn, Hur. Although he was their cousin, he was considerably older.

Ithamar dragged himself to his feet and ambled into the house. His eyes took a few moments to adjust. Reed mats hung over the windows, keeping out both insects and the heat of the day. The women were not in the communal area, furnished only with a few woven rugs on the dirt floor. Reed baskets stood in the corners, holding the family's meagre possessions and stores. He pushed aside the curtain over the doorway into his parent's room. The covering over the window had been pulled back, and both his mother and aunt were sitting on the rug on which his parents normally slept, going through a large pottery bowl of lentils, removing any remaining pods and stalks. They both looked up. 'Did your day go well, my son?' his mother asked. Her voice sounded strained.

Ithamar nodded. 'Well enough—we completed our quota. But where is Father? I did not see him outside.'

His mother stared down at the lentils. 'He has gone to see your uncle.'

'Nahshon?'

'No, not Nahshon,' she replied, seemingly concentrating on an empty pod in her hand.

'Nor any of your mother's brothers,' added Miriam.

After a few moments of silence, Ithamar's confusion suddenly melted into a wide-eyed stare as Miriam and Aaron's younger brother finally came to mind. 'Moses?' he exclaimed with incredulity, his gaze darting back and forth between the women.

Elisheba finally met his eyes and nodded. 'Yes, Moses.'

'But…' Too many questions suddenly filled his mind. 'He…he still lives? Where? Has he sent Father a message?'

'No, your father has not heard from him.'

'But—'

'Yahweh has spoken to your father,' said Miriam.

Only one matter was discussed that evening as the family shared a meal of lentil and onion stew, flavoured with garlic and herbs. There was little the two older women could tell them, however, as they scooped up the contents of the dish with bread baked by Keziah and the other wives.

Where has Father gone? East. That is all I can tell you.

How did God speak to him? He heard His voice.

Why did he leave so suddenly? Yahweh told him to go and he obeyed.

How will he know where to go? The God who spoke to him will guide him.

How long will he be gone? I don't know.

And the question, above all others, burning in Ithamar's mind: *Why has Yahweh sent him to Moses?* I don't know.

The late end to their meal left Ithamar even wearier than usual, as he lay down that night with Keziah in their tiny room within the shared house.

'You did not tell me your father had a brother,' said Keziah softly. Although the darkness in the room was all but complete, Ithamar's arm across his wife told him that she was lying on her side, facing him.

'I never knew him,' he answered. 'He fled Egypt six years before I was born.' He paused. 'It was as if he were dead to us.'

'Your mother spoke earlier of him being brought up in the Egyptian court. I wanted to know more but everyone else in the room seemed to already know of it.' Keziah prodded him playfully.

'Ow!'

'I began to wonder if I had married a man who never tells his wife anything!' Ithamar smiled to himself in the darkness. 'But I know he will now tell me all I want to know.' She tugged at him until he rolled onto his side to face her invisible form.

'Now?' he groaned. 'I want to sleep.'

'Now!' she whispered. 'Or I will give you no rest.'

Ithamar groaned again. 'My wife demands too much, but as she is a good wife I will please her.' He paused again, wondering where to begin. 'Miriam is the eldest of the three, with Aaron next. The first Thutmose was on the throne when Moses was born—'

'But he was the one, wasn't he, who ordered all our baby boys to be thrown into the Nile?'

Ithamar nodded. 'That's right. As our numbers grew ever greater, he began to fear our people. But my grandmother hid Moses for three months in the house. Or so I am told—Father was only two. She couldn't hide him there forever, though, so she took a basket, covered it with pitch, and put it amongst the reeds of the Nile. Miriam must have been seven or eight then, and she was told to wait nearby and keep a watch on the basket. But Hatshepsut came with her maids to bathe in the river. She saw the basket, sent one of her maids to retrieve it and found Moses inside. He was crying, so she felt sorry for him and decided to raise him as her own son, despite knowing he was a Hebrew boy and that her father had commanded them to be drowned.' Ithamar chuckled. 'You'll never guess what happened next though.' He heard an exasperated sigh beside him.

'You ask me to guess once more, despite always telling me I will never be able to do so!'

He chuckled again, and then yawned. 'True! So I will simply tell you. My aunt was bold and went up to pharaoh's daughter, offering to find a Hebrew woman to nurse the baby for her. She did not, of course, say that Moses was her brother! Anyway, Hatshepsut agreed, and maybe you *can* now guess what happened then.'

Keziah thought for a moment. 'Miriam fetched your grandmother…'

'There, see, you *can* guess! And Hatshepsut said that she would pay her to nurse him until he was weaned!'

'An Egyptian princess paying your grandmother to nurse her own son!' She gave a little laugh. 'You are right. I would never have imagined that.'

Ithamar fell silent, and drowsiness began to overtake him. Eventually he added softly, 'That is why my father believes the hand of Yahweh is upon us.'

'What happened then?'

'He was brought up in the palace as the son of Hatshepsut,' he mumbled, 'though he knew he was a Hebrew…' His voice became even quieter. 'Later, when Thutmose's son ruled…' He yawned again.

'The one that Hatshepsut married—her half-brother?'

There was a pause. 'No. The next pharaoh…'

'You mean the third Thutmose, Amenhotep's father?'

'Hmmm,' said Ithamar so softly that Keziah could barely hear him.

She prodded him gently until he groaned yet again. 'What happened? I just want to hear why Moses fled.'

'Moses saw Egyptian beating a Hebrew…killed him. Great crime for foreigner. Thutmose found out…wanted him dead. He escaped.' It went quiet and Ithamar's breathing became slower. If Keziah had any more questions, he didn't hear them.

'Do you remember him—from before?' Ithamar's question hung in the air for several moments, as his mother continued cutting up onions and cucumbers for the evening meal. Moses and Aaron had returned that day, and Ithamar was watching them talking to Nadab and Abihu.

She paused for a moment, wiping her arm across her eyes before glancing briefly across at the men. 'Not like that.'

'What do you mean?'

'I only saw him once or twice, and then, only from a distance. He looked like any other royal. I would not have known he was my husband's brother or even one of our people had Aaron not told me. And yet now, looking at him—' She broke off once more from her chopping. 'Now, I can see both Aaron and his father in him, whilst the Egyptian prince is nowhere to be seen.'

'He *has* changed,' said a voice softly to one side. It was Miriam who had joined them, a pottery bowl filled with choice pieces of lamb cradled in her arms. The safe return of both of her brothers demanded something special, and one of the best animals from their flock had been slaughtered.

When the lamb, together with cumin and coriander, had been added to the huge pot suspended over the fire pit, the family gathered and sat in the cool of the evening and the light of the fire. And whilst the meat bubbled away, filling the air with the rare but rich aroma of braising lamb, they listened as Moses told his story, their usual weariness forgotten.

'I travelled east when I fled the land—' he began.

'Where Thutmose was less likely to find you?' asked Aaron.

Moses nodded. 'Yes, when the pharaohs are bent on conquest, it is to the north that they look, and their fortresses stretch along the route towards Canaan. But our God kept me safe—as He has from my birth. I travelled to Midian, where I met a priest named Jethro.' A smile played across his face. 'But it was his daughters—seven of them—that I met first, at a well. They took me for an Egyptian, but when I helped water their flocks, I was invited to eat with them. I ended up staying, and one of his daughters—Zipporah—was given to me as a wife. She has given me two sons, Gershom and Eliezer.'

'They have not come with you?' asked Elisheba.

Moses shook his head. 'No, they *were* travelling with me, but then I sent them back to Jethro, deciding it would be safer for them.'

The word *safer* did not escape Ithamar's attention. *What lay ahead?*

'For many years I helped pasture Jethro's flocks. I learned to be a shepherd and a father.' Moses paused. 'But I am being called to shepherd far more than sheep and goats, now that Thutmose and the officials who sought my life are all dead. A little over a month ago, I was in the wilderness with the flock, on Mount Horeb, and Yahweh came to me. I was neither seeking nor expecting Him in the desert, but He found me.'

'How did Yahweh appear to you?' asked Nadab eagerly. 'Did you see Him?'

Ithamar straightened up, staring intently at his uncle. *Would Yahweh be like one of the Egyptian gods, with their unearthly marrying of a human body and an animal's head? Surely not! But what then?* He felt a pang of disappointment when Moses shook his head again.

'No, I did not see His form. All I saw was a bush that was burning yet unconsumed by the flames. It was such a strange sight that I went closer.' He paused. 'And that was when I heard a voice calling to me— calling my name—from the midst of the bush.'

The back of Ithamar's neck prickled, and all were still as the night, waiting for Moses to continue.

'The voice told me not to come any closer, but to remove my sandals as I was standing on holy ground. Then He said, *I am the God of your father, the God of Abraham, the God of Isaac, and the God of Jacob.* Fear filled me, and I bowed down, covering my face. He told me that He had seen the affliction and suffering of our people, and heard the cries of pain caused by the taskmasters.'

As Moses paused again, Ithamar's thoughts flitted to Khamet. *So his rod and his beatings had not gone unnoticed by their God!*

'Yahweh then told me that He had come down to deliver us from the power of the Egyptians.' Moses paused and gazed round at them all. 'He is not a God who stands far off. Just as He came down to me in the bush, He is coming to bring us up to a good and spacious land, a land flowing with milk and honey—the land of the Canaanites. He has not forgotten the covenant he made with our father Abraham.'

'He is taking us home,' murmured Aaron.

'But how?' asked Abihu. 'Are we to leave immediately?'

'No,' answered Moses. 'I am to go to Amenhotep with your father.'

14

'And there is none among the Hebrews,' interjected Aaron, looking at his brother, 'who understands the court of Pharaoh as you do. I have always said Yahweh's hand has been on our family, and now we can see His wisdom.'

Miriam smiled. 'It is true! Hatshepsut gave you what we couldn't—an education in the tongue, the ways and the warfare of our oppressors.'

'And now that knowledge is to be used against them!' exclaimed Nadab.

'But it is *Yahweh's* plan, not mine, that will deliver us,' said Moses firmly.

Ithamar studied his uncle. *The Egyptians were a proud and haughty people, and Pharaoh foremost among them. Moses may have been raised by them but he showed none of their pride.* Ithamar had seen only quietness and humility in his father's brother. *Maybe it was forty years in the desert that had done that. Maybe it was meeting Yahweh...* Ithamar's thoughts were interrupted by Moses continuing.

'We are to tell Pharaoh that our God requires us to journey into the desert to sacrifice to Him—'

'Not that we are leaving for Canaan?' interrupted Abihu.

Moses shrugged his shoulders, as a wry smile deepened the lines upon his face. 'We will say what Yahweh tells us to say. Maybe He intends to expose Pharaoh's heart by asking of him the least costly response...'

'We would be an army to match that of Pharaoh!' declared Nadab.

'In numbers only,' said Eleazar quickly.

'But Pharaoh cannot match the hand of Yahweh—the hand of the Creator,' said Aaron.

Moses nodded. 'Battles lie ahead, but not in Egypt. It is Yahweh who will deliver us from Pharaoh's grasp. The descendants of Israel have been here over four hundred years, but now it is time for the God of our fathers to take us back to the land promised to Abraham and to us, his offspring.'

A thrill of exhilaration coursed through Ithamar. Every face was bright with anticipation and every tongue stilled by awe. Eventually Nadab broke the silence. 'When do you confront Pharaoh?'

'Not before we have spoken to the elders of Israel,' replied Moses. 'Yahweh is sending us to them first.'

It was on the second evening after Moses' return that the elders of the twelve tribes were gathered together. As Ithamar and his brothers eagerly awaited the outcome of the meeting, they busied themselves by examining an aging family tent. Moses had already told them that the whole community would need to ready itself for a long journey. The land of Goshen was rich with pasture land, and there had been little need for them to travel with the flocks as their ancestors had done in Canaan. So the tents of Jacob and his family had gradually given way over the years to mudbrick houses.

'That will need patching, Ithamar,' said Nadab, pointing to an area where the goatskin had either worn thin and torn or suffered an accident.

Ithamar looked up sharply and asked with some exasperation, 'Why me?'

'Because Yahweh gave you nimble fingers,' replied Nadab, adding with a grin, 'and because you're the youngest!'

'Sorry, Brother—Nadab's right!' said Eleazar with a laugh. He pointed to another spot. 'And that is not the only place!'

Ithamar managed a wry smile. 'Then one of you can kill and skin the goat!'

All of them had found new vigour since Moses' return, their customary fatigue dispelled by thoughts of freedom. Ithamar's mind, however, was not fully on the tent. His brow suddenly furrowed. 'I know Moses said that he was to ask Pharaoh to let us journey into the desert to worship Yahweh…' he began.

'So?' said Abihu.

'Pharaoh will not agree to that, surely? Any breaks from our labours are only ever for festivals to the Egyptians' gods.'

'And Amenhotep, like all Egyptian pharaohs, believes he is a god,' added Eleazar. 'He will not respond well to foreigners telling him what to do.'

'He will have no choice!' exclaimed Nadab, tugging at another part of the heavy tent to unfold it. 'Father said that Yahweh has given Moses power to perform signs, to prove to the elders that God has sent him. Surely when Pharaoh sees the signs, he will not be able to refuse.'

Eleazar shrugged. 'Maybe. But I doubt it.' He was rarely wrong.

Ithamar suddenly saw movement out of the corner of his eye. He turned his head. 'Here they are!' Moses and Aaron were walking towards them, with Aaron carrying Moses' staff. Nahshon, their mother's brother and the leader of the tribe of Judah, was with them.

'Did it go well with the elders?' asked Eleazar.

Aaron smiled. 'It did. The message that Yahweh has heard his people's cries and is concerned for them gladdened the hearts of all.'

'And even more so,' added Nahshon, smiling broadly, 'when they were told that He will free us from slavery and take us up out of Egypt to the land promised to our father Abraham!' The smile softened into solemnity. 'If any had doubts, they were dispelled when we saw Yahweh's signs—a staff becoming a snake and then a staff again, a hand instantly becoming leprous and then just as suddenly being healed, and water drawn from the Nile falling to the ground as blood. None could deny the hand of our God!'

Moses, however, seemed strangely quiet amidst the jubilation. 'But Pharaoh will be another matter,' he said suddenly. All fell silent. 'Yahweh has told me that he will not let us go—except by being compelled and at great cost.'

Notes

1. *Many sceptics have cast doubt on the Israelites ever having been slaves in Egypt, given their complete absence from Egyptian records. However, the vast majority of papyri records have perished, and pharaohs would never have recorded their defeats on durable stone walls—particularly the successful escape of a huge number of slaves, involving also the utter defeat of the Egyptian army. However, tomb paintings from the 15th Century BC show foreign slaves making bricks under Egyptian taskmasters, mixing water and mud to create moulded bricks which are then dried. This accords well with the narrative in the book of Exodus (e.g. Exodus 1:11-14, 5:1-21).*

2. *Although specific pharaohs are named elsewhere in Scripture (e.g. Jeremiah 44:30 refers to Pharaoh Hophna and Jeremiah 46:2 to Pharaoh Necho), the practice of Egyptian rulers was not to name their enemies in their written records. Traditionally, Moses has been considered as the main author of the first five books of the Bible. Having been brought up in an Egyptian court, he could be expected to follow the same practice, hence the lack of any specific name for pharaohs in both this story and that of Joseph.*

3. *1 Kings 6:1 refers to the commencement of the building of the temple (which has been dated to 966 BC) being in 'the four hundred and eightieth year after the Israelites came out of Egypt'. If this is taken literally, this dates the Exodus to around 1446 BC—the so-called Early Date. However, some scholars take the 480 years to be figurative (twelve generations of forty years), on the grounds that archaeological evidence in Canaan may point to a dating of the Exodus to the reign of Rameses II in the 13th Century BC—the so-called Late Date. (See, for example, the case for the Late Date in K.A.Kitchen, 'On the Reliability of the Old Testament'.) Other scholars, though, see the external evidence as not incompatible with the Early Date, and point towards other Biblical verses and external data as supporting the Early Date. For example, a number of Jubilee cycles (see Leviticus 25:8) mentioned in the Talmud and Judges 11:26 may both point towards a date of around 1406 BC for the start of the conquest, forty years after the Exodus. The Early Date has been used in this account.*

4. *A papyrus from the reign of Amenhotep I (recording an astronomical observation) could, in theory, give accurate dates for Egyptian chronology and dates of the pharaohs, if the location of the observation (and therefore its latitude) are known. However, the papyrus does not record its location, but it is likely to have been in Thebes or in a Delta city such as Memphis or Heliopolis. Depending on which place is assumed, datings roughly 20-25 years apart result. These are referred to as the Low and High chronologies, respectively. The High Chronology has been chosen, as it seems to accord better with the Exodus account (if the Early Date is assumed), and this would mean that the pharaoh of the Exodus would be Amenhotep II, and 'Pharaoh's daughter' could be Hatshepsut, one of the daughters of Thutmose I. An intriguing corollary of these choices is that at some point (possibly during Amenhotep's reign) many images of Hatshepsut were*

destroyed, probably in the belief that erasing all her images would destroy her immortality. Could this have been punishment, after the Exodus, for being the one to save the life of Israel's liberator?

5. A possible problem with the Early Date is that, at that time, the capital was in Thebes, 400 miles south of the likely location of Goshen (in the eastern Nile Delta), where the Israelites lived. How could Pharaoh's daughter be in the vicinity to pull Moses out of the Nile? However, recent archaeological evidence has shown that there was a sizeable royal complex in the Nile Delta, in the vicinity of what is thought to be Goshen, during the eighteenth dynasty (see notes in Chapter (2) for more details).

6. Exodus 6:20 records that 'Amram married his father's sister Jochebed, who bore him Aaron and Moses. Amram lived 137 years.' It is likely, however, that (as elsewhere in Scriptural genealogies) there are generations not recorded between Amram and Aaron, which may also be why the story of Moses' childhood in Exodus 1 and 2 does not name his parents. If it is assumed that all generations are recorded, then there are only three generations (Levi, Kohath, Amran, Aaron) from the Israelites going to Egypt and the Exodus, which seems too few to cover the 430 years in Egypt. In the second year after leaving Egypt, Numbers 3:27-28 states: 'To Kohath belonged the clans of the Amramites, Izharites, Hebronites and Uzzielites; these were the Kohathite clans. The number of all the males a month old or more was 8,600.' This magnitude of this number (if this translation is accurate) again points to unrecorded generations.

7. Exodus 6:23 records that 'Aaron married Elisheba, daughter of Amminadab and sister of Nahshon, and she bore him Nadab and Abihu, Eleazar and Ithamar.' The names of all other wives are imagined.

8. Acts 7:23 states that Moses was forty years old when he killed the Egyptian, and also comments that he had been instructed in all the wisdom of Egypt.

9. The location of Midian and Sinai are somewhat uncertain, though it is clear the latter is south of Canaan. Here, Sinai's location is taken as the traditional site in the Sinai Peninsula, east of the Gulf of Aqaba.

10. The names Horeb and Sinai are used interchangeably in Scripture, though it is not clear why. One may be the Semitic name (Horeb), and one the non-Semitic (Sinai). The latter is probably linked with the desert of Sin nearby.

11. It is not clear where the term 'Hebrew' comes from. It is possible that the term is derived from the word 'Apiru' (or its Akkadian equivalent, 'Habiru'), which is used in Egyptian records to refer to a distinct foreign group.

12. It has been assumed (because of the references to houses, lintels and doorposts in Exodus 12) that at some point the Israelites had started living in houses rather than tents.

13. Given any lack of reference to Miriam's family (and her age) it seems not unreasonable to portray her as a widow. However, there is a rabbinic tradition that Miriam was married to a man of the tribe of Judah named Caleb and that she was the mother of Hur, mentioned in Exodus 17:10 and 24:14. This idea has been adopted here, as it gives a reason for Hur's unexplained inclusion at some key events. It is also assumed that he is quite a number of years older than Ithamar and his brothers, given his presence alongside Aaron and Moses.

2

Moses and Aaron went to Pharaoh and said, 'This is what the LORD, the God of Israel, says: "Let my people go, so that they may hold a festival to me in the wilderness."' (Exodus 5:1)

Yahweh will stretch out his hand and strike Egypt. That was what Moses had said. If his uncle knew more of its meaning, he didn't elaborate.

'Here,' said Keziah, handing Ithamar a small flat round of freshly-baked bread as he emerged from the house, yawning, in the first light of the sun.

'What kept you?' said Eleazar, looking up from the bowl into which he was dipping his bread.

'It is my wife,' replied Ithamar mischievously. 'She keeps me awake at night with her snoring.'

Keziah put both hands on her hips. 'I do not!' she exclaimed with a look of mock outrage. 'I am a summer breeze compared to your storm!'

Tirzah, Eleazar's wife, handed Ithamar a bowl of curds. 'My husband is just the same,' she said to Keziah with a wry smile. 'It is like sleeping with a pig!'

'Where are they going?' asked Ithamar suddenly, as he noticed Moses and his father, staff in hand, talking quietly together with Nadab and Abihu. They were standing a few paces beyond the clay oven beside which his brothers' wives were sitting on their haunches, baking more bread.

'They go to meet Pharaoh,' said the voice of Miriam to their left. She and Elisheba were both sitting on wooden stools milking goats.

'At Perunefer?' asked Ithamar. The palace was situated beside a harbour on the Pelusiac—the most easterly of the seven rivers into which the Nile divided before emptying into the Great Sea—and was particularly used by Amenhotep when preparing to leave by ship for battles to the north. It was also close to Goshen.

'Yes,' Miriam replied, 'they intend to seek an audience with him there.' And, as if prompted by her words, Moses and Aaron turned towards them, nodded an acknowledgement, and then left.

News of the meeting with the elders had spread among their people as swiftly as the flowing of the Nile in flood. Ithamar noticed the change in mood when he and his brothers arrived at the brickfields. The eyes of their fellow slaves turned towards them as they passed.

'Hope stirs,' remarked Eleazar. 'Maybe they begin to believe that the sound of their suffering has been heard in heaven.'

'Freedom is no longer an empty dream,' added Nadab. 'Our future lies beyond these fields!'

But the day was no easier than any other. They hauled mud and water. They tramped the pits to mix in the straw. They shaped the endless bricks for the storage cities for grain—grain that had been planted, watered, harvested and threshed by their fellow Israelites. All for the Egyptians' benefit. And Khamet's rod could keep them toiling because chariots were never far away, whose soldiers wielded swords and bone-tipped arrows, either of which could swiftly fell slaves who rebelled.

It was only after the sun had passed its zenith that the day changed. The presence of a mounted soldier approaching Khamet drew Ithamar's eyes even whilst his hands and feet continued their tasks. 'What do you think is going on?' he asked Eleazar quietly, as they worked side by side, digging up mud.

'Nothing good,' muttered Eleazar, after Khamet had pointed at Shimron, shouting, *You come!*

Khamet then glared around at the team over which he ruled, bellowing 'Keep work! No stop!'

'What does he *think* we're doing,' muttered Ithamar, as he bent down to haul his bucket onto his shoulder, before straightening up. He watched for a moment as the messenger kicked his horse off in the direction of the next team, and Khamet strode off, with Shimron following a pace or two behind. His mind immediately flitted to what they had been told that morning.

'Father and Moses must have been to the palace by now,' murmured Eleazar.

Ithamar left his hopes—and his fears—unspoken.

The annual rising of the Nile had not yet begun, but it was preceded, as always, by the increase of both the heat and the length of the day, and the brothers were still labouring when both Khamet and Shimron returned. Uneasiness rose in Ithamar's heart when he saw the expression on Shimron's face—and the smugness on Khamet's. *What had happened at the palace?*

'Come!' shouted Khamet. Ithamar stepped out of the pit, his feet heavy with mud. He quickly scraped off the worst with his hand, and joined the others as they silently approached their taskmaster. 'You listen what Pharaoh say!' began Khamet. 'Now we give you no straw. You find straw.'

'Then you will get less bricks,' shouted Nadab angrily. Shimron shifted on his feet uneasily at Khamet's side.

'No,' shouted back Khamet. 'You make same number. Not less.'

It was as if a huge boulder had been tossed into the Nile, throwing up water into the air. Bewildered exclamations erupted from the group. 'Why?' called out a voice from the back. 'What have we done?'

The smug expression returned to the taskmaster's face. 'Pharaoh say you lazy,' he said, raising his chin. 'You ask to make offering to your god so you not work. You lazy. Must work harder.' A twisted smile came to his face as he turned pointedly towards Nadab and Abihu. 'Pharaoh say you listen to lies.' He paused. 'So same number bricks.' And with that he sauntered off.

Shimron was immediately surrounded, besieged by angry questions from every side.

'Bricks without straw will be useless—they will crumble to bits!'

'Where are we supposed to get straw from?'

'How are we meant to meet our quota?'

'We cannot do what he asks!'

Eventually Shimron held up his hand for quiet and the clamour subsided. 'We cannot do without straw, but we can collect stubble. The river has not yet risen to cover the harvested fields. We must send some out to gather stubble for straw—'

'But that will leave less men for making bricks!' interrupted another voice.

Shimron sighed. 'I know. The childhood of our young ones is short enough already, but maybe some can help collecting stubble or treading the mud...' He paused and Ithamar saw a look of quiet desperation in his eyes as he cast his gaze around them. 'We must all do what we can.'

And like the light of the day, the hope of the morning had faded by the time they were all trudging home, with only darkness ahead.

Ithamar was not surprised by the account of the events at Perunefer, for he had seen what had followed. '*Who is Yahweh?* Pharaoh said, though he neither waited for nor wanted an answer,' said Aaron, shaking his head, as they sat sharing a large pot of fish stew that evening. 'He has no intention of obeying our God—'

'Or of giving us permission to worship Him,' added Moses, leaning forward to dip a piece of bread in the stew. 'As he believes himself to be a god, he does not take kindly to being told what to do.'

'Amenhotep is young and proud,' said Miriam. 'He sees his Egyptian gods as superior in every way to those of other nations.'

Nadab turned towards Moses, 'He clearly knows that you spoke to the elders. According to Khamet, Pharaoh spoke of us listening to lies.'

'I believe he wants to set our people against your father and me,' replied Moses. 'That is why he withdraws straw from us.'

Aaron nodded ruefully. 'So we become trouble-makers to our brothers.'

'Pharaoh was right in one thing he said, though,' replied Moses. All eyes turned to him, his face softened in the fading light of dusk. 'He said he did not know Yahweh. That much is true. But mark my words: he will soon know our God.'

As both men and women from the Hebrew settlements were sent out into Lower Egypt, and then south along the course of the Nile, to gather as much stubble as possible before the inundation washed it away, Ithamar felt the hostility of his fellow Israelites. Although any resentment largely remained unspoken, he'd overheard one worker direct angry words at his eldest brother: *Did your God tell you that your uncle's words would make life harder for us all?* For despite labouring throughout the longer, sweltering days of summer, their toil from dawn to dusk (with their numbers diminished by the search for straw) was often insufficient to meet the quota. And when that happened, the consequence was brutal.

Ithamar stood as motionless as if his feet were held fast by the mud in which he was ankle-deep. None of those around him spoke as they watched, helpless, as Khamet brought his rod down again and again upon Shimron's back. Each *thwack* of the rod on his bare skin was followed by a stifled cried of pain, though both were largely drowned out by Khamet's screams. 'Why you not make enough bricks? Today you do as yesterday. Not enough!'

'He knows perfectly well why we can't make enough bricks,' muttered Abihu. 'It's the fault of his pharaoh, not us.'

But despite his brother's words, Ithamar could not shake a nagging sense of guilt. *Surely his family* had *been the cause of this greater suffering of their people.*

'Shimron says that a group of the foremen are going to appeal to Pharaoh tonight,' announced Nadab, as he returned one evening, slightly after Ithamar. 'He said that none of them wants another day of beatings.'

Moses rose from the stool on which he was sitting. 'Then your father and I will go immediately to the palace, and be there to meet them when they come out.'

'But the day is late,' said Elisheba, concerned. 'And you have not eaten.'

'A full moon will be rising soon,' replied Aaron. 'We will have enough light—*and* enough strength—for the walk to Perunefer.' He paused. 'Moses is right. We must stand with our brothers.'

Ithamar and Eleazar watched them depart a short while later. They soon disappeared between the scattered mudbrick houses. 'Do you think Pharaoh will listen to what Shimron and the others have to say?' asked Ithamar.

'He will listen,' replied his brother. 'But he is stubborn as a mule and unmovable as the pyramids.'

Ithamar feared he was right.

Darkness had fallen by the time Moses and Aaron finally returned. As the family sat on rugs around the dying embers of the fire over which their meal had been cooked, with only a few scattered lamps to pierce the blackness around them, Ithamar's father related their encounter with the foremen. It didn't take long.

'Amenhotep still says the fault lies with our laziness—' began Aaron.

'That from a man who has never done a day's labouring in his life!' exclaimed Nadab, his fists clenched and his eyes flashing in the lamp-light. Ithamar felt the same.

'He will neither give us straw nor reduce the quota,' continued Aaron, ignoring the outburst from his eldest and then sighing deeply. 'But that is not the worst of it. His words *have* set the foremen against us. *May Yahweh look on you and judge you*, they said.' There was pain in his voice.

Moses finally broke his silence. 'They believe that your father and I have made them a stench to Amenhotep.' He tossed a piece of untouched bread down on the rug. 'They say that we have put a sword into the hands of the Egyptians for them to use against us.' He suddenly stood up, and without a further word walked off.

'You have not eaten your meal,' called out Miriam after him.

Moses didn't look back. 'I'm not hungry.'

They sat in silence for a few moments. *His uncle was in an almost impossible situation—Pharaoh would not listen to him and neither would the Israelites.* After Moses had disappeared into the darkness, Ithamar asked quietly, 'Where does he go at this time of night?'

'To seek Yahweh's face,' replied Aaron simply.

'I hope he finds Him,' muttered Abihu under his breath.

As the heat of the season rose to its height, and the Nile's inundation commenced, Moses and Aaron returned to Amenhotep. Yahweh had spoken again, and Moses had listened, even if the Israelites still remained deaf to their words. Moses turned to Ithamar and his brothers as they were about to leave. 'Be in no doubt,' he declared, 'the Egyptians *will* know that Yahweh is the true God when He stretches out His hand over this land. And they *will* see Yahweh bring us out of Egypt!' And with that, he and Aaron—staff in hand—departed for the palace as the first light was creeping across the sky and the smell of bread was rising around them.

'They go with the power of Yahweh,' said Miriam, as she rose from squatting beside the clay oven. 'And Pharaoh will begin to see it today.'

The sound of stone grating against stone began again, as Keziah and the other wives resumed grinding barley for bread that would be baked later in the day. It was only as they were eating the bread that evening that Ithamar discovered the meaning of Miriam's words.

'What did Pharaoh do when Father's staff became a snake before his very eyes?' asked Abihu excitedly, as Moses related the day's encounter.

'He leapt to his feet,' answered Moses, 'but that was not all. He called for Jannes and Jambres.'

Ithamar knew the names of the sorcerers—they all did. He lived in a land where magic was practiced and where countless scrolls were filled with spells and incantations. Their Egyptian neighbours sought not only favour from their hundreds of gods but also power by their chanting and charms: power over the land, over their enemies, over anything—including death itself. And amongst all of Amenhotep's magicians, the two who were best known—and most feared—were those Moses had named.

'And what did those sons of darkness do?' asked Miriam disdainfully.

'They also threw down staffs that became snakes,' replied Aaron.

'How?' asked Eleazar. 'Their gods are nothing.'

'You are right,' replied Moses. 'But there are dark powers, of that I am sure—and Jannes and Jambres are masters of them. But whether they performed their signs by trickery or dark arts I cannot say, but their snakes were real.'

'But my brother has not told you the best part yet,' said Aaron with a wry smile.

'And what is that, my husband,' said Elisheba, intrigued.

But it was Moses who answered, laughing. 'Aaron's snake swallowed up their snakes! And then Aaron reached out for the tail of his snake and it became a staff again. He stood there, staff in hand, staring at Jannes and Jambres. They were struck dumb!'

As the laughter that followed died down, Eleazar said, with a little chuckle, 'And Pharaoh sits on his throne with a gold serpent on his forehead as a sign of his divine authority! It is as if Yahweh proclaims his victory over Egypt!'

'Ah, my nephew sees as keenly as the eagle,' replied Moses with a smile.

'But what about Amenhotep?' asked Abihu eagerly. 'What did he do then?'

Moses sighed. 'The young pharaoh is as stubborn as Eleazar is wise. His heart is hard, and grows harder. He would not look at us, but signalled to his guard to escort us from the palace.'

'So what happens now?' asked Elisheba.

Ithamar sat up and looked at Moses expectantly. But his uncle's response was not what he wanted to hear. 'We wait. We wait for Yahweh to speak again.'

The wait was a short one, however. Within days, Moses and Aaron were heading for the palace again. Although the flooding of the Nile had submerged great swathes of Lower Egypt where the river divided, the irrigation channels had diverted the water away from the cities—and the palaces. But Ithamar did not have to wait until evening to find out what had happened.

The nearness of the floodwaters meant less of a trudge for mud and for water. Ithamar's tasks that day, though, were divided between treading the pits and filling the moulds. He was kneeling by a line of newly-shaped bricks when he heard it: a cry of either shock or terror. Ithamar wasn't sure which. He looked up sharply and towards where the cry had come from—the water's edge. A number of people were pointing in that direction. Shouting in both the Hebrew and the Egyptian tongue began to fill the air. His brothers were all standing and staring in the same direction, and Nadab and Abihu began running towards the commotion. It was only when Ithamar rose to his feet that he understood. The water, as far as the eye could see, had turned red. He caught his breath and his chest tightened. *It was as if the land of Egypt were bleeding.*

He ran to Eleazar's side. 'Is this the hand of Yahweh?' he asked breathlessly.

His brother nodded. 'It must be. Yahweh has done to the waters of Egypt as he did to the water that Moses poured out before the elders.' Eleazar tipped his head in the direction of Khamet. 'Look! He is afraid, and does not know what to do.' It wasn't difficult to see. The Egyptian turned this way and that, agitated, eventually deciding to seek out his fellow taskmasters. He hurried off, but without any command to keep working.

They both walked towards what had been muddied water when they'd first arrived that morning. Already fish were floating—dead— on the surface, whilst others flapped around in vain on the mud. 'The river is dying,' said Eleazar. 'This blood brings death.'

'What will we drink,' asked Ithamar suddenly.

Eleazar shrugged his shoulders. 'Yahweh will not let us die of thirst.'

For Shimron's sake, Ithamar and his brothers stayed working throughout the day, as did most others. There was no assurance that, even as the rivers of Egypt ran red, the quota would be forgotten.

Keziah ran to meet him. 'I thought you would have been home long ago,' she whispered, after throwing her arms around him.

He held her tightly for some moments, feeling her heart beating fast against his chest. 'You needn't be afraid,' he said softly. 'Fear is for the Egyptians. We are in Yahweh's hands.' He felt her nodding against his shoulder.

'If you say so.'

He released her from his embrace. 'I do,' he replied, smiling.

The question of what they were to drink had been answered by those digging out mud from near the edge of the water. The waters that seeped into the newly-made holes ran clear as the summer's sky. But greater questions loomed as Moses and Aaron related their encounter with Amenhotep.

'We met Pharaoh on the banks of the river by the palace,' began Moses, as the men sat together on woven mats on the ground, while the women finished preparing the meal. 'He was going down to bathe in the waters. We gave him Yahweh's command—*Let My people go*—and we told him that Yahweh would strike the Nile so that it turned to blood. Aaron struck the waters with the staff, and right before the eyes of Pharaoh and all those around him Yahweh did what He'd said.'

'You could see the fear in the Egyptians,' added Aaron. 'Except Amenhotep. If he was afraid, he hid it well.'

'No pharaoh would want to show fear before his servants,' said Nadab. 'Especially one as proud as him.'

'He sent for Jannes and Jambres,' continued Moses. 'And by whatever art they used, they convinced Pharaoh that they could do the same.'

'Then Amenhotep simply turned his back on us,' said Aaron, 'and went back into the palace, as if what had happened was of no consequence, as if the Nile turning to blood meant nothing to him.'

'Maybe he will change his mind when the river begins to stink,' said Miriam, as she placed a bowl of steaming bean stew in the middle of the rug. A little smile played across her face. 'We are not having fish tonight.'

Seven days later—just as the Nile's stench had begun to subside—there was a further unwelcome discharge from the river. Ithamar had never seen—or heard—anything like it. The first he knew of it was Abihu's cry, *Get out!* When he turned to look, he saw his brother tipping a frog out of the bucket into which he was about to shovel mud.

'There's another one behind you,' Ithamar said with a laugh, adding after a moment, 'Oh, and another one.' Then he went quiet. 'Abihu...'

'What?' replied his brother crossly, as the frog proceeded to jump into the hole in which he was digging.

'Look...' It was as if the Nile was suddenly bubbling over, but what was emerging was not water, but a living torrent of dark green, and a cacophony of croaking with it.

By the time the sun was overhead, work was all but impossible. The frogs were jumping into the mixing pits, over the bricks moulds, and under their feet. 'If frogs could bind the bricks together as well as straw, we would easily be reaching our quota,' said Nabad with exasperation as another frog narrowly escaped being trodden into the mud by him.

Ithamar put down his buckets. 'Here comes Shimron.' Nabad stopped tramping as they waited for the arrival of the foreman, and both Abihu and Eleazar joined them. They had not seen Khamet for some time. His reaction to the frogs had been similar to the blood in the Nile: fright followed immediately by him scurrying away.

'You may as well do what most of the others are doing,' began Shimron, raising his voice above the constant chorus and casting his eyes around at the numerous Israelites who were drifting away. 'Unless our masters desire their storehouses to be built of frogs, there is little purpose in trying to continue—I hear these creatures are everywhere. Go home to your families.'

Eleazar grimaced as a frog landed on his foot. He shook it off. 'I wonder whether the Egyptian women are still worshipping Heqet— or whether they are praying to their frog goddess to remove this plague from their land.'

Shimron gave a little wry smile. 'Either way, they will soon hate the sight of them.'

Once again, Pharaoh's magicians had mimicked the sign. 'All that Jannes and Jambres can do,' said Aaron with a laugh, however, 'is to add to the frogs that Yahweh has sent. They are scarcely helping

Pharaoh. If those sorcerers had any real power, then they would remove this plague, not make it worse!'

'But Pharaoh still refuses to let us go,' said Moses quietly. 'This has not changed his heart.'

Although the doors and windows were all covered as well as could be managed, it was impossible to keep out the noise. Both Ithamar and Keziah spent much of the night awake. Ithamar could feel his wife turning from side to side.

'They are worse than your snoring!' declared an exasperated voice suddenly in the darkness. 'There must be hundreds of the cursed beasts outside our window!'

Ithamar rolled towards his wife and put his arm over her. 'Just be thankful,' he murmured, 'that they are just that—*outside* our window. Moses told Pharaoh that they would have frogs in their bedrooms and in their beds.' His fingers found her smooth neck and tickled her. She let out a little giggle, but then Ithamar felt her small fist jabbing his side.

'Stop it! I will be dreaming of frogs crawling over me if you do that again.'

He rolled closer to her. 'Then I will make sure you dream of me instead,' he whispered, and leant over to kiss whatever part of her his lips found in the dark. It was her hair.

Sleep came to them both eventually, but it left them far more abruptly. Ithamar was jerked awake by a shriek from Keziah, followed by a croak in his ear.

'Ithamar! Get it off me!' Almost immediately, Keziah added, 'Urghh! There's two of them!'

The room was still very dim, although the first light of the day was creeping in round the covers over the windows. But it was clear that that was not all that had crept in round the mats. Ithamar had no choice but to try to catch the creatures in the gloom, helped by croaking that was far nearer than it had been during the night. First one and then the other was caught and thrown unceremoniously out of the window, although not before Ithamar had circled their small room at least three times.

A short while later, as Ithamar and his brothers were discussing—inside—whether there was any point attempting work that day, a second unexpected interruption occurred. A voice called out loudly in the Egyptian tongue. Although he did not understand many of the words, Ithamar recognised two names: that of his father and uncle. It was clearly a summons, and Ithamar was in no doubt from whom it had come.

'Pharaoh has clearly had enough of frogs,' said Miriam drily, as they all stood outside—amid the plague—watching the departure of Moses and Aaron for Perunefer.

'We all have,' muttered Abihu.

'Amenhotep says he will let us go to sacrifice to Yahweh,' explained Moses on their return later that morning, 'if we will entreat Yahweh to remove the frogs.'

'So he does acknowledge Yahweh now?' asked Miriam.

'When it is in his interests to do so,' replied Moses bluntly. 'I do not believe a short-lived affliction is sufficient to change his heart.'

'You think he will go back on what he has said?' asked Eleazar.

'We will see what happens tomorrow.'

'Tomorrow?' Nadab's question echoed Ithamar's own.

'Moses gave Pharaoh the choice,' explained Aaron, 'of when the frogs would be removed from the land, so that he would know that it has been done by Yahweh's hand.'

Elisheba moved suddenly. 'Get out!' She lunged for the kneading trough, to expel the frog that had somehow found its way into the house and into the oblong vessel in which the dough was left to rise.

Abihu laughed. 'Tomorrow can't come soon enough.'

Moses' prediction turned out to be true. As the piles of dead frogs grew (and the stench with them), so did the hardness of Amenhotep's heart. Ithamar found himself back in the brickfields rather than tasting freedom. But as the Nile fell, the days cooled and the fields were first ploughed and then planted, a third plague—of gnats—choked the air of the land, and Pharaoh's sorcerers were finally powerless to repeat the sign. Another month passed, and Moses and Aaron again confronted Pharaoh on the banks of the Nile. But this time, Ithamar only heard of the plague of flies, for—as Moses had declared to Amenhotep—Yahweh made a distinction between Goshen, where His people lived, and the rest of Egypt. Again Moses and Aaron were called to the palace, again there were assurances, later to be broken, and again there was relief when Moses prayed.

When the days were shortest and coolest, and the livestock were let out into the fields, the fifth plague fell, though not in Goshen. One chilly evening, as they all sat cramped in the largest room of the house, Moses reported, 'It is just as Yahweh decreed and just as we declared to Pharaoh. Their animals are afflicted and are dying—and not just their cattle. It is their flocks, and their horses, camels and donkeys. All are affected with a sickness that ends in death.'

'But I do not see even one animal sick among our herds,' responded Miriam, 'let alone dead!'

'And Amenhotep knows that,' said Elisheba. 'Nahshon told me that some of Pharaoh's officials came into Goshen, looking at our herds.'

'It goes beyond discomfort now,' said Aaron, as he took some of the dried dates that were finishing their meal. 'They begin to suffer loss.'

'Pharaoh's stubbornness is now hurting his people,' said Miriam. 'And yet he seems not to care.'

'The longer he resists Yahweh,' said Moses, 'the harder his heart becomes. And each time Yahweh sends a plague, another of their gods is shown to be powerless!'

'What do you mean, Uncle?' asked Ithamar.

'I was taught more than enough of their so-called gods as I grew up among them,' replied Moses. 'They worship Hapy as the god of the inundation, and yet the waters this year brought death. They suppose their frog-headed goddess, Heqet, to have power over fertility and abundance—'

'And yet the only abundance they have is frogs, gnats and flies,' interjected Eleazar.

'Indeed! Their god Apis is a bull and their goddess Hathor has the head of a cow,' continued Moses, 'yet both bulls and cows are now dying in the fields. And they believe that Hathor brings protection.' Moses paused. 'That, like all their beliefs, is false. Whether Yahweh deliberately chooses the plagues he sends to shame their gods, He has not said. But that is indeed what they do.'

There were a few moments of silence. The small lamps flickered in the warm, stuffy room, sending shadows dancing on the mud walls around them. Ithamar looked across at his uncle, and asked the only question that seemed to matter. 'And there are more plagues to come?'

Moses nodded. 'They will not cease until we have left Egypt.'

It was still the cool season of the year, when showers occasionally watered the earth, and making bricks was not so oppressive, particularly in Khamet's absence. Ithamar wasn't surprised when he was nowhere to be seen for several days. Moses had thrown soot into the air before Pharaoh, declaring that it would become boils breaking out on both man and beast—and Khamet was likely to be suffering along with other Egyptians. Jannes and Jambres had been among those afflicted.

'So their magicians have no power to heal themselves,' Abihu had announced, laughing. 'I wish I could have seen their discomfort!' And Sekhmet, Egypt's lion-headed goddess of healing, seemed just as impotent as its other gods.

'He has returned,' said Eleazar one day, nudging Ithamar, and nodding his head towards their right. Ithamar followed his gaze and saw Khamet arrive, with head still held high and rod in hand. But it was not difficult to see a number of large scabs that could not be hidden by a tunic that covered more of his body than his usual shenti.

'He will claim the tunic is because of the cold,' whispered Ithamar.

'I feel only pity for him,' said Eleazar quietly. Ithamar wasn't sure that his sympathy stretched that far. 'He suffers for Pharaoh's wilfulness,' his brother added. And Ithamar had to acknowledge that that much was true.

Another month passed before Khamet was absent once more. Early the previous morning, Moses and Aaron had gone to confront Pharaoh again, and had departed even before Ithamar had risen. 'You will see the hand of Yahweh tomorrow,' Moses had told the family. 'This time, He will send hail upon the land, such as Egypt has never seen. Only Goshen will be spared. It will be so severe that it will bring death to those who do not seek shelter for themselves and their animals.' Whilst the plague of boils had occurred out of their sight, the hail was different. With Khamet nowhere to be seen, much of the day was spent simply staring at the heavens. The sky was unlike anything they had ever witnessed. Huge dark clouds in the distance filled the sky to both the south and the west, like vast fists, towering above the earth. The sound of faraway thunder rumbled around them almost constantly, and flashes tore through the clouds, as bolts of lightning struck the ground again and again. Even Shimron seemed to have forgotten the quota.

When Ithamar and the others finally returned, after a day of little labour, Moses and Aaron were nowhere to be seen. 'Pharaoh has sent for them again,' said Miriam, before any of them had the chance to ask the question.

'But how did his men get here through the hail,' asked Ithamar.

'Eight soldiers came,' answered Elisheba. 'All carrying large bronze shields. They must have held them aloft and walked beneath them.'

'Shields that can stop a spear would stop hail,' stated Nadab, as he took a cup of barley beer from his mother.

'Except the shields were all dented when they arrived,' said Miriam, as she held out two more cups of the beer.

'Listen,' said Eleazar suddenly. They all stopped and stood still.

Ithamar heard nothing. 'The thunder has stopped.'

'Yahweh withdraws His hand,' murmured Miriam.

They continued to stand in silence for a few moments, and then Elisheba broke the mood. 'We will wait until they return to eat. If they have not left Amenhotep yet, it will not be long before they do.' She added with a smile, 'At least they will not need an escort home.'

Ithamar listened, rapt, once more, as his father and uncle related their latest encounter. 'It is no surprise that you did not see Khamet today,' said Aaron. 'The only ones out in the storm today lay dead upon the ground.' He spread his thumb and little finger as far apart as he could and held them up. 'There were hailstones *this* big lying everywhere.'

'More than enough to kill a man,' said Eleazar softly. 'It would have been like being struck by a rock.'

'It was not only those who drew breath that were felled,' said Moses grimly. 'We saw shattered trees, and crops completely battered down. They have lost both their barley and flax harvests. The wheat and spelt may survive, as their ears have not yet formed.'

Ithamar swallowed the large mouthful of lentil and leek stew that he had been chewing. 'But what of Pharaoh? What did he say this time?'

'He acknowledged that he had sinned,' answered Moses, 'and that Yahweh was in the right, and he and his people were in the wrong.'

'He said that?' exclaimed Abihu.

Moses nodded. 'He said it, though I do not believe he truly fears Yahweh yet. He asked that I beseech Yahweh so that the hail would stop. And he said he would let us go.'

'So why do we not just leave?' asked Nadab.

'Because,' answered Moses, 'Yahweh has not directed us to go yet—'

'And Pharaoh's army would block the way if we tried,' added Eleazar, 'if what Uncle has said about Pharaoh's heart is true.'

Before the new moon announced the start of the next month, the eighth plague was upon the land. The first Ithamar sensed of its approach was out in the brickfields. Khamet no longer screamed at them when they stopped. Instead he seemed fearful, as if he might be struck down then and there if he crossed Moses' nephews. Even at a distance, he still appeared nervous. Ithamar straightened up and looked around, as did Eleazar. *He had felt it too.* 'The wind changes direction.'

Eleazar turned his head slightly. 'It comes from the east now.' They both turned, squinting into the distance and shielding their eyes from the morning sun. 'But Moses said the locusts wouldn't come until tomorrow.' And Moses was right.

Ithamar lay alongside Keziah, awake. He could hear her steady breathing, and although he could see the grey light of dawn beginning to seep into the room, he felt no inclination to stir, especially as Moses had implied they might not be able to work that day. He could hear movement in the house. Elisheba was always first to rise. Despite her seventy-five years, she still saw herself as the mother of the household. The light gradually strengthened, but then came a sound outside. *Fluttering*. Except it soon became a din, as if a huge bowl of grain were being emptied out upon the ground. The morning light receded.

Keziah stirred as Ithamar pulled himself to his feet and moved over to the window. 'What is it?' she asked sleepily.

He pulled back the mat just a crack, and peered out. The air was thick with insects in flight. 'It is the locusts,' he said eventually. 'They are here, just as Moses said.'

Once again, there was little point in venturing out. 'Do goats eat locusts?' asked Tirzah, as they sat inside later, working on any final repairs to their tents. Moses had said that they would soon need to be ready.

Eleazar laughed. 'Goats eat almost anything—or at least they try to! Why do you ask?'

'I wondered if it would change their milk,' she answered.

'We will find out soon, as they will probably try them, at least,' said Ithamar. 'They are curious about most things.'

Moses appeared in the doorway, clearly having overheard their conversation. 'Your goats and all your animals will need grain, not locusts, for a while,' he said. 'The locusts *will* eat anything that is green: crops, leaves on trees and bushes, any grazing.' They fell silent. 'They will devastate the country, believe me. Although grass and weeds will begin to sprout again soon, the animals will need other feed until then.'

'Will Pharaoh summon you back again, Uncle?' asked Eleazar.

'If he has any sense, he will,' replied Moses, 'though his defiance obscures reason.'

'Do you think his heart *is* changing at all?' ventured Ithamar hesitantly.

Moses shook his head. 'Each time he goes back on his word it becomes easier for him the next time. He has hardened his heart to Yahweh, and Yahweh has further hardened his heart.'

'Why?' asked Keziah, perplexed.

Moses stern expression softened into a smile. 'You have a good heart, and maybe it is difficult to understand why Yahweh should deliberately make Pharaoh more obstinate. But, in doing so, He will reveal more of Himself to the Egyptians and more of Himself to us. When Yahweh has finished, there will be no doubt who is God—and it will not be Amenhotep.'

Ithamar had watched the locusts depart to the east, like a cloud of smoke drifting across the land, as a strong west wind drove them out. But it almost felt as if they had been transported elsewhere, so altered was the landscape around them, with nothing green remaining. Any crops that had survived the hail had been consumed by the airborne army, and even the palm trees had been stripped, so that only their bare trunks remained, like long fingers stretching up from the sand towards the heavens. It had become a place of desolation and death.

Then, as the days began to grow warmer, and the daylight lengthened to equal the night, the ninth plague fell upon Egypt with no warning to Pharaoh, as Moses stretched out his hand toward the sky. Ithamar saw it again from the brickfields, though he did not know what he saw. He happened to be looking to the west at the moment Yahweh's hand struck. He could just about make out the line of denuded trees marking the Pelusiac branch of the Nile and, in the clear light of early morning with the sun behind him, the palace and buildings of Perunefer. But before his very eyes, they suddenly disappeared, as if they had been wiped off the land as a wind would erase a line drawn in the sand. He gasped, and slowly turned to his left and towards the south. The same had happened there. He stood motionless, too stunned, too bewildered to even speak, wondering if his eyes were deceiving him, like some strange opposite of a desert mirage.

Then shouting began. *Others must have seen it too!* He ran to Eleazar standing nearby. 'What is it?' he asked, breathing heavily.

'It must be the hand of Yahweh,' replied Eleazar in a mystified tone, 'but what it is I do not know.'

Khamet's face showed utter terror as he looked towards the place where he lived—which had disappeared. And for the first time he approached them. 'What is your god done?' he asked, trembling and wide-eyed. 'My family...' he began, but then his choked voice petered out.

'We don't know,' answered Eleazar. He then added quietly, 'But our God is not cruel.'

Ithamar was not sure if Khamet took any comfort from his brother's words, but either way, he hurried off to find other Egyptians, possibly too fearful to run towards his own village.

'Let's go home,' said Eleazar suddenly.

'I want to know what's happening,' said Ithamar.

'We all do...'

The answer they sought was *darkness*. Ithamar had experienced the blinding sandstorms of Egypt, but if this was a dense sandstorm, then it was far more besides. No huge dust clouds had been seen on the horizon—*nothing* had been seen, as light was withheld from everywhere but Goshen. As the darkness persisted for three days, Ithamar couldn't help thinking that yet another of the Egyptian gods—Ra, their sun god—had been shown impotent before Yahweh.

'He tries bargaining again,' reported Moses, when he and Aaron returned from another summons to Pharaoh. 'First, when there were gnats, he said we may go but only if we stay within the land. Then when locusts arrived, he said just the men could go—'

'Knowing full well,' added Aaron, 'that we would not leave for good without our families—or our flocks.'

'And now, when darkness falls, he says we can go, even with our little ones, but leaving our flocks,' said Moses. 'But he will not change Yahweh's mind by his haggling.'

'He was so angry when we would not accept his offer,' continued Aaron, 'that he drove us out, warning us that if we saw his face again, we will die.'

After a pause, Moses suddenly said, 'Come with me.' Ithamar and his brothers followed their uncle and father out beyond their settlement, and stood in silence for some moments in the evening sun, the devastation of Egypt before them now that the darkness had lifted. 'Behold,' said Moses eventually, 'Yahweh unmakes Egypt. In creation, He made the waters swarm with life, but here He made the Nile die. He gave man dominion over the animals, but frogs and locusts, gnats and flies, have ruled this land and driven man from it. He called for light in the darkness, and has covered the land with darkness at noon. And He will send one final plague: the plague that will cause Pharaoh to expel us from Egypt. The life called forth from the dust, Yahweh is about to send back to dust again.'

Notes

1. *In ancient times, Egypt was divided into Upper Egypt, to the south, where Thebes was, and Lower Egypt, to the north, around Memphis and the Delta region.*

2. *The location of Pharaoh during the account of the plagues provides something of a challenge. Various details in the accounts suggests that Pharaoh was somewhere near Goshen, given his ability to summon Moses and Aaron—particularly in the last plague, when he summons them during the night just before they depart from Goshen. If the pharaoh of the Exodus is Amenhotep II, then his capital was Thebes, 400 miles to the south. The late Exodus date doesn't have this problem, as Pharaoh Ramesses set up a new capital, Pi-Ramesse, in the Nile Delta (at the same location as the much earlier capital of Avaris), and this is likely to have been very near Goshen, where the Israelites lived.*

However, Amenhotep II was born and brought up in Memphis, just south of the Nile Delta, maybe only 50-100 miles from Goshen, and he continued to maintain a focus in Memphis when he became pharaoh. Recent archaeological research in the Nile Delta in the 1990s has, however, uncovered a palace in the vicinity of Pi-Ramesse/Avaris, dating to early in the 18th Dynasty (16th – 14th Century BC), which would have been in use at the time of Amenhotep II, and may well have been in existence at the time of Moses' birth and earlier. One leading expert on Egyptian archaeology, Manfred Bietak, has argued that this may well be the location of the naval base, Perunefer, used by Amenhotep, and others have suggested he may well have spent much time here, not only when he was young (as stated in Egyptian records) but also when he was preparing for military campaigns which departed by ship.

3. Some scholars have suggested that the plagues all have natural explanations, some of which led through cause and effect directly to others, beginning with an extreme high flooding at the inundation. (See, for example, Kenneth Kitchen.) In the plague of locusts, God clearly uses an east wind to blow the locusts into the country (possibly from a usual migratory route from breeding grounds in east Sudan northwards into Arabia), and then a west wind to expel them. Natural phenomena are not, however, incompatible with the hand of God: the scale and speed of the plagues, the accurate foretelling of their start and end, and the discrimination between Goshen and the rest of Egypt, all speak of a divine hand at work.

4. In the book of Exodus, it appears that the sequence of plagues occurs over a short period, but there is no reason why it might not have occurred over many months. The detail of stubble in the fields suggests that Moses and Aaron first confronted Pharaoh in the period directly before the inundation (which occurred around August/September). The hail occurred at the time of the barley harvest, or just before, which would have meant in January or February. The Passover, marking the final plague and exodus, would have been around April. It is quite possible then that the plagues began at the time of the annual inundation of Nile, the previous summer.

5. The names of Jannes and Jambres, Pharaoh's magicians, are found in the New Testament in 2 Timothy 3:8.

6. *In a total eclipse, when one area of the earth's surface may be in darkness close to an area that is not, the area in darkness 'disappears' when viewed from outside the area of totality. This is simply the result of no light being reflected back from that region (reflected light from an object being the reason that it is seen). This fact has been incorporated in the description of the plague of darkness, assuming that the plague was more than just a particularly severe sandstorm.*

3

At midnight the LORD struck down all the firstborn in Egypt, from the firstborn of Pharaoh, who sat on the throne, to the firstborn of the prisoner, who was in the dungeon, and the firstborn of all the livestock as well. (Exodus 12:29)

'It is time,' said Moses.

Ithamar glanced up at the western sky. The heavens were aflame with colour, though the sun had already sunk from view. Aaron was standing, knife in hand, with Nadab kneeling before him, restraining a young, unblemished male lamb. It had been chosen from their flock four days earlier and tethered outside the house since then. Aaron nodded, and Abihu swiftly stepped forward with a pottery bowl, holding it under the creature's throat as a swift slash ended its life. Ithamar could smell the blood as it filled the bowl. He glanced around; similar rituals were being carried out nearby. All over the settlement, fire pits were already ablaze with spits set up for roasting the lambs or young goats similarly chosen and set apart.

The lamb—still with head and legs—was skinned, prepared and secured above the flames that would roast it whole. 'How long will it take?' asked Keziah, as the smell of scorched meat began to fill the air.

Aaron looked to the east. A full moon, as bright and white as any polished Egyptian marble, had just begun its climb into the sky. 'It is only a small animal. It should be cooked by the time the moon is half way to its zenith.'

'We will all need to be inside well before midnight,' added Moses quietly.

'Is that when it will happen?' began Tirzah hesitantly, with Eleazar's arm around her. 'When Yahweh will strike the firstborn?'

Moses nodded. 'Yes, He will fulfil His word and do everything He has said. Which is why,' he added, looking at his brother, 'we must do exactly as He has commanded us.'

Yahweh's instructions had been given several days earlier by Moses. The announcement of the final plague had been accompanied by a description of what Yahweh had called *His Passover*. They were not only to slaughter a lamb at twilight on the night of the full moon, but also every year as a memorial to what He was about to do. And that month, Abib, was to become the first of their year. 'The people finally believe,' Moses had said after passing on the instructions to the community. 'They finally believe that Yahweh will liberate them.' They, like Ithamar, had now witnessed the hand of their God.

Aaron picked up the bowl of blood, and, with it, a small bunch of hyssop that had been set beside it. The leaves that the locusts had stripped from the branches of the shrub had regrown, and—in obedience to Yahweh's commands—he dipped the hyssop in the blood, and began daubing it across the lintel and posts of the door into their home. The red marks around the door would protect the firstborn of their family. They watched in silence as Aaron performed the ritual to be repeated across every Israelite house in Goshen. After he'd placed the bowl on the ground again, he turned to face them all. His eyes flitted to Nadab. 'It is done.'

The silence was eventually broken by Miriam. Despite her age, she knelt beside her sister-in-law who was cooking rounds of bread without yeast on the clay oven. 'Here, I will help you.'

'Do not forget to put the oven on the cart,' said Elisheba to Aaron.

He replied with a smile that deepened the wrinkles at the edge of his eyes, 'Would you like me to do it now?'

She gave him a withering look as she dislodged a flatbread from the side of the oven with a stick, 'It depends which you prefer—having your hands burned or your bread baked!'

'You would do better to ask our youngest,' replied Aaron. 'He is the most practical of my sons.'

'I will not forget, Mother,' said Ithamar with a grin. He wandered over to the already-laden cart to attempt to make a space for it. The goatskin tents had been folded, tightly rolled around their poles, and tied with their ropes. Ithamar, with the help of Eleazar, had practised putting them up and taking them down, until he was able to carry out each task quickly and successfully. Somehow, his hands seemed to accomplish deftly what his brother's fumbled over. But among the tents was also a wooden box, containing scrolls and other writing materials that Moses had obtained. Oxen were tethered nearby, to be hitched to the carts on their departure, and donkeys were already laden with rugs, bed mats, pots, and material and garments given by Egyptians living nearby. Yahweh had instructed them to ask their neighbours for gold, silver and clothing. *Payment for our years of slavery*, Nadab had called it, when they had returned laden with the riches of Egypt. It had been clear that their neighbours were desperate for them to leave.

'Maybe they hope to placate our God by their gifts,' Abihu had responded, 'and hope that He will leave with us.'

'Pharaoh's heart may not have submitted,' added Eleazar, 'but his people have felt Yahweh's judgment.'

Egyptian gold earrings now adorned their own ears, and many of their women were wearing costly gold and silver jewellery.

But there was another cart nearby with a far more solemn burden. Two days earlier, Moses had made a journey to collect the ornately painted casket in which was held the embalmed body of Joseph, whose bones had waited four hundred years to be taken to their true home—the land that had given Joseph life and whose hills, valleys and streams would soon sustain their own.

'It's ready,' announced Aaron, after cutting into the lamb on the spit and carving off a piece of meat.

Moses looked around him and nodded in satisfaction. Other men had begun to remove their lambs or goats from the fires, and, here and there, families were disappearing inside blood-marked houses, closing doors firmly behind them. Ithamar glanced at the ascending moon once more. *Half way between sunset and midnight. His father had been right.*

'Take the meat and bread inside,' instructed Moses. 'I will join you soon.'

'He is like a shepherd,' said Miriam, as her brother disappeared from view. 'He is concerned for his flock, and goes to see that none are straying from the word of Yahweh and into danger.'

Ithamar took a final look around him before following his aunt inside. 'He cannot check every door in Goshen!'

'That is true,' said Miriam, turning to give him a smile. 'But he will do what he can. He knows that Yahweh has called him to care for His people.'

They waited for Moses' return before eating. 'We are now ready,' he declared to the eleven others as he pulled shut the door behind him.

'It is like Yahweh shutting the door of the Ark,' said Miriam, 'so Noah and his family would be saved from the judgment of the flood.'

'But blood saves us this time,' said Eleazar. 'And now the meat of the lamb will sustain us for the journey ahead.'

They stood together around the food laid out on the one remaining rug in the house. It was a meal unlike any other. The bread was flat and firm compared to what they were used to. The abundance of meat, eaten with bitter wild lettuce, was richer fare than they normally ate. And, in obedience to Yahweh's command, they ate in haste, clothed and ready for departure. The mood in the flickering lamplight was sombre and quiet, each largely left to his or her own thoughts.

Suddenly Nadab broke the silence. 'When do we leave?'

Ithamar chewed his meat more slowly as he looked across to his uncle. *It was one of the many questions on his mind.*

'I have told our people not to venture out until the morning, but Yahweh will make it clear to us when it is time.'

Ithamar wanted to know *how* Yahweh was going to make it clear but he kept his question to himself, finishing the mouthful of lamb instead.

It was impossible to tell when the moon was overhead, but a strange silence seemed to cloak the whole land. Ithamar leant against a wall, with Keziah sitting at his feet. She leant against his legs, and dozed from time to time. His father stood, staff in hand, but with eyes closed. *He was a firstborn male, as was Nadab.* Ithamar's eyes flitted to his brother. *Would Nabab now be dead if he had been outside?* He wondered if the Egyptians were mourning their dead yet. And he found himself suddenly thinking of Khamet. *Was he the firstborn among his brothers? Did he have boys? Was he alive or even now cradling a dead son in his arms?* He realised that he knew nothing of the Egyptian's life. But one thing he did know was that in every home across Egypt there would be a death that night—either that of a lamb or a child.

The sudden and harsh sound of the door being pounded by some blunt object jerked Ithamar awake. *He must have drifted off.* Outside, an Egyptian voice called out loudly, 'Moses and Aaron, Pharaoh orders you, *Come now!*'

'The hand of Yahweh has struck,' said Moses. He looked round at Ithamar and his brothers. 'Stay inside until we return. I do not believe we will be long.' And with that, he and Aaron disappeared out into the night.

Nadab walked over to a window and pulled back the reed mat that hung there. 'Four soldiers,' he said simply, 'and they are in a hurry to return.' After a short pause he added, 'The moon is in its descent.' He let the mat fall back across the window and turned to face them. 'Midnight passed some time ago.'

Ithamar's heart pounded. *Would it soon be time for them to depart and leave behind the only life he had ever known?* Although no words were spoken, he could feel the mood in the room change. Everyone was fully awake, eyes bright and expectant. First Nadab and then Abihu began to pace back and forth within the confines of the small room.

'The day of our liberation is upon us,' said Miriam quietly, her face shining.

Ithamar tried to imagine what was happening at the palace at Perunefer. He tried to picture his father and his uncle standing before Amenhotep, among the frescoes of men leaping over bulls, which had been painted—according to Moses—by foreigners from an island in the Great Sea. He tried to remember the name of Pharaoh's firstborn. *Had he called him by his own name?* His brow furrowed and he wondered if grief would now be filling the palace.

Just when Ithamar began to wonder if Moses and Aaron had been detained, the door was flung open. And for the second time in a day, Moses declared, 'It is time.'

'What happened?' asked Nadab.

'Pharaoh has ordered us to leave—all of us, with our flocks. And he asked us to bless him.'

Moses' last words seemed almost incomprehensible to Ithamar. *The proud pharaoh was actually asking Moses to pray for him?*

'The sword of Yahweh has finally pierced Pharaoh's own heart,' said Moses. 'It is no longer only his people who suffer. His eldest son lies dead.'

'It is true then?' asked Elisheba. 'The Lord has struck down all their firstborn?'

Aaron nodded gravely. 'Before we even reached the palace, we could hear the wailing. Every Egyptian house that we passed had light inside and the sound of weeping.'

'Cattle lay dead in the fields,' added Moses. 'The whole land is suffering a loss like no other. Every Egyptian we saw begged us to leave.' He paused, sweeping his gaze around the ten who had been waiting for their return. 'Come outside and see for yourselves the great sign for our departure from this land.'

Moses led them out through the door and under the blood that had saved them. Directly ahead, the full moon was low in the sky, and would soon be setting in the western sky. There was light in the east—but not of a rising sun. It was something else—something that made the hairs on the back of Ithamar's neck bristle. It was fire in the sky. A huge pillar of flaming red cast an eerie light around them. Ithamar stared at it, transfixed, his heart pounding and his mouth dry. *This was the hand of Yahweh! It could be nothing else.*

'Yahweh Himself will lead us out of the land. Nadab, Abihu— go throughout the settlement and tell everyone to make ready for our departure. Eleazar—you are to light a large fire on which our neighbours can burn any lamb left over, as the Lord has instructed. Ithamar—load anything that is left onto the carts and hitch up the oxen. And you women—gather the herds and bind up the kneading troughs with the dough you have prepared.' He paused, and then declared exultantly, '*This* is the day of our deliverance!'

As Ithamar secured the now-cold clay oven on the cart, his eyes kept darting to the pillar of fire. *No one could doubt Yahweh's presence with them now.* But it was an unexpected arrival rather than the contents of the cart that finally drew his eyes away from the fire. A kerfuffle behind him made him turn around. His mouth dropped open. Khamet was falling to the ground, prostrating himself before Moses. Beside him, two girls—whom he judged to be around six and three—and a heavily pregnant woman all followed his lead, bowing down until their foreheads were resting on the dust.

Without looking up or raising himself from his position, Khamet began to speak haltingly, shaking as he did. 'Moses, lord, I ask you permit me speak…'

There was a pause. Moses then replied in the Egyptian tongue, which resulted in a torrent of words flowing from the prostrate taskmaster, who still didn't dare look up.

Ithamar had heard that—unlike Pharaoh—many of the Egyptians, including officials, had come to hold his uncle in high regard, and now he was witnessing it for himself. He slipped alongside his father and whispered, 'What's he saying?'

'He's asking for mercy,' replied Aaron quietly. He paused to listen. 'He says his eldest brother is dead, and that three of his nephews have also died this night.' He paused again. 'He says that once he considered himself not favoured by the gods, as his first two children were girls, but he knows that if either of them had been a boy, then they would now be dead.' He listened to more of Khamet's words. 'He says that his wife's baby is due, and if she had already given birth to a son, then he would be dead.' As Aaron paused once more, Ithamar could hear Khamet's voice beginning to break and his wife quietly sobbing, and, to his surprise, he felt his heart strangely moved by the Egyptian's plight. 'He says if the child is a boy, he doesn't want him to be struck down. He knows now that Yahweh is more powerful than all the gods of his people. He knows he doesn't deserve anything but bad because of how he has treated the people of Yahweh.' Ithamar and his father waited as sobs slipped from Khamet's prone form. Another burst of rapid words followed, and then silence. 'He says,' continued Aaron, 'that one of you told him that your God isn't cruel, and so he begs to come with us and find protection from Yahweh's wrath. He says he will worship only Yahweh from now on.' Ithamar remembered Eleazar's words to the Egyptian.

Moses said nothing for a few moments. His eyes were still fixed on the small prostrated family. Curiosity at the silence was clearly too much for the youngest. A small, dark face looked up, glancing around at the strangers. The open, inquisitive face was one of innocence, and when Moses finally replied, there was gentleness in his voice. Khamet rose in response to his words, whispering to his wife and children, who also scrambled to their feet. He was still trembling and staring at the ground. As Moses continued speaking, Aaron said quietly, 'Moses says that Yahweh has already given commands concerning strangers among us. Moses says that they can join us, providing Khamet is circumcised—*and* the child, on its eighth day, if it turns out to be a boy.'

Ithamar did not need to know the Egyptian tongue to know that gratitude was pouring from Khamet and his wife. Sheer relief filled their faces when Khamet and his wife finally had the courage to look at Moses, and found him to be smiling. *Eleazar was right: Yahweh was not cruel.*

It was strange leaving behind the house in which he'd been born and grown up. Ithamar looked around as he pulled on the rope of one of the oxen hitched to a cart. Keziah was staying close to him and she led a donkey loaded with rugs.

Miriam must have been watching him. 'It was the same for our father Abraham,' she began as she came alongside. 'The Almighty called him to leave behind all he had known and all that was familiar, to go to the land promised to him. We are like Abraham, but travelling to Canaan from a different direction.'

Ithamar looked ahead, toward the east. The sun had now risen, and, as it had, the flaming pillar had transformed into a pillar of dark cloud, as if a living column stood between earth and heaven. But as they moved towards it, it never seemed to come any closer. Ithamar had concluded that it, too, was moving, leading them forward as Moses had said. 'Abraham did not have a pillar of fire and cloud leading him, though.'

'Ah, you are right!' replied Miriam, with a laugh. 'But he knew the route to Canaan. We do not know the way that Yahweh will take us.'

Ithamar thought for a moment, and then smiled wryly. 'Abraham's family was also far smaller back then!'

'The Almighty has, indeed, multiplied his descendants as He promised.'

The multitude had grown as they travelled eastwards through Goshen, gathering more of their people. Ithamar had never seen such numbers. It was as if the whole land, as far as the eye could see, was bristling with life. As well as the travellers on foot, there were many other laden carts and donkeys, as well as small herds of sheep and goats. The bleating was constant and unremitting, but to Ithamar it was a sound of joy, of elation. *They were free!*

Moses and Aaron were a little way ahead at the front of the great company, and it was only as the sun began to set behind them that Aaron finally raised his staff high into the air, and the huge company gradually began to come to a halt. Aaron walked back to meet the rest of the family. 'Moses says we will not pitch our tents until we have left Egypt,' he explained. 'We will sleep under the stars tonight, here at Succoth. Start fires and bake some of the dough you have brought.' He looked around. 'There is ample grazing for the animals. Milk the animals, but stay prepared!'

The meal that night was a simple one of lentil stew, eaten with the same unleavened bread as the previous night. At the setting of the sun, the pillar had once more become blazing fire. Ithamar still found the sight disconcerting. Far more familiar were the innumerable campfires piercing the darkness as far as the eye could see. The ground was dark and uneven in the glow of both the fires and the pillar. *It was a terrain forged by a multitude.* 'Have you any idea how many we are?' he asked Moses as the conversation paused.

Moses laughed. 'It would be easier to count the stars in the sky!'

'But that is what Yahweh told our father Abraham, isn't it, Uncle?' commented Eleazar. 'He promised that his descendants would be as numerous as the stars above or the sand beneath.'

'You are correct,' replied Moses, nodding.

'My son has a good memory for his father's stories,' said Aaron with a smile. He then paused, his gaze still on Eleazar. 'But my son also has a furrowed brow. What perplexes your mind this time?'

Eleazar glanced over towards the pillar of fire before turning towards Moses. 'Yahweh is leading us east, is He not?'

Moses nodded again. 'So?'

'The more direct route to Canaan would be to the north, along the coast…'

'Indeed, but the Way of Horus, as the Egyptians call it, is heavily guarded by forts,' explained Moses. 'It is not only the trade route to Canaan and beyond, but also the route that armies march south as well as north.'

'But surely Yahweh would fight for us if we went that way?' said Nadab. 'We have seen His power, as have the Egyptians.'

'And Yahweh *will* fight for us,' replied Moses, 'but at the time of His choosing. He says that if our people see war too soon and too close to Egypt, they may decide to turn back.' He smiled. 'Yahweh may not be taking us by the shortest route, but it will be the best.'

'But…' began Eleazar hesitantly. 'To the east lie the smaller seas, and between them canals that are deep and wide. Boats may ferry small numbers but not ours.'

'Yahweh is leading us,' replied Moses simply but firmly, 'and He will show us the way.'

As Ithamar lay awake in the chill of the night, with Keziah close to him for warmth, he looked up at the sky. *The stars were harder to see with the glow from the pillar of fire.* He also found it harder to sleep with the noises of the night much closer than usual—and with all that had happened fresh in his mind. He drew his legs up slightly as he wondered once again how many thousands were camped nearby.

'Are you awake, Ithamar?' whispered Keziah.

'I doubt I will sleep this night,' he whispered back. He felt her snuggling closer to him, and he put his arm around her. Their conversation continued in whispers.

'How long will the journey to Canaan take?' she asked.

'I have heard of another route—the Way of Shur—that leads to Canaan. Maybe if Yahweh takes us that way it could be a month, maybe less. It depends on how quickly we can travel with the flocks.'

'And do we have food enough for that journey?'

'There is grain in the carts that should last that long, and lentils and beans and dried dates. We have milk from the flocks, and we could always slaughter another animal. We will not starve!'

There was a little giggle at his side. 'They say you can eat locusts. Maybe Yahweh will send another swarm if we run out of grain.'

Ithamar smiled in the dark. 'I think I'd rather kill a goat…'

The second day's march eastward was no different to the first, and was followed by another night under the stars. But when they rose the following morning, Moses addressed the family before leading the multitude out once more.

'Yahweh has spoken,' he began. 'We are to turn back, to the west and the north—'

'Back towards Egypt?' Nadab exclaimed with incredulity. 'Why?'

'The Almighty has not finished with the Egyptians. They will be shown a final time that Yahweh is to be honoured. Pharaoh will think that we are wandering in the desert, unable to find the way out of Egypt, and Yahweh will harden his heart so that he comes after us.' He turned to Ithamar's eldest brother. '*Then*, Nadab, you will see Yahweh fighting for us.'

Ithamar was aware, as they marched, that the water that lay far off to their right was gradually coming closer. It was one of the seas to the east of Lower Egypt, and they camped that evening beside it. Its bank, lush with reeds, stretched as far as the eye could see, both to the north and the south.

The smell of baking bread was just beginning to quicken Ithamar's hunger when he heard Nadab's cry. 'Look!'

He followed Nadab's gaze and saw a cloud of sand in the distance to the west. He screwed up his eyes.

'That is no sandstorm,' said Eleazar quietly at his side. 'It is the storm of Pharaoh and his army.'

The news of the army's approach—and fear with it—spread among the people as quickly as a pack of wolves among sheep. A terrified cry went up nearby: 'They have chariots—hundreds of them!' Soon Moses and Aaron were surrounded by an alarmed crowd.

'Have you brought us here to die?' demanded a grey-haired man. 'Weren't there enough graves for us in Egypt?'

'Didn't we tell you to leave us alone?' cried a distressed woman with a baby. 'What have you done to us?'

The person standing next to her called out, 'It would have been better to stay slaves than to be slaughtered here!'

Ithamar felt an arm being wrapped around his. It was Keziah and she was trembling. 'We are trapped,' she began. 'The sea blocks our way and there is nowhere we can go!'

'It is a trap, but of Yahweh's making,' said Eleazar, resting his hand upon her shoulder. 'It is for the Egyptians, not for us.'

As the agitated crowd closed in, Moses held up his staff. His clear, strong voice rose above the commotion. 'Do not be afraid! Stand your ground and watch!' The clamour around him began to subside. 'You will behold with your own eyes this day how Yahweh will save you, and this will be the last you see of the Egyptians. Be still, and Yahweh will fight for you!' Moses fell silent, but his attention was elsewhere, as if listening to another voice.

'Yahweh speaks to him,' whispered Eleazar. Then he pointed eastwards. 'And look!'

Ithamar turned and gasped. The pillar of cloud was moving. It slowly crossed from east to west, until it stood between them and the

Egyptians. 'See!' said Ithamar to Keziah, his heart pounding. 'Yahweh protects us. The Egyptians will not dare approach.'

'But that is not all,' added Eleazar. 'Look behind you.'

Moses was by now standing facing the water, Aaron by his side. He lifted the staff and stretched out his arm, as if he was reaching out over the expanse.

For a while, nothing seemed to happen, but then Keziah whispered, 'Do you feel that?'

It was a breeze blowing onto their faces as they looked east. Within moments, however, it had strengthened, and soon the sand around their feet was being whipped up, not by the odd gust, but by a driving wind. 'What is Yahweh doing?' asked Ithamar, though not expecting an answer. He glanced round. The pillar of cloud was obscuring the setting sun but seemed unmoved by the wind.

Nabad and Abihu joined them as Aaron returned. 'What is happening?' asked Nadab, his dark eyes shining, even before any of them had greeted their father.

'Yahweh is dividing the waters for us,' replied Aaron, looking towards Moses' outstretched arm. 'He is making a path through the sea.' And before any of them could respond, he added, 'Now, go! Tell the people to be ready.'

Ithamar could not believe that the ground beneath his feet was dry. The wide expanse that had opened up through the water was by now filled with a different flow—of people, herds and flocks, carts and donkeys, all moving forwards against the strong easterly wind. Although night had fallen, light came from both the moon that had risen in front of them and the pillar of fire behind, as Moses led them across to the other side. Some distance away, both to his left and his right, there were what appeared to be walls of water, and—despite his trust in Yahweh—Ithamar was glad not to be near them. Near silence hung over the multitude, as if each were holding their breath. Only the animals seemed unconcerned about the strangeness of their pathway.

By the time every person had crossed, the moon had passed overhead and was dropping down in the sky to the west. Ithamar looked back, staring intently at the pillar of fire beside the moon. *Was it his imagination, or was it moving again.* By the time Eleazar had joined him, Ithamar was certain his eyes were not deceiving him.

'Yahweh's guiding hand returns to lead us,' said his brother, without taking his eyes off the fire to the west. 'It is as if the sea has turned to blood.'

The red glow from the pillar was indeed casting its unnatural light on the waters to either side of the pathway. 'What happens now? Surely Pharaoh would not be mad enough to follow us?'

Eleazar thought for a moment as he stared westward. 'Do not judge as slight the folly of a hardened heart.'

By the time the pillar of fire was ahead of them once again, Eleazar's wisdom had been proved true. Ithamar and his brothers stood together, watching the advance of the Egyptians. 'Do any of you see Amenhotep among them?' asked Abihu.

'They are too distant and dawn is barely upon us,' replied Nadab. 'He may hesitate to cross the sea himself, but he will have no hesitation in sending his chariots after us, now that Yahweh's pillar is no longer blocking their path.'

Around them, the mood of their fellow Israelites was one of growing alarm. Some began hurrying away from the Reed Sea. But Miriam lifted up her voice, calling out, 'Do not fear!' Heads turned towards her whilst others slowed their pace. She cried out even louder. 'Do not fear! Yahweh tells us to stand and see His salvation. Watch!' And slowly every Israelite turned to face the Egyptians, their backs to the wind.

The chariots were halfway across before they noticed anything happening. 'Look!' cried Nadab, suddenly. 'Look at the chariots!' Ithamar peered more intently into the twilight.

'They're swerving and losing their wheels!' exclaimed Abihu.

Soon Nadab yelled out again. 'They are turning back!' And his cry was taken up and echoed jubilantly across their people.

'Yahweh's hand is about to fall,' cried Miriam. And Ithamar saw the arm of Moses raised once more over the sea, but this time on its western shore with the light of daybreak behind him. The wind dropped to nothing in an instant, and the walls of water began crashing down, the sea racing from both sides towards the Egyptians who were struggling to flee.

And in the tumultuous cries of victory around them, Eleazar's words were lost to all but Ithamar: *It is finished.*

As daylight strengthened, the wreckage of the Egyptian army—including bodies of both horses and men—began to wash up on the shore. Songs of victory echoed around the multitude and praise flowed as freely as the waters of the Reed Sea had done, as words sung by Moses were repeated: *Yahweh is my strength and song. He has become my salvation. This is my God and I will praise Him!* Keziah, Tirzah and the other wives joined Miriam, as she led them in dancing, many of them striking tambourines as they went, singing again and again the words that had become their refrain: *Sing to Yahweh, for he has triumphed gloriously! The horse and his rider he has hurled into the sea.*

As they sat around the fire that night, the sound of singing and laughing was still drifting around the tents of Israel. Nadab drew in a breath and declared with satisfaction, 'Freedom at last!'

'Freedom?' replied Moses thoughtfully. His eyes lifted from the dancing flames that were warming their faces to the towering fiery pillar at the edge of the camp, like some burnished shepherd's staff standing guard over them. 'Yes, but it is freedom to serve not Pharaoh but Yahweh.'

And Miriam quietly echoed in a lilting melody words from that morning's song: *'This is my God and I will praise Him…'*

Notes

1. *In later times, the minimum number of people for sharing a single Passover lamb was ten, so it was decided to have just the immediate family sharing the meat here as there were twelve of them in this story.*
2. *The Passover lamb could be a sheep or goat, and probably born within the year, rather than necessarily being one year old.*

3. It is assumed that the term *firstborn* refers to firstborn males, given that the instruction to redeem the firstborn is explicitly firstborn males (see Exodus 13:12,15).

4. The eighteenth dynasty palace at Avaris (assumed in this chapter and the last to be the location of Perunefer) has fragments of painted frescoes of a Minoan style. There is also other evidence that Egypt had links with Crete at this time.

5. Thutmose IV was the son of and successor to Amenhotep II (assumed here, to be the pharaoh of the Exodus), and some evidence may point towards him not being Amenhotep's firstborn.

6. Moses is later instructed by Yahweh (Exodus 17:14) to write particular words down on a scroll, hence the reference to packing writing materials.

7. Joseph had been embalmed (Genesis 50:26), and it seems reasonable to assume that, following Egyptian custom, his body was then placed in a sarcophagus of some sort.

8. It is later stated (in Numbers 3:4) that Nadab and Abihu had no children at the time of the Exodus. As they are the eldest, it has been assumed that none of the four brothers had children at the start of the story.

9. Exodus 12:38 reports that a 'mixed multitude' left Egypt with the Israelites. Given the nature of a God of grace (who has revealed Himself to the Egyptians through the plagues) and Yahweh's instructions for the stranger and the sojourner to eat the Passover (Exodus 12:48), it does not seem unreasonable for some, at least, of the mixed multitude to be Egyptians. The plagues may have acted for salvation as well as judgment, although the scene involving Khamet is an entirely imagined one.

10. The assumption has been made that the Israelites used carts for the Exodus. They were obviously in possession of carts by Numbers 7:3. They would have had tents (see, for example, Exodus 33:10, Numbers 16:26,27 etc.), most likely made from goatskin. It therefore seems reasonable to assume that carts could have been used for the transporting of heavy tents.

11. Some archaeologists think that there may have been ancient canals linking the lakes (Lake Ballah, Lake Timsah and the Bitter Lakes) that lay between the north end of the Gulf of Suez and the Mediterranean, that is, along the path of the current Suez Canal. This would have acted as a defensive barrier against invasion of Egypt by armies approaching from the

east. If this is true, then it might explain a route through one of these lakes, and when they are told to turn back (Exodus 14:2) it could be along the western edge of the these waters.

12. The exact locations of the places mentioned as stopping points on the journey are uncertain, both before and after the crossing of the Red Sea (literally, 'the Sea of Reeds').

13. The Sea of Reeds seems to be a term that the Israelites applied to more than one body of water. It is used of the water they encounter to the east of the Delta and also probably to the Gulf of Suez and the Gulf of Aqaba, both of which they seem to camp beside later (see Numbers 33:10 and Numbers 21:4). To them, these may have looked similar and simply been different parts of the same body of water.

14. It need not necessarily be the case that Pharaoh perished in the sea. Although Psalm 136:15 speaks of Pharaoh and his army being overthrown in the Red Sea, this could simply be referring to the defeat of Pharaoh by the destruction of (at least part of) his army there.

15. The timings of the journey to the Red Sea are not specified. It may have been longer than implied in this chapter, which was how Pharaoh knew they were NOT taking a three day journey into the wilderness. But maybe the knowledge that they were fleeing simply came from an awareness that they had taken everything.

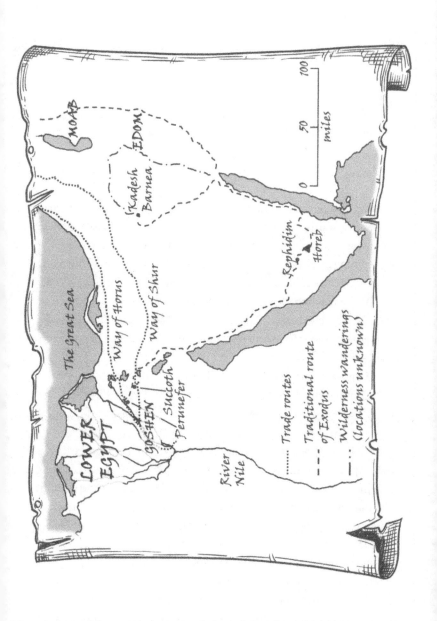

4

The people were thirsty for water…and they grumbled against Moses.
They said, 'Why did you bring us up out of Egypt to make us and our
children and livestock die of thirst?' (Exodus 17:3)

Ithamar was puzzled. 'The rising sun should be to our right if we're heading towards Canaan,' he said to Eleazar, as they set out the following morning from the Reed Sea. 'Or at least straight ahead, if we're going east by the Way of Shur, before turning north.' The rising sun was, instead, to their left, with the pillar of cloud ahead.

'We're heading south,' began Eleazar.

'Exactly! Further away from the Promised Land!'

'Moses said that Yahweh would not be leading us towards war—'

'I know,' interrupted Ithamar. 'But the opposite direction?'

Eleazar smiled. 'Patience, Brother! He said Yahweh would take us by the best way.' He laughed. 'What are you going to do about it anyway? Go and argue with Yahweh's pillar?'

Ithamar thought for a moment. 'No, but I can ask His mouthpiece!' He thrust the rope of the donkey that he was leading into his brother's hand. 'Here, hold this until I get back.' And without waiting for a response, he began running ahead, towards the front of the huge company. It didn't take him long to reach Moses and Aaron. 'Uncle, where are we going?' he blurted out.

Moses raised an eyebrow and smiled. 'Canaan.'

'But surely this is not the way!'

'Ah, but surely it *is* when Yahweh is leading us!'

'Yes, I know, but…' Ithamar paused, unsure how to question the Almighty's sense of direction.

Moses laughed. 'I am being unfair to my nephew. You wish to know why we are heading south?'

Ithamar nodded. 'Yes!'

'Do you remember where I met Yahweh in the burning bush?'

Ithamar nodded again. 'Mount Horeb. Is that where we are going?'

'Yes, and that was where your father met me on my way back to Egypt. The Almighty said that we would worship Him on the mountain on our way to the Promised Land.'

'How long will it take us to get there?'

'It was quicker for your uncle and me,' answered Aaron. 'We did not have women and children with us—or flocks and herds.'

'Two months,' said Moses. 'Maybe more, maybe less.'

'And then we go to Canaan?' asked Ithamar.

Moses smiled. 'And then we go to Canaan.'

Over the meal that evening, the journey to Mount Horeb was their main interest. 'You said it would take maybe two months to reach the mountain,' said Ithamar, after Moses had retold the story of his encounter with Yahweh in the desert.

'That is if I have guessed the pace of our journey correctly, and if we travel each day,' replied Moses. 'What of it?'

'But we only have food for a month or so,' said Keziah, voicing the matter on Ithamar's mind.

'And you wonder,' said Miriam, smiling, 'if we will starve before we get there?'

'Even if we somehow managed to make our food last to Horeb,' said Ithamar, 'we certainly wouldn't have enough for the journey to Canaan.'

'He's right,' added Nadab. 'Milk and cheese from the flocks will not be enough to sustain us.'

Moses thought for a moment. 'When we were camped by the Reed Sea, with Egyptian chariots before us and deep water behind, how many of you even imagined that Yahweh might divide the sea for us?' He looked around at each face illuminated by the dying flames of the campfire. There was silence. 'None of us knows how the Almighty will provide for us. What we *do* know, however, is that He will.'

'But we are so many,' began Abihu.

'And He is so powerful,' responded Miriam.

'My sister is right,' said Moses. 'Yahweh has not led us out into the desert to starve. The deliverance that He has begun, He will finish.' And no-one dared question his words.

Ithamar decided that sleeping in a tent was not so different to sleeping in a cramped, mudbrick house. Although Moses had his own tent, as did Aaron and Elisheba, the four sons and their wives shared a single tent. It had been divided up into different sleeping areas by means of large woven hangings, and conversations at night tended to be whispered.

'Ithamar?' said Keziah softly.

'Mmm.' Ithamar wanted to sleep rather than talk.

She rolled towards him, so that they were lying close together. 'Do you trust that Yahweh will provide for us?'

Ithamar sighed. *Sleep would have to wait.* 'I try to,' he whispered back.

'He will need to,' began Keziah. But rather than continuing, she found Ithamar's hand in the darkness, and pulled it down until it was resting on her belly, with her small hand on top of his. 'The seed you have planted is growing…'

It took Ithamar a moment, and then he was wide awake. 'You mean—'

'I am with child,' she whispered, a little laugh ringing out in the dark.

'Are you sure?' he asked, not wishing his heart to fly only to fall again to earth.

'It is two months since I last bled. And I spoke to Elisheba. She says that the way I have been feeling is the manner of those who carry new life within.'

Ithamar lay on his back, staring up into the darkness for a moment. Then he chuckled. 'So I—the youngest of my brothers—am the one who will father a child first!'

'Maybe not...' whispered Keziah, drawing the words out in a lilting manner.

He sighed again. 'Ah. So my wife has more to tell me.'

'Tirzah may be slightly ahead of me.'

'And Eleazar knows?'

'He will do tonight.'

Ithamar chuckled again. 'So my mother and my sister-in-law know before me—'

'It is the same for Eleazar.'

Ithamar was silent for a moment. 'Nadab and Abihu will not be pleased. Knowing them, I am sure they will make every effort to catch up!'

Keziah giggled. 'You should not say such things!'

Ithamar lay grinning before a sudden idea made him stop. He thought for several moments. 'So the baby may be born in seven months?'

'Yes...'

'If Moses is right, and it takes two months to reach Horeb, then even if we stay there a month, and if it takes no more than three months to reach Canaan, our child could be born in the Promised Land!'

'There are many *ifs* in what you have said,' replied Keziah, gently stroking Ithamar's hair. 'My husband may be numbering kids before his goats give birth!'

'Maybe,' he conceded. He turned his head, kissed Keziah, and murmured happily, 'Yahweh is, indeed, good to us.'

It only took three days in the wilderness for the songs of victory to become mutterings of discontent. They had come upon a watering hole, fed by a spring. But one mouthful was more than enough.

Nadab spat out the water without swallowing. 'Urghh!' Ithamar paused, water-skin in hand. 'There is salt in the water,' said his brother, shaking his head, 'and other tastes that are just as unpleasant.'

Although many others were thronging around the edge of the large pool, none were filling their empty water-skins, and any water that had been drawn was already being poured back. 'The people do not look to Yahweh in their need,' muttered Eleazar, nodding his head over to their right. Ithamar followed his gaze. There was a growing crowd around their uncle, and it wasn't difficult to hear their complaints.

'This water is bitter,' shouted out one man. 'It is fit for neither man nor beast!'

'We'll soon be dying of thirst,' called out another.

And numerous voices cried out, 'What are we going to drink?'

As the clamour continued to climb, Moses held up a hand, gradually stilling the grumbling. But he didn't reply. 'Where's he going?' asked Ithamar, as Moses walked silently away from the community.

Eleazar sighed. 'To seek Yahweh?'

The people milled around aimlessly, like a flock of scattered sheep, as they awaited Moses' return. They had already named the waters *Marah. Bitter.* But when Moses did finally reappear, Ithamar was mystified. 'What's he carrying?' he asked, craning his neck.

Eleazar sounded just as perplexed. 'It looks like the branch of a tree…'

The crowd quietened and then parted, as Moses made his way towards the water amid whispering and baffled looks.

Moses' eyes skimmed the crowd, waiting for silence. 'Yahweh has spoken,' he began eventually as an expectant hush fell. 'He is giving you a law to live by—a ruling that will test you. He says that if you listen to Him—your God—diligently, and do what He says, obeying His commands and His laws, then He will not bring upon you any of the suffering He brought upon the Egyptians. He says, *I, Yahweh, am your healer.*' And with that, he cast the branch into the water. Heads turned hesitantly this way and that, but no-one stirred.

Ithamar suddenly felt movement at his side.

Eleazar made his way forward, weaving through the crowd. When he reached the front, he knelt by the water and scooped some up with his hand, raising it to his lips and drinking. 'The water is sweet!' he called out. 'Drink of Yahweh's provision.'

A number came forward, reluctantly at first. But soon cries of joy and excitement were filling the air. 'The water *is* changed,' said Nadab, after sampling it for himself.

'Did you doubt your brother's word?' asked Ithamar with a wry smile. But Nadab just raised an eyebrow and walked away.

Eleazar was soon at his side again. 'Not only can Yahweh render the waters of the Nile undrinkable, He can also make the bitter sweet.'

Ithamar did not reply. *It was not only the waters that had been transformed.* Grumbling had become praise, as all manner of vessels were filled and animals led to drink. When he did finally speak, however, it was about another wonder. 'You're going to be a father too, then…'

Eleazar smiled and nodded. 'And you'll never guess who I saw today!'

Ithamar shrugged his shoulders. 'Then you will have to tell me, Brother.'

'Khamet. He has a baby boy.'

The wonder of the waters of Marah was followed, however, by the wonder of how quickly it was forgotten.

'That is nonsense!' exclaimed Ithamar, barely able to contain his irritation. 'Did they really claim that they ate stew every day in Egypt?'

Aaron sighed as they sat together by the entrance to Moses' tent in the evening sun. The women were busy nearby, grinding the last of their grain to make bread for what would be a very meagre evening meal. 'They may not have used the words *every day*, but their memories are short.'

'Do they not remember our Egyptian taskmasters?' said Eleazar, shaking his head in disbelief. 'And to say it would have been better if Yahweh had killed them in Egypt…' He shook his head again as his words trailed off.

'Yes, it is scandalous and insulting, given all He has done for us,' said Aaron.

'They might as well accuse Yahweh of being cruel and uncaring,' replied Eleazar.

They had now been travelling for a month, and as their supplies of food had dwindled to nothing, the grumbling of the people had grown. Nadab picked up a small stone and hurled it at a nearby rock. There was a sharp crack as it found its target and bounced off into the dust. 'They certainly accuse *you* of being uncaring,' he said, looking towards his father and uncle, 'when they claim you have brought them here to starve them to death.'

'They speak such nonsense!' exclaimed Ithamar once more. 'If they want meat, why don't they kill a goat or sheep? And if they are loath to slaughter a ewe and lose their milk and curds, surely they can spare a ram!'

Moses, who had been sitting quietly listening to them, finally spoke. 'They have also forgotten the words of Yahweh, spoken to them at Marah. They test Him, rather than trust His promises. They grumble against us rather than crying out to Him.' He rose to his feet. 'But I will do on their behalf what they won't do themselves.' And with that, he left them and walked out beyond the camp.

The following evening found Ithamar busying himself. He went down onto one knee and held the tent peg in his left hand, bringing the mallet down with his right. Moses had instructed them not to travel further south that day—the cloud hadn't moved—and Ithamar was tired of sheep. He'd decided to go around the tent as the last rays of the sun embraced the camp, checking the ropes and tent pegs, and repositioning any that had worked loose. He hit the tent peg a second time with his usual force, but it refused to go deeper into the earth. He tried again, but it wouldn't budge. He sighed. *There must be a rock or stone underneath*. He jiggled the peg until the earth around it loosened its grip, before pulling it free. He positioned it a short distance from the empty hole, and started again.

His mind flitted back to that morning, and to the words that Yahweh had spoken to Moses. They had been announced to the assembly by his own father. *I have heard the grumblings of the sons of Israel,* Yahweh had said, which didn't surprise Ithamar. But the next words did. *I will rain down bread from heaven for you,* He'd said. *At twilight you shall eat meat, and in the morning you shall be filled with bread.* And they had then seen the cloud suddenly shining as brightly as the noonday sun. *Yahweh's glory,* Moses had called it. *How could they doubt His words? But bread from heaven?* Ithamar shook his head, and began hammering. But just as he was hitting the peg for the third time, something thudded into his back. Something alive. He swung round, his knee still planted on the ground. He immediately had to dodge to one side as a small, stumpy bird flew directly towards his face. And there were more of them coming. Cries of surprise and delight were beginning to come from every side. He ducked, holding an arm up to cover his head, and felt the *swish* of air just above him, as another bird narrowly missed him. He heard a *thwack* nearby, and turned to see a quail flapping its short wings and rolling its way down the sloping roof of the tent.

'What in heaven…?' began Keziah, as she emerged from the tent. She stopped abruptly and stared around, wide-eyed.

Ithamar shook his head again, but this time in wonder. The air was by now thick with quails, most flying no higher than a man could reach up, and all descending upon the camp.

Eleazar joined them, laughing, as they, like every other Israelite around them, began chasing the birds around the ground, a quick twist bringing each captured quail's life to a swift end. '*At twilight you shall eat meat,*' he shouted as he grasped yet another bird. 'Yahweh has opened His hand and look what has flown out!'

Ithamar chuckled, calling out to Keziah, 'Get a pot of water on. We will be eating stew tonight!'

As all four brothers sat cross-legged on straw mats a short while later, plucking the small mound of birds that lay between them and laughing together, Eleazar suddenly fell quiet. 'What is it, Brother?' asked Ithamar.

'Given all that Yahweh has done for us,' he began, 'the complaints and questions of our people deserve His judgment—'

'That they do!' interjected Abihu.

'And yet the grumbling is met by Yahweh's gracious provision—and an abundance!'

Ithamar thought for a moment, and then replied. 'It shows beyond all doubt that it is better to serve Yahweh than Pharaoh.' He then chuckled again, remembering the promise for the following morning. 'And surely if being ankle-deep in quail doesn't convince them, then being rained on by bread will!' And he made up his mind not to venture out after sunrise until the loaves had fallen.

'What is it?' asked Ithamar, as he stared at the white flakes that covered the ground as far as the eye could see. If it was bread, then it was unlike any that he had ever eaten.

Keziah crouched down, put some of the flakes into her cupped hand and examined them. 'They look a little like split coriander seeds.' She then held them to her nose. 'There is very little to smell.' She gingerly put out her tongue.

'Careful...'

Keziah gave him a withering look and continued, touching the flakes with her tongue. 'But there is a hint of sweetness.' She stared upwards for a moment, as if in thought. 'Like honey.'

Ithamar crouched down beside her, put some of the flakes straight into his mouth and chewed. Not that he was hungry after a very large belly-full of quail stew the previous evening. He swallowed. *It wasn't unpleasant.* 'But I wouldn't call it bread...'

He turned and stood as he heard the deep laugh of his uncle behind him. 'Maybe you will when the women grind and bake loaves with it.'

Elisheba joined them, smiling. 'And I will try boiling it, as we did when we made barley porridge in Egypt.'

'Either way,' laughed Moses, 'it is bread from the heavens, and it looks like we will be calling it *manna*.'

They soon learned that the white flakes melted away in the heat of the sun—and that it was impossible to store it.

Ithamar recoiled from the clay jar, after Moses had held it out for them to peer into. The smell was revolting.

'That is foul!' announced Nadab, screwing his face up, after he had also looked at the worm-infested manna.

'I told the people not to leave any overnight,' said Moses, his expression stern, 'and that Yahweh would provide each morning. And yet many still do not trust His word. I have shown this to the elders, that they might warn each tribe of the folly of disobedience.' And Ithamar was glad that Keziah had heeded the command.

A few days later, however, they discovered the happy exception in Yahweh's instructions.

Ithamar lay back on the straw mat. Although the ground was still cool from the night, the morning sun was already warm. He put his hands behind his head, closed his eyes, and allowed himself the pleasure of simply lying there. *No manna to be collected. No tents to take down. No carts to load. No flocks to herd.* The peace didn't last for long, however. Even with his eyes closed, he could tell that something was now blocking out the brightness of the sun, and he felt his side being gently kicked.

'Here, lazy!'

'I thought that this was our day to rest,' he protested, opening his eyes.

Keziah was standing with the sun behind her, looking as if she herself were shining. 'So you don't want the effort of eating?'

He pulled himself up into a sitting position. 'I did not say that!'

She held out a bowl of curds which he took. She then sat down next to him, and tore off a piece of bread from a small loaf. 'And this is what we baked yesterday from the extra manna you collected.'

He inspected and then took it. 'Not a worm in sight.' He dipped it in the bowl.

Keziah tore off another piece and did the same. 'I like the idea of the Sabbath.'

'You remember the story of creation?' asked Ithamar.

'The Almighty rested on the seventh day, did He not?'

'He did, and now He commands us to do the same.' They had known nothing of a seven day pattern in Egypt. Their oppressors had divided each month into three periods of ten days. *But now they were Yahweh's own people!*

'Yahweh's word was true. There was not even a single flake of manna on the ground this morning, though I still saw some people go out looking for it.'

Ithamar sighed. 'Maybe now they will have learned their lesson.'

They hadn't.

Ithamar sat whittling a new tent peg. Little flakes of wood were falling to the dry ground and covering the earth around his feet. He smiled. *Like the flakes of Yahweh's manna—but not as appetising.* They were camped at a placed called Rephidim after a journey south during which the grumblings and accusations had become louder as the days became longer and hotter and water scarcer. They had seen, however, Yahweh miraculously bring forth the much-needed streams of water from a rock—though not before Ithamar had felt as parched as the dried-up wadi along which they had travelled east.

The sound of running suddenly drew Ithamar's eyes upwards. A young Israelite whom he didn't recognise came into sight and halted not far from him, his breathing ragged and his wide eyes darting this way and that.

'Moses! Where is Moses?'

Nadab, who had been sitting on a small stool milking a goat, rose to his feet. 'He is in his tent. Why do you ask?'

'Fetch him quickly! There has been an attack on our people.'

The goat was abandoned as Nadab ran off, and Ithamar leapt up. Eleazar dropped the newly-filled water-skins he had been carrying. 'My father, Aaron, is nearby. I will fetch him as well.'

Ithamar set down the wood and the knife. He hurried to the water-skins and removed one of the stoppers. He offered it to the red-faced stranger, laying a hand on his shoulder. He was trembling. 'Here, drink.' As the man drank deeply of the water, he added, 'I am Ithamar, son of Aaron and nephew of Moses.'

The man finally lowered the skin. 'I am Jemuel, of the tribe of Asher.'

Aaron emerged from a nearby tent just as Moses appeared. Moses dispensed with the customary greetings. 'Tell me what has happened, my son!'

'My family fell behind the company when a wheel on our cart broke and we stayed to fix it. But we were not the only ones who became separated. One family was delayed by a woman's labour and another by a lame ox. There were others beside who were simply weary and flagging. We camped together, knowing it would be easy enough to find you all when we were ready to continue. There must have been fifteen or twenty tents altogether. But they came without warning as evening fell—'

'Who?' asked Moses.

'I do not know, but they were well armed, and we had nothing to defend ourselves with. We scattered in every direction.' Fear returned to Jemuel's face. 'I picked up my second child and dragged the eldest by her hand. I shouted to my wife to run with the baby, but in the confusion we became separated. I didn't stop running until the shouting and screaming behind me had faded.' Jemuel paused and shuddered. They waited in silence for him to continue. 'By this time night had fallen, and with no moon there was nothing I could do but wait with my two children until first light. I returned to the camp, but...' His trembling voice trailed off. They waited again. 'Men, women and children had been slaughtered, and anything of value taken.' He fell silent again.

'And your wife and baby?' asked Moses gently.

He shook his head. 'I do not know. They weren't among the dead, but I had hoped that they might have found their way here.'

'We will send out men to search,' said Moses, his face grim. 'Could you say how many were in the raiding party?'

Jemuel shook his head. 'Not for certain. It happened so fast and they came from more than one direction. Fifty? One hundred maybe?'

Moses turned to Nadab. 'Gather the elders.'

Ithamar's mouth was as dry as the desert once again, but not from thirst. He glanced down at the sword in his hand, and wondered if he would be as adept with the weapon as he was with a whittling knife. They were, after all, not soldiers, but liberated slaves who had spent their lives making bricks. He sensed that those around him shared his apprehension. They were the ones who had been chosen to fight by Hoshea son of Nun, a young leader from the tribe of Ephraim whom Moses had appointed to lead them into battle. Ithamar could just about see Hoshea at the head of the small army. He judged him to be about Nadab's age, and although still relatively young, there was something about him that eased Ithamar's fear.

Their enemy also now had a name: Amalek. Scouts sent out by Moses had quickly found the source of the raiding party—and the reason for the attack against them. A little distance to the south, along the wadi that they had been following, lay a fertile oasis, clearly claimed by the Amalekites, together with the land around it. It seemed they did not want to lose their treasure.

Ithamar shifted nervously from one foot to the other. 'Moses says the Amalekites are descended from Jacob's brother, Esau,' he said to his cousin, if only to distract himself from what lay ahead. 'He knew of them when he shepherded flocks in Midian.'

'They certainly do not treat us as kin now,' replied Mishael grimly, leaning on the spear in his hand.

'How many do you think we are?'

Mishael shrugged. 'A thousand—possibly more. It is difficult to say.' He attempted a smile. 'I haven't counted them.'

Ithamar glanced around. Other Levites were there—including Nadab—and although he recognised some of the faces, most of the names were unknown to him. 'Maybe Hoshea called for two hundred from every tribe…'

'However many he has gathered,' replied Mishael, 'he will have made sure that we will more than match their numbers.'

Ithamar suddenly wondered if he would live to see the birth of his child. *The Amalekites were far more used to battle than they were.* He kept his fears to himself, and looked over towards a hill that was ahead of them. Beyond the hill lay the enemy. But it was on three small figures that were making their way to the top of the hill that Ithamar fixed his attention. Moses, Aaron and his cousin Hur would watch the battle from there. But more importantly, Moses would raise up over them the staff of God.

Ithamar steeled himself and tightened his grip upon both his sword and shield. *He would put his trust in Yahweh.* 'Numbers alone will not win this battle,' he said to Mishael. 'When the Amalekites oppose us, they are opposing our God. Yahweh divided the waters of the Reed Sea when Moses raised the staff over it. And He will divide and conquer the Amalekites when Moses lifts up the staff over this battle.' His mouth was still dry, but somehow he felt stronger for having spoken the words. *The hand of Yahweh that gave them bread from heaven would now give them victory.*

The signal to advance, when it came, quickened Ithamar's heart and heightened his senses. As they skirted the hill, he glanced up to his right and saw Moses holding the staff aloft. *This was it!* As the Amalekites came into view, their own battle cry rose like thunder and their feet hastened forward, until they were falling upon their enemy as the waters of the sea had done upon the Egyptians. They pressed ahead, into the midst of Amalek, and Ithamar's sword began to find its mark, though more than once he had to quickly raise his shield against a blow from the enemy.

But if Ithamar had hoped for a swift battle, it was not to be. The early blow that they had dealt to the Amalekites had been a weighty one, but the longer the fighting dragged on, the more the hand of Amalek seemed to strengthen. After a lengthy exchange, the outcome of which was only secured when Ithamar's opponent fell, he stood for a moment, breathing heavily. He swiftly rubbed his right forearm across his brow, in an attempt to wipe the sweat from his eyes, and as he did so, he lifted his gaze to the hill. Moses was tiring and the staff was dropping lower. *Yahweh—give him strength, and remember me also!* But there was no more time either to rest or to pray, as another Amalekite bore down on him.

Slowly but surely, however, the battle seemed to turn in their favour. The next time Ithamar glanced upwards, he saw Moses sitting on a stone, with Aaron and Hur supporting his hands, so the staff was again held high. Although Israelites lay dead or wounded, the number of Amalekites left standing was clearly dwindling, and by the time the western sky was as steeped in red as the battleground, the remaining foes had either fled or been slain. Ithamar finally stopped. His arms dropped to his side and he closed his eyes and just breathed. Having stopped, he found he could barely lift his arms, so both his sword and his shield stayed down at his side. It was as if they were now inseparable from his arms, having somehow been grafted onto his body during the battle.

'Brother!'

For a moment, his utter exhaustion was forgotten. Ithamar turned, only to find himself being wrapped in Nadab's strong embrace. His sword and shield finally separated themselves from his hands, falling to the ground, and his arms somehow found enough strength to grip his eldest brother. 'Yahweh has given us victory,' uttered Ithamar with both weariness and wonder. And as his head rested for a moment upon Nadab's shoulder, his eyes fell upon the one distant mountain that had a name. *Horeb*.

Notes

1. *The route of the Exodus has been much debated (see, for example, Kenneth Kitchen for a summary of the main discussion). Although the Bible records a number of place names in connection with the Exodus, many of them cannot now be located with certainty, especially as the region will have undergone topographical changes over three millennia. The route that seems to fit the Exodus data best, however, is known as the Southern route, going down the western side of the Sinai Peninsula, before turning north along its eastern side after the stay at Sinai. There are various watering places along the way.*

2. *The exact rate of travel of the community is not known (given that they did not necessarily travel every day). It might have been as much as 10-15 miles on a good day, although others have estimated it as 6 miles per day.*

3. *Quails fly north from Arabia to Southern Europe in March/April time.*

4. *Water from rocks has apparently been known in that area, as there is water under the sands of the coastal strips to the west and east of the Sinai Peninsula.*

5. *Manna is described both as flakes and being like coriander seeds, which are small and round. However, split coriander seeds look a little like rolled oats, so it is possible that this is what was meant. The Israelites ground the manna, and both boiled and baked it (Numbers 11:7-8). Boiling it presumably made a porridge, as was done with various grains in ancient Egypt. It is possible that boiling might also have produced something like the thick, solid, dough-like African staple of ugali, somewhat similar to the European dish of polenta. Although various natural explanations for it have been offered, probably none of these would apply to all the different terrains that the Israelites passed through.*

6. *The word, 'manna' means 'what?' in Hebrew. This word-play is obviously impossible to reproduce in English.*

7. *Deuteronomy 25:17-18 reports that the Amalekites assaulted stragglers. There is no indication of how many there were, but the implication of Exodus 17:14-16 is that the Amalekites were not wiped out by this encounter.*

8. *Rephidim may have been reached by travelling along Wadi Refayid, which intersects Wadi Feiran (a few miles north of the mountain Jebel Musa) which has a lush oasis.*

9. *Hoshea is named Joshua later when he goes into the Promised Land as a spy (Numbers 13:16). His earlier name is kept at this point in the story.*

10. *We do not know how old Joshua was at this time, only that he was 110 when he died (Joshua 24:29), which was, at the very least, 45 years after these events. However, Caleb was forty when he went with Joshua and the others to spy out Canaan, so it may be reasonable to assume that Joshua was around 30-40 at this time.*

11. *There is debate about which mountain in current-day Arabia is Mount Sinai (also called Horeb). The traditional site of Jebel Musa ('the mountain of Moses'), towards the south of the Sinai Peninsula, has been chosen here, as it has a large plain in front of it. It is also, according to Kenneth Kitchen, around a two-day journey to the Feiran oasis, which would have had an ample supply of water.*

12. *It is not clear why both names (Horeb and Sinai) are used for the mountain. Some have suggested that one applied to the general region and the other to the mountain, but in the text they both seem to apply to the mountain itself.*

5

The LORD descended to the top of Mount Sinai and called Moses to the top of the mountain. So Moses went up. (Exodus 19:20)

Ithamar wandered back into the camp with the clay jar he had just filled with manna. He stood with his back to the rising sun and gazed out over the myriad tents packed into flat, open land edged by mountains. He stared along the length of broad plain. *Maybe five times as long as it was wide*, he decided. Animals were scattered around the camp and on the slopes nearby. *The land was good for grazing—no wonder Moses had brought a flock here from Midian.* Ithamar had seen a number of brooks running down from the mountain heights, and on their way to the plain they had passed through the lush oasis previously claimed by the Amalekites. It now lay only a short distance behind them, not much more than a day's journeying with flocks.

He turned around, one hand shading his eyes from the sun peeping above the mountains to the east, whilst the other held the clay jar to his chest. Mount Horeb rose directly in front of him, like some vast, unyielding tent, whose folds were made from rock rather than woven goat's hair. He'd never seen a mountain so high. His gaze gradually moved down the rugged face of Horeb and finally came to rest on the one tent that stood apart, some distance from the camp and closer to the mountain. It was the tent that Moses always pitched as a place for meeting with Yahweh. Although Hoshea, who had become Moses' servant, didn't leave the tent, they knew when Moses was there, as the pillar of cloud would descend to cover its entrance. But the cloud wasn't over it now.

Ithamar suddenly realised that—unusually—he had not seen his uncle since the previous evening. 'Have you seen Moses?' he called out to his cousin, who was sitting on a small stool, milking a goat.

Gershom shook his head, 'Not for a while. He went up the mountain at first light and hasn't come back yet.'

Ithamar studied him for a moment. Gershom was Moses' eldest son, and he and his brother, mother and grandfather had arrived a few days earlier, just as they'd reached Horeb. *He didn't look much older than himself.* 'Does it seem very different here to living in Midian?' he asked.

Gershom glanced around. 'I have never seen so many tents, and the mountains are higher.' He grinned. 'But goats are goats.' He gave the one he'd been milking a quick slap on the rump, sending it scurrying off, and rose to his feet. 'Do you know how many you are?'

Ithamar shrugged. 'Thousands upon thousands is all I can say.' He thought for moment. 'You said that you'd heard about what happened in Egypt...'

'That's right.'

'But how?'

'Traders,' replied Gershom simply, picking up the bowl of milk from the ground. 'Those returning from Egypt kept speaking about disaster after disaster falling upon the land. Then, maybe almost two months ago, we began to hear of Israelite slaves—huge numbers of them—leaving Egypt. And tales of a sea being dried up.'

'I saw it,' said Ithamar. 'We all did.'

Gershom's eyes drifted across to the ever-present pillar of cloud. 'And you behold Yahweh's presence every day.'

'We do,' replied Ithamar, smiling. 'And we eat His bread.'

When Moses finally reappeared, sometime after noon, he immediately summoned Ithamar and his brothers. 'Gather the elders,' he declared solemnly. 'Yahweh has spoken.' He didn't elaborate but there was a fire in his eyes that intrigued Ithamar. *Whatever Yahweh had said, it was momentous.*

Ithamar was sent to his uncle Nahshon, who would gather together the elders of the tribe of Judah, and to Nethanel and Eliab, who would do the same for Issachar and Zebulun. He set off with Eleazar, who was to go to the tribes of Dan, Asher and Naphtali. 'What do you think Yahweh has said to Moses?' asked Ithamar slightly breathlessly as they hurried along. 'It sounds important.'

Eleazar turned his head towards him, one eyebrow raised. 'Does Yahweh ever say anything that is *not* important?'

He had a point. 'More important than usual, then,' he replied, grinning. 'You know what I mean.'

'I cannot and will not begin to try to guess the mind of the Almighty,' said Eleazar, shaking his head and smiling. 'But it is only right that the elders hear it first. You, my brother, will have to wait like everyone else.'

The meal that evening was a simple one of cheese from their flocks and herds and bread baked from manna. The days had lengthened, and a crescent moon hung low above the mountains in the rapidly-fading colours of the western sky. As they sat out together on mats in the cool of the evening, Moses spoke. 'Yahweh is going to make a covenant with us—a covenant that binds us, His people, to Him.'

'What are its terms?' asked Nadab, tearing some bread from a round lying with others on a platter.

'He calls us to obey His words,' replied Moses, 'and if we do so, then we will be His own treasured possession, singled out from among all the peoples of the earth. We shall be a kingdom of priests, a holy nation.'

'That was what you told the elders this afternoon?' asked Abihu.

'Yes. I declared Yahweh's intention to them, and they replied for the tribes of Israel.'

'What did they say?' asked Eleazar.

'They answered as one man.' Moses smiled. *'All that Yahweh has spoken we will do.* And tomorrow I will rise early and return to Horeb, to bear those words to Yahweh.'

Ithamar was puzzled. 'But surely Yahweh knows all things and knows what they have said.'

'He does indeed,' interjected Aaron, 'but it is a solemn covenant, requiring Moses to declare the elders' answer to Yahweh nevertheless.'

'And what happens then?' asked Ithamar.

'Then,' replied Moses, 'we will do whatever Yahweh tells us to do next.' And with that, he picked up a piece of bread, balanced some goat's cheese upon it, and ate.

'It is as well the days are so hot,' said Keziah, smiling. 'The washing will dry as swiftly as spilt milk on a bread oven.'

Ithamar laughed. 'You speak truly!'

'So...' said Keziah, drawing out the word and looking at him expectantly.

'So what?'

She sighed with exasperation. 'So give me your tunic if you want it washed and ready for tomorrow. If it didn't need washing at the start of the day, it does now!'

Ithamar looked down at his dusty clothes. *She was right.*

The camp had been transformed that day, with wet clothes seemingly hanging over every rope of every tent. When Moses had returned from Horeb again the previous day, it was with instructions from Yahweh for the whole assembly to prepare and purify themselves to meet Him, washing their garments so that they would be ready on the third day. Ithamar, his brothers, and a number of others had also spent the day erecting barriers around the base of the mountain, mainly from any spare tent poles and ropes they could find. Yahweh had made it clear that neither man nor beast was to even set foot on the mountain, and any who did so were to be put to death.

Later, as they were lying side by side that night, Keziah suddenly whispered, 'Are you nervous?'

'About meeting Yahweh tomorrow?'

'Yes.'

Ithamar thought for a moment, but instead of answering, asked, 'Why? Are you?'

'Is it not right to be afraid? After all, Moses said that anyone who even touches the mountain must not have a hand laid on them, but stoned or shot with arrows.' She paused. 'I have spent the afternoon washing, but can any preparation ever make us fit to meet Yahweh?'

Ithamar rolled onto his side so that she could feel him close and laid his arm over her. Had it been any other night, he would have comforted her by their union, but Moses had instructed them to abstain until after the third day. Ithamar moved his hand and laid it on her belly. It had been more than two months since she'd told him she was with child, and he could now feel the curve of her body that spoke of the new life within. 'Yahweh is the God of life,' he said quietly. 'And He gives us not only life, but all that is needed to sustain it. His warnings are only for our own good.' He thought for a moment more. 'We are drawn to the warmth of a fire, and it gives us heat to cook, but it is powerful and we know not to touch it. Maybe it is like that with Yahweh.'

She laid her hand over his, and squeezed it in the dark.

'But, yes,' he continued, 'I *am* nervous—even a little afraid—and maybe it is right for us to feel that way.' He heard her draw a deep breath in and let it out slowly.

'You're right.'

'Maybe we should try to sleep.' he said, 'If we can…'

After a night of fitful sleep, Ithamar rose with the dawn. But even as he pushed back the thin woollen covering, a sound rang out that he hadn't heard since the plagues in Egypt: thunder. When he pulled back the flap of the tent, he found Eleazar already outside, looking steadily south-east. He glanced, but only for a moment, in Ithamar's direction. 'Come. Look at this.'

As soon as he emerged from the tent, dressed as he had been in Egypt, in a simple loincloth, a fleeting flash illuminated the sky. A crash of thunder followed almost immediately. Not for the first time, Ithamar felt the hairs on the back of his neck rise, as his eyes were drawn towards Horeb. He stood in silence, open-mouthed. The top half of the mountain was ringed with a cloud that was both dark and thick. Most of the sky was also clouded, and although there was some light in the sky to the east, most of the grey dawn of the new day was obscured, so that an eerie twilight hung over the camp. Another flash streaked outwards across the sky from Horeb, and another thunderclap seemed to shake the very air around them.

'The whole camp will be awake now, if it wasn't before,' said Eleazar softly, his eyes not leaving the mountain.

With difficulty, Ithamar briefly tore his gaze away and glanced around. People of all ages were silently standing by the tents, transfixed. 'Some look stunned,' he murmured, 'others, terrified.'

'He is a fool who stands fearless before Yahweh,' replied his brother.

'Or undressed.' Ithamar's eyes remained on the mountain as he retrieved his clean tunic from the tent rope. *Keziah was right, it was bone dry.*

Manna was collected hastily that morning, and Elisheba made a quick meal of porridge for the family. None sat to eat and all ate in silence. The usual hubbub of chatter and laughter was absent from the camp, and others seemed to be eating as they were. Not one had their back to the mountain.

'They feel it too,' said Keziah to Ithamar, nodding in the direction of two of their goats. They were unsettled and straining at the cords that held them. All the flocks and herds had either been tethered or penned, so that none could stray onto the mountain.

'Only the dead would be unmoved by this day,' he replied, putting his arm around her. 'But Yahweh has not brought us this far only to destroy us.' She nodded, but did not speak.

Keziah begin to tremble, however, as a new sound began to build between the thunder. It was the unmistakable sound of a ram's horn, but louder than any Ithamar had ever heard. And there was no pause in the note, as if the one blowing had breath as limitless as the seas. Around them, some huddled together whilst others glanced fearfully in every direction but that of the mountain, as if deciding whether to stay or flee.

'It is the trumpet blast that Moses told us to wait for,' said Ithamar. 'It is time.'

'Yahweh summons us,' cried out Moses moments later, as he strode into the midst of the tents, holding the staff aloft. 'Come now, and pass the message through the camp. Follow me!' And with that, he turned back to face Horeb, and began walking slowly forward.

Ithamar had seen their people both on the move and camped, but never gathered together to stand in one place. He and Keziah were near the foot of Horeb. A wide strip of empty ground lay between those at the front and the barriers they had erected. No-one was pushing forward to get closer, each person wanting to stand at a safe distance. Wave upon wave of the children of Israel were arriving, and the sea of people was spreading out to the right and the left around the base of the mountain. The eyes of many were fixed upon the thick, dark cloud that encircled the top of the mountain. Others glanced up nervously before swiftly lowering their eyes again. Some were visibly shaking. And once again there was utter silence apart from the continuing blast of the trumpet and the crashes of thunder. Ithamar's mouth had become dry and, despite the heat of the summer, he found himself shivering.

Moses stood slightly apart with his back to them, but still on their side of the barrier. His staff was now planted on the ground, but his head was tilted back, his gaze—like theirs—on the cloud. And then Ithamar felt it. The ground beneath his feet began to shake, as did the mountain, gently at first, and then violently. Ithamar heard screams from behind him, and Keziah gripped him more tightly. He held her close. The cloud was no longer simply dark. Huge flames darted upwards, and thick smoke started rising up from it, as if a giant furnace had suddenly been lit upon the upper slopes of Horeb, whose fires reached to the heavens. And the trumpet blast became deafening. Ithamar wondered whether it was announcing that Yahweh Himself had now stepped down from the heavens onto the mountain. Moses raised his arms towards the cloud, but any words spoken to the Almighty were lost in the noise. A sudden crash of thunder made Keziah jump. Several babies in their mother's arms began to cry nearby, and older voices joined them. *This was no impotent Egyptian god!*

Moses moved forward, crossed the barrier and began walking up the mountain. He was not struck down. The trumpet began to fade away, as if the one wielding it had finally run out of breath, although Ithamar knew that was not the reason. His uncle became smaller and smaller, eventually disappearing into the cloud. It was only when Moses could no longer be seen that murmuring in the crowd began.

'What happens now?' whispered Keziah after a time.

'We wait.' It was the only answer he could give.

Ithamar had no real idea of how much time had passed when Moses finally emerged from the cloud. The sun was obscured, and the gloom of the day made it impossible to tell whether it was yet noon or long after. The murmuring of the crowd gradually dwindled until there was an expectant silence. It was only when Moses was standing on their side of the barrier once again that he addressed them. 'Yahweh warns you once more not to approach Him. He is veiled from your eyes and it must stay that way. Any who defy His orders will bear the penalty.'

The message was conveyed back across the huge crowd, until silence eventually returned. Not even the bleat of a goat could be heard. And then the air was suddenly rent by words that resounded around them. 'I am Yahweh, your God, who brought you out of the land of Egypt, out of the house of slavery.' It was as if the thunder had now become a voice. Or waves, like those that had come crashing down at the Sea of Reeds, were now speaking—though Keziah said later it was like music. It was unmistakable, inescapable, overwhelming, formidable. It was not the voice of Yahweh's mouthpiece, but of Yahweh Himself.

Ithamar immediately forgot every other person around him and dropped to his knees, bowing his head to the earth.

'You shall have no other gods before me,' continued the voice. 'You shall not make for yourself an image in the form of anything in heaven above or on the earth beneath or in the waters below.' And Ithamar trembled before his God.

The commandments continued, until the thunder finally ceased to be a voice. Ithamar remained with his forehead to the ground, his ears still alert. *Had Yahweh finished speaking?* He suddenly thought of Egypt. *There the gods were seen but were silent and lifeless. Their God remained hidden and yet spoke and acted. And unlike the unpredictable Egyptian deities, He had made known to them what He required.*

Eventually those around him began to stir. He cautiously raised his head. All, like him, were bowed down, but slowly people began to get to their feet, and he followed their lead, as did Keziah.

'Is it over?' she whispered.

'I don't know. We must wait until Moses instructs us further.'

It was not long, however, before the elders were gathered around Moses again, and Ithamar was close enough to hear their words. It soon became clear that they shared one burning concern, though many spoke at the same time and their voices were mingled.

'Yahweh has shown us His glory and greatness…'

'We've heard His voice from the heart of the fire…'

'God has spoken to us today and yet we live! But why should we risk death again?'

'Yes, if Yahweh speaks to us again, we'll die!'

'This terrible fire will consume us…'

'Can anyone hear the voice of the living God as we did and yet survive?'

Moses held up his hand and the clamour died down, but one of the elders spoke for them all in the silence that followed. 'Moses— you go and listen to what Yahweh says. Then tell us everything he says to you, and we will listen and obey.' His words were followed by nods of agreement and cries of *yes, that's right, that's what we want.*

Moses nodded slowly. 'You should not be terrified,' he began. 'God has come to you in this way to test you. You have seen his glory and greatness, and that should make you fear sinning against Him.' His gaze swept steadily and silently across not just the elders but also the whole assembly. There appeared to be a tenderness in his eyes. *Like a shepherd watching over his flock,* thought Ithamar. Moses nodded again. 'I will take your words to Yahweh. Wait here.' A short while later, he was disappearing from their view once more.

Although the thick cloud still covered the top half of the mountain as they waited, the flashes of lightning abated, and with it, the palpable fear. The gloom felt less intense, people spoke in low voices, and there were ripples of movement throughout the crowd. Ithamar became aware that the rumbling of thunder had been replaced by the rumbling of his stomach.

The taut lines on Keziah's face finally softened and a smile crept across her face. 'Are you hungry, my husband?'

'The bowl of porridge was a very long time ago,' he replied with a grin. 'What about you?'

She shook her head. 'No, I do not feel like eating yet.' She paused. 'Do you think we will hear Yahweh's voice again?'

Ithamar thought for a moment. 'We *will* hear His voice, but maybe from now on it will be through the mouth of Moses. You heard the words of the elders?'

She nodded. 'Yes—and they echoed the thoughts of my heart.'

He put his arm around her waist. 'But do you remember what I said this morning? Yahweh hasn't brought us out of Egypt to destroy us, but to give us a new life.'

She twisted her face upwards towards his, her eyes shining. 'I believe you, maybe because Yahweh is blessing *us* with a new life in another way.' And she guided his free hand onto her swelling belly.

They stood in an amiable silence until Ithamar's attention was drawn back to the cloud by a sudden murmuring around him and a familiar voice at his side.

'Look, Moses returns,' said Eleazar.

Although Moses was still some distance away, Ithamar studied him, trying to measure his mood. There was no weariness or hesitancy in Moses' stride. He was looking steadily ahead. 'Will all be well?' Ithamar asked, turning to his brother.

Eleazar smiled wryly and raised an eyebrow, as he was wont to do. 'You still expect me to know the mind of Yahweh, Brother?' His eyes returned to Moses and he added, 'But all appears well.'

The elders gathered around their uncle once more after he'd completed his walk back to the foot of the mountain. Moses raised his voice and spoke slowly and with solemnity. 'Hear the word of Yahweh. He says, *I have heard the words you have spoken.*' He paused, looking round at them all. 'And His response is, *You have done well in all that you have said.* So be at peace, my friends. Yahweh also says, *Return to your tents.* Therefore go now, and pass His words to the tribes of Israel.'

There was a brief silence, and then visible relief washed across the gathering like a cool breeze in the heat of the summer sun. The elders began to disperse, conversing freely. But there was something inscrutable about Moses' expression as he stood, unmoving as an ancient oak, watching over the assembly. Ithamar wasn't the only one to notice it.

'There is something else,' whispered Eleazar.

Ithamar turned to Keziah. 'You and Tirzah go ahead.' There was a question in her eyes. He smiled. 'There is a meal to prepare! We will follow soon.'

'Come, Tirzah,' she called out with laugh. 'Our husbands are in danger of fainting from hunger.' And with that, the two wives departed.

Aaron too, waited with them, as the huge crowd slowly moved away, like a mighty, wide river flowing unhurriedly but inexorably forward. The three of them approached Moses, who was watching the people depart. There was sadness in his eyes.

'What is it, my brother?' asked Aaron.

Moses' gaze didn't move from the camp and its people. 'There was more that Yahweh said,' he replied. 'Yes, He said that they had spoken well. But then He added words that pierced my soul. *Oh that they had such a heart in them, that they would always fear Me and keep all My commandments, so that it would go well with them and their sons forever.*' He fell silent, and then added quietly, 'He knows His people's heart better than I do and I fear His meaning.' And with that, he turned and began to walk slowly back up the mountain.

When Moses returned with further instructions from Yahweh, only the elders were summoned.

'At least hearing Yahweh's commands will not be so terrifying this time,' said Ithamar to Eleazar, as they stood at the edge of the gathering of Israel's leaders.

'You are right! But His words will be no less binding than if delivered by a voice of thunder.'

Ithamar thought for a moment about the ten commandments that they had heard directly from the mouth of Yahweh. 'And will this also be part of the covenant?'

Eleazar shrugged his shoulders. 'I imagine there is more to say about how we are to worship and serve Yahweh and live as His people.' They both fell silent as Moses held up his hand.

Ithamar listened with fascination as his uncle began relating Yahweh's latest—and varied—instructions. There were decrees concerning the building of altars, the treatment of slaves and reparation for injuries. Detailed laws addressed stealing sheep and seducing virgins. Others involved fires in fields, leaving land fallow and annual feasts. *These were laws for everyday life.* But it was some of Yahweh's final words through Moses about the driving out of the Canaanites that particularly caught Ithamar's attention.

'Yahweh says, *I will not drive them out before you in a single year,*' proclaimed Moses, '*as the land would become desolate and the wild animals too numerous for you.*' Ithamar strained his ears to hear what was to follow. '*Little by little I will drive them out before you, until you have increased enough to take possession of the land.*'

When Moses finally fell silent, Ithamar whispered to his brother, 'If we are to fight, then, it is not going to be over quickly.'

Eleazar turned to him, as the elders began to talk among themselves. 'What did Moses tell us before?' He smiled and didn't wait for an answer. '*Yahweh may not be taking us by the shortest route, but it will be the best.*'

Even as Ithamar was still taking in his brother's words, a spokesman for the elders called out, 'Everything Yahweh has said, we will do!'

'Then assemble the people early tomorrow,' replied Moses, 'and the covenant between Yahweh and His people will be made.' He paused and added, 'But before you leave, I will choose seventy of you to ascend the mountain with me, along with Aaron and his sons, Nadab and Abihu. We will worship Yahweh there after the covenant is sealed.'

A pang of disappointment pricked Ithamar's heart. *He and Eleazar were not included.* He glanced at his brother. There was longing in his eyes. Ithamar sighed. 'They *are* the eldest, I suppose.'

Eleazar nodded. 'Yes, but to draw close to Yahweh…' His voice trailed off.

'We *have* heard Him speak, though,' replied Ithamar. *And that had been terrifying, after all, so maybe they were being spared.* But his wistfulness remained.

When Ithamar returned from tending the sheep that afternoon, he passed near Moses' tent. The sides of the tent were hitched up to allow both the stifling air out and any cooling breeze in. Zipporah, Moses' wife, was beating a mat hanging over a tent rope with a brush, sending clouds of fine dust into the air. Ithamar caught a glimpse of Moses inside. He was sitting cross-legged with a large wooden box in front of him as a makeshift table, over which he was hunched. The box was covered with scrolls.

Ithamar, his curiosity kindled, wandered over to Zipporah, and tipped his head in Moses' direction. 'What's he doing?'

She laughed. 'Writing!'

'But what?'

'Why don't you ask him?' she replied, her dark eyes sparkling. She went back to beating the mat.

Ithamar ducked his head slightly as he entered the tent. Moses looked up and smiled. 'What is it, Nephew?'

'I was just wondering what you were writing.'

'You did me a great service, Ithamar,' began Moses, 'when you packed my writing box carefully onto the cart when we left Egypt. For if you had not done so, I would not now be able to write an account of all the words and ordinances of Yahweh.'

Ithamar stared down at the black marks on the papyrus scroll which meant nothing to him. 'Are those the words you spoke to the elders earlier?'

Moses nodded, and laid down the reed brush he was using with the ink. 'Yes, this will be the covenant with Yahweh that I read out tomorrow, but it will also preserve the memory of His words for future generations.' He picked the scroll up and held it out to Ithamar. 'Here, look.'

Ithamar took it and studied it.

'Can you read what it says?'

Ithamar shook his head. 'No, slaves had neither a need to learn nor anything to read.'

'But you are a slave no longer,' said Moses, taking the papyrus back from Ithamar. 'I will teach you—and your brothers.' He then chuckled. 'But not today.'

Ithamar grinned. 'You are busy, Uncle!'

'Ah, but no man should be too busy to teach his nephews to read the words of Yahweh. I will keep my promise.'

A rough altar of uncut stones taken from Horeb had been built by the time the people were assembled again at the foot of the mountain. Around the altar, Moses had set up twelve pillars of stone—the twelve tribes of Israel gathered around Yahweh—as they prepared to pledge their allegiance to each other in a solemn and binding covenant. Young men from each of the tribes sacrificed young bulls, with Nadab from their own tribe and Hoshea from Ephraim among them. Moses sprinkled the altar with the blood of the slaughtered animals, and the smoke and aroma from the burnt offerings rose upwards to meet the vast, dark cloud that hung over the mountain. Unlike the day of the previous assembly, however, there was no thunder and the sun made the day bright.

As the smoke continued to rise, Moses stood before the people, a scroll in his hands. 'Hear the words of the covenant that Yahweh is making with us,' he cried out, and as silence descended upon the whole assembly he began reading. *'You have seen for yourselves that I have spoken to you from heaven…'*

Ithamar didn't hear a single voice apart from that of his uncle during the entire time he was reading. But as soon as he had finished, it was as if the tribes of Israel were replying to Yahweh with their own voice of thunder, as myriad men and women standing on the plain responded with one voice: *Everything Yahweh has said, we will do. We will obey!*

Then, in view of the whole assembly, Moses sprinkled some more of the bull's blood on the elders, on the pillars representing the twelve tribes, and on any others who were close enough, sealing the agreement between their God and His people. Moses lifted up his voice once again and announced, 'This is the blood of the covenant that Yahweh has made with you in accordance with all these words.' And with that, he signalled to Aaron, Nadab and Abihu, and the seventy elders. It was now time for them to meet the God of Abraham, Isaac and Jacob.

'What was it like?' asked Ithamar eagerly as Nadab and Abihu finally returned later to the tent. Their wives simply seemed relieved to have them back safely.

'Ithamar!' chided Keziah. 'Let them sit down and have something to eat and drink first before you start demanding answers.'

'Peace, Keziah,' said Nadab with a smile. 'We have both eaten and drunk.'

'And eaten and drunk well,' added Abihu, as he lowered himself to a sitting position on the woven mats in the centre of the tent. The hangings dividing the tent into their sleeping areas were pulled back, and the four brothers and their wives sat down together to share the events of the day.

'So?' said Ithamar, as soon as they were all seated.

Nadab and Abihu looked at each other, and then Nadab began. 'It was so unlike the day we heard Yahweh's voice. No thunder or lightning—'

'Or fire or smoke,' interjected Abihu.

'All was peaceful.' Nadab then added in a quieter voice, 'More peaceful than any place I have ever been. It was as if...' He broke off for a moment, searching for the right word. 'As if the air itself was thick...or heavy...'

'And instead of dark clouds and gloom, there was light,' said Abihu, awed. 'Light as bright as the sun.' Utter silence, like that of the wilderness, pressed in on them all for several moments.

'It was coming from Him,' said Nadab eventually, his eyes full of wonder. And none needed to ask of whom he spoke. 'We couldn't raise our eyes to look at Him,' he continued, 'even if we'd had the courage to do so. The light was too blinding.'

'We could look no higher than His feet,' said Abihu. 'They were like the feet of a man, except under them...' He seemed to be struggling for words again.

'It was as if the sky was the pavement beneath His feet,' murmured Nadab.

'Like a pavement of bright blue lapis lazuli, only clear.'

They both fell silent.

'And?' asked Eleazar, his eyes bright.

'And we ate and drank in His presence,' said Nadab, with a smile and shrug of his shoulders. 'What more can we say?'

Ithamar felt a tinge of disappointment. He sensed that the questions that were tumbling through his mind would remain unanswered.

But Abihu *did* have one more thing to say. 'We saw Yahweh yet He did not stretch out His hand against us.'

'He extended instead His hand of friendship,' said Eleazar softly.

After a pause, Nadab added, 'Moses has returned to the mountain. He has taken Hoshea with him, and has instructed that we stay in the camp until they return. He's left Aaron and Hur in charge, to deal with any disputes.'

'Why?' asked Ithamar. 'Is he going to be on Horeb long?'

'He did not say,' answered Nadab drily, 'and that might be because he did not know.'

Notes

1. *The word for wilderness that is used implies grazing land rather than desert.*
2. *Deuteronomy chapters 4, 5 and 9 also recount the above events. The extra details given there have been combined with the Exodus account, and every attempt has been made to harmonise them accurately.*

3. It is not clear why Moses tells the Israelites to abstain from sex before meeting Yahweh, particularly as this was before the laws on ritual cleanliness given in Leviticus.

4. It is not explicitly said that there were physical boundaries erected around the mountain, although it seems implied in some texts (eg Exodus 19:12,23).

5. It has been assumed that the people are already at Sinai when Jethro comes with Moses' wife and sons (Exodus 18). Jethro must have known that Sinai was the goal of Israel's pilgrimage (from Exodus 5:1) and that worship there would be a fulfilment of God's promise.

6. We don't know how long it took for Moses to climb Sinai. Today, there is a steep route to the top that may take as little as an hour and a half, but as that involves steps that have been hewn out of the rocks by monks, it might be better to assume that Moses took a gentler route. The 'Camel Path' takes around 3 hours today, although we can't be sure of the exact point at which Moses began his ascent, or if he went to the summit each time.

7. When it comes to the voice of Yahweh, New Testament references have been drawn upon. Revelation 14:2 speaks of a voice from heaven, 'like the roar of rushing waters and like a loud peal of thunder…like that of harpists playing their harps.' John 12:29 also speaks of a voice from heaven that some hear as thunder, and Revelation 1:15 describes the voice of Jesus as being like the rushing of many waters.

8. The text of Exodus doesn't say that the people bowed down when they heard the voice of Yahweh, but Exodus 4:31 says: 'And when [the elders] heard that the Lord was concerned about them and had seen their misery, they bowed down and worshipped.' It is hard to imagine that when they heard the actual voice of Yahweh, they didn't do the same.

9. It is assumed that when all the people give their response in Exodus 24:3, this is through the elders as their representatives (given the difficulty of Moses communicating it verbally to the entire assembly). The repeating of the (now written) words in Exodus 24:7 is, however, taken as being the whole assembly, though it is not clear again how this would be done.

10. We are not told the identity of the young men offering sacrifices, but it was before Aaron and his sons were designated as priests. It seems reasonable to assume, therefore, that the twelve tribes would all be represented in offering sacrifices.

11. It is not clear what it means when Moses and the elders 'saw the God of Israel' (Exodus 24:8). From what is said later to Moses (in Exodus 33:20), it cannot mean that they saw the face of God, unless it was the pre-incarnate Christ (as may well have been the case with Abraham in Genesis 18). This story has used the picture of the transfigured Christ, whose face 'shone like the sun' and whose clothes 'became as white as the light' (Matthew 17:2). This would render them unable to raise their eyes to look directly at Him.

6

Then the LORD said to Moses, 'Go down, because your people, whom you brought up out of Egypt, have become corrupt. They have been quick to turn away from what I commanded them and have made themselves an idol cast in the shape of a calf.' (Exodus 32:7-8)

The mood in the camp was jubilant—at least for a while. But as Moses' absence turned from days into weeks, with the Sabbaths slipping by, Ithamar noticed a change. *The people were becoming restless.*

'They are not content to wait,' said Eleazar, as he and Ithamar began gathering the double portion of manna for that day and for the Sabbath. 'The murmurings seem to grow with each day that Moses does not return. They want to be moving.'

'But it is clear that Yahweh has not moved!' exclaimed Ithamar, as he dropped some more manna into his jar. 'All they need to do is look at the mountain to see that.' He glanced over to Horeb. Cloud and fire were still covering its summit. But he had to admit, he wished Moses were there; he had already seen the people turn against their leaders more than once. *Would it take much or many for them to do so again?*

'It is a strange thing,' replied Eleazar. 'They have seen the glory of Yahweh there every day for—what?—forty days? But the sight that once drove them to their knees has ceased to trouble them.' He then held up a piece of manna. 'Like this. The more times we gather it, the more easily we forget that it comes from the hand of Yahweh. After all, it only took three days after crossing the Sea of Reeds for the grumbling to begin.'

Ithamar straightened up. 'You are in a strange mood today, Brother!' Eleazar just grunted and shrugged his shoulders, so Ithamar continued. 'The people have heard the voice of Yahweh. Does that not change everything?'

Eleazar smiled wryly. 'It did for me.' He paused and then looked around him. 'I am not so sure it did for everyone.'

However, not long after the manna had been baked to become the first bread of the day, Nadab suddenly exclaimed, 'This looks like trouble!'

Ithamar glanced up and immediately leapt to his feet. Scores of men were streaming through the camp towards their family tents.

'This is no simple dispute,' muttered Nadab. 'We need to stand by Father. Ithamar, find Hur.'

Ithamar hurried off. He had witnessed Aaron and Hur dealing with the Israelites' quarrels: disputes over flocks or property, or maybe claims of unfaithfulness. But there had only ever been two or three of them at a time before, or a small group at most. *This was something very different.* He had seen the looks of defiance and determination on the faces of many.

Soon Ithamar was returning with Miriam as well as Hur. Although the three of them hurried back, by the time they neared Aaron's tent, they had to push their way through what had become a solid wall of people. Ithamar had no idea of how many were there, but it was a huge number, and among them he saw some of the elders. *Had this been something that they had been planning for some days?*

Ithamar and Miriam hung back, allowing Hur to join Aaron in the small clearing in the middle of the large crowd. Ithamar craned his neck, trying to see better.

A voice—he couldn't see whose it was—suddenly declared, 'Listen!' The clamour immediately faded away into silence. 'We have had enough waiting!' Cries of *Yes!* rippled around the crowd. 'Make us a god to lead us!' demanded the voice.

Ithamar stood open-mouthed in shock. *Surely this could not be happening.*

Someone else immediately spoke up. 'Yes. None of us know what's happened to this Moses who led us out of Egypt.' Voices shouted out in agreement.

Miriam turned to Ithamar. 'They behave as if my brother were a stranger to them!'

And then slowly, horrifyingly, a chant began to unite every voice in the mob, until it was deafening. *Make us a god! Make us a god! Make us a god...*

Aaron and Hur were talking together urgently. They seemed defenceless in the midst of the belligerent crowd. Although Ithamar couldn't see any weapons being carried, he knew that they didn't need them. *Their very numbers were deadly enough.* He caught sight of Eleazar. He was pale and as motionless as Horeb. Ithamar felt sick. *What on earth would the horde do if their request was denied? They could do anything they wanted—and they seemed determined to get what they desired.* Their voices were relentless.

'Yahweh, have mercy,' whispered Miriam.

The chanting only subsided when Aaron held up his hand. He appeared shaken and afraid. 'Remove the gold rings from the ears of your wives, your sons and your daughters,' announced Aaron. 'Then bring them to me.'

Ithamar turned to Miriam, stunned, but before he was able to voice a single question, she shook her head slowly, and murmured, 'He gives in to them...'

'This is wrong!' exclaimed Eleazar, as he and Ithamar stood watching their uncle, but far enough away to be out of earshot. 'It is a grievous sin!'

A huge pile of gold earrings had accumulated by noon that day, and with the aid of a large fire, Aaron had melted down the gold and was now shaping the roughly-cast idol with a tool.

'He believes he has no choice,' replied Ithamar.

'There is always a choice,' insisted Eleazar angrily. 'Father heard the words of Yahweh. We all did. *You shall have no other gods before me. You shall not make for yourself an image in the form of anything in heaven above or on the earth beneath or in the waters below. You shall not bow down to them or worship them.*'

Ithamar could not refute a single word but he kept quiet. *Would he have acted differently if he'd been confronted by a mob?* He couldn't be sure.

Eleazar went on. 'We all ate bread this morning from the hand of Yahweh. Yet now the people want their own pitiful god that will be as dumb and lifeless as they are reckless!' He shook his head vehemently. 'I cannot watch this.' He then stormed off.

By evening, a roughly formed golden calf was being carried to a space that had been cleared at the edge of the camp, at the foot of Horeb. A crowd was beginning to gather there. Despite Eleazar turning his back in disgust, Ithamar felt it prudent to keep watch. He stood with Miriam some distance away but close enough to see what was happening.

A number of the elders lifted the small and unimposing calf onto a large rock, as if that would make it more impressive. It didn't appear to be entirely stable, but cheering began to fill the air.

'We are meant to be set apart for Yahweh,' said Miriam softly, her eyes upon the idol. 'Distinct among the nations. And yet this makes us no different to the Canaanites with their bull gods.'

Ithamar had seen their worship in Lower Egypt. The Canaanite gods may have been different to those of their overlords but they were just as contemptible.

In the distance, a voice cried out, 'This is your god, O Israel, who brought you up out of Egypt.'

'Why does Yahweh not strike them down?' murmured Ithamar, glancing up at Horeb, where cloud and fire still rested on the mountain, crowning its heights. Miriam did not answer, but he did not expect her to.

As the golden light of evening spread across the camp, an altar was built from rocks and earth in front of the calf. 'Whatever sacrifices they intend to offer,' said Miriam bleakly, 'at least they will not be desecrating the altar that Moses built.'

Eventually, above the crowd, another voice rose—that of Aaron. 'Tomorrow shall be a feast to Yahweh.'

The words were met with more cheers of approval before the horde finally began to disperse. Aaron and Hur started walking towards them. Neither Miriam nor Ithamar went forward to meet them, or spoke when the men stopped in front of them.

'It was a mob, Mother,' began Hur, looked steadily at Miriam. 'A mob of hundreds of men demanding we did what they asked. Pharaoh was told we were going to hold a festival to the God of Israel in the wilderness. That is what we will make it tomorrow. It is the best we could do.'

'Calling it a feast to Yahweh,' said Miriam icily, 'does not change what it is.' She then turned and walked away.

Being the Sabbath, there was no need to gather manna the following morning, but the mood in the tent was strained as Ithamar and the others rose early. Although Tirzah had baked bread from the manna collected the previous day, none of them seemed to have an appetite for either eating or speaking.

'What are we going to do?' asked Ithamar tentatively, as he, his brothers and the four wives went out together in the early morning light.

'I will not be part of it,' replied Eleazar adamantly. 'Neither Tirzah nor I will do anything other than stand at a distance.'

'And I will not sacrifice a living bull to a lifeless one,' said Nadab.

'But we cannot simply abandon Father,' said Abihu. 'Or Hur.'

'But neither can we endorse what has been done,' insisted Eleazar.

They walked on in silence through the tents. Others eagerly walking in the same direction clearly did not share their concerns. Many carried jars or skins and drinking vessels; others, whatever food was to hand. Men, both old and young, led animals to be sacrificed. There was a mood of celebration and anticipation as the crowds thronged forward.

Beyond the tents, men, women and children were spreading out in every direction. Ithamar was relieved to see that Aaron and Hur were at least holding back, seemingly allowing the people to do as they pleased. Elders were standing near the altar, as were the young men who had previously sacrificed to Yahweh—though without Nadab.

'The last time they made offerings on an altar,' muttered Eleazar, 'it was to seal the covenant with Yahweh, a covenant in which they promised to worship and obey Him alone.'

'But this *is* meant to be a feast to Yahweh,' said Abihu.

'How *can* it be that with that thing standing there,' spat out Eleazar.

Ithamar's eyes drifted back to the golden calf, which seemed absurd and small from where he was standing—and utterly insignificant next to the cloud-ringed mountain towering over it.

As the day wore on and after the sacrifices had been offered, the feasting began. Although Ithamar knew not from whence it came, strong drink flowed freely, and soon men and women were on their feet, singing and dancing. But these were nothing like the songs of praise that Moses had taught them or the dances led by Miriam on the shores of the Reed Sea. Ithamar averted his eyes. As he did so, he noticed that others from his tribe were also staying back. Whether it was from loyalty to Yahweh, to Moses or to Aaron, he couldn't be sure.

The revelry and noise only increased with the drunkenness, and both modesty and clothing began to be abandoned. 'What can we do?' uttered Ithamar in desperation.

'Only hope and pray that Yahweh does not rain down fire upon us as he did upon Sodom,' replied Eleazar, stony-faced. 'This is no more a feast to Yahweh than an Egyptian festival to Amun-Ra.'

Nadab spat on the earth. 'Or a Canaanite fertility rite.'

Ithamar lifted his eyes to the burning cloud far above the golden calf, almost expecting to see fire fall at any moment. But a movement against the mountain caught his attention. He strained his eyes, shading them against the sun. *Maybe it was a bird he had seen. Or a mountain goat.* He kept his eyes fixed on Horeb. *There it was again!* He stared for a long time until he was sure. 'Look!' he exclaimed.

'What is it, Ithamar?' asked Keziah.

'Moses and Hoshea! They are returning!'

'Yahweh be praised,' said Eleazar, his relief evident. 'Come! Let us go to them!'

'It will be quicker to skirt the gathering,' said Nadab.

Abihu nodded. 'You're right. It is chaos there.'

Their swift progress around the edge of the debauchery drew little attention from the revellers. 'They are either too drunk to notice us or they do not care,' said Ithamar as they hurried along.

'That will soon change,' replied Eleazar grimly. 'Of that I am sure.'

'Look,' said Abihu. 'We are not the only ones making our way to Moses.' Ithamar spotted Aaron and Elisheba, together with Miriam and Hur, approaching him from the opposite direction. He glanced up towards his uncle. He was easily recognisable by now, and had two tablets of stone in his arms. He and Hoshea were nearing the base of the mountain—and the golden calf.

If Moses hadn't noticed the small bull before, he had now. He let out a terrible cry. His anger clearly fuelled his strength, and he lifted the two stone tablets as if they were made from papyrus. Then, just as Ithamar and the rest arrived, he threw them down with such force that they shattered on the rock at his feet. He then looked out on the crowd, whilst pointing at the fragments of stone. '*That*,' he shouted, 'is what they have done to our covenant with Yahweh!' Then, with eyes blazing, he turned on Aaron. 'What did these people do to you,' he asked with uncharacteristic vehemence, 'that you led them into such a terrible sin?' He glared at his brother, breathing heavily.

Aaron held out his hands to him. 'Don't be angry, my lord,' he implored. 'You know yourself what the people are like. They're prone to evil.'

His reply did nothing to lessen Moses' fury. 'How did this happen? Explain it to me!'

Aaron briefly related the requests of the crowd the previous day, though his final words were less than truthful. 'When they gave me the gold, I threw it into the fire, and out came this calf.'

'If only you knew…' said Moses forcibly, shaking his head. 'If only you knew the honour that Yahweh had planned for you and your sons! They were to be priests, but *you*—You!—were to be His High Priest. To bring the people before Yahweh. But instead you have led them away from Him!' He pointed back up the mountain, his face anguished and his eyes still on Aaron. 'Yahweh's eyes saw this sin long before I did. I had to plead with Him not to destroy you all! I stayed His hand, but the cost of this folly may still be greater that you could imagine.'

No one spoke. And in the silence, the rowdy shouting of the camp intruded upon them. Moses' gaze shifted from his brother to the horde. 'They are out of control and running wild,' he said. 'It will bring shame upon us before our enemies. This must stop—now!'

They all followed him as he strode to the edge of the camp. 'Whoever is for Yahweh,' he shouted out, 'come to me!'

It soon became clear, as men started running to Moses, that far more had abstained from the revelry than Ithamar had thought. But they were all from the tribe of Levi. 'This is what Yahweh, the God of Israel says,' declared Moses loudly as they gathered round him. 'Every man must strap a sword to his side. You are to go from one end of the camp to the other, every one of you killing his brother and friend and neighbour.'

Ithamar swallowed hard. His uncle was asking him to take the sword that had killed Amalekites and turn it on their own people. *No. It was Yahweh commanding him.* He followed his brothers, running to their tent. If any of them were reluctant to carry out the order, they did not show it. A fire burned in Eleazar's eyes. *Zeal for Yahweh*, thought Ithamar, as he fumbled to strap on his own sword. His hands were trembling.

By the time the command had been carried out, three thousand lay dead in the camp. Most had fled screaming, abandoning their indulgence, as Yahweh's judgment began to fall. Ithamar's sword felled a single fleeing Israelite. That was enough.

Ithamar walked back to Moses with Eleazar after they had done what had been required. 'There are so many dead...' he began simply.

'But the real horror is not the blood on the ground,' replied Eleazar. 'It is the heinous stain of such sin—the profanity of worshipping a golden calf.'

When they returned, a huge fire was blazing. Ithamar caught a glimpse of a lump of bright metal in the midst of the flames. As the Levites gathered around Moses once again, their tunics spattered with blood, he stood upon the rock where the calf had been. 'Today you have set yourselves apart for Yahweh's service,' he called out. 'At great cost, you have killed sons and brothers, and Yahweh will bring a blessing upon you because of it. Now, go in peace. Your hands are clean before Yahweh.'

As Moses dismissed them, he called Ithamar and his brothers to him. 'Fetch my sons and your cousins,' he commanded. 'There is a job that must be done by the end of the day.'

Ithamar soon found himself, with a score of others, carrying empty jars retrieved from the refuse of the revelry. They filled them from a nearby brook that ran down from the mountain and alongside the camp, and then emptied the water over the fire, dousing its flames. Clouds of steam rose from the embers, as the fire sputtered, hissed and finally died. And amongst those embers was a pool of rapidly hardening gold. 'Keep cooling the metal,' directed Moses. 'I want it cold enough to be pounded and then ground to dust.'

As the sun dropped lower in the sky, the constant sound of metal being hammered by rocks rang out over the camp. Ithamar brought his rock down hard again and again upon the metal taken from the fire. His hands became black with soot and sore with blisters, as the gold became tiny, bright flakes. Eventually, Moses swept up the gold dust into bowls, before addressing the young men. 'I have one last task that must be done before the sun sets on the Sabbath,' he announced. 'Go out into the camp and order the people, in my name, to fill their water jars immediately from the brook. And as they come out with their jars, I will be standing here, upstream, scattering the gold over the water. And they will drink it.'

As Ithamar walked with Eleazar into the camp, his brother turned to him. 'By tomorrow, the golden calf will be shit.' The vulgar word seemed strange on his brother's lips. *But then again, it was no more than the idol deserved. There was no polite word for an abomination.*

The assembly that Moses called together the following morning was a sombre one. The people stood before him in silence. *A guilty silence*, thought Ithamar. Most had their eyes cast to the ground. 'You have committed a great sin,' began Moses. The words seemed to resound off the mountain behind him, as if Horeb itself were throwing the accusation back at the Israelites. The only movement was the shuffling of feet. 'But now I will go up to Yahweh,' continued Moses. 'Perhaps I can make atonement for your sin.' And with that, he turned his back on them all and began once again the ascent to the cloud, alone.

The huge company did not move from the foot of the mountain, despite the summer heat being at its most fierce. The discomfort seemed fitting, as the sun rose higher and the day dragged on. 'Lean on me,' whispered Ithamar to Keziah, who was looking pale and faint. She had been with child for six months, and her protruding belly was easily visible, despite her loose tunic. As she rested her head against his chest and put an arm around the back of his waist, he wrapped both arms around her to take part of her weight. She felt damp with sweat. Several young children nearby were crying, but not a single person left the gathering for either food or water. From time to time, quiet murmuring rippled around the assembly, but mostly there was silence, broken occasionally by the cry of a bird high above them or the bleating of a faraway goat.

Ithamar's mind drifted to the words Moses had spoken to his father. *He'd spoken of the honour that Yahweh had planned for him. He was to have been the High Priest. But that was not all he'd said. Moses had stated that he and his brothers were to be priests of Yahweh. What did that mean? And was that promise as shattered now as the fragments of stone at the foot of the mountain?*

Ithamar closed his eyes and prayed. It was a simple prayer: *Have mercy upon us, Yahweh. Please do not reject your people.* His lips moved silently, as again and again he repeated his plea. And just as he was beginning to wonder if Keziah might actually faint, the crowd began to stir. 'Moses returns,' said Eleazar quietly beside him. *He was right.* Once again, a small figure was making its way across and down the mountain. Ithamar studied his uncle as he gradually drew closer, trying to discern from his movement or manner anything that might indicate his mood—or the message he was bringing from Yahweh. His stride did not seem as purposeful as usual, nor his head held as high. *But then again, the day was blisteringly hot.*

When Moses was finally close enough for Ithamar to see his face, his heart sank. *Whatever the message was, it was not going to be good.* An expectant hush fell over the gathering.

'Hear the word of Yahweh,' began Moses, staff in hand. 'He says, *Depart, leave this place, and go up to the land I promised on oath to Abraham, Isaac and Jacob, and to you, their descendants. I will send an angel before you to drive out the Canaanites. Go up to the land flowing with milk and honey.'* Moses paused, and an excited murmur rippled around the crowd. *Maybe he had misjudged his uncle's mood.* But Moses hadn't finished. 'But Yahweh also says this,' he continued. *'I will not go with you, because you are a stiff-necked people. If I were to go with you even for a moment, I might destroy you.'* Moses let the words sink in before continuing. 'If your hearts are grieved by this, as they should be, then strip yourselves of all your ornaments, and mourn as is fitting. Now go to your tents, and wait whilst Yahweh decides what to do with you.'

Ithamar felt movement against him. Keziah was already removing her earrings and bracelets. Other women nearby were lifting chains from their necks. Ithamar immediately took the gold rings from his own ears. He glanced around. *Every person was doing the same.*

'Come on, let's get you some water, Keziah,' said Ithamar, taking her jewellery in his hands. Eleazar was already helping Tirzah towards the brook into which Moses had scattered the gold the day before. Many others were also flocking towards the small stream. Ithamar helped her down onto her knees when they reached the water, and both scooped up handfuls and drank. Although the water was warm from the heat of the sun, it was as welcome as if chilled by a clear winter's night. It revived Ithamar's parched mouth and throat, and, after sprinkling a handful of water over Keziah's head, he did the same to his own.

Keziah breathed deeply several times. 'That is better.'

As Ithamar sprinkled some more water over her, Eleazar suddenly spoke.

'Father and Miriam are approaching Moses. Let us join them.' He turned to Tirzah. 'You and Keziah go back to the tent and get some rest. We will follow soon.'

As they hurried after their father, Nadab and Abihu joined them. None of them spoke. Ithamar wondered what was going through his father's head. *Did he feel that he was the one chiefly to blame?*

The assembly was rapidly dispersing as they reached Moses. There was pain in his uncle's eyes. He drew in a long breath and let it out slowly. And then he spoke, fixing Aaron with his gaze. 'This disobedience has been costly. I pleaded with Yahweh to forgive the sin, telling Him that I would stand with the people under Yahweh's wrath if He did not.' He paused, and Aaron lowered his eyes to the ground. 'But Yahweh said He would only take the lives of those who have sinned. So you can be sure there will be more deaths in the camp.'

'But He tells us to leave for the Promised Land,' blurted out Nadab, 'and that an angel would go before us. So His promises to our father Abraham will still be fulfilled.'

'Except the most precious one!' exclaimed Moses. 'Do you not see that?' His voice and face betrayed both his anger and anguish. Nadab fell silent. 'What good is it if we live in a land of milk and honey and yet are no different from any other nation? It is Yahweh's presence among us, and that alone, that sets us apart. Not where we live or what we eat!' He fell silent and then sighed, suddenly looking tired. He sat down on a nearby rock, shaking his head. 'If we leave here now, we leave without the tabernacle that was to be built for worship, and in which the glory of Yahweh would have dwelt in our midst.' He looked over towards the shattered tablets that still lay on the ground nearby. 'We leave without a covenant between our tribes and our God.' He paused and shook his head again. 'And worst of all, we leave without Yahweh. What good is Canaan to us, if He isn't there? We become just another tribe of Canaanites.'

An ominous silence hung in the air until Miriam eventually spoke. 'Will Yahweh relent if He sees the people's sorrow?' she asked softly.

'I do not know,' replied Moses. 'He has relented once, when I entreated Him on the mountain not to destroy the people. I have to believe that He will listen to me again.' He stood up wearily. 'Tell the people that tomorrow I will enter the tent and speak to Yahweh.' And with that, he left.

Ithamar looked across to the tent to which Moses referred, standing apart from the camp. There was only one thought that brought him comfort. *If Yahweh was going to listen to anybody, then it was Moses.*

True to his word, Moses approached the tent of meeting the following morning, and—as was their custom—the Israelites stood by their tents and watched. As Moses went in, the pillar of cloud descended, covering the entrance, and Ithamar, with everyone else, bowed down in worship, before rising again.

Compared to the waiting of the previous day, it felt like only a few heartbeats until Nadab suddenly exclaimed, 'The pillar of cloud is lifting. Moses has left the tent!'

Ithamar followed his brothers as they hurried to the edge of the camp. 'His head is held high,' said Eleazar as they walked out to meet their uncle. *He was right.* Ithamar allowed himself to hope that all would be well. Moses smiled and nodded when he saw them, and when they reached him, he said simply, 'Yahweh has said that He will do what I have asked. His presence will go with us.' His smile widened. 'Now find a mallet and chisel. We have stonework to do.'

Another forty days passed whilst Moses tarried alone on the mountain, summoned there once more by Yahweh. He had left with two freshly cut stone tablets to replace the ones that had been shattered. The covenant was to be renewed.

Nadab brought the news of Moses' eventual return—but this time it was different.

Ithamar looked up from milking a goat as he heard his brother's rapid strides. 'Where's Father, Ithamar?' asked Nadab breathlessly, shock on his face.

'With Miriam and Hur I think. Why? What is it?'

'You will have to see for yourself. I cannot explain it.'

'What are you talking about?'

'It's Moses. At least, I think it is.' Without uttering another word, he ran off.

'What was that all about?' asked Keziah, as she emerged from the tent.

'I have no idea,' replied Ithamar, mystified. 'But I'm going to find out.' He ran to the edge of the camp, where a small crowd had already gathered, and it didn't take him long to discover why Nadab had behaved so strangely. His eyes were immediately drawn to a bright point on the mountain. But the light was moving. He stared, open-mouthed and then froze. *The light had legs.* It was Moses.

That Moses was unaware that his face was shining soon became apparent. He had to call out to Aaron to discover why even his brother was too scared to approach him.

'He must have seen Yahweh's glory,' whispered Eleazar. 'He said, didn't he, before he left, that Yahweh had promised him that?'

Ithamar nodded, awed. 'He did.' *This was the God who would now be dwelling in their midst.*

And when Moses—face now veiled to cover Yahweh's reflected glory—finally stood before Aaron and his sons, he held in his arms two tablets. They were covered with writing that Ithamar was determined to learn to read. Despite his familiar features being hidden, Moses' voice was still the same. Except now it was devoid of all anger and full of wonder instead. 'I have seen Yahweh.'

'You looked into His face?' asked Aaron.

The veiled head shook. 'Not His face, but I saw His back as He passed by. And I have heard His name.'

'Yahweh?' asked Ithamar, confused.

'*Yahweh, the compassionate and gracious God, slow to anger, abounding in love and faithfulness, maintaining love to thousands, and forgiving wickedness, rebellion and sin.*' Moses paused, and Ithamar sensed his uncle was now smiling behind the veil. 'We have a God who forgives our rebellion, who graciously renews the covenant, and whose loving presence will go with us.' And then, causing Ithamar's heart to leap, he added, 'And you will be His priests.'

Notes

1. The supposed festival to Yahweh with the golden calf was not necessarily on the Sabbath, but this seemed the most appropriate day to declare a feast.
2. Gold melts at 1064 deg C, and a wood bonfire can exceed 1100 deg C, meaning that Aaron would have been able to melt the gold without a special furnace. It is possible that a clay pot (able to withstand such temperatures) might have been used as a crucible for the gold.
3. The word usually translated as calf simply means a young bull. However, the word calf has been used here for consistency with most Bible translations.
4. It is not clear whether it was the first or the second commandment (or both) that was being broken by the golden calf. They may have viewed the calf as a representation of Yahweh or as another god.
5. It has been assumed that fear was a large factor in Aaron capitulating to the people's desire and making the calf.
6. Although in the text Moses destroys the calf and scatters it on the water before ordering the Levites to go through the camp, the length of time that would have been required to destroy the calf implies that it probably happened later, particular as Aaron still refers to 'this calf' (Exodus 32:24) after the record of its destruction.
7. It is not clear how or when 'the LORD smote the people' (Exodus 32:35) in response to the incident with the calf. It has been alluded to in the story, but no details given.

7

'Let Aaron your brother be brought to you from among the Israelites, with his sons Nadab and Abihu, Eleazar and Ithamar, so that they may serve me as priests.' (Exodus 28:1)

Ithamar pointed over to his left. 'Over there.'

The young woman bearing a bundle of folded linen nodded, and left the front of the long line waiting to present their gifts for the building of the tabernacle.

'Add it to the pile,' he shouted after her. Ithamar smiled to himself. *Who would have imagined that the wealth of Egypt would be used to build a dwelling place for Yahweh!* He had been honoured with the responsibility of recording the contributions—and he relished it.

'And how is my nephew faring today?' said a familiar voice, as a hand rested upon his shoulder.

He turned to face Moses, smiling. 'The flow of gifts does not abate.' He glanced around at the nearby piles and baskets. 'Though you can see that yourself.' Ithamar pointed an older man towards a heap of goats' skins, all dyed red. 'Put it there.' He continued directing the offerings as he talked with Moses.

Before Ithamar was a makeshift table piled with scrolls. A brush was resting in a pot of ink. Moses pushed aside a stone and picked up one of the scrolls. Ithamar had written the word *bronze* at the top of it. Moses nodded. 'Of my brother's four sons, you alone have taken to reading and writing like an eagle to the air.'

Ithamar flushed. To learn such a skill had thrilled him, and all the more as it was for the service of Yahweh. One of his helpers— another Levite—was sitting on a stool nearby. He suddenly raised a hand, holding scales in the other. Ithamar acknowledged the signal and made a mark on a different scroll. 'Another hundred shekels of gold,' he said, as his helper tipped earrings, rings and necklaces from one of his scale-pans into a large basket. He marked a third scroll as a different hand was raised. 'And another hundred of silver.'

'They give freely and joyfully,' said Moses, gazing at those waiting patiently in line, 'as Yahweh desires. Their gold earrings made an idol, but now they rejoice in being a part, however small, of building a dwelling place for the God who has shown them mercy.' He bent down and skimmed through the sheets on the table. 'How much gold do we have now?'

'Over twenty-seven talents. And ninety-four of silver, and sixty-six of bronze.'

Moses laughed. 'I chose well when I put you in charge of this task! We will soon have all we need, and then I will have to stop the contributions.'

'But there are so many who still wish to give! It's the same at the end of each day—I have to send people away and tell them to return the next morning.'

Moses sighed. 'Many who have delayed their giving will lose their chance to share in this holy work.' He turned to Ithamar, meeting his eyes. 'Never be slow of heart in your devotion to Yahweh.'

Moses summoned Aaron's family to eat with him at the end of the day. Horeb towered over them as they sat out in the cool of the evening in a mood of celebration, the large pot in the middle all but emptied of its goat stew. Darkness was soon upon them as the days continued to shorten.

'You have done a good job of clearing a space in the middle of the camp,' said Moses to Nadab. 'In the coming days, the construction of the tabernacle can begin, so Yahweh can truly dwell in the midst of His people as He desires!'

'And He chooses to dwell in a tent as we do,' said Nadab.

'Ah, as if any building on earth could contain the Most High,' replied Moses with a smile. 'The ark of the covenant will simply be as the footstool for God's throne. A link between heaven and earth.'

He paused and smiled again. 'When I was growing up in the court in Egypt, important deeds or treaties would often be stored beneath the feet of their lifeless deities. Here, the ark will hold the two tablets of our covenant with Yahweh, the living God. Two golden cherubim will adorn its cover, and, between their wings, His presence will dwell.'

An awed silence fell on the gathering. 'And He will move with us when we move,' said Eleazar quietly.

Moses chuckled. 'You are right, although it is better said that we will move with *Him* when *He* moves.'

Eleazar laughed. 'And you are right to correct me, Uncle!'

'But who will be able to approach the ark?' asked Nadab, his eyes bright.

'Ah,' said Moses knowingly, 'my brother's firstborn wishes to know more about the honour that Yahweh bestows on them.' Nadab didn't reply. 'And that is why I have invited you here tonight.'

Ithamar had already been listening in rapt attention, but his heart quickened. Even as he had been counting gold and watching the piles of linen and brightly coloured thread growing, his mind had often flitted to what lay ahead. *To be a priest of Yahweh! An honour to be bestowed on their family alone!*

Moses looked around at them all. 'Yahweh is pure and holy, but we are not. None can stand before Him in His glory. But you are to be counted holy—belonging to Him and set apart for His service. As priests, you will approach Yahweh on behalf of the people. You will stand in their stead, like a bridge between our God and His people, and sacrifice will be at the heart of all you do. There is to be a large altar of bronze within the tabernacle.'

There was a short pause. 'Yes, but what about the ark?' began Nadab. 'Who will—?'

'Peace!' interrupted Moses with a smile, holding up his hand for silence. 'You are as impatient as ever, Nadab! And impetuous with it too. But it is fortunate for us that our sins and our failings do not bar us from Yahweh's service—I know that well!' He shook his head, as if in wonder, his thoughts clearly in some distant place.

Was he thinking of the time he killed the Egyptian? Ithamar's gaze drifted across to Aaron. *And was his father remembering the golden calf?*

'Yahweh has yet to reveal the details of your duties,' continued Moses, 'but I will tell you what I *do* know. There will be three different areas within the tabernacle. An outer court, where the bronze altar and laver for washing will stand. Wooden pillars supporting linen curtains will mark out this courtyard, which will lie east to west, twice as long as it is wide. The entrance will be at the east end, and the tent of meeting facing it at the western end of the courtyard.'

'The tent you now use to meet with Yahweh?' asked Ithamar.

Moses smiled. 'Ah, that tent is but a pale shadow of what will be built for the tabernacle. The tent of meeting will have an outer covering of goats' hair, similar to our own tents, but inside…' Moses paused, as if momentarily dazzled by a vision in his mind's eye. 'Ah, the inside will be glorious! The finest linen, with cherubim worked into the curtains of blue, purple and scarlet thread!'

Ithamar thought of the piles of materials that he had inspected earlier. *So that was to be their destiny!*

Moses went on, jolting Ithamar's attention back to the present. 'Acacia wood, covered in gold, will support the curtains. But the tent will be divided into two by another embroidered curtain. The larger section, entered first, will be known as the holy place. A lampstand, a table for bread and an altar for incense will be there, all made from or covered in gold.' His eyes drifted across to Nadab. 'But the ark will be behind the dividing curtain. And only the ark. In the holy of holies.'

There was a pause. 'But will there be no light there?' asked Elisheba.

Moses smiled. 'There is no need for a lamp where the glory of Yahweh shines!'

By the end of the evening, Ithamar knew that they would all have linen garments made for them, although not as elaborate as the high priest's robes to be worn by their father—and by Nadab, when he eventually succeeded him one day. Only the finest quality materials were to be used. And there would be a seven-day ritual to consecrate both themselves and the tabernacle for Yahweh's service, when everything was complete.

As he and Keziah retired to their part of the family tent, she stood facing him and put both her arms around his neck, her swollen belly between them. She sighed deeply as she looked up into his eyes.

'What is it?' he asked.

'Our child is not going to be born in the Promised Land, is it? It will take many weeks to build the tabernacle, and the baby is due in less than two months.'

Ithamar leant forward and kissed her. He had been thinking the same. When he opened his eyes again, he held her gaze. 'No, I'm afraid not, my love.' He thought for a moment, and then pulled her into a tight embrace, wrapping both arms around her and feeling the curve of her belly against him. 'But if a tent in the desert is good enough for Yahweh, then it will be good enough for our son—or daughter.'

She rested her head upon his shoulder. 'I suppose so. It would have been nice though.'

'He or she will see Canaan soon enough. And now that I have almost finished counting for Moses, I can begin making the tent for our new family, as Eleazar is doing.'

She paused for a moment. 'What do you think it's going to be?'

'I don't mind whether it's a girl or a boy.'

She chuckled. 'Liar!'

He released her and held her at arms' length, in mock outrage. 'Are you accusing me of trying to deceive you?'

Her eyes sparkled with laughter. 'Yes! I know you would like a boy as your firstborn.'

He drew her back into his arms. 'Ah, you see through me—'

'It is not difficult…'

'I will trust Yahweh for whatever He gives, but the Almighty *will* know that there will be a need for more priests.'

'Hmm. Well then, maybe Yahweh will give you twelve sons as He did to our father Jacob.'

'Ah, but I have only one wife, not four.'

'And you will keep it that way,' she said, holding him tighter.

He smiled. 'With you, I need no other.'

She sighed deeply. There was then a long pause. 'Ithamar?'

'Hmm?'

'What are cherubim?'

It was the question he'd hoped she wouldn't ask. He thought hard for a moment. 'The Lord placed cherubim outside Eden, to guard it and bar Adam and Eve from entering after they sinned.'

'But what *are* they?'

'Special beings. Like no creatures on earth.' *She couldn't argue with that.*

'Yes, but what do they look like?'

'They, er, have legs…' He thought quickly. 'And wings!'

She pulled apart from him, a sceptical expression on her face. 'Eagles have both wings and legs, as do locusts. Your answer doesn't help me!' She folded her arms. 'You don't know, do you?'

He sighed, rolling his eyes. 'I'll ask Moses tomorrow.'

Ithamar worked hard with Keziah for the best part of a month making their own tent, with its poles, ropes and tent-pegs. But most days, Ithamar also wandered over to the centre of the camp to see the work on the tabernacle.

Ithamar glanced around as he picked his way between open-sided shelters, under which both men and women were hunched over huge swathes of linen. Here and there, men were working with hammers, beating sheets of gold cast from the gifts of jewellery, and filling the air with a constant *tap, tap, tap*. Elsewhere, clouds of smoke rose from fires for melting silver or bronze. Ithamar spotted his cousin. 'Bezalel.'

A young man, roughly the same age as Ithamar turned and smiled. 'Ah, the priest is back to check we are doing our job!'

'I'm not a priest yet—'

'And that is just as well,' said Bezalel with a grin, 'as we are not finished yet.' He was from the tribe of Judah and the grandson of Hur, but their years were similar, despite being two generations apart. And just as Yahweh had chosen and set Ithamar apart to serve in the tabernacle, He had set Bezalel apart to be in charge of building it.

'And what are you working on today?' asked Ithamar, as he drew alongside his cousin. There were wood shavings, tools and a measuring stick lying on the ground around him.

'Can't the priest tell?'

Ithamar studied the oblong of wood in Bezalel's hands, and the four long shaped pieces nearby. 'The table for the bread,' he answered.

'It is—or will be.' Bezalel grinned. 'That wasn't exactly difficult, was it?' He picked up one of the four legs and looked along its length with one eye. He seemed satisfied. 'The acacia wood in Sinai is perfect for this. Hard and durable.'

'And the table is what the gold is being hammered for?'

'Yes, that and the ark. When it is thin enough, it will be used for overlaying them both.'

'You've almost finished the ark?'

'Yes, apart from the cover.'

Ithamar sighed, his hopes dashed.

Bezalel studied him for a moment. 'What is it?'

'Keziah asked me one night what cherubim looked like. I didn't know. But when I asked Moses, he just said it would be easier for me to see for myself rather than him trying to explain. And I know that the cover will bear two cherubim of gold.'

'But you can still see what they look like.'

'How?'

'Come with me...' Bezalel led him through the workmen, pointing and commenting as they went. 'Look—those will hold the curtains when we move: red bags of dyed goats' skin for the embroidered linen, and ones of dugong skins for the goats' hair tent.'

Ithamar constantly marvelled at the workmanship he saw. *But Yahweh deserved the best!* Soon, they came to the tent that had been set apart as a store. Another young man was already in there, poring over a makeshift table.

'Oholiab,' said Bezalel. The other man straightened up and faced them. He had also been appointed by Yahweh for the work, as Bezalel's main assistant.

'What is it?'

'Have you got the scroll with the design for the cover of the ark?'

'I'm looking at it now, checking the measurements.'

Ithamar approached the table eagerly and peered down at Bezalel's exquisitely drawn picture. *There seemed no end to his cousin's talents!*

'So that,' said Bezalel pointing, 'is what cherubim look like. Not that I've seen one! I spent an entire day with Moses, drawing and re-drawing the design from his descriptions of what Yahweh showed him on the mountain.'

Ithamar cocked his head slightly. *They certainly had both legs and wings!* The bodies appeared to be like that of a bull, as the four legs of each had hooves. They were facing inwards, with huge wings arched up and over towards each other. Each had a human face, with eyes cast downwards, as if in reverence. *No wonder Moses had suggested that he waited to see it!* Ithamar had never seen anything like it, even among the strange-looking Egyptian gods. He'd heard of the sphinx, with its lion's body and head of a man, but this was something quite different.

'They guard His throne,' explained Bezalel, as Ithamar continued to stare in fascination at the images.

'And we have to make them from gold,' added Oholiab, with a laugh.

Ithamar looked up, intrigued. 'How do you know how to?'

'Not all of us made bricks in Egypt,' replied Bezalel. 'Some were used for metalwork, others for spinning, weaving or embroidery. The skill of hand and eye come from Yahweh, but Egyptians taught us how to use those skills to the best.'

'Nowhere do they weave linen as finely as in Egypt,' added Oholiab. 'They have been doing so for hundreds of years, and their twisted thread is the best.'

'We do not have their looms in the desert,' said Bezalel, 'but we left with an abundance of linen. And now those whose fingers have been gifted by Yahweh are working cherubim into curtains of that linen for the tent of meeting.'

Ithamar sighed contentedly. 'I will not keep either of you from your work any longer—I have a tent for my wife that I must finish.' His face broke into a broad smile. 'No cherubim though...'

Keziah had been right. Tirzah was ahead of her and her baby was born first—a boy. Phinehas, as they named him, would be the first of the next generation of priests. Three weeks later Gaddiel entered the world. Ithamar had chosen the name: *God has given fortune.* He had, of course, seen many babies, but it was his own son—a perfect, tiny, beautiful creation—that awakened a sense of wonder like never before.

'We are truly made in the image of Yahweh,' he murmured, as he gazed down at the small bundle in Keziah's arms.

'What makes you say that?' she asked, not taking her eyes off the child.

'He is a master craftsman, fashioning His intricate designs, not in gold or wood or thread, but in human flesh.' He paused and ran a finger lightly over Gaddiel's soft, downy cheek. 'And yet He has placed within human hands the skill to also create intricate beauty.' Tiny lips began to move, though Gaddiel's eyes remained closed. He breathed out a quivering sigh. 'The tabernacle will be glorious,' continued Ithamar in a hushed, reverent tone, 'but it will still only be a pale reflection of His own exquisite workmanship.' With that, a pair of small, dark eyes opened—and Ithamar considered himself blessed beyond measure.

Ithamar was not the only regular visitor to the open-air workshop. Often, he would see his uncle inspecting the works, making sure that Yahweh's directions were followed, down to the last detail. That morning was no exception. Ithamar wandered over to where Moses was standing, peering over Bezalel as he knelt beside a log, measuring it with a rod.

Moses turned to Ithamar. 'This is the most joyous sight, is it not?'

'A log?'

'You must look beyond what it is now to what it will become.'

'Which is?'

'The altar for the courtyard, for the offerings of the people.'

Bezalel glanced up. 'The wooden frame will be covered in hammered bronze, with an out-turned horn at each corner.'

Moses ran his hand up and down the wood. 'And you, Ithamar, will burn the sweet-smelling sacrifices on it.' After a pause, Moses straightened up. 'Come with me, Nephew, and see the latest of our treasures to be completed.'

As they passed men and women engrossed in all manner of craftsmanship, Moses paused beside a man huddled over a sheet of gold hammered thinner than fine linen. He was cutting it into long narrow strips. *Like strands of golden hair,* thought Ithamar. His uncle turned to him. 'Can you guess what this is for?'

Ithamar shook his head. 'No.'

'It is for the high priest's breastplate. These gold threads will be woven into linen of blue, purple and scarlet. It will rival anything worn by an Egyptian pharaoh. Twelve precious stones will be mounted on a pouch of the material, each engraved with the name of one of the tribes. They will be borne over your father's breast—held close to the high priest's heart, as all God's people should be.' He turned to face Ithamar. 'And they must be held close to yours too.'

They resumed walking. 'Your cousin Bezalel does everything well. It is little wonder Yahweh chose him. He is not only a skilful workman, but a faithful one too.'

'What do you mean?'

'He makes everything exactly according to Yahweh's plan. Yahweh gives us much freedom in life. But in matters of holiness and worship, it is only *His* will and *His* way that matter.'

Ithamar thought for a moment. 'To follow our own way rather than His is to repeat the sin of our ancestors Adam and Eve, isn't it?'

Moses nodded. 'It is the nature of *all* sin.' As they approached a tent that stood apart from the others, its flaps closed, Moses stopped and turned to Ithamar. 'Ah! But there is a message for our fallen race in the tabernacle.' Ithamar studied him, intrigued. 'Your father has told you the story of Eden many times I know. Do you remember where the Almighty stationed the cherubim to guard the way to the garden and the tree of life?'

Ithamar thought for a moment. 'The east side?'

'Indeed,' smiled Moses. 'It is to the east that the tabernacle opens. It is our way back into Yahweh's presence…' And with that, he stepped forward and pulled back the tent-flap, inviting Ithamar to go in.

It was as if he had stepped into a different world. The dim light of the tent couldn't hide the lustre of the gold. The wooden table that he'd watch Bezalel assembling now gleamed, completely covered in the precious metal. The ark stood, silent and majestic, with the cherubim—wings extending upwards—as if frozen in gold. He'd seen both before, but that did not lessen his sense of wonder. But it was the newly-finished lampstand that soon drew his attention. 'Magnificent, isn't it?' murmured Moses.

Ithamar slowly moved closer, awed by its beauty. *Like a golden tree, raising its branches to Yahweh in worship.* Almond buds and blossoms, with their five petals of gold, had been worked into both the central upright stem and the three pairs of branches on either side. Seven golden lamps were mounted upon them. 'Eden had its tree of life,' said Moses softly. 'We will have a tree of light, a sign of God's presence with us.' He moved silently towards the table, running a loving hand along the ornate golden rim that Bezalel had fashioned for its edges. 'A light will burn constantly in the house of God, and what more welcoming sight than bread set out for a meal. He invites us back to Eden and to fellowship with Him.'

Ithamar shuffled his feet and stared at the ground. He had never been so nervous. A little over six months had passed since the work on the tabernacle had begun. At the new moon—the first day of the first month of their second year—and under the direction of Moses and Bezalel, a small army of those who had worked on the tabernacle set everything in place early in the morning. Keziah had washed his clothes, and Ithamar was now waiting with his family, though no-one uttered a word. Eliezer was fiddling with the sash around his tunic. *His brother was as tense as he was!* Nadab and Abihu alone seemed without fear.

'Here comes Moses,' said Nadab suddenly. And Ithamar's heart quickened.

'We are ready for you now,' said Moses simply. Ithamar turned to Keziah, and kissed both her and his four-month-old whom she cradled in her arms. *He would not see them for a whole week.*

They walked in silence behind Moses. Soon, a huge multitude came into view, gathered around the newly-erected tabernacle. Ithamar drew in a sharp breath. As they approached, the crowd parted like the Reed Sea, allowing them to pass through. With myriad eyes upon him, Ithamar kept his gaze turned downwards, but still felt himself flushing. When he did briefly glance up and around, he caught sight of the tent of meeting rising above the curtains of the tabernacle courtyard. He also saw heads craning to catch a view of himself and his brothers. He swiftly looked down again. Moses had told them that the ceremony to consecrate them as priests would be a public one. *This was everybody!*

As they approached the only entrance into the courtyard of the tabernacle, he found the courage—fuelled by curiosity—to look up. He had not yet seen everything in place. The colourful curtains of blue, purple and scarlet that formed the gateway were pulled back and the bronze altar was directly ahead. Crowds filled both sides of the courtyard with the elders of Israel prominent. But it was the majestic tent of meeting that drew Ithamar's eyes, its curtains—identical to those of the gateway—veiling the glory inside.

They passed the altar and stopped near the bronze laver. A young bull and two goats were tethered nearby, disinterested. A basket of bread and cakes was a safe distance from the goats. An expectant hush fell upon the gathering, all murmuring dying away. When he had silence, Moses looked out at the congregation and raised his voice. 'This is what Yahweh has commanded us to do.' He paused, as if challenging any who might question the granting of the priesthood to his brother and nephews. None demurred. Moses moved to the laver and summoned Aaron, Ithamar and his brothers. 'Come near.'

They stripped down to their new linen undergarments and, as the multitudes watched, Moses took a bronze bowl and ladled water over each of them, starting with Aaron and finishing with Ithamar, the youngest. *Not that he was dirty. Keziah had seen to that, saying that she was not going to have her husband shaming her by having so much as a dirty fingernail in front of the congregation.* Ithamar was surprised his skin wasn't still smarting and bright red from her attentions. The water drawn from the mountain stream was cool and refreshing, untouched by the gentle warmth of the spring day.

Ithamar shivered slightly as he stood barefoot, watching his father being dressed in the rich and ornate robes of the high priest. Small golden bells around the hem of his blue robe tinkled as it was put on over his head. The ephod—the patterned tabard of vibrant blue, purple and scarlet—sparkled in the morning light as the sun caught the strands of gold that had been worked into the material. As Moses secured it with a sash, Ithamar wondered if any earthly king had ever worn such glorious garments.

Once the breastplate was in place, Moses dropped into the pouch two stones—Urim and Thummin—one dark and one light. They would be used by his father to discern the will of Yahweh, drawing out a single stone and repeating the action a number of times, to determine if Yahweh was answering their question with a *yes* or *no*. The final element of his clothing was a plate of pure gold which was fixed with blue cords to the front of a white linen turban. The plate was engraved with just three words: *Holy to Yahweh*.

His father looked like a different man, standing straight and tall. He had been clothed, not only with garments but with dignity, honour and authority. As Ithamar's shivering subsided, the warmth of the sun drying his bare body, Moses took a flask of perfumed oil and entered the tent to anoint and consecrate all that was in it. When he emerged a short time later, he poured oil from the same flask on his father's head. It trickled down from his turban onto his face and beard, and Aaron made no attempt to brush away the drips. Ithamar breathed in deeply. The air was rich with the heady fragrance of spiced myrrh.

Moses then beckoned each of his brothers forward, in age order, clothing them with the simpler priests' garments: a linen tunic and sash, and a cloth cap that was bound on the head with ties. *They would need them in the heat of the sun.* Ithamar felt himself flush when he was left as the only one unclothed. *Every eye would be upon him.* The linen tunic, when it came, felt soft on his skin compared to his normal clothes. *He had never worn such fine and costly material. It was an honour of which he did not feel worthy.* He glanced sideways at his brothers. Eleazar stood with his head bowed, but the two eldest held theirs high, seemingly enjoying the attention. *A lack of confidence had never been their problem.*

Soon the fragrance of the oil was overwhelmed by the smell of fresh blood. A young bull, the sin offering, had been led into their midst, and after Ithamar and the others had lain their hands on its head it was slaughtered by Moses beside the bronze altar. As the bull staggered and then crumpled to the ground, Aaron held a bronze dish to the ugly scarlet slash across its neck, collecting the blood. *The life of a bull for his own,* thought Ithamar. *Yes, he was unworthy, but this was the provision of Yahweh for the forgiveness of his sins: blood for blood, life for life.*

Moses smeared the blood on the four horns of the altar to purify it. The rest was poured out at its base, staining the sandy earth dark red. Ithamar and his brothers carried the lifeless bull to a nearby table, where Moses cut it open along its belly. His hands were red when he pulled out the offering of the kidneys and the fat around its innards. *Sin and sacrifice were a messy affair.* He kindled a fire on the altar, and the smells of burning meat and fat mingled with those of myrrh and blood. Two rams were slaughtered next, and Ithamar stood motionless, his head bowed, as blood was daubed upon him three times by Moses, who had done the same to his brothers. On his right ear: *he was set apart to listen to the voice of Yahweh.* On his right thumb: *to devote his hands to the sacred tasks.* On the big toe of his right foot: *he must walk in the ways of Yahweh.*

Ithamar's hands were soon performing their first priestly task, lifting up high a portion of fat from the second ram together with some bread—a wave offering—before lowering it again. Ithamar breathed again. *It hadn't slid off his hands.* Whilst Moses took the offerings and laid them on the altar, Ithamar glanced down at his hands—they were greasy and bloodied. *His tunic wouldn't be clean for long.* But Ithamar wasn't the first to mark the virgin cloth. Moses sprinkled each of their garments with the anointing oil, filling the air once more with the heady scent of myrrh. But he then sprinkled them all with blood from the second ram, sending splashes of bright red across Ithamar's tunic.

And that was it—he was consecrated to Yahweh.

Moses turned to them. 'Boil the rest of the ram's meat and then eat it at the doorway to the tent with the rest of the bread from ordination offerings. Burn up whatever you don't eat. You must stay here until your ordination is complete.' He then raised his voice, so that all gathered there could hear. 'What has been done today was commanded by Yahweh, making atonement for Aaron and his sons.' He turned back to them, but his voice was still raised. 'You must stay at the doorway of the tent of meeting, day and night, for seven days, as Yahweh requires, so that you may not die. That is the command Yahweh gave to me.'

Ithamar lay down under the night sky with a full stomach. Instead of the familiar family tent, the linen walls of the tabernacle surrounded them, with Yahweh's heavenly canopy overhead. In the dark, he could see fire still burning on the bronze altar nearby. They had added more wood before nightfall, to ensure it would burn throughout the night.

'It is like when we were young,' whispered the voice of Eleazar beside him. 'The four of us sleeping together.'

'Except I do not have Nadab kicking me,' replied Ithamar softly.

Another voice nearby answered. 'If you moved a little closer, I could oblige...'

Ithamar smiled to himself in the dark, staring upwards. The stars were silent and inscrutable as they looked down upon him. But the eyes of Yahweh were upon them too. Moses' words about staying in the tabernacle ran through his mind: *as Yahweh requires, so that you may not die.* After several moments he spoke even more softly, for Eleazar's

ears alone. 'Moses said we will die if we leave before seven days...'
He left the words hanging.

A long pause followed. 'If Yahweh said it, then it is true. To walk
in obedience is the only safe path.' And beyond his brothers, Aaron
began to snore.

The following day, a second bull was sacrificed to continue the
purification and consecration of the bronze altar. Moses then had
them sit on the ground around him. The gold plate on Aaron's
turban flashed in the sun.

'Yahweh has spoken further,' he began. He then gestured around
with a sweep of his arm. 'Now the tabernacle is standing, He is
revealing more of how we are to be His people, and the sacrifices we
are to offer so that He can continue to dwell in our midst. All that is
needful will be revealed before your consecration is complete.' And
with that he began to describe what they must do when an Israelite
brought a burnt offering.

Each day fell into a similar pattern: the sacrifice of a bull and
instruction from Moses on the different types of offerings. Ithamar's
head spun each night as he lay under the stars: *which offerings to burn
whole, and which required only the fat and kidneys to be laid on the altar; when
the meat of the sin offering was to be eaten and when it was to be burned outside
the camp; which animal skins belonged to them and which did not; where
to put the ashes from the altar and how to carry them outside the camp.* He
was grateful that Moses was recording it all in detail. *At least he could
keep reading it until it was etched upon his mind. And he had the example of
Moses, who was offering the sacrifices on their behalf until their consecration
was complete.* He watched intently every time, taking in each detail.
Whilst he was content to observe and learn, however, he couldn't help
noticing that Nadab and Abihu seemed eager—almost impatient—to
perform the priestly tasks themselves. *But they would have to wait.*

'The laver is there for a purpose,' said Moses one day in response
to a question from Abihu. 'Apart from the grain offering, the shedding
of blood is at the heart of each offering. So, *yes*, you *will* have to keep
washing your hands.'

'Must blood always be shed for forgiveness?' asked Nadab.

'The animal dies in the place of the sinner, paying the penalty for their sin,' answered Moses. 'So Yahweh has ordained it. Its blood must be shed, not by you, but by the sinner who brings the offering, covering their sins before our holy God. And as the blood is the animal's life, it is not to be eaten, because all life belongs to Yahweh.'

'In Egypt, they offered food for their gods...' began Abihu.

'Their gods needed feeding,' replied Moses. 'Yahweh does not. The fat and kidneys are not laid on the altar because He is hungry. They are showing that we give the very best—the choice portions— to Yahweh. So we eat neither blood nor fat.'

However many details were swirling around in Ithamar's mind, he was sure about one thing: *worship of Yahweh was a serious matter.*

Ithamar felt a thrill of nervous anticipation course through him. *The seven days had ended and they were now ready to begin serving Yahweh as His priests!* The elders were gathered in the courtyard again, and the entire congregation at the tabernacle. The first of the daily offerings—a one-year-old lamb—was offered up by Aaron, who then offered a young bull and a ram for himself. Then, at Moses' command, he stood before the elders and addressed them.

'Take a male goat as a sin offering,' began Aaron, 'and a grain offering mixed with oil; for this very day, Yahweh shall appear to you.'

His father's final words quickened Ithamar's heart and sharpened his attention. *He would do exactly as he had been taught.*

The offerings continued as the sun rose higher, performed exactly as Moses had instructed. 'You have done well, my brother,' he said softly to Aaron. 'All that remains is for you to bless the people.'

With that, Aaron approached the elders and the people, lifting up his hands before them. In a clear, loud voice he cried out: 'Yahweh bless you and keep you; Yahweh make his face shine on you and be gracious to you; Yahweh turn his face towards you and give you peace.' And then, for the first time, he entered the tent with Moses.

Ithamar's heart stirred. *What would it be like to behold God's glory?*

When his father and uncle eventually emerged from the tent, Ithamar and the others joined them as they once more approached the people to bless them. But a great shout suddenly went up and the crowd stared, wide-eyed. Ithamar spun around. The fiery cloud they had seen upon Horeb had descended upon the tent. *It was so near!* A light as bright as the sun flashed out from the cloud and a loud *crack* split the air. Ithamar shielded his eyes, but when he looked again, huge flames were rising from the altar, consuming the offerings there. Another great shout resounded, echoing around the plain as the mountains threw back the cry. Ithamar cast himself face down on the ground with every other person. *Yahweh had appeared to them, just as his father had said!*

The cloud continued to rest on the tent, and even after Moses had dismissed the congregation later, there was still more to be done.

'Nadab and Abihu,' began Aaron, 'you are to take the ashes from the burnt offerings to the place outside the camp that Moses will show you. As Yahweh has instructed, you must change out of your priestly tunics first.'

'Yes, Father,' answered Nadab. He seemed to take everything in his stride.

'Eleazar and I will follow you,' continued Aaron, 'with the carcass of the sin offering to burn it in the same place.'

Ithamar looked at his father expectantly. 'And me, Father?'

'You stay and ensure that the fire on the altar is kept burning. And put fresh wood in the fire pit for cooking the meat from the other sin offering.'

'Yes, Father.'

As the others began their tasks and then left, Ithamar relished being left in charge of the tabernacle, even if it was only to make a fire. For a while, he stood looking at the tent. It was his father's responsibility, both morning and evening, to tend the lampstand and burn incense on the altar there, and to set out the bread every week. *Nadab would, in time, take on those roles, but would he, the youngest, be allowed to serve within the tent at all?*

He set about building a fire and thought of Keziah and Gaddiel. *He would finally be able to return to them that night after the offering of the evening sacrifice.* He smiled.

He had almost finished laying out the fresh wood when he heard movement behind him. He turned his head as he knelt beside the firepit. Nadab and Abihu had returned, but there was something strange about their mood. *Why were they so animated?* A sudden thought crossed his mind: *had they been drinking in the time they had been gone?* Ithamar chided himself for even thinking such a thought. But they seemed eager—even excited—to change back into their priest's tunics. Ithamar studied them for a few moments and then turned back to the wood.

When he had finally finished, he brushed his hands together to rid them of fragments of bark, rose to feet and turned round. He froze, panic and fear rising within him. Nadab and Abihu were standing at the altar, filling long-handled pans with burning embers. 'What are you doing?'

Their eyes were bright and their faces flushed with excitement. 'We are going to offer incense before Yahweh,' replied Nadab.

'You mustn't,' stammered Ithamar wide-eyed, his mouth suddenly dry. 'Moses said nothing about us doing that!' He looked around him in desperation, frantically hoping for the return of his father or uncle.

'Yahweh has consecrated us as priests to serve Him,' replied Nadab, 'and that is what we are going to do.'

'Why provide these censers for the service of the tabernacle,' added Abihu, 'if we are not to use them?'

'Just wait until Father returns,' pleaded Ithamar.

'We are holy to Yahweh, too,' said Nadab, as he took his pan over to where the incense was stored. 'And I will be high priest one day.'

Ithamar hesitated, helpless. *Should he run to fetch Moses or his father or try to stop them?* 'Please don't!' he pleaded once again. 'Yahweh has not spoken of this! Wait and ask Moses!'

The rich smell of the incense began to rise from the censers. 'We are ready!' said Nadab. They walked towards the tent, while

Ithamar stood frozen in indecision and horror. Nadab pulled back the entrance curtain, and he and Abihu entered, leaving a cloud of fragrant smoke hanging in the air behind them. Ithamar held his breath. Then he saw it. A flash lighting up the tent curtains from within, and for the second time that day, there was a deafening *crack*. Then clattering and two heavy *thud*s.

'No!' Ithamar ran towards the tent. 'Nadab! Abihu!' There was no response. He shouted louder. 'Nadab!' Nothing. He dared not pull back the curtain, so turned and ran. *He must find Moses or his father!* But before he even reached the entrance to the tabernacle, they hurried through it with Eleazar. *They must have heard the sound.* His eyes met those of his father, and the colour drained from Aaron's face.

'What has happened?' demanded Moses.

'Nadab and Abihu,' began Ithamar, his mouth still dry as sand. He faltered, and turned to face the tent. 'They went in.' All four ran towards it, Eleazar arriving first. He held the curtain to one side for Moses and Aaron to enter.

An agonised wail sullied the air. 'My sons! My sons!'

'Do not touch them!' said Moses sharply. 'You must not defile yourself with the dead.' Another distraught cry tore Ithamar's heart.

'You can look,' said Eleazar softly to Ithamar.

Ithamar forced his gaze inside. His brothers were lying haphazardly on the ground in front of the altar of incense, both motionless. Smoke was still curling up from the embers that had been strewn over the ground. The censers lay upside-down nearby. The priestly tunics of Nadab and Abihu seemed untouched, but their faces and hands told a different story—blackened, as if by fire. Ithamar's stomach lurched.

Moses turned to Aaron. 'They have borne the penalty for treating the commands of Yahweh lightly. This is what Yahweh said: *Among those who approach me I will be proved holy; in the sight of all the people I will be honoured.*' Aaron did not reply, but just stood staring at the two lifeless forms at his feet. Moses turned to Ithamar and Eleazar. 'You must not make yourselves unclean by touching them—you have further duties you must perform today. I will fetch Mishael and Elzaphan. They must carry your brothers and bury them outside the camp. All of you must stay within the tabernacle until you have finished dealing with the offerings from this morning.'

As Moses departed to find their cousins, Ithamar continued staring numbly at the charred bodies of his brothers. Aaron was kneeling beside them, weeping. 'I should have stopped them,' Ithamar whispered. 'It's my fault.' He felt Eleazar's hand on his shoulder.

'You are not to blame. I doubt you could have prevented it.'

'You don't know that…'

'I know my brothers—I know what they are like,' replied Eleazar softly. He corrected himself. 'What they *were* like.'

Ithamar felt as if he were dreaming as he watched first Nadab and then Abihu, both still in their priest's tunics, being carried away by his cousins. As Abihu's body disappeared from the tabernacle, Moses began speaking to the three of them again. 'You must not remove your turban or caps or tear your clothes in mourning or you will die…' The words washed over Ithamar and the rest of the day passed in a haze. He forced down the bread—the priest's share—of the grain offering, though he had no appetite. They sat in silence as they tried to eat, and Ithamar barely cared when Moses rebuked him and his brother for burning rather than eating the rest of the meat.

Whilst Aaron tended the lamps within the tent, Eleazar (under Moses' watchful eyes) removed the ashes from the altar before offering the evening sacrifice of a one-year-old lamb. Ithamar added enough wood to keep it burning throughout the night, though he was shaking as he did it, stealing a look at the cloud that still rested on the tent. *What if he dishonoured Yahweh without realising?* He felt a hand upon his shoulder and it calmed him.

'I will sleep here tonight and make sure the fire remains alight,' said Eleazar. 'You and Father can return to your tents.' *It was as if the mantle of the firstborn was now resting upon his shoulders.* Ithamar nodded wearily. *It would not be the joyful reunion with Keziah he had looked forward to.*

'I will go in and stand before Yahweh,' said Moses simply when Aaron emerged, still looking dazed. 'I will seek His face this night.' And with that, he entered the tent.

Ithamar and Aaron finally laid aside the priestly garments, changing back into the clothes they had worn seven days earlier as they'd entered the tabernacle for the first time. Neither of them spoke. Ithamar couldn't bear to look at his father's anguished face, but even as his fingers fumbled with the belt around his waist, a haunting song began to fill the evening air. Ithamar had not heard the melody before, but there was strange beauty about it. The words sung by Moses, however, pierced his heart:

Lord, You have been our dwelling place
> *in all generations.*
Before the mountains were born,
> *or You gave birth to the earth and the world,*
> *from everlasting to everlasting You are God.*
You turn man back into dust
> *and say, 'Return, O children of man!'*
For a thousand years in Your sight
> *are but as yesterday when it passes by,*
> *or as a watch in the night.*
You have swept them away like a flood; they fall asleep;
> *in the morning they are like grass that sprouts anew.*
In the morning it flourishes and is renewed;
> *in the evening it fades and withers.*
For we are brought to an end by Your anger;
> *by Your wrath we are dismayed.*
You have placed our iniquities before You,
> *our secret sins in the light of Your presence.*

Ithamar finally wept.

Notes

1. *That Ithamar had a leading role in recording the materials given for the tabernacle is stated in Exodus 38:21.*

2. The exact chronology of these events is not easy to determine. Different parts
    are recorded in three different books (Exodus, Leviticus and Numbers) and
    the ordering of the accounts in Leviticus and Numbers are not necessarily
    chronological. Some events may also occur concurrently. We are told that
    the people arrived at Sinai/Horeb on the first day of the third month of the
    first year, and that the tabernacle is erected on the first day of the second
    year. Given that Moses spends two periods of forty days on the mountain,
    it is assumed that the contributions for the tabernacle don't start before the
    sixth month of the first year at the earliest, giving up to six months for the
    construction of the tabernacle.

3. It has been assumed that the appearance of the glory of the Lord in Exodus
    40 and in Leviticus 9 are the same event. This may or may not be correct!
    This assumption is based on the following:

    (a) Exodus 29:43-44 links the appearance of the glory of the Lord
        with the consecration;

    (b) Leviticus 9:6 again links the completion of the consecration/
        ordination ceremonies with the Lord's glory;

    (c) Exodus 40:1-16 treats the setting up of the tabernacle, its
        consecration and the consecration of the priests as together fulfilling
        what God had commanded.

4. It seems that the deaths of Nadab and Abihu happen on the same day as
    the start of priestly duties, as Moses' comments in Leviticus 10:14,16 relate
    to the specific offerings that had been offered that day (Leviticus 9:3,21).

5. In Bibles, the various terms for the tabernacle seem to be used
    interchangeably, and it is not always clear whether the tent or the whole
    structure including the courtyard is being referred to. Here, purely for
    reasons of clarity, the terms 'tent', 'tent of meeting' and 'sanctuary' are
    adopted as interchangeable terms for the central covered structure that made
    up the holy place and the most holy place, whereas the term 'tabernacle' is
    used for the whole enclosure, including the open courtyard.

6. The garments for the high priest are quite complex and the meaning of
    some of the words (e.g. ephod) is no longer clear. The same is true for
    Urim and Thummin. They are clearly some form of sacred items for
    casting lots, but it is not clear either what they looked like or how they were
    used. It appears that they were used for guidance, and may have involved

some sort of way of determining the answer to a yes/no question, though it appears that it was also possible for no answer to be given through them. For reference to its use, see for example Numbers 27:21, 1 Samuel 28:6, Ezra 2:63. In an Assyrian document, two stones of different materials are drawn, and only if the same stone is drawn three times in a row is the answer confirmed. Urim is the word for 'lights' and so would probably refer to a bright or white stone.

7. *The idea of the ark being God's footstool is explicit in 1 Chronicles 28:2.*

8. *Cherubim also appear in Genesis 3, Ezekiel 1 and Revelation 1. They may have had features of a number of different creatures, similar to the Egyptian sphinx. They clearly have wings and may have had a four-legged animal body. In ancient art, they often appear flanking thrones, both of kings and gods. For a fuller discussion of the appearance of cherubim, see for example, Nick Page's book, 'Whatever Happened to the Ark of the Covenant?'*

9. *There is no record in Scripture of the names of Ithamar's descendants, though Eleazar's firstborn is named as Phinehas.*

10. *Bezalel is recorded as being Hur's grandson. It is assumed here that it is the same Hur mentioned elsewhere in Exodus, as (unlike Oholiab) the name of not just his father but his grandfather (Hur) is given. This seems to imply that his grandfather was of significance, i.e. known.*

11. *It has been assumed that Israelites from tribes other than Levi were permitted into the courtyard of the tabernacle.*

12. *Some commentators suggest that the ram/dugong skin covers were tent bags, rather than extra layers over the tent of meeting, given the lack of specific dimensions as for the other coverings. Two extra layers over the goat hair covering seem redundant and very heavy! One skin covering might be understandable, but two seems excessive. This suggestion has been adopted.*

13. *The precise nature of the sin of Nadab and Abihu is not clear, but was certainly an act of disobedience. Moses' response in Leviticus 10:8-9 may imply that alcohol was a factor in their actions.*

14. *Psalm 90 is attributed to Moses, but its use at this point is guesswork. It seems appropriate, however.*

8

The LORD said to Moses, 'Send some men to explore the land of Canaan, which I am giving to the Israelites. From each ancestral tribe send one of its leaders.' (Numbers 13:1-2)

For Ithamar, the mud and misery of Egypt had been exchanged for blood and butchery. He shared with his father and brother the twice daily tasks of slaughtering a lamb, skinning it and cutting it into pieces, before burning it on the bronze altar. But those sacrifices were as a single drop in a deluge when it came to the Passover.

'Yahweh has spoken again,' Moses declared to them just after their consecration. 'As He decreed when we were still in Egypt, in this first month of the year we are to commemorate our liberation. We are to observe the Passover at twilight on the fourteenth day.'

'What must we do?' asked Eleazar.

'Yahweh has already commanded,' continued Moses, 'that any animals to be eaten, be they an ox, lamb or goat, must be brought to the tabernacle and slaughtered there, and their blood brought to the altar.'

Ithamar stared at his uncle. 'But that will mean thousands of lambs!'

Moses nodded. 'The three of you will be busy.' Ithamar caught the fleeting look of pain on his father's face. *Three rather than five...* The Passover would be less than a week since his brothers' deaths.

When it came, there was little time to dwell on the absence of Nadab and Abihu, however. The steady flow of Israelites through the entrance to the tabernacle in the afternoon was rapidly leading to a small pool of blood around the base of the altar, as Ithamar, his father and brother constantly sprinkled the altar with the blood of the lambs and poured out the rest at its base. Even though the sandy soil afforded good drainage, it was becoming difficult to avoid stepping in the ever-spreading expanse of red. The smell was almost overwhelming.

'Should we move the altar?' said Ithamar, pausing briefly, as the day lengthened and the sun fell lower in the sky. 'Must it stay exactly here?'

Both Aaron and Eleazar thought for a moment. 'Surely it simply needs to be between the entrance and the laver,' said Eleazar. He glanced around. 'There is plenty of space to move it—and many still arrive with lambs.'

Aaron remained silent, clearly weighing up his sons' words. Then his shoulders drooped, as if suddenly pressed down by the weight of a heavy burden, his eyes full of unspoken grief. 'We will do nothing without asking Moses.'

Two weeks after the Passover, as a new moon marked the start of the second month, Moses had another announcement. Ithamar looked up from washing the blood from his hands after the morning offering, as his uncle emerged from the tent of meeting. 'Yahweh wants us to take a census,' said Moses.

Aaron, who was already drying his hands on a towel, asked 'Of all the congregation?'

'Of the men twenty years old and above—those who will be able to fight.'

'Entering the Promised Land will mean battles, like when we fought the Amalekites then?' asked Ithamar. He shook the water from his hands, remembering the time when they wielded a sword.

'And Yahweh will give us the victory,' added Eleazar

'Yes,' replied Moses. 'Except you will not be fighting. Neither will any others from our tribe.'

'None of the Levites?' asked Eleazar.

Ithamar took the towel offered by his father. *Eleazar was clearly as puzzled as he was.*

Moses shook his head. 'No. Just as you have been set apart as priests, Yahweh is now setting apart the whole tribe of Levi. They are to help you as you serve at the tabernacle. And that means you are all dedicated to the worship of Yahweh, rather than to fighting His wars.

So you will not be numbered with the fighting men—you will be counted separately afterwards. But more of that later.'

'You are counting only eleven tribes then?' asked Ithamar.

'Yes, but the sons of Joseph are to be counted as two tribes— Ephraim and Manasseh—so that there will be twelve tribes of fighting men to march out.' Moses turned to face Aaron. 'Hence we have a job to do now, which is likely to take the rest of the day.'

Ithamar's mouth dropped open. 'You're going to count everyone in one day?'

Moses laughed. It was the first time Ithamar had heard him do so since the deaths of Nadab and Abihu. 'No, my nephew—at least, not *just* your father and I. The leader of each tribe is to help. And now I must go and find your cousins to send them out to fetch those men.'

Ithamar and Eleazar were left in charge of the tabernacle for the day. Not that many brought offerings with the census taking place. It was only as twilight approached that they saw Aaron again.

'Is the census complete?' asked Eleazar, after greeting his father.

Aaron nodded wearily. 'Everything apart from adding up the final numbers.' He looked at Ithamar. 'Moses wants you to help with that—but only when we have finished our tasks for the day.'

Curiosity about the census lifted Ithamar's heart from its grief as he and Eleazar made the evening sacrifice. Whilst his brother killed and prepared the one-year-old lamb, Ithamar carefully added more wood to the altar fire, and then measured out the fine flour for the grain offering, mixing it with oil, and then the wine for the drink offering. By the time Eleazar had carefully positioned the pieces of lamb on the now-roaring fire, and Ithamar had both scattered the grain offering on the fire and poured out the wine on the altar, Aaron was emerging from the tent, having tended the lamps and burned incense on the gold altar.

'I should have said,' began Aaron, as they all began changing out of their priestly robes, 'we are to eat with Moses tonight.'

'Before or after we look at the numbers from the census?' asked Ithamar.

'After.' Aaron smiled, but it seemed forced.

A short time later, Ithamar was standing in his uncle's tent. He stooped down and picked up one of the scrolls from the rug in Moses' tent, unrolling it and then studying how the ink marks upon it were grouped.

"Each of those marks represents ten men,' said Moses.

As Ithamar started counting, his brother looked around at the twelve piles of scrolls. 'We knew we were many thousands,' said Eleazar. 'But this...' He trailed off in wonder.

'*This*,' responded Moses, 'is the fulfilment of Yahweh's promise to our father Abraham.'

Ithamar glanced up. 'There are not just tens of thousands here, surely, but hundreds!"

'And that is why I have called you to help me now,' said Moses. 'And does my other nephew desire to assist us?'

Eleazar shook his head. 'Forgive me, Uncle, but I think I would hinder rather than help. Besides, the smell of supper draws me outside.'

'Don't start before we join you,' protested Ithamar.

'Do not fear, Brother. I merely wish to stir my appetite, not sate it!'

As Eleazar disappeared into the ever-deepening evening, Ithamar and Moses worked by the light of several oil lamps scattered around the tent. Together they checked and re-checked each of the twelve piles until they were sure of the count for each tribe.

'Judah numbers at least ten thousand more than any other tribe,' said Ithamar.

'Our father Jacob saw clearly when he prophesied blessing upon him. He said that Judah's brothers would praise him and that he would rule over the tribes of Israel.' Moses smiled. 'And yet Yahweh is the shepherd of His people, counting His flock. Each sheep is known by Him and matters to Him.' He paused, and then continued, awed. 'Israel was only seventy people when he travelled to Egypt. Look at us now!' He laid his hand on Ithamar's shoulder, his smile broadening. 'And are you now ready for the final numbering?'

True to the word of his brother, the family had waited for Ithamar and his uncle. After Moses had said the blessing, the three priests, their wives and children sat with Moses' family around a larger-than-usual selection of pots and platters. A goat had been killed for the occasion, although meat was now less of a rarity to them, as many of the offerings had a portion that belonged to the priest and his family. And although they may not have had the onions, leeks and garlic of Egypt, Zipporah knew the ways of the desert and the herbs that grew in the wilderness, and had cultivated a small patch beside their tent. Ithamar was glad that Keziah was keen to learn from her.

The meal had the feel of a celebration, although each time Ithamar's heart was ready to fly, the memory of his eldest brothers stole its wings. Still, the sight of six-month-old Gaddiel at Keziah's breast cheered him, as did the news they shared as they ate.

Eleazar, his eyes wide, repeated his uncle's words. 'Over six hundred thousand?'

Moses nodded. 'Six hundred and three.'

'And five hundred and fifty,' added Ithamar. He then leant over to dip his bread in the stew.

Moses smiled. 'Ah, we must not forget those—or those who have not been numbered. The women and children—'

'And Levites!' interjected Eleazar.

'Indeed. The Almighty told our father Abraham that a great nation would come from him. He has fulfilled His word.'

'And He will surely fulfil more of it soon,' said Eleazar, 'when He leads us into the land He promised to Abraham.'

'The census of fighting men is preparation for that,' said Moses. 'It will not be long before Yahweh directs us to break camp.'

'When will that be?' asked Elisheba quietly. Her grief for her sons was no less than Aaron's.

'A final wash of the priestly garments,' added Tirzah, 'would be wise whilst we have ready access to water.'

'We will move only when the pillar of cloud moves,' replied Moses. 'And that will be when we are ready.'

'Uncle,' began Ithamar, 'you spoke this morning of the rest of the tribe of Levi also being set apart to serve Yahweh. What does that mean?'

'Every firstborn male belongs to Yahweh since He struck down the firstborn in Egypt. But instead of dedicating to Himself the first issue from every womb in every tribe, He is taking the whole tribe of Levi. That is the blessing He is bestowing upon the Levites for remaining faithful when their brothers prostrated themselves before the golden calf.'

'But how are they to serve?' asked Ithamar.

'They are to take down and carry the tabernacle every time we set out at Yahweh's command, and they are to put it up wherever Yahweh directs us to stop.' Moses then looked straight at Ithamar. 'And they will do so under your supervision.' He turned to Eleazar. 'And under yours. It is another solemn responsibility that you will both bear, but I know you will bear it well.'

Ithamar's heart swelled. It was a great honour and he relished the challenge. 'We will not fail you, Uncle.'

'The Levites will also encamp around the tabernacle, as will you, and they will guard the house of Yahweh, day and night, so that only those who are permitted and prepared approach the holy things.'

Ithamar pictured the contents of the tent. He knew how much gold was there—he had counted it.

Moses continued: 'Your ancestor Levi had three sons—Gershon, Kohath and Merari.'

'And we are descended from Kohath,' added Eleazar.

'Our next task will be to number their descendants. Three family lines to be assigned to three forms of service.'

The next few days were spent re-arranging the camp for the journey that lay ahead. At the centre of the camp was the tabernacle—the dwelling place of Yahweh—with the people grouped around it in tribes.

Ithamar stood staring at the banner that had been made for the tribe of Judah—an impressive lion had been worked into the linen.

Moses had chosen symbols for each tribe from the prophecy that Jacob had uttered concerning his sons.

'There is much wisdom,' began Eleazar, as he drew alongside Ithamar, 'in how Yahweh has arranged the camp.'

'How so?'

'Four groups of three on each side of the tabernacle to camp and to march together. The tribe of Judah camps to the east of the tabernacle—the place of favour, nearest its entrance—and Judah will lead us out—'

'The biggest tribe. Moses said Judah would rule over Israel.'

'So Yahweh does not put Judah together with the tribes of his elder brothers who could resent his leadership. Instead, he is with Leah's youngest sons, Issachar and Zebulun.'

'And Reuben and Simeon instead,' offered Ithamar, 'to the south with the eldest son of Leah's maid—Gad. With Reuben leading.'

'Exactly. To the west of the tabernacle are the sons of Rachel—Ephraim, Manasseh and Benjamin…'

'And Ephraim has the rights of the firstborn, so leads that group.'

'Leaving the other sons of the maids to the north,' finished Eleazar, 'with the eldest son, Dan, leading.'

Ithamar thought for a moment. 'They all camp at a distance from the tabernacle, but the Levites encircle it to the south, west and north, with Yahweh's priests closest to its entrance on the east.'

Eleazar nodded. 'We are blessed indeed.' He took his eyes off the tribe of Judah and turned towards the tabernacle, with the cloud still over the tent, directly above the ark. 'And at the heart of our camp and the centre of our lives is Yahweh, our God.'

Ithamar soon discovered that his relative Bezalel could also turn his skills to making musical instruments. Though *musical* may not have been the most fitting word when Moses presented him and his brother with a silver trumpet each. Ithamar took his with some confusion. 'These are to be used,' began Moses, 'for summoning the congregation, for signalling that it is time to set out, for sounding an alarm, and for announcing the new month or a festival. And the sons of Aaron are to have the honour of blowing them.'

Ithamar stared down at the trumpet. He then looked up. 'But I don't know how.'

'And that is why Ethan,' continued Moses, gesturing towards a stranger at his side, 'is here. He is a Gershonite and a gifted musician. He will teach you.'

Moses then left them in Ethan's care and under their father's watchful eyes. However, despite Ethan's careful explanation and demonstration of a clear, steady note, their first efforts were less than successful.

'That sounded like a strangled cow,' said Ithamar, laughing, after his brother's first attempt. However, his was even worse—there was no sound other than that of him blowing.

'But your cow is dead!' said Eleazar, grinning.

'Remember,' said Ethan patiently, 'keep your lips close together, and make a sound like the buzzing of an Egyptian fly. Just as I showed you.'

Ithamar tried again. *At least he was now making a sound.*

Eleazar laughed. 'Your cow lives! But it is both strangled *and* giving birth!'

Aaron gave them a look of reproof. 'Try again—both of you.'

But as Ithamar raised the trumpet to his lips, he caught his brother's eye. They both burst out laughing.

Aaron sighed. 'Be serious.'

But their father's disapproval only seemed to make it worse. Ithamar raised the trumpet again but could see Eleazar's shoulders shaking out of the corner of his eye. The trumpet didn't even make it to his lips. After two more failed attempts, both had tears streaming down their faces. It was the first time Ithamar's heart had truly felt light since the death of his brothers, and the laughter felt like a draught of cool, refreshing water to a parched and weary soul.

Aaron sighed once again and shook his head, but even his face now wore a wry smile. 'Please, Ethan, instil some sense and some skill into my sons…however long it takes.' And with that, he turned and left.

'Ithamar!'

The sound of his name drew Ithamar from the depths of sleep. He groped around in the darkness for his tunic, before pulling it clumsily over his head and stumbling to his feet.

'What is it?' asked Keziah, sleepily.

'Father is calling me.' There was no further explanation he could give. He pushed the tent flap aside and emerged into the cool greyness of dawn. 'What is it, Father?' But even as the words were leaving his lips, he knew the answer: the cloud that had rested upon the tent of meeting for fifty days had lifted. Before his father could answer, a long, loud, steady blast sounded from Eleazar's trumpet. Both of them had been practising.

Aaron turned to him. 'It is time to set out. We are leaving Horeb. There will be no morning sacrifice today, and Eleazar has given the signal to summon the leaders of the tribes. They will be told to rouse and alert their people. You know what to do now.'

Ithamar nodded, 'Yes, Father.'

'Good.' And with that, Aaron was gone.

Ithamar hurried back inside the tent. Keziah was just lifting their son to her breast. 'We are leaving today,' said Ithamar. 'I will go now to collect manna for the day. I will be back by the time you have fed Gaddiel. Whilst you bake bread, I will pack up the tent. Do you have cheese or curds ready?'

'Both.'

'Good—that with bread will be sufficient for a swift meal. I will need to be at the tabernacle as soon as I am able. You can pack the rest of the things when I go.'

'I will be quick!'

He bent down with a smile and kissed her. 'I know you will.' And with that he left.

Ithamar raised his trumpet to his lips and blew. Unlike his brother's long blast, his was a series of short bursts—the alarm. It was to alert the first division of Israelites—those camped to the east of the tabernacle—that it was time for them to set out. The cloud, which

143

had lifted at dawn from the tent of meeting, now stood ahead of them, to the north-east—the direction in which Canaan lay.

'You did well,' said Moses, as Ithamar lowered the trumpet.

'He did indeed,' added Aaron with a wry smile.

'Your uncle Nahshon will be leading the tribe of Judah out,' continued Moses, 'with the tribes of Issachar and Zebulun behind him.'

'And it is now time, is it not,' said Eleazar, 'for us to begin taking the tabernacle down?'

'That is right,' replied Moses. 'I will be nearby to help ensure that all is done correctly.'

'We will start immediately,' said Aaron.

Whilst Moses remained in the courtyard, the three of them entered the tent and unhooked the embroidered veil that hung in front of the ark. They folded it carefully and laid it over the ark to cover it. Eleazar then laid a second cover made from skins over the ark, leaving just the two gold rings on each side of the ark exposed. As Aaron spread a final cloth of pure, bright blue over the top, Ithamar and Eleazar carried between them the two wooden poles overlaid with gold for carrying the ark, and guided each of them in turn through the pairs of rings.

The golden altar, table and lampstand were then draped with cloths upon which any utensils were carefully stowed, after which they were also covered with skins and mounted on gold-covered poles. And whilst Ithamar took away the ashes from the bronze altar, his father and brother covered it in a similar way, before its bronze-covered poles were inserted.

'You have done well,' said Moses as Eleazar adjusted one of the poles slightly. 'All has been done as Yahweh commanded. He turned to Ithamar. 'While Eleazar deals with the oil and the incense, it is now time for you to demonstrate the careful planning and preparation I know you have done.'

'Yes, Uncle,' replied Ithamar, nodding. As he walked towards the gateway of the courtyard, he prayed nervously under his breath. 'Yahweh, please help me to honour You now. Let nothing be forgotten!'

The sight outside calmed his heart. He had instructed chosen men from two out of the three divisions of the Levites—the sons of Gershon and the sons of Merari—to assemble in separate groups at the entrance to the tabernacle when they heard the first alarm. He smiled at them. *He still couldn't believe he had oversight of so many!* And those before him were a fraction of the almost 6000 men of Gershon and Merari who were of age to serve at the tabernacle. Six covered carts, each pulled by two oxen, were behind the two groups—two on one side and four on the other. 'Gershonites,' he began, turning to his left, 'we are now ready for you.'

Eleazar stood at Ithamar's side, shaking his head. 'How long did this take you to plan?' he asked, a note of wonder in his voice. He had watched as the first group of Levites had suddenly invaded the tabernacle like a small swarm of locusts, denuding every pillar and bar of the curtains they supported. Each curtain was carefully folded, whether the richly embroidered ones that formed the tent or the goatshair ones that covered it; the colourful ones for the screens or the plain linen ones that formed the courtyard. They were then stowed safely with any cords on a cart. The skeleton that was left was then set upon by a small army of Merarites. Each seemed to know exactly which pillar or supporting socket, board, cord or tent-peg they were assigned to.

Ithamar laughed. 'It took a while—and much ink and papyrus.'

'It is as well Yahweh assigned you rather than me to the task!'

They stood in silence for a while, watching as the outline of the tabernacle disappeared before their eyes, like wind erasing marks in the sand. Beyond where the curtains had been, the rest of the Levites, who had been camped on three sides of what had been the courtyard, were finishing their preparations for the journey.

Not one man taking down the tabernacle had approached Ithamar with a question. Meticulous preparation ensured that every single item was collected and taken to the appropriate cart, spreading the weight between them. Now all that remained of the tabernacle were the five covered treasures to be carried on poles by the remaining

Levites—the Kohathites. The ark alone had the bright blue covering, marking it out so that none approached it unawares.

Aaron joined Ithamar and his brother as they scoured the dry ground, ensuring nothing had been left. 'Well done, my son,' began Aaron, laying a hand on Ithamar's shoulder. 'You have honoured Yahweh by your careful work. He has gifted you with an able mind, but you have used it wisely and well.'

'Thank you, Father.'

'And you both know what to do next?'

'Wait until the first three tribes have completely departed,' replied Ithamar. 'Then I will instruct all the families of Gershon and Merari to depart with the carts, and I will travel with them.'

'After that,' continued Eleazar, 'I will sound the alarm for the tribes to the south, led by Reuben, to set out, and I will then follow with the Kohathites and the holy things. The symbols of the presence of Yahweh will be at the heart of the whole company. Then the second half of the tribes will follow—the division under Ephraim and finally those with Dan.'

'All following Yahweh's pillar of cloud, as we leave Horeb,' finished Aaron. His gaze swept around the wide plain where they had spent over a year. He then sighed deeply.

Ithamar understood. *They were also leaving behind the bodies of his brothers in the sand.* However, the cloud over his heart lifted—as the one over the tent had done that morning—when the distant blast of Eleazar's trumpet sounded. *They were, once again, on their way to the Promised Land!*

If Ithamar had hoped that thirteen months of camping at the foot of Horeb might have cured the Israelites of their complaints, that hope was shattered within days. The wilderness they were crossing was more barren than any land they had so far encountered, and the only thing that seemed to grow there was the people's discontent. Like a persistent weed, it even entangled Aaron and Miriam.

Ithamar shook his head slowly. He and Eleazar were watching the evening sacrifice being consumed by flames as they camped for a fifth night by a place named Hazeroth. 'Why did our father and Miriam grumble against Moses? Why criticise him now for having a foreign wife?'

Eleazar shrugged his shoulders and sighed. 'Maybe that wasn't the real reason...'

'They were quick enough to point out that Yahweh had spoken through them as well.'

'Maybe the heat of the desert ails them too, and they grow jealous of the leadership of their younger brother.' Eleazar paused. 'Whatever the reason, they displeased Yahweh. If our father had not had the sacred anointing oil upon him, I am sure he would have been punished like Miriam.'

'Mercifully the Almighty only struck her with a week of leprosy rather than striking her dead as with others who have defied Him.'

Ithamar took a bronze poker and stirred the fire up. 'At least our journey will be over soon.'

The eleven day journey from Horeb to the border of Canaan took around two months, slowed both by the size and the sin of the company, and they finally arrived at the fertile oasis at Kadesh Barnea at the height of the summer heat. As at every camp, Ithamar had arrived before his brother so that the tabernacle could be set up and ready by the time Eleazar and the Kohathites arrived with the ark. The mood in the camp was jubilant.

Moses entered the tent of meeting when all had finally arrived. He emerged sometime later, smiling broadly.

'What is it, Uncle?' asked Ithamar, removing ashes from the bronze altar with a shovel.

'Yahweh directs us to explore the land, sending a scout from every tribe numbered among the fighting men.'

Ithamar paused. 'Has Yahweh told you who?'

'No, only that they are to be leaders in their tribes.'

'Will you send Uncle Nahshon then?'

Moses shook his head. 'No, I need younger leaders—those around forty. There is a good man from Judah named Caleb.

Nahshon speaks well of him. I will also send Hoshea from Ephraim. He served me well at Horeb, and proved his worth with a sword and with men when he led you and others against Amalek.' Moses smiled. 'But I have a new name for him—Joshua. No longer will he be called *salvation*, but *Yahweh is salvation*.'

'How long will they be gone?'

'As long as it takes to go through Canaan—and spy out its people, its cities and its land.'

Whilst the twelve spies were away, life in the camp continued. Standing beside the bronze altar was almost unbearable at times, with the heat of the fire adding to that of the day. Ithamar was grateful for his linen cap and glad that the regular daily sacrifices were, at least, in the cooler parts of the day. It was after one such sacrifice that the spies finally returned after forty days.

'Eleazar! Ithamar!'

Ithamar turned towards Moses, arms still full of wood and the air rich with the smell of roasting lamb, as the evening sacrifice burned on the altar. 'What is it, Uncle?'

'Where's your brother?'

'Here, Uncle,' said Eleazar, emerging from the tent, where he had been checking the oil in the lamps to ensure they would burn through the night. Ithamar caught a hint of fragrant incense from the altar inside.

'Finish what you are doing quickly, both of you, and then bring your trumpets to the entrance to the tabernacle. You need to summon the congregation—those spying out the land have returned.'

As twilight deepened, Ithamar raised his silver trumpet to his lips, as did his brother. They knew the signal they were to give—a long blast on both trumpets. *The people would know its meaning.* As Ithamar lowered the trumpet, he caught sight of Keziah standing at the entrance to their tent, not far away, Gaddiel in her arms. She smiled and waved. He returned the smile, but his gaze swiftly drifted to the group of twelve standing nearby. Two carried between them a pole on which was strung various fruits. There were pomegranates and figs, and a branch cut from a vine, on which was hanging a single enormous bunch of grapes. *It wouldn't be long now until they could taste the fruits of Canaan for themselves! What a blessed time to enter the land!* His gaze then settled upon two men in particular. Joshua looked every part the leader. *Tall, strong, confident.* His face seemed to brim with resolve and optimism. The man beside him, Caleb, seemed to share a similar disposition.

'They do not look as they should do,' said Eleazar suddenly in a lowered voice, as hundreds began to approach, answering the summons.

'Who? The crowds?'

'No—the spies.'

'Joshua and Caleb seem satisfied enough.'

'I was not looking at them…'

Ithamar began studying the others. *His brother was right. They were different.* Ithamar could not read their expressions fully in the dim light. *Was it unease or fear or some sort of grim determination?* He couldn't be sure, but there was distance between them and Joshua and Caleb.

When the entrance to the tabernacle was surrounded by people as far as the eye could see, and torches had been lit and held aloft, Moses invited the men to speak. One immediately stepped forward, as if presenting himself as the group's spokesman. He had the bearing of a leader. 'That's Shammua,' whispered Eleazar, 'from the tribe of Reuben.'

Shammua cast his gaze around the assembly before speaking, and then lifted up his voice so that all could hear. 'We went into the land as we were instructed, from the Negev in the south, through the hill country, and up to the north. It is indeed a land that flows with milk and honey.' He nodded to the men holding the pole who then lifted it high. 'This is its fruit.' Snatches of excited murmuring rippled around the gathering. When it died down, Shammua went on. 'However—' He paused, and then took a deep breath. '—the people who live in the land are powerful. Their cities are very large and fortified.' Silence fell upon the company. 'We saw the descendants of Anak there.' Shammua paused again, as if to let his words sink in. All, including

Ithamar, had heard the stories of those descended from giants. Here and there, muttering broke out in the crowd. 'There are Amalekites in the Negev; Hittites, Jebusites and Amorites in the hill country, and Canaanites living near the sea and along the Jordan.' His tone was one of defeat.

The words had an immediate effect. The muttering became a clamour, as many alarmed voices started talking at once. 'He speaks of the land as if it belongs to those who live there,' said Eleazar angrily. 'Yahweh gave it to Abraham and He will give it to us as He has promised! Have they forgotten how many we are?'

'Look, Eleazar!' replied Ithamar. 'Caleb holds his hand up to speak.'

They fell silent as Caleb slowly quietened the people. And when he spoke, it was with conviction. 'We should go up and take possession of the land. We can certainly do it!'

'We cannot!' The angry new voice rose from the ten men who stood together. 'They are stronger than us!'

'The land we explored devours those living in it,' exclaimed the man standing next to him, adding, 'all the people who live there are huge!'

'The Nephilim are there,' cried out another. 'We were as small as grasshoppers next to them—and they knew it.'

Ithamar's mouth went dry and his stomach churned. *This could not be happening!*

'They see only men,' exclaimed Eleazar vehemently, 'and they forget Yahweh!' But his words were lost to all but Ithamar in the outcry that rose around them. As the darkness of night descended upon the assembly, so did despair. The torchlight illuminated only faces contorted in panic, fear or anger.

'Why do they cry out and weep?' said Ithamar, shaking his head in disbelief as the tumult around them continued. 'Do they *still* not trust Yahweh?'

'They have failed to trust Him each time hardship has come their way,' replied Eleazar, his eyes blazing. 'They have not changed since the day we left Egypt! They see only obstacles, not Yahweh's powerful hand. They *will not* believe what He says. And look…' He gestured suddenly towards one particular knot of men, who were now pointing at Moses and Aaron. 'They are now doing what they have always done—'

'Blaming their leaders,' said Ithamar.

'It would have been better if we had died in Egypt!' shouted one of the knot of men in a sudden lull.

'They surely cannot *still* be thinking that!' exclaimed Ithamar in frustration. But no-one heard him, as other cries rang out.

'Or better if we had died in the desert!'

'Is Yahweh bringing us here so we can be slaughtered by swords, with our women and children taken as plunder?'

And then they heard the sickeningly familiar words, 'Wouldn't it be better to go back to Egypt?' The question was answered by murmurs of approval from the crowd.

'How can they even think that?' said Ithamar, incredulous. 'Have they forgotten what it was like to be slaves? Have they learned nothing of Yahweh and His power?'

But before Eleazar had a chance to reply, the response of the crowd distilled into a single, defiant cry. 'Let's appoint a leader and return to Egypt!'

'No!' whispered Eleazar. 'They are turning their backs on the purposes of Yahweh and will bring down His wrath!'

Ithamar shook his head slowly. His lips moved but only his heart uttered his prayer. *Yahweh! Have mercy!* Joshua and Caleb were tearing their garments in grief. *Their clothing was now rent like their hearts.* Moses and Aaron had already fallen to the ground, prostrating themselves towards the tabernacle. *Maybe Yahweh would hear their entreaties and prevent the disaster!*

But then Joshua stepped forward and raised both his arms, palms forward, to still the crowd. The storm before them slowly subsided, though Ithamar wondered for how long. 'Maybe their words will turn the people and rekindle their faith—'

'What faith?' spat out Eleazar.

Then Joshua began to speak. 'The land we explored was exceedingly good.' He began his appeal speaking each word slowly, loudly and deliberately. 'If Yahweh is pleased with us, He *will* lead us into the land—a land, that Shammua rightly says, flows with milk and honey. Yahweh *will* give the land to us.' He looked out at them, and then implored, 'Only do *not* rebel against Yahweh. You need not be afraid of those living in the land! We will swallow them up! Don't you see? Yahweh is with us—what protection do they have? You have no need to fear them!'

An uneasy quiet hung over the crowd for several moments, then a cry rang out. 'We should stone them!'

The tiny flame of hope that had flickered in Ithamar's heart sputtered and died. He couldn't see who had shouted out the words, but it didn't matter.

'Yes, stone them—now!' The words were echoed around the angry crowd and many began to crouch down and search the ground for the means to do it.

Ithamar suddenly thought of Keziah and Gaddiel nearby—and struggled to draw breath. *They had no one to protect them!* He was soon wrenched from his terrified thoughts as Eleazar grabbed hold of him.

'Quick, Ithamar! We must raise Moses and Aaron to their feet.'

A few quick strides and they were at Aaron's side. 'Father! You must get up,' cried Ithamar, tugging at him. But suddenly the sun in all its radiance rose behind them—or that was how it felt to Ithamar. The blazing light was reflected in hundreds of faces, frozen in fear, their torches now feeble smudges in the brilliance around them.

Ithamar swung around. *The glory of the Almighty was upon the tent of meeting.* He and Eleazar hastily helped their father and uncle to their feet.

The crowd started backing nervously away, many of them now shielding their eyes from the blinding light. Moses turned to Aaron. 'Quick, we must stand before Yahweh before His wrath falls on this people.'

As they hurried into the tabernacle and towards Yahweh's presence, Ithamar and his brother immediately joined Caleb and

Joshua. Joshua took charge. 'We must entreat Yahweh too. He has forgiven His people for their rebellion before. We must beg Him to do so once more.'

The four of them were still praying when Moses emerged from the tabernacle sometime later, the glory of the Lord shining brightly behind him, casting deep shadows into the crowd. The looks of defiance had faded, and some shifted uneasily as Moses walked forward to address the assembly. He did not need to signal for silence. If a lamb had bleated on the far side of the camp, they would have heard it. Every eye was upon him.

'Now hear the words of Yahweh, people of Israel!' he began in a loud voice. '*As surely as I live*, declares Yahweh, *I will do to you the very things I have heard you say.*' He paused. There was not even a single murmur. '*Your bodies will fall in this desert—every one of you twenty years or more, numbered in the census, and who has grumbled against Me. Not one of you shall enter the land I swore to give you, except Caleb son of Jephunneh and Joshua son of Nun. Your children, however, whom you said would be taken as plunder—I will bring them in to enjoy the land you have rejected. But you—your bodies will fall in this wilderness. Your sons will be shepherds for forty years in the desert, suffering for your unfaithfulness, until all your corpses lie dead in the sand. For forty years—a year for every day you explored the land—you will bear the guilt of your sin. You will know what it is to have Me against you. I, Yahweh, have spoken, and I will do all these things to this wicked community which has stood against Me. They will meet their end in this desert. Here they will die.*'

Ithamar stared at his uncle, stunned. *Forty years! It was a lifetime!* It was as if he had held within his hands a model of Canaan crafted from sand, only to watch it collapse and then run through his hands.

The entire assembly had stood in silence as Moses delivered the judgment upon them. Now the only sound that could be heard was people weeping softly.

'Their sorrow is too late,' whispered Eleazar, his cheeks wet with tears.

'But it has not stopped Yahweh's hand falling,' said Joshua grimly. For a moment, Ithamar did not grasp his meaning, but gasps drew his eyes towards the ten men who had journeyed with Caleb and Joshua. Some had already fallen to their knees; others were grasping their necks, terror in their eyes. All of them appeared grey in the light that still blazed from the tent. Those near them backed swiftly away, clearly fearful of being struck by the same fate. Ithamar watched horrified as, one by one, the ten men slumped to the ground, and lay there unmoving. *Yahweh's hand of judgment had indeed fallen.*

As Moses and Aaron dismissed the people, Ithamar stood as silent and unmoving as the mountains. *Forty years! Would he and Keziah never have a home in the Promised Land?* Eleazar laid a hand upon his shoulder, but said nothing. *What was there to say?* Neither Caleb nor Joshua spoke either. Both stood silently shaking their heads, one staring at the dirt, the other into the night sky.

Eventually, when every Israelite had disappeared quietly into the night, Moses and Aaron joined them. 'The word of Yahweh was devastating,' said Caleb, subdued, 'but we cannot question its justice.'

'The people have brought it upon themselves,' said Eleazar sadly. 'It is no more than they deserve.'

'It is less—much less,' replied Moses. 'And it is a mercy. Even now, He abounds in love and forgiveness. He pardons and chastens rather than rejecting and destroying, as He threatened first.' He looked towards the tent. 'He will remain among us, but the people must learn His ways before He can lead them into the land. It will be the next generation that enjoys the milk and honey of Canaan. His promises will yet be fulfilled.'

'But what of us,' said Ithamar softly. 'Are we never to enter the Promised Land?'

Moses smiled wearily and gently laid a hand on his nephew's shoulder. 'Neither you, Ithamar, nor your brother, were among those numbered in the census of fighting men, twenty years or older, or among those who grumbled against Yahweh. And you are His anointed priests. You are not under His judgment and will not fall in the desert.'

'But forty years!' blurted out Ithamar. 'It is so long to wait! I will be old when I enter Canaan…'

'We all will,' said Joshua ruefully.

'Not as old as some,' added Moses with a sigh. 'Still, our father Jacob was one hundred and thirty years when he entered Egypt. Your father and I are both over eighty now, but Yahweh is able to breathe enough life into us so that we may yet see the land that Israel called home.' He paused and then sighed deeply once more. 'I have lived forty years in the desert once before, waiting. I endured it then by the goodness of Yahweh, and I will do so again. We all will.'

Ithamar couldn't believe it. The night had passed, but not the people's folly.

'They are doing what?' exclaimed Eleazar.

'You heard me rightly the first time,' said Aaron, as he joined them on the early walk to the tabernacle to offer the morning sacrifice. 'A number have left the camp and headed up towards the hill country, intending to enter Canaan. According to Moses, their words were, *We have sinned, but we will now go up to the place Yahweh has promised*.'

'Did they hear nothing of what Moses said last night?' asked Ithamar, baffled, as they pushed back the blue, purple and scarlet screen to enter the courtyard.

'You can be sure they heard it,' replied Aaron, pausing to let the curtain fall back into place behind them. 'They heard it, but didn't like it. Moses told them not to go, and told them they would be defeated because Yahweh would not go with them.' They resumed their walk towards the bronze altar.

'They still fail to believe His words,' said Eleazar. 'If they truly repented, they would change and humble themselves before Him. All they are doing now is adding to their sin!'

'It is little wonder,' said Aaron, 'that the first thing we do *each* day is sacrifice a burnt offering, to atone for sin and to seek Yahweh's favour. And mercifully He continues to dwell in our midst.'

Ithamar glanced upwards. The cloud of Yahweh's presence was, indeed, still above the tent.

They remained camped at Kadesh Barnea for many days after the failed attempt to enter Canaan, but when Ithamar eventually blew the trumpet once more to signal that they were to move, the pillar of cloud that went before them had moved to the south. To lead them back into the wilderness—and away from the Promised Land.

Notes

1. *The first fourteen chapters of Numbers, from which these events are taken, are not arranged in strictly chronological order.*

2. *It is not clear how the slaughtering of the Passover animals at the tabernacle was carried out at twilight, given the command (in Leviticus 17:3-4) that the blood of all animals was to be offered there and the numbers involved. By New Testament times, the lambs were being slaughtered in the afternoon at the Temple, so that the Passover meal could be eaten that evening after sunset.*

3. *Only the blood of the sin offering is recorded as being poured out at the base of the altar after sprinkling it there. The blood of other sacrifices is to be sprinkled over the altar, but it is not specifically stated that the rest is poured out at the base. It seems most sensible to assume that it was. Some (much later) Jewish writings point towards there being a drainage system at the base of the altar in Herod's temple, to carry the blood away.*

4. *There has been much debate and disagreement over the numbers recorded in the census. An excellent summary of the issues is given in Gordon Wenham's Tyndale commentary on Numbers. He concludes: 'In short, there is no obvious solution to the problems caused by these census figures.' In this account, they are taken as stated. The figures behave in all ways as literal numbers. The logistics of moving such huge numbers (possibly up to two million) are obvious, but, as others have pointed out, the Exodus from Egypt and journey to Canaan are, already, one remarkable miracle.*

5. *The exact form of the trumpet signals is unclear, but it seems reasonable to assume that an alarm consisted of a number of short blasts.*

6. *There seems to be a difference between Numbers 10:21 (which implies that the ark was at the centre of the company) and Numbers 10:33 (which*

states that the ark went ahead). It is possible that a different configuration was used for different situations. The ark definitely preceded the Israelites at the crossing of the Jordan, and maybe on the inaugural stage of the journey it again went before the people.

7. A land 'flowing with milk and honey' probably reflects the idea of abundance for those with a pastoral (rather than an agricultural) lifestyle, with milk flowing from herds and abundant provision from nature, though honey may refer to date syrup rather than to bees' honey.

8. Although it may seem that only Joshua and Caleb (of those twenty years or older) enter the Promised Land (see, for example, Numbers 26:64-65), the text actually seems to imply that the Levites might escape this judgment for the following reasons:

    (a) they were not numbered in the census of those over twenty that Moses refers to in the judgment (Numbers 14:29);

    (b) they were set apart for Yahweh and possibly remained loyal to Moses;

    (c) it is clear that Eleazar enters the Canaan (Joshua 17:4) and he is surely over twenty at the time of the judgment in Numbers 14, given his consecration as a priest. Also, Moses is kept from entering, not because of this judgment, but because of his personal sin in Numbers 20:12.

9

The LORD's anger burned against Israel and he made them wander in the wilderness for forty years, until the whole generation of those who had done evil in his sight was gone. (Numbers 32:13)

The sight was a familiar one to Ithamar: his uncle sitting cross-legged at the front of his tent, bent over his writing. He had seen it numerous times during their long wanderings in the desert. Ithamar glanced around; there were hills some distance off to the east, but the land on which they were now camped was flat and open—the plains of Moab. In the other direction, though currently hidden behind the tents, was the line of trees and greenery that marked the course of the Jordan as it flowed south along the border of Canaan, towards the Salt Sea. But in the distance, to the west, he could just about see the highest hills of the Promised Land. His gaze returned to Moses, and he stood silently watching him for several moments. *The thirty-eight years since the rebellion at Kadesh Barnea had left their mark on his features, though not on his strength or his zeal. But leaving a mark was precisely what his uncle was doing now.*

Ithamar began walking towards to the tent. 'Moses!' He had ceased calling him *Uncle* many years earlier—at around the same time that Phinehas had started saying *Uncle Ithamar.*

Moses looked up and smiled. He rested his brush in the tiny pot of ink on his makeshift table. 'There are not many I would want to interrupt this sacred task, but I make an exception for you. Is all well at the tabernacle?'

Ithamar grinned, crinkling the skin around the corners of his aging eyes. 'Phinehas and Gaddiel keep their younger brothers in order well enough, and although they are kept busy, it is not like when there were only three of us!'

'Like our father Jacob and his twelve sons, Yahweh has blessed you and Eleazar richly in the children he has bestowed!' The two brothers had eleven sons between them.

'The Almighty knew His people would need more priests.'

'Indeed,' said Moses with a smile. 'But a daughter is also a blessing.'

'And Keziah and I are grateful for her. After all, he gave Dinah to Jacob—'

'And Serah to Asher,' added Moses.

'Serah?' replied Ithamar, intrigued. 'I do not remember that name.'

'Ah!' said Moses. 'But she is in here.' With that he twisted his body slightly and tapped the large, ornate wooden box behind him that contained the innumerable scrolls upon which he had been writing the history of their people and Yahweh's words to them. 'And not only is Jacob's granddaughter here, but also many others you may not have heard of—or remembered.' Their years in the wilderness had given Moses—and others—plenty of starlit nights around a campfire or evening meal to share the stories passed down through countless generations. 'As I have told you before, the story of the people of Israel did not *begin* with Israel, or even his father, Isaac, or his grandfather Abraham. It began with our first father, Adam, and runs like a golden thread through his descendants to Noah, and then through the line of Shem, his second son.'

Ithamar paused for a moment, his brow furrowed. 'Neither Abraham nor Jacob were firstborn sons, were they? And now Judah is head over Reuben and Ephraim over Manasseh. Why is it that Yahweh so often chooses not the firstborn, but a younger son?'

'Because His ways are not our ways,' replied Moses simply. 'The heart is more important to Him than the year of one's birth.'

'*His ways are not our ways*,' echoed Ithamar softly, before falling silent.

'What troubles you?'

'You have written of the deaths of Nadab and Abihu, have you not?'

Moses nodded. 'Yes, it is part of our history.'

'Will generations to come only know of my brothers that they were struck down by Yahweh when they transgressed His commands?'

Moses drew a deep breath and let it out in a long sigh. 'Sometimes it is as important—may be more so—for those that follow to be warned against what is wrong rather than told of what was right.' He paused. 'But Yahweh knows the story of *all* their days and all that was in their hearts.'

When Ithamar fell silent once again, Moses reached for the brush. But as his fingers lifted it, Ithamar spoke again. 'Where are you up to now?'

Moses smiled wryly and put the brush down again. 'Where was I the *last* time you asked?'

'You were part way through the story of the rebellion of Korah and those with him, and how they challenged your authority and that of my father after we left Kadesh Barnea. You had just written of how Yahweh made the ground open up so that it swallowed them and their tents.' He paused, his mind's eye momentarily resting upon another time and another place. 'I remember the screams of those nearby,' he murmured.

'None who witnessed that day will quickly forget it,' said Moses. 'But it is followed by the account of how Yahweh attested the authority of your father and of the tribe of Levi to minister before Him, by making Aaron's rod blossom and bear almonds overnight.'

'It did stop the grumbling, for a while at least...'

'There was not much to write of our years of wandering.' Moses shrugged. 'Men died and others were born. It did not take much ink. But I did write of Miriam's death in the first month of this year— and of all that followed when the people grumbled of a lack of water at Meribah—and when your father and I failed to fully carry out the command of Yahweh before the people. Yes, those who follow will read of your brothers' sin, but they will also read of mine.' A shadow passed across the face of Moses, but he quickly continued. 'I have written of how Eleazar succeeded your father as high priest when Aaron died at Mount Hor, and how we passed around the land of Edom. I have written of the poisonous snakes that Yahweh sent amongst the people when they spoke against Him once again, and of the bronze snake that He told us to make, so that all who were bitten and looked at it would live. I have told of how we defeated Sihon, king of the Amorites, and Og, king of Bashan, as we journeyed north towards Moab. And I have written of how we finally arrived here at Shittim, on the plains of Moab, and how Moab tried to oppose us, firstly through their prophet Balaam, and then by leading the people away from Yahweh through harlotry with their women and their gods.' He paused. 'But the zeal of your nephew Phinehas will not be forgotten!'

'You have written of him spearing Zimri whilst he lay with the Midianite woman?'

'Lay brazenly and openly—and whilst the people were weeping at the tent of meeting because of Yahweh's judgment on such behaviour.'

Ithamar remembered well his nephew's fury and outrage, and how he had suddenly grabbed a nearby spear and run towards Zimri's tent. '*Zeal* describes him well.'

'Zeal for Yahweh—and he turned aside His wrath by his actions. More would have died that day if it weren't for Phinehas.' Moses paused. 'He will be a worthy successor to Eleazar one day.'

Ithamar nodded. 'He will. So what are you writing of now? The second census?'

Moses gently fingered the scroll that lay before him. 'No, I am further than that. I have written of how we appointed Joshua to lead the people after I am gone, and of Yahweh's further commands about offerings and vows. The people must possess every detail of Yahweh's words to us.' He looked up from the table and met Ithamar's eyes. 'It is not enough to know how He has guided us in the past; we must know how He wants us to live every day—both today and in the Promised Land.'

Ithamar held his gaze for several moments, and then looked down at his feet. 'Moses…?'

'Speak…'

'Yahweh has relented before and not brought the judgment of which He has spoken...'

'He has, more than once, yes.'

'May He not yet relent, and allow you to enter Canaan? It just... doesn't seem fair. You have served Yahweh better than any other person in this camp. It was only the once that you did not do exactly what Yahweh said. And water still came from the rock at Meribah, even though you hit the rock rather than speaking to it.'

Moses sighed. 'But I did not obey Him fully and so did not honour Him as I should have done before the people.'

Ithamar marvelled at his uncle's honesty. *He was more humble than anyone else he'd known, and was freely recording his own failings for the generations to come.* Ithamar wasn't sure that he would have done the same had he been writing Israel's history, and couldn't help thinking that his uncle still deserved to enter the land far more than he did. He looked up. 'But what if you asked Yahweh again? He listens to you like no-one else!'

Moses shook his head slowly, seemingly resigned to his fate. 'I *have* pleaded with Him, believe me.'

'And what did He say?'

'He told me that I would see the land for myself from the summit of Pisgah, but that it would be Joshua who would lead the people across the Jordan and not me. And He told me not to speak of it further.' He then added ruefully, 'I will not disobey Him again.' Ithamar stayed silent and, after a pause, Moses continued: 'And so I will not grumble at Yahweh's words or His judgments. He has given me less than my sins warrant and blessed me with far more than I deserve. He has allowed me to speak to Him as a friend, face to face, and I have stood in His presence and beheld His glory. Yes, I would dearly love to set foot in the land promised to our father Abraham. But my hands have received a far greater treasure. Canaan's bounty and beauty can never compare to that of its Creator—and of Him I have tasted and been satisfied.' He smiled at Ithamar. 'I have made my peace with Him. So if my dear nephew will allow me, I will now continue writing, so that God's people will know how Joshua led twelve thousand men against the Midianites, to execute Yahweh's judgment on them, and returned here victorious to find that not one single man had been lost in battle. And how it was that the tribes of Reuben and Gad and half the tribe of Manasseh chose an inheritance of land this side of the Jordan.'

'I will leave you in peace,' said Ithamar. But as he put his hand on the tent flap, he turned. 'I will readily write down your words if your hand ever tires.'

Moses' brush was poised, unmoving, over the scroll. He smiled. 'I may yet need you.'

Ithamar pushed the grey hairs out of Keziah's eyes and kissed her. 'I think I love my wife now even more than when we left Egypt.' As she smiled, her age and vivacity revealed themselves more visibly. She had passed the age of child-bearing some years earlier, but not before giving him five more children after Gaddiel. And the wife of their firstborn had borne four sons, one of whom would start serving as a priest within five years.

She kissed him back. 'And I have few complaints about my husband.' She raised her eyebrows. 'Even if he muddles the names of his grandchildren at times.'

'But there are so many of them…'

'There are only twelve!'

He kissed her again. 'But I have passed three score years and ten.'

'Is that meant to be an excuse?'

He declined to reply. 'Are you ready?'

She nodded, 'Yes,' and then adjusted his priest's cap. 'And you are now too.'

With all their children married, they had none to harry before they left the tent. Ithamar shivered as they stepped outside. The days had scarcely begun to lengthen, and although the early morning sun was shining, the day was cool and there were still plenty of clouds in the sky. He had worn something warmer when he had gone out soon after dawn for the daily manna, but now was dressed only in his priest's linen tunic. They walked towards the tabernacle, where people were beginning to gather. It would be a solemn day. They were to enter into a fresh covenant with Yahweh before they left the plains of Moab to cross the Jordan into the Promised Land. *It was hard to believe that thirty-eight years had finally passed and it was now time to enter Canaan.*

A wooden platform had been constructed for the special occasion, allowing the people to see and hear better. Eleazar stood beside the platform in his high priest's robes. As he faced east, the sun glinted off the golden plate on his turban, and each time he moved slightly, other tiny flashes of light emanated from the gold strands woven into the ephod and from the clasps holding the twelve stones on the breastplate. *He looked noble and majestic, as their father had done before him.* Joshua was standing on the opposite side, sword strapped to his belt, as if reminding them all of the battles that lay ahead. And in between them, upon the platform, was Moses, the scrolls of the covenant before him on a stand. Despite his one hundred and twenty years, he stood unaided, straight and tall. He looked this way and that as the people assembled. *Like a shepherd watching over his sheep, checking that none were missing or injured.* His care for the people of Israel had never once faltered or failed.

As they neared the tabernacle, Ithamar left Keziah and went to join his sons and nephews, all attired as he was. It was six months to the day since his father had died, and in ten weeks it would be forty years since they had left Egypt. He studied the second generation of priests as he approached them. *Not one of them had witnessed the plagues or the crossing of the Sea of Reeds.* It was the same for many of those now gathering before the platform. The bodies of all the fighting men numbered in the first census were now scattered in the wilderness—only Joshua and Caleb remained. Yahweh's words had come to pass. The disobedience of the people had been costly.

Moses squinted slightly as he looked east over the people, the low sun shining in his eyes. By the time he was ready to speak, clouds had obscured the rising sun, making it easier for him. The crowds fell silent. 'Yahweh spoke to us at Horeb, saying, *You have stayed long enough at this mountain.*' And so began the words of the covenant made on the plains of Moab.

The ceremony finished some time before noon. As the generation before them had done at Horeb, the people responded, declaring that Yahweh was their God and that they would listen to Him and obey Him. But it was the final words of the covenant which impressed themselves on Ithamar's heart like ink upon papyrus. Moses paused and looked out on the whole assembly, every face turned towards him. 'Today I call heaven and earth to witness against you,' he cried out, his voice not weakened by age, 'that I have set before you life and death, blessings and curses.' His gaze swept across the mass of people, as if searching their hearts. 'So choose life.'

But there was more to come. 'Uncle Ithamar…?'

Ithamar turned. Eleazar's sixth son (and the youngest priest) was watching as Moses summoned Joshua forward. 'Yes, what is it, Malchiel?'

'Is Joshua to be commissioned now?'

'Yes.'

'Then why is Father also going up onto the platform with him?'

'It is right that Joshua is not only appointed before the whole congregation but also before the high priest—Yahweh's representative.'

Moses' voice rang out once again, as he faced Joshua: 'Be strong and courageous…' Malchiel fell silent and listened, but not for long.

'Why is Moses laying his hands on him?' he whispered.

Without taking his eyes off the ceremony, Ithamar shushed him. It was only when all three men were descending from the platform that he answered his nephew. 'You were asking about Moses laying his hands on Joshua, Malchiel.'

He nodded. 'We lay our hands on the heads of the animals that we bring for sacrifice. So why is Moses doing it?'

Ithamar smiled. 'It is a good question!' He noticed that one of his other nephews and two of his own sons were also listening. 'When we place our hands on an animal's head, it is as if our sins pass to the animal, to be carried by the lamb or the goat or the bull, rather than us. When Moses laid his hands upon Joshua, it was a symbol, not of sin but of authority passing to him, setting him apart for the work that

Yahweh has for him. Yahweh's authority has been upon Moses for the last forty years; now it will be upon Joshua, for it is he, not Moses, who will lead us into the Promised Land.' His nephew opened his mouth again. 'Not now, Malchiel. We are being summoned to Moses.'

As the sons and grandsons of Aaron walked towards the platform, Ithamar glanced at Phinehas. *He would be the next high priest, and his son Abishua after him.* And for just a moment he thought of Nadab. *Would it have been different if he had been Yahweh's anointed?* But the thought had passed by the time they were standing in front of the platform.

Moses began addressing them all, the scrolls from which he had read in his hands. 'Take this book of the law and place it beside the ark of the covenant of Yahweh, your God.' He handed the scrolls to Ithamar. 'At the end of every seven years, the time of cancelling debts, at the Feast of Tabernacles, when all Israel comes to appear before Yahweh in the land you are about to possess, you shall read this law to all the people—to the men, women and children, and to the alien who is with you, so that they may hear and learn and fear Yahweh, and obey all the words of your God in this law.'

Ithamar stared at the papyrus scrolls in his hands. *They were so light and yet were a greater treasure than all the gold of Egypt.*

Ithamar leant over to blow out the one remaining lamp in the tent, and then lay back down and pulled the covers up. Keziah snuggled closer and laid her arm over him. The clouds of the morning had cleared by sunset, gifting them a clear, star-filled evening but a chilly night. For a while they lay in silence, Ithamar listening in the dark to his wife's breathing. Her skin next to his was not as smooth as it used to be, but he didn't care. She was the mother of his children, a beloved grandmother to their offspring, and his faithful companion of more than forty years. And she loved him. But hers was not the only love to have touched his life. He turned onto his side, so that he was facing her. It was new moon, so there was no light outside, and although he could not see Keziah, he could feel her breath upon him.

'Do you know what struck me today as I listened to Moses?'

Keziah laughed. 'I have rarely been able to guess what is going through my husband's head, no matter how many times he asks me!'

Ithamar smiled. 'Then I will ask you another question! Do you know how many times Moses spoke of love earlier—of Yahweh's love for us and of our calling to love Him?'

'No. How many was it?' She then added playfully, 'Were you keeping one of your records again?'

'It was too late to start counting by the time I noticed how often he mentioned it.'

'Then you will have to read the book of the law again and count them.'

'Eleazar has already put the scrolls by the ark in the holy of holies—and I am not permitted to enter there. But exact numbers do not matter. It is enough to know that our covenant with Yahweh is, as Moses said, a covenant of love.'

'Like our marriage...' said Keziah softly.

Ithamar paused. 'He said that Yahweh didn't love us or choose us because we were a great people, but because He is a God who loves. And we are not just to obey and serve Him but to love Him—with all our heart, soul and strength.' He pondered the words. 'I do not think any Egyptian would ever say that of their god.'

'Neither do I.'

'We have always loved and wanted it to go well for our children. It is the same with Yahweh and His people.'

Keziah was silent for several moments and then whispered. 'But what of the curses? There were so many that Moses spoke of...'

Ithamar drew in a deep breath and let it out slowly as he thought. 'We have tasted of Yahweh's goodness and love, and that should draw us to love and obey Him in return. But we should also rightly fear turning our backs on our Creator. We should fear it greatly for no good ever comes of disobeying Him. Maybe it is as well to know what lies ahead on the path of rebellion, so that we never set our feet on it. After all, did we not warn our own children many times in their youth? We warned them because we did not wish them to be hurt.'

Keziah was silent, and in the distance, a creature of the night screeched. She sighed. 'You speak truly. Where does your wisdom come from?'

'My brother,' he said with a chuckle, but then added, 'but we have spoken enough.' And he pulled her closer.

The day was still cool and fresh when Moses walked through the gate of the tabernacle, Joshua at his side. Ithamar and Gaddiel were still attending to the morning offering, with Malchiel watching closely and learning. Ithamar paused and waited for Moses to reach the bronze altar upon which they had just placed the slaughtered lamb. *The day could be another significant one.*

'Is Eleazar still in the tent?' asked Moses.

'He should have finished burning the incense soon,' replied Ithamar. 'He has been inside for a while.'

And just then, Eleazar emerged through the patterned veil. 'I heard your voices,' he said. 'Do you need me?'

'I need the sanctuary,' replied Moses. 'Yahweh Himself is to commission Joshua there.'

Many questions formed in Ithamar's mind though they remained unspoken. Eleazar joined them as the two men disappeared inside. As the firewood crackled in the flames and the fat of the offering began to sizzle, the pillar of cloud over the tent descended, covering the doorway. *It was as if the cloud was barring or guarding the entrance.* None of them spoke. They heard the sound of a voice within, but could not easily determine the words. Eleazar whispered, 'Yahweh stands with them and speaks to them.'

More time passed than Ithamar had expected, but eventually the cloud lifted and Moses and Joshua reappeared. There was something different about Moses, though exactly what was as elusive to Ithamar as a fly in the air. 'Yahweh has spoken,' he began. 'The time is near for me to leave you.' Ithamar waited. *Did Moses' words mean what he thought they meant?* He continued, 'I will address the sons of Israel, this day, one last time.' He turned to Eleazar. 'You and Joshua are to gather the people—all the men, women and children.' He then glanced up at the sun. 'Tell them to assemble as soon as noon has passed—the day will not be an unduly hot one.' He nodded to them. 'Go now.' He then turned to Gaddiel. 'You are to go to my tent—take Malchiel with you. Just inside you will find a large carved wooden box. It contains my writing materials.'

Gaddiel nodded, 'I know it, Uncle. I have seen it there before.'

'Good. You and your cousin are to bring it back here straight away.'

'We will be quick, Uncle,' said Gaddiel solemnly, clearly sensing the mood of the day, and they hurried off.

Ithamar was left alone with Moses. He waited for his instructions, even if they were simply to continue with his priestly duties. Moses smiled. 'Today, my nephew, I would value both your swift writing and your company. It will be quicker if you are my hands, so my heart can simply remember the words of the song that Yahweh has given to me. As I speak them, record them on a scroll.'

'A song?' said Ithamar, surprised.

'More of a lament.' He paused. 'A lament and a warning. The Almighty has given me a song to teach to His people, so when they turn away from Him to other gods, it will be a witness against them. They will know from it the reason why the curses of the covenant have come upon them. Yahweh will be blameless, for He has been gracious to them, blessing them beyond measure. They will have brought the misfortunes down upon their own heads.' He paused again, but then added, 'But they will also know where to turn when disaster overtakes them.'

'You speak as if that future is sure,' said Ithamar quietly. 'You say *when they turn away from Him…*'

Moses shook his head slowly and sighed deeply. 'Rebellion is in our hearts. It has been there since Adam, and thousands of years have not removed it. We should not be surprised that forty years have not done so either.' He looked Ithamar in the eye. 'Yahweh will chasten and punish His people, but He will not abandon the descendants of Abraham.'

Finally Ithamar broached the matter that had left his heart as restless as the waters from a mountain spring. 'You said that it was nearly time to leave us…' He left the words hanging.

'Yahweh has told me that I am about to lie down with my fathers.' Moses looked eastwards and away from the Promised Land. He lifted his eyes to the mountains beyond the plains of Moab, visible above the curtains of the courtyard. 'Just as Mount Hor was the resting place for your father, so those mountains will be mine. I will climb them and I will not return.'

'When?' asked Ithamar weakly.

And, without taking his eyes off the mountains, Moses gave the answer that had been the heartbeat of his life: 'When Yahweh tells me.'

After a few moments of silence, Ithamar asked, 'Are you fearful?'

Moses turned to face him. 'What is there to fear? I have stood in the presence of Yahweh, the Eternal One, the One whose name is *I AM WHO I AM*. And I will still be in His presence when I die.'

'But what will happen to you?' asked Ithamar suddenly, though more lay behind his question than simply his uncle's fate.

'Ah!' said Moses. '*That* I cannot tell you. As with the holy of holies, a veil separates and hides from us what lies beyond. But when Yahweh met me in the bush that burned on Mount Horeb, over forty years ago, he said of Himself, *I am the God of your father—the God of Abraham, Isaac and Jacob*. He is *still* the God of those who have gone before.' He suddenly smiled. 'Do you remember, Ithamar, the story of Enoch, who lived in the time between Adam to Noah?'

Ithamar cast back in his memory, but then shook his head. 'No. What of it?'

'It is said of him that he walked with God, but then was not, for God took him.'

'Took him where?'

'Beyond the veil,' said Moses. 'Beyond it without having to go through it. But it is not so with the rest of us. So I will walk with Yahweh up the mountain, He will show me from a distance the land promised to our father Abraham, and then I will die and be gathered to my people. Yahweh Himself will bury me.' He paused once more. 'But there is another matter of which I must speak.'

'What is it?'

'Whether it is by your hand or that of your brother, or by the hand of Joshua, the record of our people must continue.' He looked Ithamar in the eye again. 'And you must ensure that it is so.'

'I will, Moses...I promise.' A sudden noise and movement at the entrance of the tabernacle drew Ithamar's eyes away. Gaddiel and Malchiel hurried in, bearing the box between them.

'They have been *very* swift,' said Moses, suddenly amused.

Ithamar took one look at their faces. 'They ran...'

Notes

1. The only named son of either Eleazar or Ithamar is Phinehas, Eleazar's firstborn (who in turn has a firstborn named Abishua). That they had a large number of sons between them is presumed from the fact that there are at least four priests carrying the ark and a further seven priests blowing trumpets at the fall of Jericho (Joshua 6:6), though the exact number is a guess.

2. It is assumed that the majority of the book of Deuteronomy (through to 31:13, maybe) occurs on a single day, given that:

    (a) there is only one date reference given in the whole book: 'In the fortieth year, on the first day of the eleventh month, Moses proclaimed to the Israelites all that the Lord had commanded him concerning them.' (1:3);

    (b) the term 'today' is used a staggering forty-seven times in Deuteronomy (out of a total of 171 in the Old Testament), the last of which is in 30:16, with a further twelve references to 'this day' before 31:13;

    (c) the book is essentially a record of a covenant ceremony (29:1,12). This is further confirmed by the fact that commentators have seen in the structure of the book of Deuteronomy a standard form of an ancient treaty. Given that the whole book could be read in a little over two and a half hours, it does not seem unreasonable for the majority of the book to be a single ceremony on one particular day. Although none of the responses of the people are recorded, this was normal in ancient written treaties. That such responses did occur is implied by the text: 'You have declared this day that the LORD is your God and that you will walk in obedience to him, that you will keep his decrees, commands and laws – that you will listen to him.' (26:17).

3. *When the covenant at Sinai occurred, God spoke to Moses (Exodus 20:1-23:33), he wrote the words down (24:4), he read the words of 'the book of the covenant' to them (24:7), and they responded (24:7). It is assumed that the covenant ceremony in Deuteronomy involves Moses reading from a book of the covenant once more, given (a) God had already spoken the words to him (1:3), (b) the length of the address, (c) the six references at the end of the ceremony to what was written 'in this book' (eg 28:58) and the instructions to the Levitical priests as to what to do with the book (31:26). The Hebrew word, sefer, translated here as 'book' can refer to any written document, so could be translated variously as book, letter, writing, document, scroll. It is assumed that papyrus scrolls are the most likely material for Moses to have used.*

4. *The commissioning of Joshua by Moses before the congregation in Numbers 27:18-23 is assumed to be the same occasion as recorded in Deuteronomy 31:7-8 (and referenced in 34:9). It appears that there is a separate occasion where God Himself commissioned Joshua at the tent of meeting (Deuteronomy 31:14,15,23) on the same day that Moses wrote and spoke the words of the song to Israel.*

5. *It is assumed that there is a gap between the Lord telling Moses, 'the time for you to die is near' and his death. This also gives time for the formal commissioning of Joshua (31:14,23) and the writing and relaying of the Song of Moses (31:19,22,28-30). God also speaks to Moses on other subjects (before or after the covenant day) at the plains of Moab—see Numbers 33:50-36:13.*

6. *Although the writings of the Pentateuch are unattributed, there has been a long tradition of Mosaic authorship within both Christianity and Judaism. If that is largely the case (with editorial notes and explanations possibly added by later individuals), a different person would have had to record the death of Moses. Some assume that this was Joshua or Eleazar, but maybe it was the person who was already known to have made records (Exodus 38:21).*

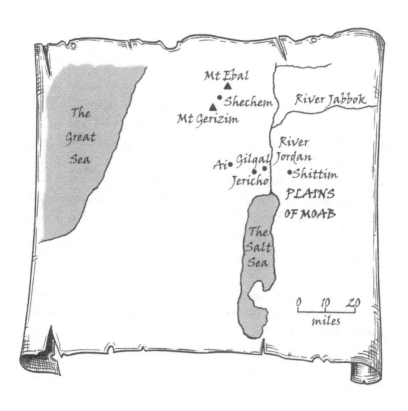

Mt Ebal ▲
● Shechem
Mt Gerizim ▲

River Jabbok

The Great Sea

River Jordan
Ai ● Gilgal
● ● Shittim
Jericho
PLAINS OF MOAB

The Salt Sea

0   10   20
miles

10

After the death of Moses the servant of the LORD, the LORD said to Joshua son of Nun, Moses' assistant: 'Moses my servant is dead. Now then, you and all these people, get ready to cross the River Jordan into the land I am about to give to them – to the Israelites.' (Joshua 1:1-2)

The mourning for Moses lasted a month. After teaching the Israelites the song transcribed by the hand of Ithamar, Moses had blessed the people—and then was gone, his final resting place known only to Yahweh. Shortly after the thirty days were over, Joshua sent messengers throughout the camp at Shittim.

Ithamar rushed back to the tent with the news. 'That soon?' exclaimed Keziah, pausing as she knelt beside the kneading trough, preparing bread from the daily manna.

He looked down at her, smiling broadly. 'That's what they said. Within three days we will be crossing the Jordan.'

She scraped the dough from her hands, and raised her aging body to her feet. Her eyes were shining. 'So, this is it—we enter the Promised Land at last!'

He nodded. 'Yes, and we are to prepare provisions for ourselves.'

'*We?*' she said, raising an eyebrow.

He leant over and kissed her. 'You will do it so much better than me.'

She placed a floury hand on his face. 'It is as well that you admit it.'

'I have learned what is good for me,' he replied, grinning. 'I will leave you to it.'

'Where are you going?'

'Joshua has summoned Eleazar and me to his tent.'

She folded her arms. 'Then you'd better wipe the flour from your beard.'

'Do you know why Joshua wants to see us?' Ithamar asked, as he and his brother walked around the outside of the tabernacle to reach the west side of the camp and the tribe of Ephraim.

'I assume it's about crossing the Jordan.'

An image from many years earlier rose in Ithamar's mind: of Moses standing with his staff stretched out over the Sea of Reeds. His uncle had always been there as they faced each new challenge. *But Yahweh's faithful servant now lay dead on Mount Nebo. Would the people fear to enter Canaan with their leader gone?* 'It will be strange to leave here without Moses,' he said eventually.

'Yahweh's hand is no less powerful than it was before…'

Eleazar was right, of course. They walked in silence for some moments, and Ithamar glanced to his left, towards the south. Only the tents of Simeon remained. The tribes of Reuben and Gad, who had previously camped there, had departed to fortify the cities taken from the Amorites, moving their families into them and building pens for their livestock. Together with half of Manasseh, they had been permitted lands to the east of the Jordan, provided they sent armed men to help with the conquest of Canaan.

'I wonder,' mused Eleazar, 'how many men from the eastern tribes will be crossing ahead of us.'

Ithamar thought for a moment. 'Reuben and Gad have—what?—almost eighty-five thousand men of fighting age between them. Manasseh numbers over fifty-two, but that is the whole tribe…'

Eleazar grinned. 'Only you would carry those numbers in your head!'

Ithamar smiled wryly. 'But how many of each tribe will go before us, I do not know. After all, they will need to leave men to defend their towns and cities.' Ithamar's eyes returned to the tents to the south. 'It is strange to see the camp so diminished.'

'Our days of living in tents are certainly numbered.'

As their destination came into view, Ithamar added, 'I wonder if we will ever be gathered together again as we have been—as one people.' Neither knew the answer.

Joshua was sitting on a rug just inside his tent when they found him, poring over scrolls in the shade. He looked up as they approached, then carefully rolled up the scrolls, laid them to one side and stood. After greeting them, he gestured to the rug. 'Sit, please.' Joshua's wife appeared from the rear of the tent.

'I will bring drinks for our guests,' she said, smiling, and then disappeared outside.

Eleazar glanced across at the scrolls. 'The book of law?'

Joshua nodded. 'Yes, Yahweh has instructed me to meditate on it day and night. And so I do. He has said that to succeed I must be careful to do all that Moses commanded.' He looked straight back at them both. 'The more I read the words, the deeper they will be inscribed on my heart.' A smiled then played on his lips. 'But I have not asked you here to tell you what you already know.' He paused. 'The Jordan lies before us, and when we cross, it will be the ark of the covenant before us, not the pillar of cloud. But when the people see the ark, they will know that Yahweh still goes before us and is with us.'

'Phinehas and Gaddiel and two of their brothers will bear it,' replied Eleazar, 'as they have done many times before.'

'Good,' said Joshua nodding. 'The armed men of the eastern tribes will be close behind, and then the rest of the tribes will follow in their usual manner.'

'But where and how are we to cross the Jordan?' Ithamar's question was left hanging as Joshua's wife returned, with not only a pitcher of water and cups, but also a platter with almonds, dried figs and dates.

'Ah, the fruits of Midian,' said Joshua, thanking his wife before she left. 'The gold, silver and bronze plundered from their cities may have added to our riches…' He leaned over and took a date. 'But you cannot eat gold.'

Ithamar followed his lead. The fruit was sticky and sweet.

Eleazar smiled. 'We have surely waited long enough to taste the bounty of these lands.'

Joshua suddenly became serious, however, and looked out through the tent flaps, as if checking that no-one was close. He lowered his voice. 'You asked, Ithamar, about the Jordan. I have sent two men, faithful to Yahweh, to cross the river and spy out the land between here and Jericho. None know of it. You are the only ones I have told, and it must stay that way.' He paused. 'If they return with news of obstacles in our way—whether of flesh or stone or water—I do not want the camp to hear of it. They must not be disheartened.' The rebellion at Kadesh Barnea did not need to be named—it was seared on their memories.

'You have not sent them farther?' asked Eleazar, breaking the silence that had fallen.

'There is no need: I saw enough before. I have sent them instead to the Jordan and to Jericho. The city will be fortified, no doubt, but we will discover more of their defences and numbers when the men return. With the help of Yahweh, we will know if they are prepared for an attack or a siege.' He paused again. 'But whatever news they bring, we *will* prevail by Yahweh's hand.'

It wasn't long before they were summoned once more. When they entered Joshua's tent, there were two others present. 'This is Kemuel,' began Joshua, indicating the larger and darker of the two men. He then gestured to the other. 'And Othniel. They are the ones I sent over the Jordan.'

Ithamar's eyes darted from one to the other. *So these were the spies!*

'We will hear their report together,' continued Joshua, gesturing for them to seat themselves on the orange and brown patterned rug. Although a platter of bread and bowl of curds were in the centre, Ithamar barely noticed the food. Joshua nodded to them. 'Now tell us what you have seen.'

'It is maybe half a morning's march from the Jordan to Jericho,' began Kemuel, 'following the road that leads to the hill country to the west. The valley is wide there, and the land between the river and the city is a broad, flat plain. It will be easy to camp there, near to the city. The land is also used for crops—fields of barley are ripe and the flax harvest has already begun.'

'The grain will be ours for the taking,' added Othniel. 'And there are springs both within the city and without. Palm trees abound.'

'You entered Jericho, then?' asked Joshua.

Kemuel nodded. 'Yes, and as you would expect, there is only one way in, through the city gates on the south side. The city rises within its walls, with streets leading up into the centre of Jericho. Its defences are strong; with the gates closed, it could easily repel an attack.'

'And with a ready supply of water inside,' continued Othniel, 'a siege could take many months.'

'Do you have any idea of how many the city numbers?' asked Joshua.

'Two thousand, we were told,' said Kemuel, 'though maybe more at the moment, with those from surrounding farms and villages having come into the city for safety.'

'If it were not for that,' added Othniel, 'the barley might already have been harvested.'

'Who did you speak to?' asked Joshua, his eyes narrowing slightly.

'A woman named Rahab,' said Kemuel. 'We stayed with her.' He then glanced at Othniel before adding, 'She's a harlot.'

When Joshua raised his eyebrows, Othniel grinned. 'The only service we paid for was lodgings.'

'That was shrewd,' responded Joshua. 'Strangers staying there would not be unusual or arouse suspicion. Did she know you were sons of Israel?'

Othniel nodded. 'Yes, and you will all want to hear what she told us. She said she knows that Yahweh has given us this land. They have all heard how Yahweh parted the waters of the Sea of Reeds for us, and how we utterly destroyed the Amorite kings, Sihon and Og.'

'She said that the hearts of all the people have melted!' continued Kemuel, his eyes bright. 'They are terrified of us.'

'And what is more, she acknowledged that Yahweh is God in heaven above and on earth beneath!'

Eleazar shook his head in wonder at Othniel's words. He murmured in awe, 'Our God has truly gone before us.'

'Yes, and surely He led you there to hear those words.' Joshua paused. 'But did others know who you were?'

'Somehow the king had discovered we were in the city and were there to search out the land,' replied Othniel.

'*And* that we were staying with Rahab.'

Ithamar had been listening intently but quietly. *Discovery would have meant death for both men.* 'What happened?' he suddenly blurted out. 'How did you escape?'

'Yahweh's hand was upon us again,' continued Kemuel eagerly. 'Rahab knew men were coming, and took us up onto the roof of her house. Flax from the harvest that she'd soaked was drying there, and she hid us under it.'

Othniel laughed. 'We were both sodden and stinking when we came out.'

Eleazar was clearly keen to know more. 'Did the men of Jericho look for you up there?'

'Rahab didn't deny we'd been there,' replied Kemuel, 'but said she didn't know we were Israelites and that we'd left before the city gates were shut at dusk.'

'She even suggested that they would catch us if they went quickly,' added Othniel, smiling. 'I do not know if all harlots have the shrewdness of Rahab, but hers served us well. Apparently they went off searching for us along the road to the Jordan.'

Ithamar's thoughts were racing. 'But how did you manage to leave the city unseen?'

'It would not have been possible to leave through the gates,' said Kemuel. 'Rahab was sure they would be checking every person who entered or left when they were opened the next morning.'

'But you said that was the only way out,' said Ithamar, 'so how did you escape?'

Kemuel laughed. 'No, I said that the gates were the only way *in*. I said nothing about them being the only way *out*.'

Ithamar looked at him, perplexed. 'What do you mean?'

'Her house was built into the city wall and she had a window looking out. She let us down by rope.'

Othniel continued, 'She made us swear an oath by Yahweh before we left, though: that in return for her kindness, she and her family would be spared when our God gives us this land.'

'She has greater faith in Yahweh than many of our people,' murmured Joshua. 'And we will honour that oath.'

'We told her to gather her family into the house when we come upon Jericho, and to tie a red cord in the window in the wall, so all our men will know which dwelling is to be spared.'

'It will be done,' replied Joshua. 'And you clearly made good your escape.'

Kemuel nodded. 'Yes, we were blessed with clouds and a waxing moon to the west. There was sufficient light to see our way clear of the city, but not enough to be seen from there. After the moon set, we waited until dawn, and then made our way up into the hills to the west of Jericho.'

'It would have been too dangerous to make our way east, along the road to the fords at the Jordan,' added Othniel, 'as they were looking for us there.'

'Did you glean anything else from Rahab?'

'As you would have learned when you spied out the land before,' replied Kemuel, 'the land is made up of many kingdoms. Most fortified cities have their own kings, who rule not only the city but the villages and land nearby, each with his own small army.'

'It is as I expected,' replied Joshua, nodding.

'But there is one more thing you should know,' said Othniel. He paused, and the two men exchanged glances. 'The River Jordan is in flood. The coming of spring has melted the snows in the mountains to the north, so the waters are swift and the river much deeper and wider than usual. We had to pay a boatman at the fords to bear us over.'

'Rahab also told us that the banks are much steeper to the north,' continued Kemuel, 'and that the fords near Jericho are still the best crossing place. But it would be nigh on impossible to cross without a boat, and certainly impassable to a multitude.' He paused. 'A multitude, that is, without Yahweh. And the people of this land have heard what He did for us when we left Egypt. No wonder their hearts melt in terror.'

'Before Yahweh, *mountains* melt,' said Eleazar solemnly. 'And seas part.'

'He has not brought us this far for the Jordan to defeat us,' added Joshua.

Ithamar turned to Kemuel and Othniel. 'Your story has shown us once more the hand of Yahweh at work.'

Both men had fire in their eyes, and Kemuel's words ignited Ithamar's heart: 'Surely Yahweh has given all of Canaan into our hands.'

The following morning they rose early at Joshua's command to break camp at Shittim, and to make the short journey west to the Jordan.

'Ithamar!' There was shock in Keziah's voice as she stepped outside the tent.

'What is it?' he said as he followed her, though the answer was apparent, even as the words left his lips.

'The pillar of cloud! Where is it?' She looked around in every direction, as if Yahweh might have hidden it. 'What has happened?'

It had been their constant companion for forty years. Although its absence felt strange, Ithamar smiled. 'There is no need to fear. Yahweh will be guiding us from now on through the mouth of Joshua. We are to look to His servant, not to His skies.'

The other difference in their trek westwards was that they were preceded by a huge column of men from Reuben, Gad and the half-tribe tribe of Manasseh—all armed and prepared for battle.

'Are you any clearer, brother,' began Eleazar as he joined Ithamar by the banks of the Jordan that evening, 'how many men are with us from the eastern tribes?'

Ithamar tried not to look smug. 'Forty thousand.' He turned his gaze from the swollen river and looked his brother in the eye. 'I counted them myself.'

Eleazar shook his head and laughed. 'You did not!'

Ithamar's weathered face broke into a grin. 'I added up the three numbers I was given when I asked each tribe.' His eyes wandered back to the water and the land to the west beyond.

'So it wasn't an outright lie.'

'I would not lie to my brother.' They stood in silence for some moments, watching the churning waters of the Jordan. There was no sign of any boatman. Ithamar imagined he must have paddled himself across the river or downstream at the first sign of a horde of heavily armed men. Bushes covered in lush greenery were everywhere, and trees stretched to the north and the south on both sides of the river, some of which were now islands in the water. *Presumably where the banks of the river normally lay.* The setting sun was transforming the sky before them, and tinging the brown, swirling waters with pink and orange.

Eventually Eleazar spoke. 'Joshua is sending word throughout the camp for the people to follow the ark in the morning. He tells them to consecrate themselves, for they are to see Yahweh do wonders tomorrow.'

The sun finally disappeared from their sight, dropping behind the hills to the west which ran like a backbone through Canaan. The colours in the sky and the clouds deepened and strengthened. 'So the God who paints the heavens,' murmured Ithamar, 'is about to touch the earth once more…'

The tenth day of the first month dawned cloudless. Ithamar began dressing swiftly in his priest's robes as the early morning light crept into the tent. Keziah packed away their belongings, as she had done so many times before. 'It is forty years ago to this day,' said Ithamar, pulling his linen tunic over his head, 'that we started preparing to leave Egypt. We set aside a lamb at Yahweh's command, three days before the angel of death passed through the land.' His heart soared. 'And tonight, on the other side of the Jordan, we shall do the same.' He laid his arm upon Keziah to stay her movements, and then took her hands in his, so that they faced each other. 'We will celebrate the Passover in the Promised Land!' He pulled her into an embrace.

'Has this day finally come?' she whispered.

'Its coming was always as certain as the rising of the sun,' he said, before pulling away enough to kiss her. 'But it has been a very long night.'

The sun was still low in the sky when Joshua called the people to him. Eleazar stood at his side, dazzling, in his high priest's robes, the sun's rays rendering his face more radiant. Behind them, some way off, lay the Jordan, its swirling waters catching the sunlight here and there and sending back tiny bursts of light. And near the river stood four men, shrunk by distance, but the white of their priestly tunics and caps still clearly visible. Golden poles also shone in the sun, as they waited to bear their bright blue burden. Joshua moved his gaze over the sea of people before him, and then cried out in a loud voice. 'By this you will know that the living God is among you, and that He will surely drive out before you the nations of this land.' He half-turned towards the Jordan, gesturing behind him with his right arm. 'Behold, the ark of the covenant of the Lord of all the earth is crossing over ahead of you into the Jordan.' He faced them again. 'And as soon as the priests who carry the ark of Yahweh—the Lord of all the earth—set foot in the Jordan, its waters flowing downstream will be cut off and stand up in a heap.' Excited murmurs rippled through the crowd. Joshua waited until he had an expectant silence once more. 'Now, people of Yahweh, return to your own standards—the banners of your fathers' households—and see for yourselves, this day, the wonders that the hand of Yahweh will perform in your sight.'

Ithamar took his usual place with the Levites and the ox-carts that carried the tabernacle. His sons were nearby, save his eldest two who would bear the ark with their cousins. And then he waited. Moving the thousands upon thousands of the children of Israel never happened quickly. But as he gazed around, he suddenly felt a small hand slide into his. He looked down. It was his second son's third—a six-year-old boy. Ithamar thought furiously. 'And what are you doing here, Abidan?'

His grandson sighed an enormous sigh and then rolled his eyes. *He'd picked that up from his father!* 'I'm Eliab, Grandpapa! Abidan's my cousin!'

'Of course you are! I'm sorry.'

'That's alright.'

'But why aren't you with your mother?'

Eliab gave another big sigh. 'I'm bored.' He then turned his large brown eyes upwards. 'And I'd rather be with you, Grandpapa Ithamar.' Ithamar's heart melted. 'And with the cows.'

He should have known… He smiled. 'They're oxen.'

It soon became clear that what Eliab really wanted was to ride on the cart, and before long he was seated beside the Levite who was holding the reins, clearly delighted at his elevation—both in height and importance—and beaming as he gazed around. However, the sun was nearing its zenith by the time the oxen eventually began straining against their yoke and the cartwheels began to turn. And Eliab was not the only one excited that they were finally moving forward: the mood of the company was jubilant. Ithamar walked alongside the cart, but as they moved westwards, the huge company soon began to part in two, half veering to the north, and half to the south. They had all been instructed by Joshua to come no closer than two thousand cubits to the ark. But the parting of the people enabled them to witness the power of Yahweh at work. For the surging torrents that he had looked upon the previous evening were nowhere to be seen. What he saw instead was the bearers of the ark standing on dry ground.

As the cart began to move to the left, Ithamar looked up at his grandson. 'Can you see your father, Eliab?' he asked, pointing towards the priests in the middle of the riverbed ahead of them, although they were too far away to recognise.

Delight lit up Eliab's face, 'Yes, Grandpapa!' and he started waving madly, despite the distance between them—and the fact that the priests were facing the other way.

But soon Ithamar was reaching up to his grandson. 'Come down and walk with me now, Eliab. Your feet need to be touching the ground.'

'Why?' There was a small pout on his face.

'Because you will want to be able to tell your own children one day that your feet walked across the Jordan River.' The Levite pulled back on the reins so that Ithamar could lift him safely down, and soon they were walking hand-in-hand on the same dry ground that was under the ark. But the wonder didn't last long.

'I can't see,' whined Eliab, turning his pleading eyes upwards. 'Can I ride on your shoulders, Grandpapa Ithamar?'

A voice beside them answered. 'Not while he is wearing his priestly tunic.' A young Levite, aged around twenty, smiled down at him. 'But if our young priest would like a ride on my shoulders, then I would be honoured!' Eliab flushed with pleasure and pride at the title he had been given, and the beam quickly returned to his face as his little head rose above all others around.

Before too long, they had drawn level with the ark, far off to their right, but still visible. *They were now in the middle of the Jordan! Yahweh's faithfulness and power were as unchanging as the hills of Canaan!*

A short time later, Ithamar spoke firmly once more. 'It is time to walk with me again, Eliab,' he said, as the jubilation of those not far ahead of them became songs of joy. 'Just as your feet have walked through the Jordan, they must now walk into the land promised to our ancestors.' The Levite swung him down, and his hand was soon securely in that of his grandfather. As they walked together, Ithamar felt a slow but steady rise of the earth beneath him. He studied the ground eagerly. And soon he saw what he was looking for: green tufts—trampled, but unmistakably grass. His heart soared to new heights and he gave Eliab's hand a squeeze. With tears in his eyes and songs on the lips of those around him, Ithamar turned to his grandson. 'I have waited a lifetime for this moment, Eliab. We are in the Promised Land!'

Within a day, however, the cries of joy had become groans of pain. They had pitched their tents to the east of Jericho, and their first day in the Promised Land was filled with the sound of stone striking stone. None of those born during the wilderness years, when they had wandered in the desert under Yahweh's judgment, had been circumcised. But the time of discipline had passed, a new day had come, and Yahweh now commanded that every male be circumcised. Razor-sharp flakes of flint sliced away every remaining foreskin in the camp, from those of men born thirty-eight years earlier, just after the rebellion, to the tender flesh of baby boys. And the fresh wounds needed time to heal.

The tabernacle was quiet the following day. Only the morning and evening sacrifices needed to be made, which was as well, given that among the next generation of priests, only Gaddiel and Phinehas had no need of circumcision.

'It has been, what—a score of years since there were so few of us serving at the tabernacle?' said Eleazar, as he and Ithamar walked away from the altar after the morning offering, leaving their sons in charge.

Ithamar was silent for a few moments. 'There would have been many more priests had Nadab and Abihu lived,' he said ruefully. The memory of their charred bodies flashed through his mind. His brother didn't reply. But the image soon left him as they went out through the colourful curtain marking the entrance of the tabernacle. A new sight met them. They walked towards the large stack of twelve stones, all taken from the middle of the Jordan at Joshua's command before the priests bearing the ark left the riverbed and the waters returned. Joshua had set the stones up at the centre of the camp by his own hand. They paused beside the memorial to Yahweh's power.

'If any of the people doubted,' began Ithamar, 'that Yahweh is with Joshua as He was with Moses, then surely they do so no longer.'

'Yahweh has exalted him in their eyes,' replied Eleazar. 'And for good reason. The conquest of Canaan will not be swift. More than once Yahweh has told us that He will only drive out its nations before us little by little. The sons of Israel need to know they have a strong and trusted leader.'

'Joshua is certainly that.'

After a few moments, Eleazar suddenly said, 'Have you heard the new name that Joshua has given this place?'

'No, tell me.'

'Gilgal—*the rolling*. Yahweh told him that the disgrace of our slavery has now been rolled away.'

Ithamar smiled. 'It is far shorter than *Gibeath-haaraloth*.'

They resumed their amiable amble back, Ithamar eventually leaving his brother and wandering off to the right as they neared the tents of all the priestly families. He passed the lamb that was tethered beside his own tent, set apart for the Passover. The day was pleasantly warm, and Keziah was seated on a small wooden stool outside, brushing the hair of Eliab's sister—their only granddaughter so far. The girl's mother was on her knees, pounding the dough in the wooden kneading trough nearby. None were aware of his approach. 'The men all expect our sympathy,' said the younger woman to Keziah, clearly indignant, 'and believe we should wait upon their every need. As if no one has ever known pain like theirs!' She thumped the dough. 'They should try giving birth!'

'I will not argue with my daughter-in-law,' said Ithamar. The women looked up, smiling but unapologetic.

'And neither will I,' said Keziah. 'She speaks more sense than many!'

Before their conversation could continue any further, a small, but furious storm swept into their midst. 'You're dead!' shrieked Eliab, madly swinging a short, thin and denuded branch around his head.

'No, I'm not,' protested his cousin, 'your sword never touched me!'

'Eliab! Watch what you're doing!' called out his mother. 'You will put out Abidan's eye if you do not take care.'

Eliab paid no attention to her words. 'Die! Die! Die, horrible Canaanite!' he shouted, bringing his weapon down with each *Die*, as his cousin did his best to block the blows with his own stick. It was only when Ithamar stepped in that they lowered their weapons and fell silent.

'They clearly heal quicker than their fathers,' said his daughter-in-law dryly.

'The young do,' replied Ithamar, 'and they also become bored quicker.'

'We're practising for the army, Grandpapa,' explained Eliab. 'So we can kill Canaanites when we're older.'

'They're living in our land,' exclaimed Abidan, as if it needed explaining. 'It doesn't belong to them!'

With some effort, Ithamar crouched down to be on their level. 'You are to have the honour of serving Yahweh as priests,' he said, looking into their flushed faces. 'And that means that you will not be bearing swords for Him.' They looked crest-fallen, a family likeness etched in their features. *They would pass as brothers.* He thought for a moment. 'Have you seen the stones from the Jordan yet?' he asked suddenly. They shook their heads glumly. 'Then come with me,' He straightened up and held out his arms to take their hands. 'You can bring your swords.' They brightened, and Abidan swapped his stick into his other hand as they each took one of their grandfather's.

Ithamar started retracing his recent steps. The boys both continued swinging their makeshift weapons around as they walked together. 'Yahweh does not want His people to be men of war forever,' he began. 'He brought us out of Egypt and is bringing us into this land so that one day we may live in peace and safety, free from fear and free to serve our God.' His grandsons listened closely. 'But there *are* battles ahead of us—'

'Because they're in our land!' said Abidan indignantly, clearly feeling the need to restate his point.

'But that is not why Yahweh commands us to destroy them,' replied Ithamar. 'We only call Canaan *our* land because Yahweh promised it to our father Abraham. But *all* the earth, including Canaan, belongs to the God who created it.' They passed Eleazar's tent, but he was nowhere to be seen. 'And Yahweh cares how men live in His world. A long, long time ago, the people of earth were very, very bad—hurting one another, hurting the world and hurting God. And God couldn't let it go on. So he stopped the evil in the world by sending something at the time of Noah. Do you remember the story?'

'He sent a flood!' exclaimed Eliab.

'And everyone died except Noah and his family,' added Abidan.

'*And* the cows and the sheep and the goats and all the other animals on the ark,' said Eliab triumphantly, giving a little flourish of his stick.

'That's right,' said Ithamar. 'And, like then, the people here in Canaan have been living very bad lives and hurting each other.' *He wasn't going to sully their young minds by speaking of immorality and abominations, curses and magic, or incest and idolatry. The abhorrent sacrificing of their children upon the altars of their Canaanite gods was too appalling to even think of, let alone name.* Ithamar simply added, 'And, as happened at the time of Noah, they have been getting worse and worse for a very long time. Six hundred years ago, Yahweh told Abraham that one day the people in this land would be *so* bad, that his descendants would live in the land instead—and that is what is happening now.' He stopped for a moment, and the boys both looked up at him. 'But how can Yahweh rid the land of the evil—evil like that at the time of Noah?' He waited for them.

'Send another flood?' offered Abidan.

It was the answer Ithamar had hoped they would give. 'Ah, but God promised that He would never again send a flood on the earth as He did at that time.' He began walking again. 'So instead, we are to be God's flood of judgment on the people of this land. We wield the sword *only* at Yahweh's command, and He commands us to wipe out the evil completely, as the flood did. No good will come if Canaanites continue their evil among us.' Ithamar hoped his words to his grandsons had not strayed too far from Yahweh's.

There was a long pause. Eventually Eliab ventured, 'So we are better than them.' He looked up at Ithamar for his assent.

Ithamar thought for moment. 'Do you remember, just over two months ago, that Moses spoke to us all when we were on the other side of the Jordan?'

Eliab nodded solemnly. 'He went on for a *very, very, very* long time.' Ithamar suspected that the word *boring* was once again in his mind.

'Moses told us that we shouldn't say that Yahweh is driving out the Canaanites and giving us the land because of our righteousness…' He adjusted his words for their young ears. 'Because of our goodness. No, it is because of the wickedness of the people here, and because He is keeping the oath He swore to our fathers, to Abraham, Isaac and Jacob.'

They had reached the pile of stones. Ithamar hoped they had understood his words. 'This is what Joshua built to remind the people in years to come of how Yahweh dried up the Jordan. Eliab— these stones were taken from where your father was standing.' He let go of their hands, and both boys crouched down next to the stones, still clutching their precious sticks. Each stroked the large stones with his free hand, their surfaces smoothed by countless years of the Jordan's flow. They would have struggled to lift even one of the stones between them. 'We have all seen Yahweh dry up a raging torrent,' said Ithamar. 'And if He can do that, He can also defeat any raging Canaanites. And He will. Never forget, either of you, the one true God—Yahweh—dwells among us. We are not great people, but we have a great God.'

The following day, they observed Passover, beginning the seven-day feast of unleavened bread. Offering the blood of the Passover lambs was far easier with thirteen priests than the three they had been at Horeb. Then, they had celebrated the festival just before setting out for Canaan; now they were doing so with the land before them. The day after eating the lamb, they ate of the grain of the land, gathered from the patches of ripened barley that surrounded the camp, and milled and baked into unleavened cakes. For many it was the first bread they had tasted made from anything other than manna.

Ithamar yawned in the cool, early morning light, as he emerged from his tent the next morning. He looked blearily at the ground nearby. Then he peered more closely, suddenly perplexed. He glanced up, and noticed the same bewilderment in his sons and nephews who had come out with their pottery jars as he had. 'Where's the manna?' called out one of Eleazar's sons.

The others shrugged their shoulders. But then it dawned on Ithamar. 'Yahweh has withdrawn it, because we do not need it now.' *Their God had provided bread from heaven for forty years, but now He provided it from the earth.* 'The grain from the land around us is now the gift from His hand.'

But the day still held another surprise for Ithamar when Joshua summoned him and his brother later. Ithamar noticed the difference in him immediately, though he struggled to put his finger upon what it was. He wondered if Eleazar sensed it too. *It was almost as if he stood taller.* His curiosity was short-lived.

'The captain of Yahweh's host has appeared to me,' he began, as the three of them stood together outside his tent in the morning sunshine. 'He stood before me, bearing a drawn sword, telling me that Yahweh has given Jericho, its king and its warriors into our hands. We may be unskilled in warfare, but He is not. He has instructed us as to how we are to take the city...'

Noon had passed by the time they were ready to carry out the instructions they had been given. The armed men of the eastern tribes were gathered in battle array, standing line upon line. Ithamar stood behind them, trumpet in hand. It was not the long, silver trumpet for signalling the people; it was a shofar—the curved instrument made from ram's horn. Beside him stood six of his sons and nephews, each with his own shofar. And behind them was the ark of the covenant, covered, as always, with its rich blue cloth, with the same four bearers beside it. Then came the remaining two priests—Eleazar and Malchiel, the oldest and the youngest—followed by the rear guard.

Joshua, sword strapped to his side, strode up to them. He addressed Ithamar and those behind him. 'We are ready. The people all know what they are to do.' Phinehas, Gaddiel and their brothers hoisted golden poles to their shoulders, raising the ark so that the cloth-covered cherubim stood higher than any around. Joshua took one final look up and down the long column of men and nodded to Ithamar. 'You may begin.'

Ithamar raised the shofar to his lips and blew. The others with him followed his lead. It was the signal for those at the front to begin marching around the city. It was some time before the forward movement rippled far enough through the column for Ithamar to begin walking. Joshua had ordered those at the front to keep their distance from Jericho, to stay out of reach of anything launched or fired from the walls. As they circled the city, however, aside from blasts of the trumpets, the tramping of countless feet was the only sound. Although the shofar never left his lips, from time to time Ithamar cast his eyes sideways, towards the city. Occasionally he saw a face at one of the small windows in the high stone walls, or a head peeping over the top of the ramparts. He wondered what they made of the eerie march. *It probably only heightened their terror.* And when they had circled the city, the armed men led them back to the camp at Gilgal.

For the five days that followed, they rose early and repeated the march in exactly the same manner. And each day, Ithamar's eyes found the red cord hanging from a window in the western wall, marking out the house of Rahab.

On the seventh day at dawn, they prepared for another march— but this would be different. As Ithamar stood in silence, waiting once more for Joshua's command, he could sense a keener mood: a sense of anticipation, an excitement that animated impatient feet. It was as if the people were a young bull straining at its leash, longing to break free. But all held their silence. Once more, at Joshua's word, the braying of the shofars rang out, thrusting the army forward. But when they had circled the city, they did not stop. A second then a third and a fourth march around Jericho followed. Ithamar's lips began to feel sore and his chest ached as he continued to blow his trumpet. *But he mustn't stop!* And each time he passed the red cord hanging down, he was sure there were faces at the window.

As they neared the end of their seventh circling of Jericho, Ithamar's heart began to race. The thrill coursing through his whole body supplied the fresh strength he would need to complete his final task. As soon as their feet returned to their starting point for the last time, Joshua turned to Ithamar. 'Now!'

He drew in a colossal breath, filling his chest with air, and blew it out through the trumpet in a long, sustained blast, the six beside him doing the same. Joshua's cry rang out with them: 'Shout! For Yahweh has given you the city.' And immediately, thousands of voices that had kept silent for seven days were unleashed in a deafening cacophony. Every face was now turned towards Jericho, myriad raised swords glinting in the sun. As the terrible cry continued, a new sound suddenly joined it. Ithamar felt it first under his feet. A tremor. Then a low rumble, as if the ground were joining the shout. And then the walls before him began to shake. One stone, and then another broke off from the top and then tumbled to the ground. Then it was as if a dam had broken, but the flow that coursed down was one of rock, as the walls fell to the ground. Joshua held his sword out towards the city, the armed men surged forward, and Ithamar finally lowered his shofar. He was trembling.

Eleazar joined him. The priests and the ark were the only ones left outside Jericho. They stood in silence for a while, the clamour from the city easily reaching their ears. There was only one small part of the walls still standing: a small section on the western edge—and Ithamar knew why.

'The people of Canaan will hear of this,' murmured Eleazar.

'Will many flee the land, do you think?' asked Ithamar, his eyes not moving from the scene of destruction before him.

Eleazar did not reply immediately. 'Do not forget,' he said eventually, 'the whole of the land is under Yahweh's judgment. And we saw the folly of Amenhotep. Yahweh hardened his heart, and he lost all reason in his opposition to us. Maybe it will be the same with the nations here…'

'You mean they will stay and fight when sense should compel them to leave?'

'Exactly. The Canaanites *already* know enough of Yahweh's power and purpose to send them fleeing. And yet they stay.'

They fell silent again, but before too long a trickle and then a stream of men emerged from the rubble of Jericho, and made their way towards the ark. Each bore plunder in his arms. 'Remember,' said Eleazar to the younger priests, as the first of the men approached them, 'the city is under Yahweh's ban. Everything within the walls belongs to Him and is dedicated to destruction. Only that which may pass through fire—the gold and silver, the iron and bronze—may be brought out of the city and into Yahweh's treasury. If anything else is brought to us—anything—it must be taken back within the walls to be burned as an offering to Yahweh.'

Jewellery and ornaments, pieces of silver and gold, utensils and weapons, were all added to a constantly growing pile before the ark. As Ithamar took a sizeable bar of gold from the hand of an Israelite and leaned down to add it to the treasures, he glanced towards the city. He straightened up. 'Look,' he said to his brother, nodding in the direction of Jericho. Eleazar followed his gaze. Walking away from the city were Kemuel and Othniel. With them were a group of ten or twelve people, both men and women, and of varying ages. All of them looked this way and that, bewildered. *Like lambs taken from their mother,* thought Ithamar. The only one with any poise was a woman dressed in a brightly coloured tunic, walking beside Othniel. 'That must be Rahab and her family,' he said quietly. *So here was the harlot who acknowledged their God.*

'The only Canaanites to escape with their lives,' replied Eleazar. 'Yahweh even now shows mercy.'

As they came closer, Ithamar studied Rahab. She appeared to be the same age as his younger sons. He glimpsed bangles of gold around her wrists, and strands of coloured beads hung around her bare neck. The ringlets of her raven hair were oiled so that they shone, and tumbled down over her shoulders. *Her trade was not a surprise.* She looked in his direction, but her gaze was not brazen. She dropped her eyes to the ground before Ithamar did.

Smoke began rising from the city, and the stream out of the city became a river, with swords being cleaned and sheathed, and hands wiped on dirty tunics. *War was never pleasant.* Soon flames could be seen above Jericho, feeding on wood and straw—and the fat of all that had drawn breath. The air was still, and the thick black smoke rose high into the sky. 'It will easily be seen from every direction,' said Ithamar to his brother. 'The people of this land will fear even more.'

'And fear they should,' replied Eleazar. 'Yahweh's wrath begins to fall.'

But where the wrath fell next stunned the whole camp.

'Driven back?' exclaimed Ithamar, struggling to comprehend what he had been told.

Malchiel had run back to the tents to tell them the news. His nephew gulped in air, nodding, and then continued between breaths. 'The men of Ai all came out...and chased our army from their city... They struck down over thirty men.'

Ithamar stared at him, bewildered. *But Yahweh had given the cities and people of Canaan into their hands. He had said so!* 'How could this have happened?' The question was left hanging. They had no answer.

The shock spread through the camp with the speed of a swooping eagle. The mood of confidence after the fall of Jericho disappeared like a morning mist. Soon Joshua and elders of the people had gathered before the tent of meeting. Whilst Joshua and Eleazar went into the tent to prostrate themselves before the ark, Ithamar remained outside with the others. All of them cast themselves, face down, on the earth. They didn't move until evening. Over and over, Ithamar pleaded silently with Yahweh to speak and dispel their confusion— and to restore the honour of His name.

'Rise up!'

Ithamar lifted his head. Joshua and Eleazar had emerged from the holy place. All around him, men began to raise themselves to their feet, dust still in their hair where they had scattered it. It was their sign of grief; Joshua's was his torn robes. All waited in silence.

'Yahweh has spoken,' began Joshua. 'The people have sinned and disobeyed His command. They have stolen from Yahweh, and taken from Jericho things under the ban.' Murmurs of shock spread through the elders. 'Until we find and destroy them, we will not be able to stand before our enemies.' Joshua's face was set like flint. 'Tell the people to consecrate themselves. Tomorrow we will remove the offence from our midst, so that Yahweh will go with us once more. Without Him, even the smallest town will overcome us.'

Eleazar, in his high priest's robes, stood with Joshua the following morning. The Urim and Thummin within his ephod were to be used to single out those whose guilt had brought their defeat. Again and again, Eleazar cast the lots and Yahweh gave the answer: the tribe of Judah, then the line of Zerah, then the family of Zabdi. Finally, Achan son of Carmi stood alone before Joshua, trembling. All colour had drained from his face.

'My son,' began Joshua calmly. 'Give glory and praise to Yahweh, the God of Israel, and tell me what you have done. Do not hide it from me.'

Achan replied in a wavering voice. 'It is true, I have sinned against Yahweh. I saw in Jericho a beautiful cloak, two hundred shekels of silver and a bar of gold. I desired them for myself, so I took them. They are hidden under earth in my tent.'

As Joshua sent men to investigate, Gaddiel whispered, 'He will pay a high price, surely, for Jericho's spoil.'

'Sin always has a price,' said Ithamar grimly. 'It is often born by bulls and goats upon the altar. But that will not be so today. He has taken into his hands what was under the ban. In doing so, he brings the ban upon himself and his family.'

Ithamar and Eleazar stood in silence in a valley near the camp as the people returned to their tents. *The deed had been done. The price had been paid.* Not far away from them was a huge mound of stones, some of which had brought death upon Achan, his family and his animals, as together they were stoned by the assembly. Their bodies now lay under the mound together with all Achan's possessions—and the spoil of Jericho. All burned as Jericho had been.

'The family line of Achan is no more,' said Ithamar eventually. 'It is a terrible fate. But did he really think that the God of all the earth would not see?'

'Sin deceives and can blind men to the obvious,' replied Eleazar. 'Maybe at least the people will now be afraid of sinning.'

Eleazar sighed. 'I am afraid they will never fear it enough.'

Notes

1. The last time reference before the death of Moses is the first of the eleventh month of the fortieth year (Deuteronomy 1:3). Although Moses is mourned for 30 days, the next time reference is at the crossing of the Jordan, on the tenth of the first month (Joshua 4:19)—over two months later. Some of this time may be accounted for by Reuben, Gad and the half-tribe of Manasseh building sheepfolds and 'cities for our little ones' before the crossing of the Jordan. They lived in Transjordan cities, such as Heshbon and Jazer, taken from Sihon and Og. (See Numbers 21:25,31-32 and 32:24-27.)

2. Unlike the previous spies who were sent into Canaan, we do not know the names of the two spies sent by Joshua. The names of a leader of the tribe of Ephraim and of Caleb's son have been chosen, but there is no Biblical basis for this.

3. Although Jericho is referred to as a city in Scripture, it is more likely to have been similar to a small, mediaeval walled town. It was probably crowded and compact.

4. The fact that the spies were able to freely converse with Rahab implies that there was a huge amount of commonality of language between the Israelites and the Canaanites.

5. It is not easy to reconcile the timings in the first three chapters of Joshua (see 1:11; 2:1,22; 3:1-2). It has been assumed that the three days referred to in 3:2 are the same three days that had earlier been referred to in 1:11, so that the Israelites spend one night, rather than three, camped by the Jordan. This may or may not be correct.

6. It is not made explicit in Scripture when the pillar of cloud stops leading the Israelites. However, Numbers 33 lists all the places they journeyed, 'by the command of Yahweh' (i.e. by the direction of the cloud and fire), but the lists ends at Abel Shittim, on the Plains of Moab (Numbers 33:49), from where they crossed into the Promised Land. It is Joshua who announces that they are to cross the Jordan after three days, so the presumption is that the miraculous guidance has ceased at this point.

7. Mudslides are known to block the Jordan. Just south of where the Jabbok joins the Jordan, eighteen miles north of the fords at Jericho, there are steep

banks which are susceptible to mudslides due to the high volume of water there. There is a well-documented collapse of one of the banks after an earthquake in 1927, which completely dammed the river for 21 hours.

8. Entering Canaan near Jericho enabled Joshua to effectively split the land in two with the initial conquests. He was then able to conduct a southern campaign (Joshua 6) and then a northern campaign (Joshua 11).

9. It is not clear if circumcision was deliberately forbidden by Yahweh after the failed entry into the Promised Land, or whether it was simply not done after that point, or not done after leaving Egypt. The text simply says in Joshua 5:5 that it wasn't done in the wilderness. Here the first option has been assumed, so that Gaddiel and Phinehas are the only ones of the next priestly generation who have already been circumcised.

10. In the act of judicial stoning, no one person bears the responsibility for the death of the guilty party.

11. It has been suggested that Achan's family must have known of his sin (which is perfectly possible if he buried the banned items in their family tent), hence their inclusion in the punishment. But this is not stated in the text.

12. The reason for the wholesale slaughter of the Canaanites is clearly given on a number of occasions, being God's judgment on their prolonged wickedness. (See, for example, Genesis 15:16, Deuteronomy 9:4-5; 12:31, Joshua 11:20.) It is made abundantly clear that if the Canaanites remain in the land, they will be a snare to the Israelites, leading them away from Yahweh, e.g. Exodus 34:12-16, Deuteronomy 7:1-14.

13. It is possible that the story of Rahab shows that if a Canaanite had turned to Yahweh in faith and obedience, changing allegiance from the pagan nations to the people of God, then their lives might have been saved.

II

*Then Joshua built on Mount Ebal an altar to the LORD, the God
of Israel…There was not a word of all that Moses had commanded
that Joshua did not read to the whole assembly of Israel, including
the women and children, and the foreigners who lived among them.*
(Joshua 8:30,35)

The smoke of Ai was clearly visible in the distance from the camp at
Gilgal. After the sin of Achan had been removed, Joshua did to the
city and its king as he had done to Jericho. But when he returned, it
was not battles on his mind.

'We cannot wait any longer,' he began, after he had sought out
Eleazar at the tabernacle. Ithamar was with him. 'There are two
ceremonies we must perform—two obligations we must fulfil—
before we continue with the conquest of Canaan. To do both we
must travel north, but the ark will not be the only precious chest to
accompany us.'

'Where are we going?' asked Eleazar.

'To Mount Ebal and Mount Gerizim—and to Shechem that lies
between them.'

Eleazar nodded, comprehension dawning on his face. 'To proclaim
the blessings and curses of the covenant, as Moses commanded—'

'And to keep a four-hundred-and-fifty-year-old promise that our
fathers made to Joseph.'

The mood of the company was jubilant as it made its way north-west
into the hill country of central Canaan. Although some had to stay
to guard the camp, the tabernacle and the livestock, or because of
age or infirmity, most made the journey. The ark led them forward

once again, and—apart from Ithamar and his brother—all the priests shared the task of bearing it ever upwards into the hills. Behind the ark came the ox-drawn cart that had travelled with them from Egypt. The covering that had usually lain over its priceless load had been removed, revealing the painted coffin that held the bones of Joseph, son of Jacob. And then came the people—men and women, old and young, Israelites and the foreigners who lived among them.

It was only a day's journey to Shechem. They were travelling light, with no herds, tents or possessions to slow them down, and they would only be away two nights. Rugs, blankets and food were borne by shoulders or donkeys. Sheep and goats for offerings trotted along amongst them, often having to be tugged forwards by the ropes around their necks when they attempted to graze.

'I sometimes forget they have been through the land before,' said Ithamar, looking ahead to where Joshua and Caleb walked in front of the ark, leading the company.

'They remember it well,' his brother replied, as they walked side by side behind the ark. 'Even if it was forty years ago that they last set foot here.'

Ithamar looked beyond them. The mountains of Ebal and Gerizim, which were merged in the distance when first seen, were now two separate peaks. He smiled. 'It is many years since we spent a night under the stars. And now we will spend two.'

Eleazar was silent for some moments. 'I still remember the stars in the sky above us when we slept at the tabernacle during our consecration.' He paused. 'But we will not have the heat from the altar fire to keep us warm tonight.'

Ithamar grinned. 'No, but we will have our wives!' Eleazar laughed.

It was late afternoon by the time they arrived near Shechem. Light from the sinking sun was still streaming into the fertile valley, running east to west, which formed a pass between the mountains. The people began dividing, as Joshua had instructed, into two camps—one at the base and on the slopes of Mount Gerizim to the south, the other facing them on Mount Ebal to the north.

'There is work to be done before we eat,' declared Joshua. 'Caleb—find a few young men from each tribe, and then bring them to me at Mount Ebal.' He then turned to Eleazar and Ithamar. 'We will find somewhere suitable to build the altar to Yahweh.'

Ithamar had never felt so at one with his ancestors as they searched for a large, level area. Abraham had passed through the valley when he had reached Canaan, hundreds of years before them, and Jacob had purchased land just outside Shechem to pitch his tent when he had returned from exile. And both had built altars and sacrificed to Yahweh there.

After inspecting several possible sites—and rejecting them—Eleazar pointed to a sizeable and open piece of ground. 'How about there?'

The three of them walked over and looked around. 'This will serve us well,' said Joshua. As elsewhere, the hillside was scattered with variously sized rocks and stones. 'We have all we will need to build the altar.' While they waited for Caleb's men, each cast his gaze over the surrounding land. 'There is a spring down there,' said Joshua, pointing, 'near the base of Mount Gerizim. The land here is good.'

'It is all good,' laughed Ithamar, 'when you have lived in a wilderness for so long!'

As they continued looking down into the valley, Joshua pointed to their left. 'You can see some of the fertile land around the Jordan from here. And if we climbed to the top of this mountain, we would see the snows of Mount Hermon to the north, and the wide plain to the west reaching down to the Great Sea.'

'*A land of milk and honey*, indeed,' murmured Eleazar. 'Yahweh gives us fields and vineyards in which we have not laboured, and cities which we have not built.'

'And forty-eight of those cities,' responded Joshua, 'with their pasture lands, will belong to the sons of Levi.' They were not to be allotted land within Canaan as the other tribes, but would be dispersed throughout the territories of each tribe.

'We have been blessed,' said Eleazar, 'with a different inheritance: the offerings of the people, the priesthood, and Yahweh Himself.'

Ithamar suddenly remembered something he'd been told. 'Moses said that the forty-eight cities would fulfil the words that our father Jacob spoke over his sons before he died. He cursed the anger and violence of Simeon and Levi, and said they would be scattered in Israel.'

Eleazar chuckled and shook his head in wonder. 'And yet now it seems that Yahweh has turned it to a blessing for the tribe of Levi!'

'And for all the tribes,' said Joshua. 'You will be among the people to teach them His ways when you are not serving at the sanctuary.' He became serious. 'You *must* ensure they continue to hear the word of Yahweh. I am not the only one who must meditate on it day and night.' His head suddenly turned. 'But now it is time to build.'

Ithamar counted thirty-six men approaching with Caleb. They quickly gathered before Joshua, clearly eager for his instructions. 'Moses commanded that when we had crossed the Jordan,' began Joshua, 'we build an altar to our God on this mountain—an altar of uncut stones on which to offer burnt offerings and peace offerings.' He cast his gaze to the hillside. 'Look around you—the stones are in our midst. So let us begin the task so that tomorrow we may sacrifice to Yahweh in this place, as our fathers did.'

Joshua, Eleazar and Ithamar marked out a substantial square for the base of the altar, and watched over the placing of the large, rough stones, one upon another. As the young men went back and forth, one of them stirred something in Ithamar's memory. *But what was it? There was almost something Egyptian about him.* It was only when the young man returned to the site of the altar for the third time that it suddenly dawned on him. He touched Eleazar's arm, and nodded in the direction of the man, whispering, 'Does he remind you of anyone?'

Eleazar's brow furrowed, and then softened after some moments as a wry smile played on his face. 'Khamet!' he said. 'Though it is clearly not him. Besides, he is far too young.'

Ithamar continued to watch him, more and more convinced of the likeness. The man suddenly seemed to be aware that he was being watched, and glanced at Ithamar nervously. Ithamar smiled and walked over to him. 'What is your name?'

'Pawara, my lord,' he answered, casting his eyes to the ground as Eleazar came to join them.

There was no hint of an accent. *But it was an Egyptian name.* 'And that of your father?'

'Khamet.'

'Do you know why we ask?' said Eleazar.

He looked up shyly, nodding. 'You knew my father. He told me of you both and the story of how our family left Egypt.' He smiled. 'And then he repeated the story to each of my children, right up until the day he died.'

Ithamar found his heart unexpectedly warmed. 'When was that?'

'Five years ago. He was three score and five. It was a very good age!'

Eleazar sighed. 'He left Egypt but the only land he found with us was the wilderness. Did he ever regret leaving?'

Pawara thought for a moment, but then shook his head. 'No. He used to say to me, *Yahweh is a good God. He is not cruel like Egyptian gods.*' He paused. 'I never lived in Egypt, but my father always said that your laws were more wise and fair than those of his land. He said that the sons of Israel loved their families the same as the sons of Egypt, but that they treated strangers better.' And then he added with a hesitant smile, 'My father told me much of his nation. It seems that Egyptians had to live under laws of men and leaders who thought themselves gods. But you—we—have the laws of God and leaders who know they are men.'

'You have spoken much truth,' said Eleazar, smiling broadly.

Pawara flushed, but then chuckled. 'But my father never stopped missing barley beer.'

Ithamar suddenly gestured towards an Israelite a little distance away, who was standing next to a large rock and clearly waiting. 'Do you know him?'

Pawara's face lit up. 'He is my brother-in-law—from the tribe of Asher. I married his sister. She is a very good wife, and I am with her tribe now!'

'You'd better go and help him!' said Eleazar, smiling. As Pawara moved out of earshot, he added softly, 'Yahweh does not judge other nations because they aren't sons of Israel, but He welcomes them when they embrace our God.'

Ithamar and his brother returned to their wives on the lower slopes of Mount Gerizim as soon the altar was finished, when the setting sun was filling the sky at the western end of the valley with colour. But Keziah barely let them lift their cups of water to their lips before she blurted out excitedly, 'You'll never guess what we learned today!'

Ithamar swallowed his mouthful and sat down on the rug that they had laid out on a level piece of ground. *Keziah suddenly looked like the wife of his youth again, her eyes bright and sparkling.* 'You play me at my own game.'

'It is about one of your cousins!' said Tirzah, looking at each of them in turn, clearly eager to tell more.

Eleazar joined Ithamar on the rug. 'Which one?' he asked, more amused than interested. 'We have many.'

'Salmon!' replied Tirzah.

'The son of your uncle Nahshon,' added Keziah, as both women sat down next to their husbands.

'We know who Salmon is,' said Ithamar dryly.

'He is going to marry Rahab!' exclaimed Keziah in a lowered voice, clearly conscious of the other families around. Both women seemed pleased by the reaction of the men.

'Rahab?' said Ithamar, astounded, adding in a lowered voice, 'The harlot from Jericho?'

Both women nodded enthusiastically. 'His niece told us when we were drawing water,' said Tirzah.

Ithamar raised an eyebrow. 'Maybe she will finally bear him a son.'

Keziah sighed. 'His wife never did before she died.'

'She gave him four daughters though.' Tirzah paused. 'How old is he now?'

'Between fifty and sixty,' replied Ithamar. 'He was blessed with being too young to be numbered among the fighting men in the first census.'

Eleazar had been sitting quietly, his eyes fixed on the rug, as if studying the pattern woven into it in green and brown wool. He suddenly looked up. 'Salmon is a good man, and Rahab has shown herself to be a woman who not only believes in Yahweh, but risks her life to do so.' He gave a little laugh. 'Even a Canaanite harlot can find a place among our people by turning to the one true God.'

Ithamar nodded slowly in agreement. 'We are not the only ones to receive His mercy.'

Eleazar drained his cup. 'May Yahweh indeed bless her with a son whose faith is as great as hers!'

The day that followed was both solemn and joyful. Near the altar, as Moses had directed, Joshua set up the white, lime-coated stones he had prepared at Gilgal. On these he had written the ten commandments that Yahweh Himself had inscribed upon the two stone tablets, now in the ark of the covenant. Every one of the sons of Aaron was kept busy at the altar, as whole burnt offerings and the fat of peace offerings were placed upon the huge stone altar to be consumed by fire. The heat became intense as the fire grew fierce, the flames feeding on countless portions of fat. As the smoke of the offerings rose up, high into the sky, the people gathered, with half of the tribes beneath the peak of Mount Gerizim, and the other half facing them beneath Mount Ebal. And at the heart of their assembly was the ark, with Ithamar, Eleazar and all the priests now standing beside it with Joshua.

As the murmuring of the people began to die away, Ithamar looked out across the vast gathering. Everywhere faces were turning towards the ark in anticipation: faces of mothers with young children in their arms; of girls and boys straining to get a better view; of the aged who had borne every year in the wilderness, and of men who had so recently seen battle. *If they had needed a reminder of the blessings of obedience and the curses of rebellion, then they need look no further than Jericho and Ai. Yahweh was faithful in both blessing and judgment.*

All finally became still, and the cry of a bird carried across the silence. Joshua lifted up his voice and cried out, 'Hear, O Israel…' It was as if his words—the words of Yahweh's own law—were somehow strengthened by the air, as if the very mountains themselves were adding their voice. And the people listened as Joshua recited all that it meant to be the people of God.

Then it was the turn of the Levitical priests. All but Eleazar stood with Mount Ebal behind them, to pronounce the twelve curses as Moses had instructed. Phinehas began: 'Cursed is anyone who makes an idol—' His voice rang out as Joshua's had done. '—an abomination to Yahweh, the work of a craftsman's hands, and sets it up in secret.' There was a pause, and then a thunderous *Amen* filled the valley, echoing off the mountains before it faded. *Yes,* thought Ithamar, *these were a Father's loving warning to His child.* Gaddiel was next, and one by one the sons of Aaron proclaimed the curses, each one garnering the same response. And finally Ithamar raised his voice. It sounded unnaturally loud to his ears. 'Cursed is anyone who does not confirm the words of this law by doing them.' And a twelfth *Amen* shook the valley for a final time.

Silence fell. And then, from under Mount Gerizim, one last voice rang out: that of Eleazar. The one who was both brother and high priest spoke over them all the words first heard on the lips of their father: 'Yahweh bless you and keep you; Yahweh make his face shine on you and be gracious to you; Yahweh turn his face towards you and give you peace.'

And the last word of blessing seemed to hang in the air longer than any other.

They rose early the next morning. Ithamar's belly still felt full from the feasting upon the meat of the peace offerings that followed Eleazar's blessing. Smoke was still curling lazily up from the altar into the clear blue sky. They would return to Gilgal that day, but first there was one last sacred duty to perform.

Scouts sent out by Joshua had already found the plot of land that had been bought by Jacob—and there they were to bury Joseph's bones.

A solemn procession set out from the assembly. At its head, leading the cart, were Joshua and Caleb, together with Eleazar and Ithamar. The four were the oldest living of those who had set out on the journey from Egypt with Joseph's coffin. And they would now lead it to that journey's end. Behind the cart were the elders from the tribes of Ephraim and Manasseh, the sons of Joseph. And finally there were some of the youngest of those tribes—the next generation of Joseph's descendants made manifest, but their hands still in those of their parents

When they arrived at the plot of ground, a short distance from the town of Shechem, there was nothing to mark the land as ever having belonged to Jacob. 'Not a single piece of stonework,' murmured Ithamar, as his eyes swept the patch of land. 'Nothing but bushes and trees.'

'They dwelt in tents,' replied Eleazar. 'All they would have left is footprints in the dust.'

Before the coffin was lifted down from the cart, Eleazar and Ithamar stepped apart from the company. The high priest would be defiled by the dead, however long past they had breathed their last. They found an olive tree a short distance away, and stood in its shade, watching. There was no burial cave on the land as there had been in the field bought by Abraham, so the sons of Joseph began digging near an oak.

Ithamar's gaze drifted slowly around. Large stones were scattered, here and there, among the trees. *Maybe some of them were once part of the altar their ancestor built on the land!*

He was clearly not alone in that thought. '*Mighty is the God of Israel*,' said Eleazar softly. 'Is that not the name our father Jacob gave to his altar?'

'It is,' replied Ithamar, and then added, 'after Yahweh gave him the name *Israel*.'

'But what if one of these stones came from the altar of Abraham?' mused Eleazar. 'What a wondrous thing *that* would be!'

Ithamar pondered the idea. It thrilled him. But then he added, 'Now, though, we bring into the Promised Land altars of gold and bronze and a tent of fine linen.'

Eleazar didn't respond immediately. The only sounds were a breeze gently rustling the leaves of the olive tree and the steady *thud* of shovels striking the ground. 'It is here, at Shechem, that Yahweh first promised Abraham this land. Any other would have thought Yahweh's promises empty or impossible—whether of countless descendants or of possessing the land.' He paused. 'Yet our father Abraham believed.'

After a few moments, Ithamar smiled wryly. 'Yahweh was certainly not in any haste to bring about His word. He *did* multiply Abraham's seed, but slowly, and it is only now that we stand in Canaan.' He paused. 'Yet even now many battles still lie ahead, and securing the land will take time.'

'But the passing of years do not nullify His promise,' replied Eleazar. 'They merely display His faithfulness when the seed of His word finally bears its fruit.'

Ithamar's gaze returned to the digging. A memory suddenly stirred. 'Do you remember when we slaved in the brickfields?' he asked. 'Half-naked and covered from the hair on our heads to the soles of our feet in mud!' He chuckled. 'I do not believe we could have looked any *less* like the people of Yahweh!'

Eleazar turned to his brother and smiled. 'He delights in working in ways that confound the wisdom of men.'

Ithamar knew it to be true. *Their flight from Egypt and journey to Canaan were nothing less than one long wonder wrought by the hand of Yahweh.*

Eleazar looked back towards the others. 'As with Joseph, our story can only be told because of Him.'

The memory of golden calves and grumbling surfaced, however, in Ithamar's mind. *They had seen both in the wilderness.* 'Even our rebellion could not thwart His purposes.'

'Sin is not that powerful!' exclaimed Eleazar. 'Our lack of faithfulness never changes His.'

They fell silent as the digging stopped and spades were set aside. Neither spoke as what was left of Joseph's embalmed body was lifted from the painted casket. It was still held together by the cloth that had been wound tightly round it in the manner of Egyptian princes. It was then slowly and reverently lowered into the ground. After the earth was replaced, every hand of those gathered chose a stone from the ground nearby, and together they raised a mound over the grave. Finally, Joshua set up pillar—a lime-washed stone like those inscribed with the law. But this stone bore Joseph's name and the blessing of Yahweh.

The group then began to disperse, but Ithamar and Eleazar lingered. 'Joseph only lived here seventeen years, but to him this was home.'

'You are wrong, Brother,' declared Ithamar with some delight.

Eleazar turned to face him, his expression sceptical but good-natured. 'You challenge the high priest?'

'It was *less* than seventeen years,' said Ithamar firmly. 'You forget that he was born elsewhere, in Paddan-aram. He lived here—' He cast his eyes upwards for several moments. '—maybe for only eleven.'

Eleazar threw his head back and laughed loudly. 'You are *still* counting?'

'Always,' he replied, 'especially my years!'

Eleazar turned his gaze one last time towards the mound of stones. '*However* many years Joseph spent here before Egypt, he is home now.'

Ithamar's eyes wandered across the hills of Canaan. He drew in a deep breath of its air, savouring it before releasing it slowly. He smiled. 'And so are we.'

Notes

1. *It is not clear what happened with the camp at Gilgal when the people went to Mount Ebal. Although the text speaks of 'all Israel' being there, presumably some must have stayed with the tabernacle and camp. They are certainly still camped at Gilgal afterwards (Joshua 9:6, 10:6,43, 14:6), and seem to stay there until they start to take possession of the conquered land, or move with the tabernacle to a new base at Shiloh (Joshua 18:1). Moses' instructions about the ceremony in Deuteronomy 27:12,13 also indicate that the Transjordan tribes should be there. It seems more likely, however, that the armed men represented them.*

2. Only Matthew 1:5 records that Rahab is the mother of Boaz (his father being Salmon). Given that Salmon is the son of Nahshon, Aaron's brother-in-law, it seems best to assume that he was under twenty when they left Egypt. This has largely been included for continuity with what comes next.

3. Mount Ebal and Mount Gerizim form a natural amphitheatre, with Shechem between. That voices can carry across the valley has been demonstrated in modern times, and is illustrated in Scripture, not only in this episode, but also in Judges 9:7.

4. Eleazar is clearly still alive after the conquest (Joshua 21:1). This story has presumed the same for Ithamar.

5. Only three cities are recorded as being destroyed during the conquest of Canaan—Jericho, Ai and Hazor—leaving the other existing cities for the Israelites to move into (see Joshua 24:13, for example). They will have taken over not only cities but also fields and crops. The archaeological record, therefore, will not necessarily show great discontinuities as a result of the conquest.

6. It seems that the main conquest lasted around seven years, as Caleb speaks of it being 45 years from the time of the rebellion at Kadesh Barnea to the end of the military campaign (see Joshua 14:10).

7. It has been assumed that Joseph was buried soon after entering Canaan, although it isn't recorded until the end of the book of Joshua (chapter 24). This may be hinted at when Joshua 24:32 states that the land on which Joseph was buried 'became the inheritance of Joseph's sons', despite the burial being recorded after the allotment of land. It seems hard to believe that the Israelites would only have buried Joseph's bones at the end of Joshua's life, which was maybe 25 years after the initial seven years of conquest, and therefore around thirty-two years after crossing the Jordan. Shechem, the burial place of Joseph, was directly between Mount Ebal and Mount Gerizim where they went for the ceremony in Joshua 8. (It ended up, through God's providence, virtually on the border of the lands of Ephraim and Manasseh, Joseph's two sons.) The placing of Joseph's burial in Joshua 24 may possibly be more thematic: in the last five verses of the book, three faithful Israelites—Joshua, Joseph and Eleazar—are all buried in their allotted inheritance in the Promised Land, ending the book with an emphasis on the faithfulness of Yahweh to His promises.

Naomi

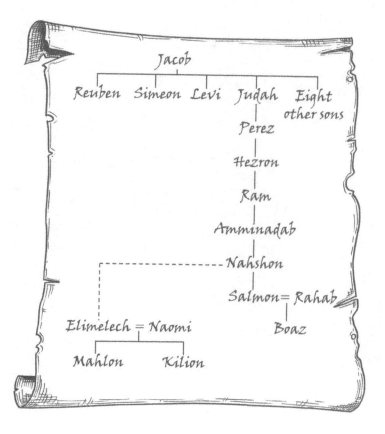

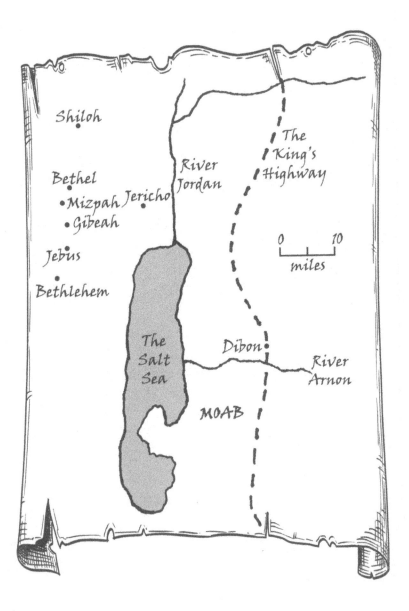

Shiloh

Bethel
Mizpah Jericho
Gibeah

Jebus
Bethlehem

River
Jordan

The
King's
Highway

The
Salt
Sea

Dibon

River
Arnon

MOAB

0   10
miles

I

In those days Israel had no king; everyone did as they saw fit.
(Judges 21:25)

Naomi's exasperation erupted in a sharp rebuke. 'Mahlon! Don't you dare prod the goat with that stick. Put it back!' The two-year-old grinned cheekily, withdrawing the stick from near the animal's rump but keeping it firmly within his grasp. Naomi sighed, shaking her head. The scolding of her firstborn was as constant as the dripping of a leaky roof in the autumn rains. He started prodding one of the large flat stones on which he was standing instead. 'I said, *Put it back!*'

Winter was slowly surrendering to the first signs of spring, and a day of sunshine had warmed the courtyard where rounds of bread for the evening meal were now baking on the hot stones at the base of the clay oven. Nearby, a cooking pot filled with lentil stew was bubbling gently, suspended over the firepit. On one side of the courtyard were five wooden pillars, beyond which a selection of goats and two ewes were tethered, having been returned to the house by one of the town's shepherds. He had earlier led them—and others—to pasture beyond the nearby fields for the day. Above the animals' pen was a roof of clay and earth compacted on brushwood, which had been laid over beams stretching from the top of the pillars to the outside stone wall of the house. On the opposite side was the same arrangement, though half of it was bricked in to form a storeroom. The half that was open to the courtyard functioned as the kitchen and workshop.

Naomi arched her aching back and rubbed it with one hand, her other resting for a moment on her belly. Not for the first time she pondered whether new life was beginning to stir beneath her orange tunic—she had missed her monthly bleed. She lifted her eyes to where clothes were drying on the flat roof above the kitchen and storeroom. *She would bring them in after she had fetched the water.* Her gaze returned to the oven. The small hand that had finally laid the stick down next to it was reaching into the woven basket into which the fresh rounds were being piled. 'Just one!' The cheeky grin returned, and Mahlon wandered off on his chubby legs.

She went over to the basket, picked up the stick, and crouched down beside the clay dome, looking in through the hole at the base. She had earlier kindled a wood fire there, and then brushed out its ashes when the fire had died down, and both the oven and the stones on which it rested were far too hot to touch. *The bread was baked.* She deftly flicked the two remaining loaves out from the hot floor of the oven and added them to the basket. She then checked that the stew had enough water in and gave it a stir, before going into the kitchen and placing the stick out of Mahlon's reach on one of the shelves set into the outside wall. She lifted a large empty clay water jar onto her shoulder. 'Come on, Mahlon. We're leaving.' She held out the hand that wasn't steadying the jar. 'Now!' He toddled over, still munching on the fresh bread.

Naomi left the courtyard door open behind her. *The animals were safely tied up—they wouldn't be going anywhere.* Within a few paces, she was at her neighbour's door. 'Haggith!'

A young woman came into view. She smiled. 'Naomi!' Her eyes flitted between the jar on her shoulder and her son. 'Do you wish me to take Mahlon while you go to the well?'

'Yahweh bless you! If I take him, I might not get there before nightfall!'

Haggith laughed. 'Gladly. He might keep Caleb out of mischief for a while if the two of them can play together without squabbling.'

'Or double your woe!'

Haggith shrugged her shoulders. 'You suffer my son just as often.'

Naomi let go of Mahlon and gently urged him forward through the door. 'Go and find Caleb.' He trotted off.

'Is Elimelech still planting?'

Naomi nodded. 'Yes, but he hopes to have finished the lentils and chick peas by the Sabbath. And Shammai?'

'Planting onions.'

'Yahweh has truly blessed the land with good rain over the winter.' Naomi's eyes fell on Haggith's belly. 'And you will be having another harvest before the wheat is threshed!'

Haggith looked down. 'For a woman, there is never a good time to have a third child!'

Naomi laughed again. 'Unless it is when the men are well out of the way and busy with harvesting. I will still be here for you when your time comes.'

A shriek and a cry drew both women's eyes into the courtyard. 'I fear my words are needed elsewhere,' sighed Haggith.

'I will not be long,' promised Naomi. 'I wish you the patience of Yahweh!'

'I may need it.'

As Haggith disappeared back inside, Naomi continued towards the gate of Bethlehem. She passed a number of doors that opened off the narrow street, which was, in truth, little more than an alley. It wound this way and that through the space left between the houses crowded together within the town's solid walls. Naomi turned a corner and then emerged into the open space between the overlapping and offset city walls that formed part of the town gates. The area was filled with familiar faces. *But then, everyone knew everyone in Bethlehem.* Various men were sitting on benches on opposite sides of the roughly square area that led to the gates themselves. This was where disputes were resolved, business was done and agreements were forged, with witnesses always to hand.

Naomi nodded to Haggith's father, and then to Salmon. He was one of Bethlehem's most respected elders, though now over ninety, and a leader of the tribe of Judah. He had fought alongside Joshua in the conquest of Canaan, some forty years earlier, and had married Rahab, the Canaanite woman who had hidden the Israelite spies in the city of Jericho.

Naomi passed through the heavy wooden gates that were opened at sunrise each day and shut tightly as the sun set. Bethlehem's well immediately came into view—and she smiled. 'Rizpah!'

A woman dressed in a green tunic that fell to her ankles turned towards her. She returned the smile and the greeting. 'Naomi! I wondered if I would see you here.' She emptied the leather bucket into her water jar and set it down. 'Come, sit with me a while. I have news to tell you!'

'What news?' asked Naomi, perching on the small, circular wall that ran around the top of the well.

'Reumah's back!'

Naomi's brow furrowed for a moment. 'You mean Uri's daughter? The one who became a concubine to that Levite from Ephraim?'

'Yes!'

'What was his name?'

'Assir son of Mahli.'

'That's right, I remember now. But what of Reumah?'

Rizpah leant in slightly. 'She arrived back in Bethlehem last night, or at least that's what Helah tells me.'

Naomi smiled wryly. 'You cannot always believe all that Helah says.'

'But she saw Reumah herself.'

'And what brings her back?'

Rizpah raised her eyebrows. 'I can guess. Knowing Reumah, she was never going to take easily to being Hagar to her husband's Sarah.'

Naomi shrugged. 'It was a good enough match given that she had no dowry to bring to a marriage.'

'True enough. She brought a fertile womb instead.' Rizpah leant forward again. 'But can you see her living happily alongside a barren wife? I would not be surprised if an argument with the husband or the wife is what sent her scurrying back here.'

'It certainly did not end happily for Hagar, running away from her mistress and then being sent away by Abraham.'

'And Reumah's words always flowed as readily as a wadi in winter—too readily for her own good.'

Naomi nodded and gave a little laugh. 'She is not the first!'

Rizpah glanced around. 'But that is not all Helah told me.' She lowered her voice. 'She said that Merab was with child—and lost it again.'

Naomi sighed. 'Poor woman. She is running out of time to bear Boaz a child.' Merab's husband was both Salmon's son and a cousin of Elimelech.

'It is strange that Yahweh leaves such a faithful man without an heir. He blesses Boaz with wealth but gives him no one to pass it on to.'

Naomi shrugged again. 'Who can know the ways of Yahweh?' After a pause, she smiled. 'But I know the way of my husband. Elimelech is like a growling bear when his belly rumbles, and he'll be back from the fields soon.' She stood and picked up the leather bucket, casting it into the darkened depths of the well. The rope on the wall rapidly followed it, until the sound of the bucket hitting the water rose up from below.

'I must go too,' said Rizpah, raising her water jar to her shoulder. 'Planting sharpens a man's thirst like a salty stew.'

Naomi started pulling on the rope, hand over hand. 'If only they were like camels...'

Rizpah's dark eyes sparkled. 'But my husband already spits like one.'

The barley ripened and was reaped as the heat of the summer grew. But it was only as the wheat harvest, a month behind the barley, was coming to an end that the conversation at the well turned to the concubine once again.

'Assir the Levite has returned for Reumah!' said her neighbour, Haggith, as soon as Naomi had reached the well and before she had even set down her water jar. The women gathered there had clearly been discussing it before her arrival.

Naomi removed a bag filled with bread from her other shoulder and placed it next to the jar. 'Will she go with him? She's been back—what?—four months?'

'Thereabouts,' replied Rizpah. 'But I was just telling the others that her father welcomed him.'

'They were feasting together last night,' said Helah. 'And he arrived with two spare donkeys. He must be intending to take her back.'

'She has no choice if her father sends her,' said Haggith. 'Besides, she is bound to him. She may not be his wife, but there was still an agreement.'

'I would not want to exchange living in Judah for Ephraim,' said Rizpah. 'Their hold on the land is less secure than ours.' Although Joshua's battles had established the Israelites in the land, there was still much of Canaan that remained to be taken. The men of Judah had soon driven the Canaanites from the hill country but not from the portion of Judah's land to the west, towards the Great Sea, where Canaanite iron chariots ruled the plains. Ephraim had taken Bethel, but not the towns on the lower land to the west. The tribes in the north had fared even worse.

'Boaz says that the Canaanites live among the men of Ephraim,' replied Merab, breaking her silence, 'as they have failed to drive them out.'

Helah shrugged. 'That may be so, but I hear that Assir comes from a remote area, to the north.'

'If Reumah goes with him,' said Rizpah with an air of finality as she picked up her jar and raised it to her shoulder, 'the Levite will have to take better care of her if we are not to see her back in Bethlehem again.' Her words carried more foresight than any of them realised.

Naomi's jar was soon full and she resumed her errand, having left Mahlon with Haggith's daughter, who was also watching over the new baby, born to her neighbour some ten days earlier. She followed the outside walls of the town, passing the flat, hard ground of the threshing floor which lay below the ridge on which Bethlehem was situated. One or two were beating ears of wheat with rods. Another was using an ox to trample it for the same purpose—to separate the grain from the stalks and chaff. Naomi guessed they would wait until later to exchange their rods for winnowing forks. The evening breeze would blow away the chaff and straw more readily as they tossed the threshed wheat high into the air in the cool of the day.

Once on the other side of Bethlehem, Naomi began descending a gentle slope. Some of those still harvesting were already resting in the shade under small shelters scattered among the fields of ripened wheat. Here and there, smoke rose up in wispy columns into the bright blue sky, as small bundles of fresh grain were roasted over fires of thorn bushes. The parched grain that was left when the chaff had burned off could then be enjoyed by the harvesters.

Naomi passed a number of the stones set up to mark the boundary of one man's field with another, until Elimelech's land came in sight. *He was hungry.* Elimelech's furrowed brow and the way he hacked at the remaining wheat told her as much. They had married when she was fifteen and he was two years older, and nine years of marriage had been more than enough to become familiar with his moods. But Elimelech and the worker he had hired to help with the harvest weren't the only ones there. Naomi recognised one of the widows of Bethlehem nervously standing at the edge of the field, a child of around five or six clinging to the skirt of her dress. Naomi's heart went out to her. Their eyes met, but the other woman looked away swiftly. *Waiting to scavenge grain that had been left or dropped by harvesters was a pitiful way to live. But at least it* was *a way.*

'I had begun to think my wife had forgotten her duty!'

Naomi's eyes returned to her husband. 'Fresh bread doesn't bake itself.' She walked across the low stalks left after the sickle had cut down the ripe wheat. A young lad of twelve by the name of Zerah was busy tying bundles of the cut stalks into sheaves, using one or two stalks wrapped tightly around them to secure them. The men were dressed in simple tunics and sandals. Elimelech laying down his sickle was the sign for the other reaper and the lad to join him in the shade of their own small shelter erected in a corner of the field. Naomi lowered the water jar from her shoulder and poured it into the almost-empty jar already standing there. She then took a wooden platter from her bag and placed the rounds of bread on it, completing the simple meal by pouring wine vinegar from a small stoppered jar into a bowl into which they could dip the bread.

As the men began eating, Naomi took one of the cups from beside the newly replenished jar and filled it. Her gaze moved from the jar to the widow, who was already searching the newly-harvested ground.

'She can get water herself from the town well,' muttered Elimelech.

'The water comes freely from Yahweh's hand and it is only a cupful.' Naomi neither met his eyes nor waited for an answer. *The woman could glean more grain if she didn't have to return to Bethlehem for water.* Naomi knew her own life wasn't all milk and honey, but she would never barter it for that of a lone widow.

When Reumah finally departed with Assir four days later, Naomi gave her no further thought, and the conversations at the well and across the flat roofs of their houses moved on. Until, that is, a further six days had passed. Naomi was on the roof above the animals' stall when the sound of running and shouting grew near. She looked up from the loom on which she was weaving woollen cloth.

'Something stirs Bethlehem,' said Haggith on the neighbouring roof, where she had been laying out washing to dry. She put down a wet cloth that had been used to wrap her newborn, and moved towards the edge of the roof nearest the street.

Naomi followed her lead. 'What do you think is happening?'

But before either woman could answer, Zerah came into view. The twelve-year-old looked up at them, breathing heavily. 'Elimelech and Shammai are needed at the gate!'

'Elimelech's tending the vines,' said Naomi. Since harvesting and storing the wheat, her husband's attentions had turned to the next crop to be gathered.

'And so is Shammai,' added Haggith. 'Can't it wait till they return?'

'No! They are needed now. All the elders and men of the town are gathering. Can you fetch them?'

'They won't be the only ones out on the hills,' said Haggith impatiently. 'Why the urgency? Women have work to do too!'

Zerah paused, looking back along the narrow street in the direction of the gate. He turned back to them. 'Something terrible has happened.' His face told the same story. 'They need to come now.' And before Naomi had the chance to voice any of the myriad questions that were crowding her mind like animals around a feeding trough, Zerah was gone, running further up the street.

Both women hurried towards the ladders they had used to climb up onto the roofs. 'What can have happened?' began Haggith.

Naomi paused with her hand on the top of the ladder. 'I don't know.'

But then the sound of a baby's cry rose up from Haggith's courtyard. She sighed. 'The child is hungry. I was waiting until after I'd finished the washing to feed him.'

'If you can take Mahlon, I'll fetch Shammai as well as Elimelech.'

Haggith looked at Naomi's swelling belly—she was in her fifth month. 'Do not run, my friend.'

Naomi smiled ruefully, as she turned and put her foot carefully on the top rung. 'Hurrying will be less trouble than watching four children.'

But hurrying through Bethlehem's now crowded and noisy alleys was not easy. As she approached the gate her curiosity—and foreboding—grew. The sound of wailing rose above the commotion, and as Naomi wormed her way through the mass of people, she caught sight of Reumah's mother. Hers were the agonised cries that sullied the air. She was with a group that was forming a tight knot around something on the ground. Naomi began to hear Reumah's name on the lips of those she passed—all of whose faces carried the same expressions of shock and disbelief. She spotted Rizpah in the crowd. 'What is it?' whispered Naomi as the two met.

'All I know is that Reumah is dead—' Her gaze suddenly shifted to the huddle by the distraught mother. '—and that her head has been delivered to Bethlehem.'

Bethlehem felt quiet and empty with so many of the men gone. Naomi knelt by the millstone and pushed the upper stone back

221

and forth over the wheat, both hands gripping the upper curved surface of the stone, whilst the flat lower surface crushed the grain. There were fewer grains to grind with one less mouth to feed. But her thoughts were elsewhere. As she felt a tiny stirring within her womb, the question that so greatly troubled her mind returned with a vengeance: *would the child have a father when it was born?*

The news that had left the town reeling had been followed by a meeting of the elders from across the tribe of Judah. The gruesome delivery had been a call to action, which was answered by the departure of most of the tribe's fighting men. Elimelech left with a bronze sword hanging from his belt as they set out to march north through the hill country towards Mizpah, less than a day's journey away. All the tribes were being summoned to an assembly there. All the women could do was wait.

'Naomi!' She had been oblivious of the approaching footsteps, but the sound of Rizpah's voice roused her. She looked up, half in hope, half in fear. 'Izhah has returned—and there is news.' But before Naomi could ask about Rizpah's husband, she went on. 'I will fetch Haggith, and then I will tell you both what I know.'

The news from the north was grim. 'Izhah has returned wounded,' began Rizpah as they stood together in Naomi's courtyard. 'He will heal, but he cannot fight any more.'

'There has been a battle?' said Naomi, her heart fearful. 'Against the Canaanites?'

'A battle, yes, but against the men of Benjamin.'

Naomi could not believe what she was hearing. 'What, against our own people?' she asked, aghast. 'How can that be?'

'I will tell it from the beginning—from Reumah's departure— and then you will understand.' Rizpah took a deep breath. 'When Assir left Bethlehem with her, it was not until well past midday. They travelled north, past Jebus, and only reached Gibeah in Benjamin by nightfall. A man took them in, but during the night the men of the city surrounded the house. They took Reumah, and raped and abused her through the night. It killed her.'

'Yahweh have mercy!' whispered Haggith before falling silent.

Naomi was too appalled to speak. She could neither comprehend how this had been done in Israel nor begin to imagine the horrors that Reumah had endured at the mercy of the mob—passed from man to man to satisfy their lust and then cast aside like an empty wineskin once their desire was sated. *No, she could not think of them as men. They were like hungry wolves, and Reumah had been their prey, to be toyed with and then devoured.* 'Are the men of Gibeah no better than a pack of animals?' she murmured.

'Or the men of Sodom?' added Rizpah. No one answered.

Haggith drew in a breath eventually. 'What of the Levite? Where was he?'

'He said the men of the city were going to kill him.' There was disdain in Rizpah's voice.

'So he just abandoned her!' exclaimed Haggith, her face darkening.

Naomi's revulsion turned to anger. 'Or maybe offered her to the mob to save his own skin!'

'Izhah did not say. Only that she was raped and died.'

'But how could this happen among the people of Yahweh?' continued Naomi. 'It is an outrage!'

Rizpah nodded. 'Maybe that is why Assir did something just as outrageous.' She looked repulsed. 'It was not only our own tribe that received a portion of Reumah. They all did—to summon the tribes.'

'May that Levite's name not be spoken in Israel!' Haggith's expression soon changed, however. 'But what was the response of the tribes? You said there was a battle against Benjamin…' Her voice was anxious. Battles meant death—and a husband was a woman's only real security.

'The Benjamites ignored the summons to Mizpah and sided with the men of Gibeah—'

'How could they ally themselves with such behaviour?' interrupted Naomi, spitting out the words. 'Do their blood bonds mean more to them than their covenant with Yahweh?'

Rizpah shrugged. 'The whole of Benjamin came out to fight with Gibeah against the tribes. And there was not one battle but three. The men had taken the ark from the Tent of Meeting at Shiloh when they gathered to fight, and Phinehas the high priest was with them. Three times Yahweh directed them to go up against the city of Gibeah. Twice they fell before the Benjamites but on the third attack they ambushed them and prevailed. That's when Izhah was injured. The last he knew was that those still fighting were pursuing the men of Benjamin who had fled the battle.'

'And what of the men of Bethlehem?' asked Naomi, her voice strained. 'How did they fare?'

'Attai fell in the first attack and Jahath was injured in the second. Izhah knew of no others.'

Naomi breathed more freely again, more for what Rizpah did not say than for what she did.

Over the next four months, the news of what had happened flowed back to Bethlehem. It came with the men who returned safely after fighting—including Elimelech and Shammai—or from further assemblies. So the women learned from fathers, husbands and brothers of the retribution that had fallen on all the towns of Benjamin and their people. As wives and daughters carried their water jars, they shared in the town's winding streets and narrow alleys the tales of the desperate attempts by the grieving elders of Israel to find wives for the few remaining Benjamites—the six hundred that had taken refuge at the rock of Rimmon, the strangely shaped hill just to east of Bethel. Despite the appalling sin, none wanted a tribe of Israel to be wiped out. And the story was shared across Bethlehem's flat rooftops of how men of Benjamin were allowed to snatch wives for themselves from among the virgins who danced at Shiloh as the festival of Tabernacles was celebrated. Naomi wondered, however, if that had been the command of Yahweh or the desperation of their leaders, forging a plan that seemed right in their own eyes.

But it was at the well, once again, that Naomi and the women of Bethlehem gave voice to their thoughts on all they had heard.

'This would not have happened if Joshua was still alive,' said Naomi. Her water jar was already full, but she had no intention of leaving immediately, particularly as the wall of the well gave her the opportunity to sit down and rest. 'The men of Gibeah would not have dared to behave as they did.' She had only been fourteen years old when the man who had led the Israelites into Canaan had died at the age of a hundred and ten. She had never seen him—but she had heard of him. They all had.

Merab poured the water from the bucket she'd just raised into her water jar. She paused. 'But Yahweh has not raised up a leader to follow Joshua.' She dropped the bucket into the well for a second time. 'And Boaz tells me that, besides his father, there are only a few left who were there when our people left Egypt.'

'All too old to lead the people,' added Helah. 'But the tribes have their leaders and each town its elders. Is that not enough?'

'Maybe it would be,' replied Merab, as she pulled up the bucket, 'if they heeded Yahweh's commands and His directions through Phinehas.'

Rizpah nodded. 'The men of Gibeah did not. They lived among Canaanites and began to behave like them.'

'But surely they are not the only ones,' said Helah. 'There are rumours, are there not, of idols and household gods being used by some among the tribes in the north?'

'Rumours do not mean that something happens,' replied Rizpah.

Helah folded her arms. 'But neither do they mean that it doesn't.'

Naomi's mind was still in the south, however. 'There is still one matter I do not understand,' she said, her hand resting on her enormous belly. 'We were told that Yahweh directed the Israelites three times to go up against the men of Benjamin at Gibeah, and yet twice they were defeated before they prevailed. Why would Yahweh send them into battle, only to be defeated?'

The women fell quiet—even Helah, who rarely lacked something to say. But after Merab had tipped the second bucket into her water jar, she spoke again. 'Maybe men too easily think they will triumph by their own strength and need to be humbled first.' Naomi suspected she spoke with the wisdom gleaned from the lips of her husband, Boaz. 'There is, though, another matter that troubles me more.' Merab cast her gaze around the others. 'Why is it that the men of Israel can unite from Dan to Beersheba to fight one of its own tribes but seem unable to join together to drive out the Canaanites who still live among us?'

Naomi's brow furrowed. It was, indeed, a good question.

Helah paused, the bucket now in her hand. 'The tribe of Benjamin do not have iron chariots.'

Merab raised her jar to her shoulder. 'But the Canaanites do not have Yahweh.'

As Naomi walked slowly back with Haggith, her mind returned to the conversation at the well as her friend chattered. *If such terrible events could take place whilst Phinehas and the older generation who had witnessed the powerful Hand of Yahweh still lived, what would happen when they joined Joshua in death, which would surely be soon?* It was a troubling thought, but it did not stay with her for long. She felt a sudden rush of water leaving her. She stopped and looked down at the darkened dust on the ground. 'Haggith...'

The other woman stopped and turned. Her eyes went from Naomi's face to her feet. 'I will fetch the midwife.'

Notes

1. *This chapter takes the character of Naomi from the book of Ruth, and links her with an event that happens in the book of Judges. However, this is conjecture. There is no consensus about either the dating of Ruth—the events of which take place 'In the days when the judges ruled,' (Ruth 1:1)—or the chronology of the book of Judges. Even if the date of the Exodus is known, the dating beyond that is difficult because of a variety of factors, including the following:*

   (a) *the period of decline and apostasy started after the elders who outlived Joshua had died (Judges 2:7,10). However, it is not clear when Joshua died—at the age of 110 (Judges 2:8). At the Exodus, he was young enough to be described as a 'young man' (Exodus 33:11), but there is nothing about his age beyond this.*

(b) it is not clear by how many years the elders outlived Joshua, or how soon the apostasy began after their deaths.

(c) even if the Exodus and the end of the period of Judges (the start of the reign of Saul) are fixed, some of the judges may have overlapped and the lengths of some of their periods of rule may be rounded. However, there is also uncertainty about the length of reign of Saul (see Bible footnotes on 1 Samuel 13:1).

Here, it has been assumed that the elders who outlived Joshua would have been those who saw and remembered the events of the Exodus around 1446 BC (aged 15-20?), and it is assumed they died off around 1365 BC. An early date for Ruth has been chosen, as the spiritual state of the nation (as exemplified by Bethlehem) is good, and therefore possibly earlier in the period of the Judges, as there appears to be a general overall spiritual decay during Judges. Also, if Boaz is the son of Salmon and Rahab (as implied by Matthew 1:5 – see point 6 below), that would put Boaz in the first generation born after the conquest of Canaan. It is likely that there are generations missing in the genealogy at the end of Ruth 4 (echoed in Matthew 1 and elsewhere in Scripture), as there do not seem enough generations to cover the period from the conquest to the monarchy (even if a late Exodus date is chosen). Any missing generations are assumed here to have been between Obed and Jesse. This is tentative guesswork, however.

2. The events concerning the concubine from Bethlehem seem to be quite early in the period of the Judges, despite being placed at the end of the book (Judges 19-21). Phinehas is mentioned (but not Joshua), and the tribes are still functioning as one.

3. A concubine would have had a marriage contract, but would have been a secondary wife, maybe coming to the marriage without a dowry, and specifically to raise up an heir because of the first wife being infertile. They would undoubtedly be of lesser status than a regular wife.

4. The Levite is not named in Scripture, possibly because of the heinous nature of what happened. Although he is initially given a name for convenience here, his name is then deliberately 'blotted out' in the story.

5. It is not clear from Scripture how Elimelech and Boaz were related. The general term 'cousin' has been chosen to allow them to be of the same

generation, with some flexibility about closeness, as there was one other kinsman who was closer to Elimelech.

6. We only know that Boaz is the son of Rahab from Matthew 1:5. Although genealogies may have missing (less important) generations, in the other three cases in Matthew where women are mentioned (Tamar, Bathsheba, Mary), they are the actual mothers of the named offspring and not more distant ancestors.

7. Ruth 4:12 is best explained if Boaz was childless. He is unlikely to be a bachelor (as he appears to be much older than Ruth), so it has been assumed that he was a widower, with no children from his previous marriage.

8. Bethlehem had no spring and relied on cisterns to collect water. A well, however, is mentioned in 2 Samuel 23:15 in the time of David, and it has been assumed that this was already in existence at the time of Ruth. Bethlehem is also portrayed as a walled town with gates, with a threshing floor outside the town.

9. Jebus is another (possibly early?) name for Jerusalem (Judges 19:10); those living there are called Jebusites. Given that this name for the city is used in Judges, it has been adopted here.

10. Judges 20:26-28 is the only reference to the ark of the covenant in the book of Judges. For most of the book it is not known where it is kept or how it is being used. The pattern of the religious life of the nation is also unclear; for example, it is not known the extent to which sacrifices were being offered or festivals celebrated. It is thought by some that the ark possibly changed location during this time, being variously at Shechem, Bethel and Shiloh (maybe more than once). In Joshua's time, however, the Tent of Meeting was set up at Shiloh (Joshua 18:1, c/f Judges 18:31), and Kitchen comments: 'and there it stayed most of time down to Eli and Samuel's epoch. It remained a focus for annual festivals down to that time... but its role was modest' (Kitchen, p221). It is assumed here that the Tent of Meeting stayed at Shiloh, and hence 'the annual festival of the Lord' being held there (Judges 21:19)—presumably Tabernacles, as there was dancing.

11. 'From Dan to Beersheba' became a saying that referred to the whole of the country, with the city of Dan in the far north, and Beersheba in the south (e.g. Judges 20:1, 1 Samuel 3:20, 2 Samuel 3:10).

12. Under Joshua, there was never a complete conquest and occupation of the land. Victories were decisive, but possession of Canaan was far from complete.

2

After that whole generation had been gathered to their ancestors, another generation grew up who knew neither the L<small>ORD</small> nor what he had done for Israel. Then the Israelites did evil in the eyes of the L<small>ORD</small> and served the Baals. (Judges 2:10-11)

Salmon died shortly after Kilion had drawn his first breath. The changes that crept across the land with the passing of the generation that had known Moses were not slow in following, and few could escape them, even among the young.

'Mahlon! What did I tell you? Keep hold of your brother's hand, unless you want your ears battered by his screams when he stumbles and falls.'

'But I want to go ahead with Caleb…' he whined.

'And I want you to hold Kilion's hand. He's only four.'

The seven-year-old rolled his eyes and reluctantly took his brother's hand. He proceeded to sulk.

Haggith laughed. 'He's not a leper, Mahlon!'

The furrows on his forehead only deepened. Despite the warmth of the sun, he coughed twice. He was not the most robust child.

The late summer's day was pleasant, and the walk to the hillside on which some of Bethlehem's vines were planted was unhurried, given the pace of the children accompanying them—six between the two women, with Haggith carrying her fourth on her hip. Naomi carried the food for both families: bread, cheese, raisin cakes from the previous year's harvest, and two generous skins of milk for quenching thirsts. A day of harvesting grapes lay ahead—their husbands were already at the vines. Naomi glanced around the countryside—others were picking ripe figs from the stumpy, dark-leaved trees, whilst sheep and goats tugged at anything green that was still growing in their shade. Her gaze drifted to the top of the nearest hill. She narrowed her eyes and squinted. 'What's that?' she asked, pointing to a mound of stones or earth that had not been there before. She feared she knew the answer, however.

The small party stopped. 'I can run up with Mahlon and find out!' suggested Caleb.

'I know well enough what that is without my son leaving my side,' said Haggith drily. She turned to Naomi, her cheerful mood gone. 'It is another high place.'

Caleb seemed puzzled. 'But it's not very high. There are bigger hills over there,' he said, pointing north.

'That's not what Haggith means,' explained Naomi.

'It's where people build an altar,' said Haggith's twelve-year-old daughter, Judith, clearly keen to demonstrate the superior knowledge of the firstborn. 'They make sacrifices to their god there.'

'*They make sacrifices to their god there,*' echoed Caleb, mimicking his sister's condescending tone.

'That's enough!' interjected Haggith.

'Is it like the altar at Shiloh?' said Mahlon, clearly interested.

'No, it is not,' said Haggith curtly.

'It cannot be a Canaanite shrine,' murmured Naomi. 'There are none living near here.'

'It's most likely the work of one of our neighbours.'

Naomi spotted an upright piece of carved wood nearby. 'I hope it is only *one* of them, because whoever it is, they have raised an Asherah pole there too.'

'What's that?' asked Mahlon.

Naomi sighed, and turned towards Haggith, a questioning look on her face.

Haggith shrugged her shoulders. 'It is better that they hear it from our lips and with our instruction than from others.' The two women deliberately drew the six children into a small circle. Both Naomi and Haggith crouched down to be on the level of the younger children. 'We know that the one true God is Yahweh, but the Canaanites believe in many gods. They have a god called El, and they believe that he has a wife called Asherah and a son called Baal. They think Baal controls the rains and the storms, though we know that it's really Yahweh who does that.'

'But what's the Ash…Ashrah pole?' asked Mahlon.

'The Canaanites put up a piece of wood when they worship Asherah.'

'Why?' asked Caleb.

'You may well ask!' replied his mother.

'Can we go, just to have a look?' Mahlon's plaintive question was accompanied by a pitiful expression.

'Do not think I am any more ready to allow it than Haggith. And you would be puffing all the way up—I know you.' He looked crestfallen but Naomi continued their instruction in the ways of their own God. 'Such a place should not be used by the people of Yahweh. We have a proper altar to Yahweh at the Tent of Meeting at Shiloh. The Canaanites worship gods who are no gods at all. We are not to be like them.'

It was only when the younger children were chattering among themselves as they resumed their walk that Judith spoke again. 'Leah says that it does no harm to worship Baal as well as Yahweh.'

Naomi was shocked. 'Helah's daughter says that?'

'Yes.'

'Helah should know better,' said Haggith forcefully, 'than to let her daughter speak like that, because she is wrong.'

'But she says that both her mother and father told her that.'

Naomi shook her head. 'Just because Helah and Jether say something doesn't make it right.' She hoped it would be the last time she would have to defend the ways of Yahweh, but feared otherwise.

By the time Kilion had seen his tenth autumn, the land was plagued not only by high places, but by reports from the north of raiding and plundering by the king of Aram, and, closer to home, by drought. The winter clouds held on to their water, and the spring rains that should have followed also failed. Although the water of Bethlehem's well remained pure, the words that were shared around it did not.

Rizpah thumped her water jar down on the dry earth. 'You will not guess what we saw when we went to Shiloh!' She immediately had the attention of the other four women at the well.

Naomi suspected from her darkened face that the news would not be welcome, at least to her. 'Tell us, Rizpah.'

'It is bad enough that there is an altar to Baal with its shrine on the way to Jebus, but there is now one barely a thousand paces from the Tent of Meeting, together with its Asherah pole and shrine prostitute!'

'But look around you.'

Naomi had heard Helah speak freely about Baal before and guessed she was about to do so again.

'Yahweh may have created the earth,' continued Helah, 'but it is Baal who makes the land fertile.' Naomi opened her mouth to respond but Helah hadn't finished. 'Worshipping Yahweh does nothing to bring us the rains we need. If we all worshipped Baal, they would come.'

'It is true,' said another woman, whose daughter had married a Jebusite. 'It has always been that way in this land. We may worship Yahweh, but it is only right that we honour the gods of Canaan too.'

'Do you not care if your husband lies with a prostitute of Baal?' challenged Rizpah, folding her arms deliberately.

'It is a small price to pay for grain to grind and bread in our bellies,' replied Helah casually. 'Besides, Jether is not the only man from Bethlehem to do so. Yahweh is certainly not bringing us rain, and if more did as my husband, then Baal would restore fertility to this land—as he has done for me.' She proudly displayed her swollen belly.

Just at that moment, Naomi saw Rizpah's gaze shift. She followed it. Merab, the wife of Boaz, had just walked through the town gate and was walking towards them.

'And maybe if her husband had done the same,' continued Helah, who had clearly also spotted her, 'her body would have become fertile too. It is too late for her now.' Both Naomi and Rizpah swung back to face Helah. She shrugged her shoulders. 'He clings to Yahweh alone and yet it has not brought him an heir.'

Rizpah's eyes flashed. 'Boaz is a better man than your husband—and you know it!'

Helah shrugged again and picked up her water jar. 'Then ask yourself—whose wife is the barren desert where nothing grows?' With that she strutted off with the other two.

Naomi watched as Helah deliberately paraded her belly past Merab. It sickened her. Merab kept looking straight ahead, as if she didn't see Helah and her friends.

'I do wonder why Boaz hasn't taken a second wife,' murmured Rizpah. 'He wouldn't be the first to do so.'

'Boaz believes that one wife is Yahweh's way. Or so Elimelech says.' Naomi turned her gaze back to her friend. 'And I believe Boaz is right. After all, tell me when you have seen contentment among women when they share a man?' She picked up the leather bucket and tossed it for a last time into the well.

'Never!'

Merab arrived just as Naomi was tipping the water into her jar. 'Yahweh bless you, my friends.' Merab glanced back over her shoulder. 'Was there some disagreement with Helah?'

'She continues to believe that Baal is the answer to the land's distress—'

'The answer?' interjected Merab indignantly. 'It is the worship of Canaanite gods that is the cause of it! The worship *and* all that goes with it.'

'I have seen another shrine near Shiloh,' said Rizpah, repeating her news for the new arrival. 'And one of its prostitutes.'

'Helah claimed she was happy enough to have Jether use them.'

Merab shook her head slowly. 'Tell a man that the gods, not to mention the fertility of the land, require him to lie with a temple prostitute and he will readily embrace the idea—'

'And the whore!' said Rizpah.

'But Yahweh calls it adultery—'

'And so should the wife,' added Naomi.

'Boaz says that the Canaanites think it strange that Yahweh does not have a consort as Baal has,' continued Merab, 'because they simply make up gods who behave as they would.'

Rizpah snorted. 'And gods who are as forgetful as they are! So to bring fertility on the land, Baal and his consort need to be reminded to copulate by seeing men doing so with shrine prostitutes! It is ridiculous—and shameful.'

'Yet our people run after such gods,' sighed Merab. 'Gods who need to be appeased and persuaded rather than obeyed and trusted, as the true God must be. We allowed the Canaanites to remain in the land and now we become like them.' She paused and then murmured, 'No wonder Yahweh brings judgment on the land.'

Naomi lifted her eyes to the parched hills which should have been green in spring. 'You truly think the drought is brought by the worship of Baal?'

Merab nodded. 'The drought *and* the raids. Boaz says that when God made His covenant with us before we entered this land, He told Moses that He would curse the land if the people disobeyed Him. And what was the first command He gave us at Sinai? To have no other gods but Him.'

Naomi suspected that Merab—and Boaz—spoke truth.

It had been hard settling the boys that evening. Both had been tetchy after bouts of sickness. As soon as they stopped squabbling and it seemed that they might finally go to sleep, she re-joined Elimelech. He appeared deep in thought but glanced up as she lowered herself onto the patterned rug.

'I met a trader from Moab at the gate this morning. We talked.'

Naomi held her peace. *Interrupting her husband with questions would only irritate him in the mood he had been in recently. He was worried. And why shouldn't he be, when there was likely to be little, if anything, to replenish the grain store that year?*

'He said that Moab is afflicted neither by droughts nor by the king of Aram, and that there are no shortages there.' He paused and she waited. 'Pasture for the animals is limited here, and we only have a little barley left for feed. Even now, anyone with as little wit as that of an ass can see that the crops will fail again. So I have made my decision—we must leave for Moab.'

'Leave our home?' replied Naomi, incredulous.

'We leave and live or stay and die. The choice is simple.'

'But what of others in Bethlehem? Surely it is better to face these troubles with our own people!'

'I am not alone in considering it—'

'But are others actually going?'

'What others do is of no concern to me,' he snapped. 'I have two growing sons to consider.'

And a wife. Naomi became anxious. *Leave Bethlehem, their home, their friends? Leave God's people and the Promised Land?* But it was as if he knew her thoughts.

'Look, Naomi,' he said more softly, 'you know the stories of our ancestors as well as I do. Abraham, Isaac and Jacob all faced famine, as we do, and each of them travelled elsewhere to find food and live—even to Egypt. Why should it be different for us? And we won't be going that far. You can see the fields of Moab from one of the ridges outside Bethlehem when the day is clear! It will probably take us less than a week to get there.'

Maybe he was right. But that thought did not entirely sweep away the sense of unease that continued to pester her like a persistent fly. *Yahweh had not spoken of this.* 'And how long would we go for?'

'We *will* go,' said Elimelech with a slight edge in his voice, 'for as long as the famine lasts. A year or two, maybe. Who knows?' And before Naomi had time to ask her next question, Elimelech was answering it. 'We will leave as soon as I buy a cart for what we need to take.'

Naomi didn't bother arguing. *There was no point. The decision had been made.*

'Naomi! We are waiting!'

Elimelech's impatience tore into her thoughts. *There were so many memories!* She glanced for one last time around their largest room, now bare after being stripped of all rugs, cushions and lamps. It felt empty and devoid of life. She turned and walked out into the courtyard. The morning sun had barely begun its descent of their east-facing wall. The courtyard was just a shell, and her kitchen was now no different from the covered area where the animals had been tethered—with two exceptions. Elimelech had announced two days earlier that the clay oven would take up too much room. *Besides,* he had said, *it would be simple and inexpensive to barter for a new one in Moab.* For the same reasons, one of their two water jars was also to be left behind. So both were

236

now tucked away in a corner of what had been her kitchen, and before the sun had barely risen, Naomi had baked enough bread for several days. The empty grain jars had been left in their storeroom, next to the stone-lined pit that was sunk into the ground there. Normally it would have held the grain for planting the following year, but it too was empty. Their rest of their life in Bethlehem was piled onto a cart with what remained of their grain. What couldn't be fitted on the cart was strapped onto a second donkey, now waiting outside in the narrow street which was barely wider than the cart.

Mahlon and Kilion—now twelve and nine—were chattering excitedly and waving sticks around as Naomi finally left the house. She pulled the door of the courtyard shut behind her. There was no need for a lock, even if they'd had the means to buy one. There was nothing left to steal, and everyone in Bethlehem knew it was their house. It would still be there, waiting empty for them, when they finally returned. *Whenever that was.*

'Boys!' They immediately stopped what they were doing and looked at their father. 'Watch what you're doing with those sticks. They're for herding the goats, not swords!' He turned to Naomi. 'You lead the second donkey. I'll take the cart.' And with that, he took the first step of their journey to Moab.

Naomi was glad that she had already said her farewells. She couldn't face seeing Haggith or Rizpah again, and kept her eyes forward as they passed the open door of her neighbour's courtyard. It would only upset her to see Haggith or her children again. Unlike her, Mahlon and Kilion seemed to care little about leaving their friends behind, with the excitement of all that lay ahead and with their sicknesses finally thrown off. The furthest they had been before was Shiloh, and that was less than a day's journey. Now they were travelling to Moab. To them it was a great adventure. But to Naomi, it was abandoning her home.

They travelled north to Jebus, then descended from the hill country as they travelled north-east on the road to the ruins of Jericho. Everything was dry. As they approached the piles of rocks and stones that had once been a city but was now simply the haunt of jackals and owls, the boys became quiet. For a few moments they all stood in silence and in awe, remembering Jericho's downfall at the hand of Yahweh. *But where was the God of Joshua now?* Naomi had no answer.

Their pause was only a brief one, and soon they were heading east towards the Jordan.

'There it is,' said Elimelech after a little while, pointing ahead of them. Naomi lifted her eyes and glimpsed sunlight glinting on water between trees in the distance. The line of green running from north to south was the first fertile land they had seen in some time.

'How are we going to cross the river?' asked Mahlon.

'There are fords just beyond the trees,' replied Elimelech, 'and there has been little rain in the north. It will not be deep. The King's Highway is not too far beyond the Jordan—maybe a day's journey. When we meet it, we will turn south. That will take us through the territory of Gad and Reuben, and then on into Moab. We will keep travelling south until we find somewhere good to live.'

But when Naomi's feet stood in the water, she was not thinking of the future. *Their people had crossed the Jordan more than fifty years earlier, but then they had been entering the Promised Land, not leaving it. Maybe Elimelech was right. Maybe this was best for them. After all, it seemed that Yahweh was no longer blessing their land.* But as she began crossing, she still had to silence the nagging doubt that maybe in leaving Canaan they were stepping outside the purposes of Yahweh.

Notes

1. *It is not clear what caused the famine mentioned in Ruth 1:1. Annual rains in Palestine are not assured, and so times of drought (leading to famine) were not uncommon in ancient times (e.g. Genesis 12:10; 26:1; 42:5). Foreign raiders plundering grain stores could also have brought on famine. It is likely, however, that readers familiar with the terms of God's covenant with Israel would see such blights on the land as the fulfilment of, for example, the curses of Leviticus 26:19-20,26 and Deuteronomy 28:22-25, and the result of*

disobedience to the covenant. This story has chosen to place the famine in the period of apostasy mentioned in Judges 3:7-8.

2. Baal (also called Hadad) was the most important of the Canaanite deities, and had a number of local variations. Ashtoreth (also rendered Astarte—from the Septuagint—in some Bible translations) seems to be the consort of Baal (see, for example, Judges 2:13). The term Asherah is used both for El's consort and for the seemingly wooden pole or image to represent her (the plural being rendered Asherahs or Asherim in different translations), though she is also linked with Baal (Judges 3:7). Some scholars believe that in popular religion, Asherah came to be seen by some as Yahweh's consort. There is much scholarly debate on the subject. (See, for example, the article 'Asherah and the Asherim: Goddess or Cult Symbol?' on www.biblicalarchaeology.org.)

3. There seems to be some ambiguity regarding the use of high places in the period prior to the temple. Whilst Moses issued clear instructions to demolish Canaanite high places (see, for example, Numbers 33:51-52), it seems that either existing high places or possibly new ones were used at times as local religious centres for the worship of Yahweh. See, for example, the occasion of Samuel doing this in 1 Samuel 9:11-14, and 1 Kings 3:2 ('The people, however, were still sacrificing at the high places, because a temple had not yet been built for the Name of the LORD'). So before the temple in Jerusalem, it seems to have been acceptable for the people to sacrifice at these local sanctuaries, of which there seem to have been quite a number.

4. Scripture is silent on Elimelech's decision to leave Canaan (Ruth 1:1-2), but the fact that Yahweh is not mentioned may point to this being an ungodly decision, especially given its consequences in Moab.

5. There is no indication of the ages of Mahlon and Kilion when the family leave Bethlehem. However, given they were not yet married but were both wed within ten years, it is probable that they were children approaching (or not too far from) adolescence when they left.

6. Daniel I. Block, in his commentary on Ruth, 'The King is Coming', suggests that the names of Mahlon and Kilion might both be linked with words for sickness and frailty, and 'nicknames' to prepare the readers for what follows, rather than their given names at birth. However, here those connotations are simply used to suggest weaknesses in both boys.

7. *Leviticus 11:35 speaks about smashing a clay oven that has become unclean. This seems to imply that they were easily replaced, hence the decision in the story to leave it behind. The story of the Gibeonite deception (in Joshua 9:1-13) also implies that bread for a number of days could be taken on journeys, obviously becoming increasingly stale the longer the journey continued.*

3

Naomi was left without her two sons and her husband. (Ruth 1:5)

Naomi stared through reddened eyes at the small pile of stones that covered the newly dug grave. It felt as if she had wept every single tear stored within her, leaving her as empty and dry as a discarded almond shell. She had buried Elimelech first, and then Kilion. Finally, the death of her firstborn had stolen her last and most precious possession. *We leave and live or stay and die, Elimelech had said. But he had been wrong, so wrong. Death was the crop they had reaped in Moab—and it had been Yahweh who had sent her that harvest. All had come from His hand.*

She suddenly became aware of another hand, one resting lightly upon her shoulder.

'Mother—you must come and eat. We have made leek and barley soup.' The gentle voice was that of Ruth, the wife of Mahlon until the previous day and now his widow.

'I'm not hungry.'

Another voice joined Ruth's. 'But you have not eaten for so many days,' said Orpah, Kilion's widow. 'You are already weak. Please come and eat.'

A sigh from the depths of her being made Naomi's whole body shudder. *She could not stand there forever. Continuing to grieve at a son's grave was a luxury only the wealthy could afford. It would not provide for three mouths.* She turned to face her daughters-in-law. She gave an almost imperceptible nod of acquiescence. *She would eat, if only for them.* 'I will take a little.'

Long and lingering sicknesses and then one death after another had slowly stripped her small family of their means of support and of most of their supplies, the latter dwindling before her eyes over the years. As Naomi lay awake on her mat that night, in the small mudbrick house that Elimelech and her sons had built for them in the land of Moab, the future loomed large, like some nameless beast, waiting to devour her. *What future did she have now, with neither a husband nor sons to support her? She had no place, no purpose any more.* The only future she could see was a lonely one. *After all, what reason was there for either Ruth or Orpah to stay with her? She had nothing to offer them now. At least if they returned to their families, they would both have what she could not have—a chance of marrying again. Both were young.*

Naomi sighed wearily and turned onto her other side, sleep continuing to elude her. *How would she live? Their flock that had fed on the rich pasturelands of Moab had dwindled to one goat, whose recently born kid had been bartered for oil. The goat would at least provide them with milk for some months. They only had a small vegetable plot and the jar of grain was half empty. Moab was not as kind to widows as Israel, but Yahweh had turned His hand against His people and the land—as He had done now to her. She was trapped between a pit and a famished bear.*

Sleep eventually overtook her, but her dreams were of being mired in a deep muddy pit from which there was no escape.

A week after she had buried Mahlon, Naomi ventured to the well. It was a short distance from the unwalled Moabite settlement of which their humble dwelling was a part. Despite the sunshine, the warmth of the spring day brought her no joy, and her eyes were mainly on the dirt beneath her sandalled feet. But suddenly her gaze was drawn upwards by the voices of men. The women were not the only ones at the well. A group of travelling merchants were laying out their wares, clearly keen to draw the interest of the women who might then return with their husbands to barter for whatever was being offered. Naomi left her jar at the well and wandered over to the colourful material spread out on the ground for displaying their goods. She had neither the inclination nor the means to buy anything—only the desire not to stand out by being left alone at the well.

She mingled with the excited throng, her eyes wandering idly and unfocused over the bronze dishes, dyes and spices. She didn't even have the strength to feign interest. The comments and questions around her washed over her like a river over rocks.

'…and do you have blue?'

'How much for the cinnamon?'

'…they were offering it at half the price!'

But amongst the hubbub, her ears were suddenly drawn like a moth to a flame.

'…from Shechem, Bethel and Jebus.'

She looked up sharply, her eyes searching for the speaker.

'We joined the King's Highway after crossing the Jordan,' said a man with a blue and green striped scarf wrapped around his head. 'We're travelling south through Moab before we return to Damascus.'

Suddenly there was only one question in Naomi's mind. She waited until most of the women had drifted away, and then approached the man with the blue and green scarf. He looked up.

'What is it you seek? What do wish to know?' His eyes scanned what was left on the large square of orange cloth at his feet.

The words tumbled awkwardly out of Naomi's mouth. 'No. No, thank you. Your wares do not interest me. What I mean is, I do not wish for anything today, though I can see your bowls are well-made.' A small smile played on his lips, seemingly amused by her flustered attempts to say what she wanted.

'How may I help you then?'

Naomi drew in a breath to steady herself. She let it out slowly. 'I heard you speak of Jebus. I used to live near there, in a place called Bethlehem.'

'I know it…'

'I…I wondered how my people fare? Is the land still troubled by famine?'

He seemed slightly perplexed and shook his slowly. 'We traded well there. There was no shortage of food.' He thought for a moment and then shrugged his shoulders, smiling. 'They seemed well-fed, and we had no trouble buying bread and meat for our journey from them.'

'When we left, the land was also troubled by raiding parties from Aram.'

'All was peaceful when we passed through.' He paused for a moment, as if in thought. 'I heard them speak of a man, though—a man named Othniel. He seems to be a leader of the people of Israel now.'

The name did not mean much to Naomi, but his other words meant everything. She thanked him and wandered back to the well. Even before her jar was filled, she knew what she must do. *Ten years before, she and Elimelech had sought to escape hardship by travelling to Moab. Now, to escape destitution, she must return. If Yahweh was blessing His people again, then it was better to be with them than in the land of Moab.* But even with that thought, there was another that was bitter as wormwood. *Yahweh had, however, turned His hand against her.*

At the end of their meagre evening meal of bread dipped in a thin lentil stew, Naomi took in her second deep breath of the day. She stared at the empty bowl between them. 'I have made a decision, my daughters.' She sensed them become still and raised her eyes. 'It is time for me to leave Moab and return to my own people. I have nothing here now and there is bread once more in Bethlehem.'

Ruth and Orpah looked at each other and then back at Naomi. 'We had wondered if you would,' said Ruth quietly.

'And we will come with you,' added Orpah. 'We will not leave you.'

Naomi smiled at them, but her heart was heavy. 'You are both kind.'

'You are our mother now,' said Ruth, 'and we love you and will take care of you.'

Orpah nodded. 'We will. When are we to leave?'

Naomi glanced around the almost-bare room. 'There is little for us to pack, and tomorrow is as good a day as any that will follow. We will leave when we have milked the goat and baked enough bread for the journey.' She smiled at them again. 'At least we will not have to be burdened by the oven. I left one behind in Bethlehem.'

Naomi watched them as they disappeared outside to wash the dish and grind flour from the little grain that was left, already discussing who would carry what on the journey. She had no intention, however, of letting them go with her, but neither could she face the journey north through Moab alone. *She would tell them to return to their homes when they reached the Arnon gorge, beyond which lay the land of the tribe of Reuben. The future of her daughters-in-law—if they were to have one—lay in Moab.* Of that she was sure.

They travelled northwards the following morning mostly in silence, each with their own thoughts. Naomi's only burden, apart from a waterskin, was the mat on which she slept, now rolled up with her cloak and slung on her back. She also led the goat on a tether. Both Ruth and Orpah also carried their mats, but each had a bag over a shoulder, so that between them they carried the millstones, the few small utensils and cups from the kitchen, a couple of small clay lamps, and a small bronze cooking pot which Naomi had brought with her from Bethlehem. The journey across the rolling plateau of Moab was not an arduous one. It lay above and to the east of the Salt Sea, and by the time the sun had set, they had made a simple camp just to the south of the Arnon River.

Before she allowed sleep to take her, Naomi silently ran through the words that she had prepared and which she would finally have to give voice to the following morning. She had lost count of the number of times she had rehearsed them in her mind since setting out, but wondered if, when the time came, she would be able to say them without tears choking her words. Already she could feel her throat tightening at the thought of bidding farewell to those who had been her only source of comfort and love in recent days. Both young women were dearer to her than she could say. They had been devoted to her since wedding Mahlon and Kilion. She called them daughters, for that was truly what they had become to her. *But Bethlehem would be no place for them. They were Moabites—they would find no husbands there. No, their hope of a better life and of security lay in returning to their own mothers. It was only there that they had a chance of finding another marriage and a home and family of their own. If they parted first thing in the morning, they could be back in their father's house by nightfall.* Tears welled up in her eyes. In the darkness, she could afford to let them silently spill out. *Tomorrow would be different. She would need to be strong to send them away.*

The following day dawned clear, with the exception of a few small fair-weather clouds dotting the sky like scattered sheep. After a simple meal of bread and fresh milk from the goat, they packed up their mats, and headed for the edge of the gorge, where the King's Highway would take them down to the Arnon river, and then up the other side into the lands of Reuben. As they drew near to the point where the track began to descend, Naomi slowed her pace and stopped, looking north.

'Why are we stopping, Mother? Are you feeling unwell?'

'No, Ruth.' She turned back to face them. 'We are stopping because this is where we must part.' They stared at her, either not understanding her or not wanting to. Naomi sighed deeply. 'You must go back, each of you, to your mother's home. And may Yahweh show you His kindness, just as you have shown kindness to Mahlon and Kilion and to me. May Yahweh grant both of you another husband, and a home where you can lay your head and find rest.' Her voice finally broke as she spoke the last few words. She had said what she needed to say, but could speak no more. She kissed them both as tears coursed down her cheeks. Both Ruth and Orpah started weeping.

'No, Mother, please don't send us away,' said Ruth through her anguish, as both young women wrapped their arms around Naomi.

'We will go back with you,' sobbed Orpah. 'Back with you to your people.'

It was breaking Naomi's heart. She slowly and agonisingly untangled herself from their embraces, then pulled back, holding them at arm's length. She had, for the moment, control of her voice once more. 'No, my daughters,' she began softly. 'You must return to your homes.' Ruth made to speak again, but Naomi quickly continued. 'What reason is there for you to come with me? Am I going to have any more sons who could become your husbands?' She shook her head, and went on. 'I am too old to have another husband. And even if I married this very night and then gave birth to sons, would you wait and remain unmarried until they grew up? No, my daughters. So return home. It is better for you that way, for Yahweh's hand has turned against me! The path I have to walk is one of bitterness. So return home and be at peace.'

Both young women began weeping again, and Naomi allowed them to embrace her once more. They held her until their tears eventually subsided. Orpah kissed her, and then stepped back, nodding her reluctant agreement. She took off the bag from her shoulder and handed it to Naomi. 'Farewell, Mother. And may your God watch over you.'

Naomi still had in her other hand the thin rope to which the goat was attached. It was tugging at a small bush nearby, tearing off leaves and oblivious of the lives being torn apart at the other end of the tether. Naomi glanced at the goat and then back at Orpah. 'You should not return home empty-handed,' and she held out the rope to her. Orpah hesitated. 'Take it. I will not have your family thinking I have left you with nothing.' *She would give Ruth the bronze pot.*

Orpah stepped forward and took the tether. 'Thank you, Mother.' She then looked at Ruth, clearly waiting for her to join her.

Ruth quickly went over to Orpah, kissing and embracing her. But as Naomi watched, Ruth whispered in her sister-in-law's ear. They stood apart for a moment, Orpah looking questioningly at Ruth, then back at Naomi and then Ruth again. She nodded, turned southwards and began her journey home.

Ruth returned to Naomi. 'I am going with you—I will live with you in Bethlehem.'

Naomi sighed. It was almost too much to have to repeat it all. 'Look,' she began wearily, 'your sister-in-law is going back to her people and her gods. Go back with her.'

Ruth shook her head. 'No, don't urge me to leave you or to turn back from you.' She looked straight at her mother-in-law. 'Where you go I will go, and where you stay I will stay. Your people will be my people and your God my God. Where you die I will die, and there I will be buried.' There was no doubting the determination in her voice. She then raised the edge of her hand to her throat and made a quick motion, as if she was an animal being slaughtered. 'May Yahweh do this to me, and worse, if anything but death parts me from you.'

She had made an oath in the name of Yahweh. Naomi's face finally softened, and tears welled up in her eyes once more—but this time not from the pain of parting. The sweetness of Ruth's kindness and love had pierced the bitterness of her soul. She knew now her daughter-in-law would not leave her, whatever her protests, but she had to remind her one last time what lay ahead. 'You know I have nothing left to provide for you,' she began. 'All I have is gone.'

Ruth laid her hand very gently on Naomi's arm. 'But that is why I *will not* leave you. You lost Elimelech and then your two sons. I could not let you lose both your daughters too.'

The tears spilled over. Naomi had no defence against her daughter's love. Ruth wrapped her arms around her, and held Naomi whilst she sobbed.

Eventually Naomi's sobbing subsided, and she shuddered slightly as a deep sigh escaped from her. Ruth released her and Naomi kissed her on the forehead and then stepped back. 'We still have the rest of our journey ahead of us.'

Ruth smiled. 'Then let us begin! Your future is my future.'

Together they turned north and followed the snaking path down into the gorge. After fording the Arnon, they climbed back up to plateau on the other side, and continued along the King's Highway towards the town of Dibon. After they had walked some time in silence, Naomi suddenly said, 'When you spoke after Orpah left us, you said that Yahweh would be your God...' She left the comment hanging, inviting Ruth to say more.

'I have no desire to honour Chemosh anymore, and I have vowed never to return to Moab.' She paused. 'Ever since I have known you, I have heard the stories of your God. And even in Moab, it is said that Yahweh parted the waters and led the sons of Israel through them and out of Egypt, and we know of what He did at Jericho. When you speak of Yahweh, Mother, you speak of a God who cares and provides and acts for the good of His people.'

'And the same is not said of Chemosh...' Naomi's words were not a question. The mere thought of the Moabite god was detestable.

'How could that ever be said of a god whose favour is sought by offering children as burnt offerings on his altars?' Ruth fell silent, shaking her head, as if in disbelief. 'I will gladly never speak his name again,' she murmured eventually. She suddenly turned to Naomi. 'But will Yahweh welcome me? I am not one of His people, after all.'

It was a question that had never occurred to Naomi, and she had had no reason to consider its answer before. She thought for a moment. *What could she say? The Moabites had, after all, opposed Israel after they had left Egypt and as they were on the way to Canaan.* She pondered in silence, the only sound being their sandals on the dry earth. Then suddenly it was as if a ray of light had illumined her mind. 'But Yahweh is not like the other gods. He is the Creator of the heavens and the earth. He is not only the God of the people of Israel. He rules over every nation. He is God over Moab, whether they bow before Him or not.'

'So I can say that He is my God now?'

Naomi smiled at her. 'I can only tell you what I know.' But the smile faded as she faced forward again. *The Creator had made her life bitter.* There was another thought that also troubled her. *How would Ruth be treated once they reached Bethlehem? Would the people shun her?* She could only find comfort in knowing that some of the same blood ran in their two peoples. *The story was hard to forget.*

'Do you remember Mahlon telling a tale about one of our fathers called Abraham?'

Ruth thought for a moment. 'Did Yahweh give him a son in his old age?'

'When he was a hundred, that's right.'

'I cannot remember the name of his wife, though...'

'Sarah. But Abraham also had a nephew whose name was Lot. And do you know the name of one of his sons?' Naomi thought it wise to leave unsaid the unsavoury detail of how Lot's two sons were conceived—by his daughters getting him drunk and then lying with him.

Ruth peered round at Naomi, clearly curious. 'Should I know his name?'

Naomi smiled again. 'It is the name of your forefather, Moab.'

'I did not know that! So our people are related?'

'Yes they are.' But that was not the whole story, and Canaan was drawing closer with every step. *She must at least prepare Ruth for what might lay ahead.* 'The people of my town will see that I treat you as my daughter.' She paused to consider her words. 'But I cannot say whether all will welcome you as they would a daughter of Israel, though I would wish it.' After another pause she added, 'I would also wish to welcome you into a house with some comforts. But gleaners cannot choose their grain.'

'You mean that the unfortunate must take what they can?'

'I do.' They fell silent again. Within three days they would be across the Jordan, and there were only two thoughts in which Naomi found comfort. *It was the time of the barley harvest, and Moses had said that foreigners were to be permitted to glean in the fields of Israel.*

Notes

1. *There is no indication of how Naomi and the family lived in Moab (e.g. in tents or a house, growing crops or farming animals, living in a town or a city or elsewhere), and there seemed little purpose in engaging in speculation. The ESV Bible Atlas does comment, however: 'A sojourner was one who was an alien in a foreign land, who worked in that country but had few of the rights and privileges of a citizen. He did not own his own land but was generally in the service of a native master and protector.' Another source believes that Moabites and Israelites could probably understand each other's languages (see www.bibleodyssey.org/en/places/main-articles/ moab). It is also not clear how living 'for a while' in Moab (Ruth 1:1) became ten years.*

2. *Although there are no comments on the deaths of Elimelech, Mahlon and Kilion in Scripture, it may be that the writer views their deaths as another consequence of the spiritual malaise of Israel. The cause of their deaths*

is not specified, though 'long and lingering sicknesses' has been suggested here (and is maybe implied by their names) to help explain how the family became destitute in Moab, as the book of Ruth implies that Naomi returned in poverty.

3. There is no indication in Scripture of the ages of Ruth and Orpah, although both must have still been young. The implication of Ruth 1:3-4 is that Mahlon and Kilion did not marry until after their father's death. It may then be reasonable to assume they had been married anywhere between roughly three to eight years before the deaths of the sons, and therefore Ruth and Orpah may have been late teens or early twenties, given the generally early ages at which girls would have been married.

4. As previously stated, there is nothing definite to determine where the story of Ruth occurs within the period of the Judges. However, given that Naomi stays ten years in Moab, and there is a period of eight years of oppression before God sends Othniel—the first judge—to save Israel (after which it presumably takes some time for the land to recover), he seems a particularly suitable Judge to choose, particularly if Boaz is the son of Rahab and the story therefore takes place sooner rather than later in this period.

5. Apparently Naomi doesn't consider at this point that there is the possibility of either of her daughters-in-law remarrying within Israel through the legal mechanism that is used in Ruth 4:5.

6. Scripture gives no indication of where, on the journey back to Bethlehem, the exchange in Ruth 1:8-16 occurs. Although possible places may have been at the Jordan, or the point at which they would have left the King's Highway to turn west towards the river, it seems less likely that Naomi would take her daughters-in-law 2-3 days journey beyond Moab, only to send them back again. The point chosen, the Arnon gorge, marked the border between Moab and the territory held by the tribe of Reuben.

7. The words in Ruth 1:17 may imply that Ruth made a gesture to, in some way, indicate her own death. One commentator has suggested it might have involved touching her throat, and this has been woven into the story.

4

When they arrived in Bethlehem, the whole town was stirred because of them, and the women exclaimed, 'Can this be Naomi?' (Ruth 1:19)

'There it is.' Naomi pointed just to the left of the track they were following south. After crossing the plain of the Jordan, they had steadily climbed westwards into the hill country of Judah, before turning south near Jebus. Bethlehem was finally visible on the familiar ridge.

Ruth glanced towards the western sky. The sun had already lost some of its heat, and was halfway between its zenith and the horizon. 'We will easily reach it before sunset.'

'We will indeed.' Naomi set her face forward, though could tell from the corner of her eye that Ruth was watching her. She was relieved, however, when her daughter-in-law held her peace and turned her attention to the uneven track instead. The nearer Bethlehem loomed, the greater Naomi's disquiet. *How could she face those who had known her when she'd left? Then, she'd had a husband and sons, animals and grain. Now what did she have? Nothing but the shame of having suffered the harshness of Yahweh's hand. She had been a wife and a mother, with a husband who was respected in the gate. Now what was she? A destitute widow...* The thoughts only served to heighten Naomi's mortification. If she could have, she would have crept into Bethlehem under the cover of darkness, hidden from curious or prying eyes. But the gates were shut when the shadows of evening fell, and there was no way in, save in daylight. *Besides, she couldn't avoid familiar faces forever.*

'How many live there?'

Ruth's question wrested Naomi's mind away from her troubles, if only fleetingly. 'With those who live on land around the town, maybe several hundred? Beyond that I cannot say, and I do not know how it has changed since I left. Much can happen in ten years.' *She knew that only too well.* Both women fell silent once more, allowing the sounds around them to drift in on their ears: the occasional buzz of an insect, distant voices of those labouring on the land, and their own dull footfall on the dirt track.

As Bethlehem and its walls grew closer, sizeable tracts of the countryside began to be covered in the yellow-white of ripe barley. Other patches were greener where the wheat, which would be harvested later, had yet to ripen. 'These are the fields belonging to the town,' explained Naomi.

'Who owns them?'

'Different families. There are large stones that mark the boundaries between the land of one family and that of another, and people know their own field and those of their neighbours.'

Ruth turned her gaze back to her mother-in-law. 'And you have land here too?'

Naomi nodded. 'Yes. It is on the other side of the town, but I doubt that much grows there now except weeds. I will visit it soon.'

'Won't others have taken the land?'

'Our land is sacred, given by God to be shared fairly among the people and kept within families. Even if I decide to sell Elimelech's land, it is not to go beyond our clan to a stranger.' Naomi studied Ruth's expression, and—despite her heavy heart—managed a smile. 'You marvel at our laws?'

Ruth returned the smile. 'It is not like Moab. You have laws that are wise and fair.'

'That is because our God is wise and fair.' But even as she spoke of Yahweh, her heart sank. *That Yahweh was wise and fair was not something she doubted, but neither was the conviction that His hand was against her.* Naomi tore her thoughts away from heaven and brought them back to earth. One or two makeshift shelters were visible above the tops of the ripe grain. She pointed towards them. 'Look—some have started harvesting already.' They soon drew alongside some of the fields. Naomi stopped and fingered one of the heads of barley that was bowed down under its own weight. The head was packed with hard grain amongst the familiar long awns of the barley, which stuck out from the head like a spikey beard. 'The crop will be good.' She surveyed the land again. 'Within a day or two, the fields will be full of reapers. Any grain that is missed should be left for those in need among the people.'

'Then let me go and find it!'

Naomi resumed her walk and Ruth followed her lead. 'We can both go. There could not have been a better time for us to return. We will, at least, be able to find some food for our bellies. The laws of Yahweh say that all who are poor may glean, both of what is dropped or missed and of what is left at the edge of the field.'

'Even Moabites?'

'Even Moabites.'

'And those who own the fields are glad to follow such a law?' asked Ruth, clearly curious.

Naomi gave a little shrug. 'I do not say that, but the right to glean is not meant to rest on the whim of men. There may be some, though, who make it more difficult for the unfortunate.' It wasn't unheard of for reapers to beat or take advantage of those who gleaned, and it wasn't hard to make them feel unwelcome. Naomi was not about to voice those concerns, however. *Not at that moment, anyway.* She pointed in another direction. 'And there is the town's threshing floor…'

It wasn't long before both the town's gates and well came into view. Naomi's mouth became dry. She glanced over at the well. Two women were there, but there would soon be more. She didn't immediately recognise them, but as soon as they looked in her direction, she dropped both her gaze and her head, allowing her shawl to swing forward, covering the sides of face. *She was not yet ready to greet them.*

Ruth rearranged the bags she was carrying and took Naomi's arm in hers. 'It is alright, Mother,' she whispered. 'I am here.'

Her daughter-in-law knew her too well. For a brief moment, Naomi wondered what it would have been like had Ruth not stayed with her, and as they approached the opening in the walls, she had never been more grateful for her company.

It was impossible to keep her gaze completely on the ground as they walked through the hubbub of activity in the gate. The elderly sat on benches lining the walls, as they had always done, discussing the day's news. A merchant had spread out various wares on some green cloth on the ground, whilst others conducted business. Naomi caught sight of townsfolk staring at her. Even after she hastily looked away, she was still aware of their gaze. It did not take long for the whispering to start, as curiosity became recognition in the eyes of those who saw her. More than once she caught her name being spoken in a hushed and questioning tone.

The short walk from the gate to her house felt like a dream to Naomi—the sort of dream in which escape is hindered by having to wade through a thick mire. Her heart was thumping by the time she reached the door that she had closed ten years earlier. She lifted the latch and pushed the door open. She paused. The empty courtyard before her felt like a distant memory, another life. 'Here we are.' She stepped inside.

Naomi put down her mat and bag. Her heart sank, seeing the changes wrought by her ten-year absence. The courtyard was now littered with leaves and twigs from ten autumns, and grass and weeds had taken root seemingly everywhere. But the most dismal sight was the flat roofs around the courtyard. With the lack of the usual repairs after winter rains, most of the flattened and dried mud and brushwood had collapsed onto the ground beneath, forming small mounds in which seeds, borne on the wind or by birds, had sprouted. Largely-bare timbers were left where the roofs had been. Naomi shook her head slowly. She then turned and watched as Ruth's eyes, full of curiosity, took in everything.

'It will be a good house when we have repaired it.'

'But I have nothing to fill it,' sighed Naomi. *It was devoid of the life that had completed it before. But it would have felt far emptier without Ruth.*

'We will still make it our home.' Ruth added her bags and mat to the tiny pile. 'I shall go and fetch some water.'

'You should rest from the journey first.'

'It is better that I go to the well whilst I am still on my feet,' replied Ruth with a smile. She picked her way through the remnants of the roof, to where the water jar was still visible in the corner of what had been the kitchen. She lifted the jar, peered into it and grimaced. As she tipped it up, dirt, leaves and what appeared to be the shrivelled body of a small rat tumbled out from it. 'I will wash it out first.' She lifted the jar to her shoulder before retracing her steps. 'I will not be long.'

Naomi smiled wearily. 'Thank you.' As Ruth disappeared out of the door, Naomi turned back to the small pile of belongings. *It was all they had.* She sighed once again, and bent over to begin unpacking. *She would easily be finished before Ruth returned.* However, she'd barely opened her bag when the sounds of hurrying feet that stopped by her door told her she had company. She straightened up and turned round. Recognition took only a moment. Both women's faces were worn in a way they had not been before, and the older woman's hair showed signs of grey. But Haggith and Rizpah were unmistakable.

They both stared at her, breathing heavily. 'Naomi, is it really you?' said Haggith, in not much more than a whisper.

Naomi was suddenly conscious that grief had probably aged her far more than her friends.

'Helah was at my door,' added Rizpah, 'telling me she thought she'd seen you passing through the gate—and it *is* you Naomi!'

Her name on Hebrew lips suddenly seemed utterly wrong. It meant *pleasant. The word was a mockery of what her life had become. Her life was bitter—and there was a word for that.* Before they could embrace her, she held up her hand. 'Don't call me Naomi. No, call me Mara instead, because the Almighty has made my life very bitter. I went away full—' She gestured around the bare courtyard. '—but Yahweh has brought me back empty. Why call me Naomi, when Yahweh has turned against me and brought misfortune upon me?'

The look of wonder on Haggith's face ebbed away. She spoke gently. 'Elimelech.?'

Naomi shook her head. 'He lies in a grave in Moab, as do both my sons.'

An anguished *No!* slipped from Rizpah's lips, whilst Haggith wailed softly. Both women stepped forward and embraced her.

Naomi knew it was not so much an embrace of welcome as of pity, her emptiness mirrored by that of the courtyard. Even as they were still holding her, she said quietly. 'Now you can understand why *Mara* is a better name...'

When they finally let go of her, both faces were wet with tears. Haggith looked at the small pile of belongings near their feet. 'Is that all you have?'

'It is all, apart from the Moabite daughter-in-law who has chosen to stay with me. She has gone to fetch water.'

'Was it her we passed in the street—the young woman with the green shawl?'

Naomi nodded. 'Yes, her name is Ruth.' She suddenly felt tired. She didn't want any more questions. *It was too painful.* 'I must prepare the house as best I can for her return.'

'We will help—' began Haggith.

'That is kind, but it will at least give me something to do.' *She had no family to care for, no mouths to feed.*

Her two friends glanced around and seemed to understand. 'We will leave you for now, then' said Rizpah. 'And you will need to rest after your journey.'

'Have you food with you?' asked Haggith.

'We have enough, thank you,' replied Naomi, unwilling to admit that it was only a handful of grain and bread that was now several days old. *Although if Ruth was able to collect some firewood, she could at least revive it slightly by dampening it and warming it in the oven.*

Both women embraced her once more, and departed with the promise that they would see her again the following day.

Naomi turned back to the bags and mats. *All that remained from the years in Moab, aside from the clothes on her back and a foreign daughter-in-law.* She sighed deeply, and picked up the mats, taking them into the room off the back of the courtyard that she had shared with Elimelech. She dared not linger there. As she re-emerged into the late afternoon sun, Ruth walked in through the doorway. She not only carried the water jar on her shoulder, steadied by her right hand, but was also holding a pottery jug against her. Naomi looked questioningly at her.

'Your neighbour pressed it into my hand as I passed—it is full of milk.'

Naomi managed a tired smile. 'Her name is Haggith.'

Before night fell, Naomi and Ruth sat together inside, with the door open for light, sharing warm—if somewhat stale—bread washed down with cups of fresh milk. Naomi pulled her shawl around her against the cool of the evening. Although the roof above them had holes in, it was at least partially intact, largely because there was a small upper room above it. With the warm, dry weather they would at least not be rained upon as they slept.

'I will use the last of the grain to make porridge tomorrow morning. It will sustain us as we glean.'

Ruth was silent for a moment, staring at the ground. 'I have been thinking, Mother...' She looked up. 'Let me go by myself to glean tomorrow. I am a stranger here, so it will be no hardship for me.'

It was Naomi's turn to lower her eyes to the woven mats on which they were sitting. 'What you mean,' she said quietly, 'is that you would not feel the same shame as me...'

Ruth laid her hand gently on Naomi's arm. 'You have no reason to feel shame.'

'But I would feel it nevertheless.'

'So it is better that you do not feel it at all!'

Naomi was touched by her earnestness, born of her compassion and care. She raised her eyes—but Ruth had not finished.

'If I work hard, I could glean enough to sustain us both. Let me go alone tomorrow, Mother! If Yahweh blesses me, there may be no need for the two of us to labour. Besides, the house needs cleaning and you wanted to visit your field—why not do that tomorrow instead?'

Naomi let out a long and lingering breath. *She would not miss the back-breaking work, and Ruth was a score and five years younger. Her body would be far more able to bend down and pick up stalks of grain than hers.* She smiled. 'So be it—go ahead, my daughter.' Ruth returned her smile. 'But you must be careful to glean only where the harvesters have finished, and do not stray too close to them. Look for a field where there are a good number of reapers.'

'The more reapers, the more hands there are to drop grain!' laughed Ruth.

Naomi nodded and smiled again. 'That is the hope.' Her smiled faded. 'If any treat you harshly, find another field.'

'I will glean only behind those in whose eyes I find favour.'

Naomi paused as Ruth finished her cup of milk. Twilight was upon them, and with no oil for the lamps, they found themselves sitting in near darkness. *Soon there would be little point in doing anything other than sleeping. Besides, she was tired from their long journey.*

'You may find the customs of this land different...'

Ruth laid her hand on Naomi's arm once more. 'Do not be anxious, Mother.'

Naomi laid her own hand over Ruth's, and lightly tapped it. 'I cannot help it.' She could not find the words to express how precious Ruth had become, so she spoke of what lay ahead instead. 'The wheat harvest will follow the barley. If we are fortunate, there may be six or seven weeks of harvesting.' She didn't want to think about what might lie beyond that—especially if the hand of Yahweh was still against her.

Naomi put her hands on her hips and shook her head slowly. The miserable courtyard looked no better under a clear sky, still streaked with the pinks and oranges of a new day. She had slept only fitfully, despite her weariness. The uncertainty of their futures hadn't left her as she had lain down for the night. They had both risen at first light, and Ruth had departed shortly after sunrise. If she had been nervous about facing strangers in a foreign land, she had not shown it. Naomi had tried to mirror Ruth's confidence, but it was difficult not to be anxious.

The sounds of Bethlehem coming to life drifted in from outside: cheerful voices and footsteps from the street as men headed out to the fields; children laughing in a nearby house, whilst a baby's cry rose from another; the soft scraping of stone upon stone, as Haggith ground grain next door. Naomi tried to force her mind onto the day's tasks. *After a trip to the well, she would borrow a broom from Haggith when she* returned her jar, so she could start sweeping out the courtyard. If she could scavenge some large pottery shards, she could start removing the remains of the roof. She would pile them in what had been the pen for the goats and sheep. It occurred to her that, had she still owned a goat, it would have made short work of the grass and weeds in the house. She would then visit her field, and whilst she was out, she would collect firewood in the hope that they would have grain from which to bake bread that evening. Her day would be full.

With that thought, however, Naomi's mind flitted back to Ruth. Had she found a field in which to glean yet? If so, was she already labouring under eyes filled with reproach or resentment? What if every land-owner chased her away from their harvest? She fidgeted with the edge of her shawl. Worrying would not, however, get her own work done. She drew the shawl over her head, picked up the water jar, and drew in a deep breath. She could not avoid the stares and the whispering any longer.

Naomi's gaze swept across the hills and the fields surrounding her. She still had not caught sight of Ruth. Her eyes then returned to what lay in front of her. It did not need boundary stones to mark out Elimelech's field: it stood out. It was the only piece of uncultivated land and was little more than a patch of briers and thistles, tares and stinkweed. It also appeared to have become a wasteland for stones and rocks from adjoining fields. It could be grazing for a goat, but nothing else. To clear it, plough it and plant it—even if they had grain for that—would be beyond the skill and strength of two women. Naomi sighed. It felt as if sorrow and sighing were her constant companions. She raised her eyes to heaven and asked—not for the first time—what wrong she had done to deserve such misfortune. But, as on every previous occasion, heaven remained silent.

She then surveyed the tangled mess of weeds and stones once more. At least she did have a field—a field that might be sold to purchase goats and sheep. Maybe when the barley harvest was over, she would mention it in the gate. She could not imagine that any of Bethlehem's men would be doing much business until at least the first harvest was safely gathered and the grain threshed. Ruth crept into her mind again. She had said *that she would only glean behind those with whom she had found favour. Had Yahweh granted her that?* It was not the first time that day that Naomi had pondered the question.

Eventually she turned from the field, and began her journey back to the town, searching the ground for firewood as she went. She had tarried at the well that morning, as Rizpah and others had asked after her, and she had told them not only of her sorrows but of Ruth's faithfulness. In turn, the women had begun to impart to her what, in their eyes, was most noteworthy of ten years of Bethlehem's news. She learned of women who had given birth, families that had been joined through marriage, and those who were with them no more. She was told how Yahweh had raised up a leader from the tribe of Judah—a nephew of Caleb by the name of Othniel. He had delivered them all from the hand of the Arameans, when the people of Israel had finally turned back to their own God in their distress, abandoning the Canaanite gods that had not saved them and crying out to Yahweh instead. After eight years of oppression, the land was once more enjoying freedom from attack and affliction, and they were seeing the restoration of Yahweh's favour.

Much had changed whilst she had been in Moab, but of all she was told, Naomi's greatest sadness had been hearing that her old friend Merab had died—still childless.

By the time the light began to fade, Ruth had still not returned. Naomi started to pace backwards and forwards in the newly-swept courtyard. She barely noticed her growling stomach, and had little to distract her from her growing concern for her daughter-in-law. Her eyes darted to the sky. The light blue of late afternoon had been replaced by the colours of sunset. Naomi was just beginning to wonder if she should go to the gate and ask if any had seen her, when a sudden clattering immediately drew her attention to the courtyard door. Ruth staggered through the doorway, breathing heavily. She was clutching at her shoulder the corners of her shawl, which had become an enormous bundle slung on her back. Her cheeks were flushed and her arms and face had caught the sun. Naomi rushed forward to help, but the bundle was on the courtyard floor before she reached Ruth. Still too breathless to speak, Ruth let go of the crumpled cloth in her hands. As the corners fell silently to the ground, the shawl revealed its contents—grain spilling outwards to form a mound.

Naomi's gaze flitted between the two equally unexpected sights—the huge pile of barley and Ruth's face, lit up by the light in her eyes and an exultant smile. For a moment, Naomi was too stunned to speak. Eventually, she managed a single word as she stared at the grain. 'How…?'

'I will tell you as we eat,' said Ruth, still smiling broadly. 'You must be hungry!'

The hunger that had been banished by worry suddenly returned. 'I will get the millstones…'

Ruth laughed. 'There is no need, Mother—at least, not tonight.' She rummaged down through the pile of grain and pulled out a small cloth bundle. She unwrapped it, revealing pieces of bread together with roasted barley. She held it out for Naomi to see, 'Look! We already have a meal.'

Naomi stared at her, incredulous. She looked from the bread to the pile of grain and then back again. 'Where did you glean today? Blessed be the man who took notice of you!'

'Show me first where we should store the grain, and then you will hear all.'

When the barley was safely in one of the empty grain jars in what had been the storeroom, the two women sat together inside, sharing the simple meal which was now placed between them on the mat. Ruth began her story, as Naomi ate.

'When I left you this morning, I soon found a field with a good number of harvesters, including some girls who were tying the barley into sheaves. I looked for the man in charge and asked his permission to glean.'

'You did well to request that of him, even though it is your right.'

Ruth leaned forward slightly, and looked at her mother-in-law through her long, dark eyelashes. 'I also requested him to allow me to glean among the sheaves.'

Naomi put down the piece of bread that she'd had in her hand. 'You asked for the privilege of gleaning before they had finished?' she exclaimed, astounded.

'That way I would easily know if I had found favour in his eyes.'

'And did he grant it?'

'He did!'

'The Almighty be praised!'

'I thought that the field must belong to him. I kept working and was allowed to rest for a short while in the shelter when the heat was too much for me. But then later another man came out from Bethlehem to join us. He was older and I could tell he was a man of standing.' Ruth paused, her eyes shining once more. 'He greeted the workers in the name of Yahweh! I soon realised that *he* must be the owner of the field. I kept on working, but I could tell he was looking at me. He then started talking to the overseer, still glancing in my direction. He did not seem the sort of man who would send me away, but my heartbeat was like the flight of a bird when he approached me! He told me not to glean in any other field, but to stay with the women who worked for him, and follow the harvesters as they did. He said I would be safe with his men, and even said that I should stay with them until *all* his grain was harvested. He also told me that I could freely drink from the water jars his workers were using.'

Naomi had listened up till that point in stunned silence, the meal forgotten. *It was far more than she could have dared hope.* 'Favour upon favour! How did you answer the man?'

'I bowed down with my face to the ground, and asked why a foreigner should find such favour in his eyes.' She looked at her mother-in-law in wonder. 'He said that he had heard all about me. He knew that I had left my family in Moab and chosen to live with you here.'

Naomi shook her head and laughed. 'It does not take long for news to travel from Bethlehem's well to its gate! They say women chatter too much, but I swear the men are as bad...'

Ruth gave a little laugh but then became quiet. 'He spoke again to me,' she began softly. 'I remember every word. He said, *May*

Yahweh repay you for what you have done. May you be richly rewarded by Yahweh, the God of Israel, under whose wings you have come to take refuge.'

'Praise be to God,' breathed Naomi. She shook her head in wonder once more before meeting Ruth's eyes. 'And do you know the name of this godly man?'

'Boaz.'

'May he be blessed by Yahweh,' she exclaimed, 'who is still showing His kindness to both the living and the dead!'

Ruth stared at Naomi. 'Do you know him?'

'He is not only a man of great standing in Bethlehem, but he is also from the same clan as Elimelech! He is one of our closest kin—*and* a redeemer!'

'What do you mean, Mother?'

'Yahweh tells us that kinsmen must show care for those in their family who suffer hardship through death or poverty. Do you remember how I told you that if I sold Elimelech's land, it could not to go outside our clan?'

Ruth nodded. 'I remember.'

'Boaz, or another kinsman like him, would have to buy the field—or buy it back if it had gone to another. That is why I spoke of him as a redeemer.'

'So Yahweh led me to a man who would be more ready to show us favour—'

'And a man who had already heard of your kindness to his kin. That you have also bound yourself to the God of Israel and put your trust in Him will be no small matter to Boaz.'

Naomi could hardly take in what she had heard. For the first time in more months than she cared to remember, hope began to rise in her heart and she finally dared to believe that Yahweh might not have abandoned her completely. *Maybe His heart had been stirred by her misery, after all.*

Ruth interrupted Naomi's thoughts, pushing some bread towards her. 'Eat, Mother.'

'But where did this bread come from?'

'When the harvesters gathered to rest and to eat, Boaz invited me to join them. He offered me bread and wine vinegar to dip it in, and barley that had been roasted over a fire. I ate all I wanted but still had plenty left over, and this meal is what I had left.' She paused and her face lit up with another smile. 'But that is not all. As I gleaned after the meal, I saw some of the men deliberately pulling out stalks of barley from their bundles and leaving them for me. I think Boaz must have told them to do that.'

Naomi chuckled. 'Favour upon favour, and wonder upon wonder.' She then leaned over and took Ruth's hand, lifting it to her lips and kissing it before letting go. 'It was not only the favour of Boaz that multiplied your grain though. You clearly laboured hard and long, and you threshed the barley too.'

'I was glad you had pointed out the threshing floor on our way in to Bethlehem.' Ruth picked up a handful of the barley. 'I will do the same tomorrow.'

Naomi smiled. 'I will take some of what you have threshed and barter it for some oil in the morning. After all, we already have enough grain for maybe two weeks. And if you continue to glean as you have done this day, it will not be long until we can afford a goat.' She picked up the last of the parched grain. 'It will be good for you, my daughter, to stay with the women who work for Boaz. In someone else's field you might be harmed.' Then together, in the deepening twilight, they finished their simple meal.

As the barley harvest progressed and their store of grain—and, with it, their fortunes—improved, an idea began to form in Naomi's mind. Whilst their daily needs were being met, she was keenly aware that the harvest would soon be over, and that she and Ruth still lacked protection. Their future was far from certain. *If Ruth were to marry, however, that would change for them both.*

Laying at night under the broken roof which offered little shelter, her thoughts again and again drifted to the man who could spread his cover over them. *Boaz had neither wife nor heir. He was old enough to be Ruth's father, yet he would still have seed to sow within his loins, and Ruth was* young and most likely a fertile field. She hadn't conceived with Mahlon, but they had not been married long. And if Yahweh's favour continued...

She allowed herself to hope, and as she pondered, her idea became a plan.

Notes

1. It is not clear why Naomi did not also glean. It could have been embarrassment at her poverty (as assumed here), or some sort of physical condition, or being kept busy with the house. Gleaning would certainly be hard work.

2. Scripture does not describe in any detail the clothing worn by Israelites. Some depictions have been found among some ancient paintings and reliefs (mostly from Egypt and Assyria), although these are likely to be stylised. From Deuteronomy 22:5, it is clear that the clothes of men and women differed, possibly more in colour and decoration than in general design. It seems that some sort of knee-length or full-length tunic (with or without sleeves) was worn, with a belt or girdle, an over-garment or cloak, and sandals. In addition, there was likely to be a head-covering for a man, maybe like a Bedouin scarf from current times, or a turban. The woman's cloak may have been her head-covering, going from her forehead to the full length of her back, and this idea has been chosen here, and described using the word shawl. However, there seems no definite consensus on the finer details of clothing.

3. The beginning of the barley harvest was in mid- to late-April, as the rainy season finished. This was the first harvest and ended in May, when it blended into the wheat harvest, which would have finished in June, giving a total of around seven weeks of harvesting.

4. The role of the women in the harvest is unknown. They may have also been involved in the reaping, or may have tied the cut grain to make sheaves. It certainly seems the case that the urgency of harvesting demanded as many hands and as much effort as possible.

5. Ruth 2:15 seems to imply that gleaning among the sheaves was a special privilege, possibly because it was before the reapers had completely finished in an area.

5

One day Ruth's mother-in-law Naomi said to her, 'My daughter,
I must find a home for you, where you will be well provided for.'
(Ruth 3:1)

As the barley harvest drew to a close, and the men of Bethlehem
exchanged their sickles for threshing sledges and winnowing forks,
Naomi was busy. She let it be known in the gate that she was intending
to sell Elimelech's field, ensuring that Boaz was present when she
did. She bartered with one of the passing merchants, buying a small
vial of scented oil in return for grain. Then, when she learned that
Boaz had finished threshing his barley, she washed every garment
that Ruth wore. She lent her daughter-in-law her own shawl as the
clothes dried in the hot summer sun. *She would tell Ruth her plan soon,*
but she had one more task to perform first.

'I am going to the well for more water,' said Naomi, hoisting the
water jar onto her shoulder once again.

'There is nothing left to wash, Mother!' laughed Ruth.

'Do not be so sure, my daughter,' replied Naomi playfully.

'It is good to see you with a light heart.'

Naomi just smiled. 'I will be back shortly.' The full jars of barley
and her plan had both lifted her spirits in recent days. Sorrow and
sighing were no longer her constant companions, and as she entered
the street outside her house, she prayed silently to Yahweh as she
had done so many times in recent days. *Faithful God, who has poured*
kindness and blessing on this daughter of Israel, grant me success this day, I
pray.

When Naomi returned, Ruth was sitting in the shade in the
courtyard, the shawl still wrapped around her. 'The clothes are

almost dry, Mother. Then you can have your shawl again, and I can fetch the water rather than you!'

Naomi put down the water jar, and knelt by Ruth in the shade. She took her daughter-in-law's hands in her own. 'You have blessed me so richly, not only with food to eat but by your faithful love. Now my daughter, I must find a home for you, where *you* will be well provided for.'

'But I have a home here with you, Mother.'

'You deserve better, and with Yahweh's blessing, you will have it.' Ruth looked at her inquiringly, but held her peace. 'As you know, Boaz, with whose women you have worked, is our kin. Tonight he will be winnowing the barley on the threshing floor. So wash yourself in the fresh water—I have scented oil for you to use too. Then dress yourself and go down to the threshing-floor. Do not let him know you are there, however. When the winnowing is completed, he will feast there and celebrate the end of the barley harvest with his workers. After he has eaten and drunk his fill, he will stay overnight with the grain, guarding it with his men. Take note of where he lies down, and when all is still, go and uncover his feet and lie down there. When the cold wakes him, say this: *Spread your covering over your maidservant, for you are a redeemer.* He will know what to do when you say that.'

Ruth was silent for a moment, and then said hesitantly, 'Does that mean…?' Her voice trailed off.

Naomi smiled tenderly. 'Yes, my daughter. It means that you are asking him to protect you, not by being a father, though he is old enough to be that, but by marrying you.'

'But will he?'

The fretful note in Ruth's voice touched Naomi's heart, and instead of answering the question, she asked another, although she already knew the answer. 'You like him?'

Ruth flushed and lowered her eyes. 'I know he is many years my elder, but there is no finer man in Bethlehem. Any woman would be honoured and richly blessed if Boaz took her to be his own.'

Naomi lifted Ruth's chin gently with the tips of her fingers and looked into her eyes. 'He has lost a wife and you have lost a husband. He is a good man and will know how well you are spoken of in Bethlehem. By now, the whole town knows of the kindness and faithfulness you have shown to me.' Naomi stood, raising Ruth to her feet and looked her up and down, smiling playfully once more. 'Besides, you are young and beautiful, my daughter. What man would not desire you?'

Ruth smiled shyly, but then her face clouded, as if the sun had suddenly been veiled. 'But I am a Moabite…'

Naomi looked into Ruth's anxious eyes and said softly, 'And Boaz is the son of a Canaanite mother. Now wash yourself, my daughter.'

Naomi walked beside Ruth through the streets of Bethlehem. She stole a look at her. Her daughter-in-law's dainty feet were free from dust, and her dark hair shone under her shawl with the oil that Naomi had worked into it when it was dry. *The orange tunic suited her—which was as well, as it was the only one she had, and the embroidery around her green shawl matched it.* Her eyes returned to the street.

They went out through the town gates and descended from the ridge, following the road that eventually went to Jebus. The threshing floor was heard before it was seen. The sound of music, laughter and singing drifted up towards them. 'I will go no further,' said Naomi, stopping as it came into view. She turned to her daughter-in-law and adjusted the shawl that was draped over her forehead, to hide Ruth's face. *She had done the same for herself only the previous month. Then it had been to hide her shame; it was different this time.* 'There, that is better.' She ran her eyes over her one last time and nodded in satisfaction. 'You are ready. Now, remember—stay hidden until Boaz lies down, and only go to him when all is quiet.'

Ruth nodded. 'Yes, Mother.' But there was a slight waver in her voice.

Naomi rested her hands on Ruth's shoulders and met her eyes. 'Do you remember what Boaz said to you—those words you remembered when you returned from his field on that first day?' She didn't wait for an answer. 'He said, *May you be richly rewarded by Yahweh, the God of Israel, under whose wings you have come to take refuge.*

Yahweh *will* reward you, my daughter, and Boaz himself will fulfil his own blessing upon you.' She then leaned forward and kissed Ruth on the forehead. 'Now go, and may Yahweh indeed repay you richly.'

Without a further word, Ruth turned and began to make her way to the threshing floor. The breeze caught her perfume and it hung in the air for some moments, rich and heady, like wine on the tongue. As the colours of sunset set the sky ablaze, Naomi lifted her eyes, and whispered a prayer: 'Cover my daughter with your wings of protection, O Yahweh, and prosper your servant's design this night.'

Haggith stood in her courtyard door as Naomi returned. She glanced around—no-one else was near. 'Has she gone to the threshing floor?'

Naomi stopped beside her. Haggith had been one of the two friends in whom she had confided, Rizpah being the other. 'She should be there by now. I have told her to wait in the shadows until Boaz is asleep and all is quiet.'

'You are wise, my friend. For her to be seen there would usually mean only one thing.' She folded her arms. 'Bethlehem may not be Jebus, but I don't doubt that some men use the floor for more than threshing grain, particularly when they have drunk too much beer and there is a willing woman to hand.'

Naomi nodded, but her brow then furrowed. 'Boaz and Ruth are both held in high regard in the gate, and I would not want the town's wagging tongues to have any fuel for their fire.'

Haggith glanced around again and dropped her voice as Naomi had done. 'You and I know that Boaz will not take advantage of her, but are you sure he will take her as his wife?'

'He will be left in no doubt that it is not only Elimelech's field that needs redeeming, but Ruth too, and that she is looking to him as her redeemer. He will be ready to obey Yahweh and fulfil his duty—and will do so gladly. Of that I am sure.'

'Yet your brow remains furrowed…'

Naomi sighed. 'There is one matter that is out of my hands. Geshan is also a kinsman of Elimelech and is closer to us than Boaz. He might yet step forward and not only buy the field but also take Ruth.'

'That would still give protection for you and for Ruth—'

'But I know he would not love her as Boaz would. I want the best for my daughter.'

'Is there nothing you can do to prevent that?'

'Only one thing—trust that Boaz will know what to do.'

Naomi lay awake for most of the night, with the darkness expanding her fears. *What if Ruth was seen? Would some drunken man spy her and force himself upon her? Might Boaz be angry or refuse her request?* Her anxious thoughts went around and around. As quickly as she tried to dispel them, they scurried back again, like wasps round a honey-pot. It was only when dawn was approaching that she finally fell asleep, having murmured yet again, *Be with her, Yahweh.*

After what felt like the blink of an eye, she awoke with a start. *Something had touched her.* The room was still dark but she was suddenly aware of a presence with her. 'Is that you, Ruth?'

'Yes, Mother. I am here.'

Naomi pulled herself up into a sitting position. 'How did it go, my daughter?' She was by now completely awake, her senses sharpened by the knowledge that their futures lay in the answer to her question. The moment waiting for Ruth to speak seemed like the passing of years. She noticed that the grey light of day was creeping in through the partly-patched holes in the roof.

'All is well, Mother.'

Relief swept over Naomi, and in the dimness she could just about see Ruth smiling as she crouched by her mat. Naomi pulled her shawl, which had been lying over as she'd slept, around her. 'What happened?'

Ruth sat down, tucking her legs beside her. 'I did exactly as you said. I waited until the singing and dancing stopped and everyone was settling down for the night. They'd lit fires for light and warmth which made it easier to see where Boaz lay down. He slept beside his pile of grain, slightly apart from the others.'

'Little wonder,' interrupted Naomi. 'Only a fool or a sluggard would entrust their entire harvest to another.'

'I waited until all was quiet and then crept over to Boaz. I listened to make sure he was breathing steadily and then uncovered his feet as you'd told me to do. I lay down and waited. I couldn't sleep, but it didn't matter. It wasn't long before I suddenly felt him wake with a start. His feet found my body, and he immediately sat up. I could see his outline but no more. He reached forward and touched me, and asked who I was. I answered with the words you gave me and then waited.' Ruth paused, and when she spoke, there was wonder in her voice. 'He blessed me in the name of Yahweh, and said that I had shown great kindness, choosing him rather than a younger man. He told me not to fear, and said that he would do all that I asked.' She paused again, and bowed her head slightly. 'He spoke well of me, as if I deserved praise.'

'It does not surprise me,' said Naomi tenderly, laying her hand upon Ruth's arm. 'You do.'

'But he mentioned another—' Her voice was anxious.

'I know of him, my daughter, and he has the right of redemption before Boaz.'

'He said if the other kinsman will not redeem me, then he will, as surely as Yahweh lives. He then told me to stay where I was until the morning, and that he would settle the matter today. I have come from there now, in the first light of dawn. He made sure he sent me away before anyone saw me there. But that was not all—' She broke off and rose to her feet, holding her hands out to Naomi. 'Come with me, Mother!'

Naomi took her hands and stood up, pulling her shawl around her once more. She followed Ruth out into the coolness of the early morning. Even in the dim light, she could see there was a new shape in the courtyard near the oven: a pile of grain not unlike the one she had returned with after her first day of gleaning.

'He said that I shouldn't return to you empty-handed!'

Naomi drew in a deep breath and let it out, her heart lifting. *It was true; all was going well.* Though she knew it was not over yet. 'Boaz has certainly showered us with his bounty. But now we must be patient, my daughter, and wait for him to act. I know Boaz, and he will not rest until he has done so.' She smiled. 'Let's light a fire and warm ourselves—and you must be hungry.'

Ruth returned the smile. 'I will fetch the millstones.'

Naomi stood with Ruth on one side and Haggith on the other. 'Here she is,' she murmured, as she caught sight of Rizpah weaving her way through the already-crowded gate.

Rizpah smiled as she caught sight of them, and was soon standing with them. 'Has Geshan passed through yet?'

'No,' replied Naomi, 'but he is likely to go out to his field soon.' Her eyes were on Boaz, who was standing near the benches along one side of the square that formed the gate. He appeared to be talking easily with those near him, though his eyes were not on them. 'Boaz is keeping a careful watch for him.'

'When he is not glancing at Ruth, that is,' added Haggith.

The flitting of his eyes towards the young woman had not gone unnoticed. Naomi studied him. *Was he already thinking of Ruth as his bride?*

The four women stood in silence for a while, tucked away in a corner of the gate, where they could see all that happened without obstructing those heading into or out of Bethlehem. The eyes of Boaz were suddenly set on a point beyond them and he swiftly seated himself on the bench.

'He must have seen Geshan,' whispered Naomi. And sure enough, her kinsman came into view, clearly intending to pass through the gate.

Boaz called out to him. 'Turn aside, my friend, and join me here.' He gestured to the bench. Once Geshan was seated, Boaz rose again and spoke to the older men nearby. Ten of them joined him on the benches, two of which were moved so that they formed a crescent. Others in the gate stopped to watch.

'He has called some of the town's elders to join them,' whispered Naomi to Ruth. 'They will be witnesses to the transaction, whichever way it goes, and make it lawful and binding.' Despite her confidence in Boaz, Naomi's heart was thudding within her. Ruth remained silent, her gaze fixed on Boaz.

'Naomi, who has come back from the land of Moab,' began Boaz, addressing Geshan in a strong, clear voice so that all could hear, 'has to sell the piece of land which belonged to our brother Elimelech.' He paused. 'So I thought I should inform you of this, so that you may buy it in the presence of those who are here, and in the presence of the elders of my people. If you will redeem it, redeem it; but if not, tell me so that I may know. There is no one who has a greater right to redeem it, and I am after you.' Whether deliberately or not, he glanced over at Ruth.

Naomi held her breath.

'I will redeem it,' replied Geshan, and murmuring rippled around the gate.

Naomi's heart sank, but she felt Haggith's hand upon her shoulder and caught Rizpah's whispered words to Ruth.

'It is not over yet. Boaz knows both the ways of men and the heart of Geshan.'

When the murmuring had died down, Boaz spoke again. 'On the day you buy the land from Naomi, you also acquire Ruth the Moabite, the dead man's widow, in order to restore the name of the dead to his inheritance.' The murmuring began again, though this time it was more than a ripple. Geshan fell silent, stroking his beard.

Ruth turned to Naomi, bewildered. 'What does that mean?'

'It means, my daughter,' whispered Naomi, 'that if you were to have children by him, your first son would be counted as the offspring of Mahlon and the field would then belong to him.'

'Why would that be so?'

Rizpah answered, however. 'So that the line of Elimelech and Mahlon would continue, and not die out.'

'It is the law of Yahweh,' added Naomi.

Rizpah went on. 'And it is also why Geshan may forego the land. Not only would he have to support you and Naomi, but if you bear a son, he will also lose both the field and the money he paid for it.' As the murmuring began to subside once more, she added in a whisper, 'So rather than gaining a field, his own sons will end up with less.'

All attention returned to Geshan. Naomi could barely breathe.

His hand finally left his beard and returned to resting on his knee. He looked straight at Boaz. 'I cannot redeem the land else I might harm my own inheritance. Redeem it yourself!' As the elders began talking among themselves, Geshan then reached down to his foot—and Naomi breathed freely again.

'What is he doing?' asked Ruth, puzzled.

The other three women were smiling broadly. 'It is our custom—watch and you will see!' laughed Haggith.

Geshan unfastened his sandal and passed it to Boaz.

'I do not understand,' whispered Ruth, as Boaz rose to his feet. 'Why has he done that?'

'Who knows what is in the minds of men when they establish such customs!' chuckled Rizpah, as Boaz swept his gaze across the gathering and held the sandal aloft for all to see. 'But there can be no mistake in any mind that the transaction has occurred.'

'Today you are witnesses,' Boaz cried out to them, 'that I have bought this day from the hand of Naomi all the property of Elimelech, Kilion and Mahlon. I have also acquired Ruth the Moabite, Mahlon's widow, as my wife, in order to restore the name of the dead to his inheritance, so that his name will not disappear from among his family or from Bethlehem.' Boaz looked at the elders and all those in the gate again, and, with a note of triumph that he could not hide, cried out again, 'Today you are witnesses!'

'We are witnesses,' replied the crowd as one. And among the voices, two of the loudest were those of Haggith and Rizpah.

Naomi smiled as her heart soared. *Their witness as women would hardly be valued, but to her, it meant everything.*

As the cry died down, Boaz beckoned Naomi and Ruth forward, but the elders had not finished. While Naomi and Ruth were still making their way through the crowd, the ten men gathered around Boaz. One of them addressed him, but so that all could hear. 'May Yahweh make the woman who is coming into your home like Rachel and Leah, both of whom built the house of Israel!'

'May He grant you strength in Ephrathah and fame in Bethlehem,' added another.

As the women reached the front of the crowd, a third elder saw them and spoke. 'May your house be like the house of Perez whom Tamar bore to Judah, through the offspring which Yahweh will give you by this young woman.'

Ruth took her place at the side of Boaz, both of them radiant. But Naomi's face shone just as brightly. *That Ruth was a Moabite seemed of no concern to the elders—they had spoken as if she were a true daughter of Israel. Boaz, for his part, had taken Ruth from the edge of his field to the centre of his heart.* 'Favour upon favour, wonder upon wonder, and now blessing upon blessing,' murmured Naomi, whether any were listening or not.

The few short days between the barley and wheat harvest were filled with celebration as Boaz wed his bride. Naomi left behind her house, still lacking its roofs, and moved—with Ruth—into the much larger house of Boaz. No longer was she surrounded by bare walls and floors, but by colour, comfort and plenty. She no longer lay down at night with an empty stomach, a weary body or a heavy heart. If her empty cup was now filled, however, it was soon to be overflowing.

Naomi walked arm in arm with Ruth to the field of Boaz, on a day that was cooled by the advance of autumn. The hills—yellowed and dried by the summer sun—were now showing more patches of green, as the early rains began to water the parched earth. They walked in silence, enjoying the sight of eagles soaring high in the sky above them.

Whilst Naomi's eyes were still fixed in the heavens, Ruth suddenly said, 'You will soon be not only a mother but a grandmother.'

Naomi stopped abruptly and stared at Ruth, scarcely daring to believe her words. But if she had had any doubt of their truth, the light in her daughter-in-law's face was enough to convince her. 'When did you last bleed?'

'I have not done so since before I was wed,' said Ruth shyly.

Naomi laid her hand lightly over Ruth's belly, and—sure enough—could feel a swelling. 'Why did you not tell me earlier?' she exclaimed, though there was no reproach in her words.

'I wanted to be sure. I did not want to disappoint you.'

'You could never disappoint me, my daughter,' said Naomi, with affection filling her heart and a smile gracing her face.

'You have a son!' said the midwife with a broad smile, as she held the newborn in her hands. 'May he become famous throughout Israel!'

With the midwife's blessings in her ears and her heart, Naomi removed her hand from her daughter-in-law's shoulder where it had rested during the birth. Ruth was still panting, crouched on the birthing stones. Naomi leaned down towards her forehead, glistening from her labour, and kissed it. 'Well done, my daughter.'

'Praise be to be Yahweh!' breathed Haggith, as she held the baby whilst the midwife cut the cord. She turned her eyes from the child to Naomi. 'This day our God has given you a redeemer. The child will renew your life and sustain you in your old age.'

The words of blessing were rich, like a jug of fine wine being poured out, and Naomi smiled as she beheld her grandson for the first time. *Haggith's words were true. If Boaz were to die before her, which was likely, all he owned would now pass to Ruth's son. Her future, and Ruth's, were secure.* She did not doubt Yahweh's hand in the birth, and although Mahlon and Kilion had died, she had no fear of the same happening again. Her face was radiant as she marvelled at the shock of dark brown curls, and she gazed into the tiny brown eyes as they opened for a few heartbeats, before the face screwed up and he let out a cry. *It did not matter that he was not of her blood—the bond was just as real.*

Naomi and Rizpah then helped Ruth off the birthstones and laid her back against some pillows to rest. As the midwife began clearing up after the birth, Rizpah attended to Ruth. Naomi helped Haggith as together they performed the usual rituals: washing the baby and rubbing it gently with salt, before swaddling it from its middle to its feet in long strips of cloth.

'Do you know what I think?' said Rizpah suddenly, as she gently wiped Ruth's face with a damp cloth.

Naomi paused and looked up. 'What's that, my friend?'

'I think your daughter-in-law, who loves you so faithfully, is better to you than seven sons.'

Ruth smiled coyly.

'You could not have praised her more highly,' responded Haggith, 'or more truly.'

Naomi looked from the faces of her friends to that of her daughter-in-law. Their eyes met. 'I know it.' There could be no greater blessing than to have many sons—or so most would have thought. But Naomi knew differently. *She had once questioned the goodness of Yahweh towards her, but Ruth had shown her such faithfulness and love, and brought such blessing. Had not the Almighty been showing His goodness through her?* She did not doubt it. She turned back to Haggith. 'When I arrived back in Bethlehem, I said that I had come back empty.' Her eyes returned to Ruth. 'I was wrong but did not realise it. I was already blessed.'

The midwife then left them to find Boaz whilst Haggith wrapped the newly-swaddled baby in a blanket and handed him to Naomi.

He lay quietly in her arms as she looked fully upon his tiny features, marvelling once again at the perfectly formed little fingers and minute mouth that was silently opening and closing.

'Look,' said Rizpah. 'Naomi has a son!'

Naomi smiled, her gaze still fixed upon the child. She was captivated by his little face. *She had expected nothing but loneliness and poverty in her old age after Elimelech and her sons had died, but now she had a new family in a new home. She had also said that Yahweh had made her life bitter. Yet she could barely contain the sweetness now in her heart. She had told them not to use her name—a name meaning pleasant. But now that seemed too slight for her joy.* She suddenly looked up. 'My daughter—what will you call your son?' She already knew that Boaz had bestowed that honour upon Ruth.

'What do *you* think he should be called, Mother? I could name him *Elimelech*...'

'No, not *Elimelech*,' replied Naomi, moving to Ruth's side and lowering the tiny bundle into her daughter-in-law's waiting arms. 'That name looks back to a painful past,' she added softly. 'Our eyes should be on what is ahead.'

'How about *Habazziniah*?' suggested Rizpah with a twinkle in her eye. 'I had an uncle with that name. It is impressive, is it not?'

'He is *not* going to be called that!' insisted Naomi with a wry smile. 'Imagine trying to rebuke him swiftly when he goes near the fire. The boy would be burned before you had his name out of your mouth!' Ruth and Rizpah both laughed.

But Haggith appeared deep in thought. 'You could call him *Obed*...' she said quietly.

The name hung in the air for several moments. *One who serves.* Naomi nodded to herself. *Yes, that would be a good name. For the baby was already serving as their redeemer simply by being born a boy.* She glanced across at Ruth who was smiling.

'I like it.'

'And so do I, my daughter. Then that is what he shall be called.' She turned to Haggith. 'You have named him well, my friend.'

A sudden movement at the door of the room drew Naomi's attention away from the child. Boaz entered the room.

'You have a son, my lord,' said Ruth shyly, the radiance in her face soon mirrored in that of her husband. 'His name is Obed.'

As Boaz lifted his son, cradling him in his arms, Naomi thought about the midwife's blessing: *May he become famous throughout Israel.* It seemed a great deal to ask of a tiny child of a Moabite mother. But then Yahweh had shown to her that He was not bound by either weakness or poverty, and was able to bless beyond anything she could conceive. Maybe Obed's name and story would be spoken of to generations yet to come. Her gaze drifted back to Ruth, but she then lifted her eyes to heaven—even though a mud roof stood between her and the sky—and smiled to herself.

Haggith interrupted her musings. 'What are you thinking?' she whispered, as Boaz and Ruth continued speaking quietly to one other. 'What thought brings such a smile to your face?'

'I am thinking that, when he is old enough, I will tell Obed the story of how he came to have Moabite bone and flesh within him.'

'It is a good story,' replied Rizpah softly, 'and deserves to be told.'

'And Ruth should be honoured in its telling.' Naomi then shrugged. 'But it is still only the story of two women—it is hardly likely to be remembered or shared over the exploits of men.'

'Obed at least should know it,' whispered Haggith, 'and his sons and his grandsons.'

But as the eyes of all three women returned to mother and child, Naomi suddenly realised she had been at fault in her words. 'No, I am wrong,' she murmured. 'It is not only the story of two women.' She thought about how Ruth had seemingly happened upon the field of Boaz, but knew nothing had happened by chance. 'It is also the story of Yahweh's faithfulness and goodness. Boaz has been our redeemer and Obed will yet be, but the true redeemer is Yahweh Himself.'

And for once, the three women had nothing more to say.

Notes

1. *Ruth 2:23 states that 'Ruth stayed close to the women of Boaz to glean until the barley and wheat harvests were finished'. This does not preclude Ruth 3 and the threshing of the barley occurring at the end of the barley harvest rather than at the end of both harvests, as 2:23 could refer to either the permission or the intention to glean. It would seem more likely that the barley was threshed before the wheat was harvested, and that understanding of the verse has been chosen here.*

2. *Although some commentators ascribe sexual impropriety to Ruth both in going to Boaz at the threshing floor at night and 'uncovering his feet', Boaz has only praise for her actions and immediately describes her as 'a woman of noble character' (3:11). Although the exact nature of some of the customs in the book of Ruth are unclear, the words of Boaz imply that Ruth's character remains unblemished.*

3. *The precise laws of inheritance are not obvious. Although Numbers 27:8-11 seems to preclude widows inheriting a husband's property when there are no sons, maybe in practice this was not enforced. Naomi seems to have rights to the land, given her ability to sell Elimelech's field, but the legal*

process by which that ownership came about is not clear. There also seems to have been some custom linking the sale of the land to Ruth, as the land cannot be redeemed unless she is redeemed with it. These customs are clearly linked with the concepts of redemption of land in Leviticus 25:23-28 and with what is known as levirate marriage, described in Deuteronomy 25:5-10, where a man is required to raise up the line of a brother who dies without an heir by marrying his widow. Neither Boaz nor the other kinsman was a brother of Elimelech or Mahlon, but it must be assumed that a similar custom still applied in this case.

4. The Hebrew in Ruth 3:3 does not necessarily imply best clothes, and there is obviously the question of whether Ruth would have had any, given their poverty.

5. Ezekiel 16:4 gives some interesting details concerning childbirth. These have been included here, and it has also been assumed that, as in the time of the Exodus, both midwives and birthing stones (on which the women crouched) were used (see Exodus 1:15-16).

6. It seems unusual for women outside the family to be involved in the naming of a child. There could be some custom concerning this, or it may simply be that Ruth and Boaz were open to and liked their suggestion. Women were certainly involved in the naming of their children on many occasions recorded in the Old Testament.

7. 'Bone and flesh' is the Hebrew equivalent of 'flesh and blood', and occurs a number of times in the Old Testament (see, for example, Genesis 29:14, Judges 9:2 and 2 Samuel 5:1).

8. Genesis 49:10 foretells a king coming from the tribe of Judah, and the story of Ruth tells how this comes about.

Abigail

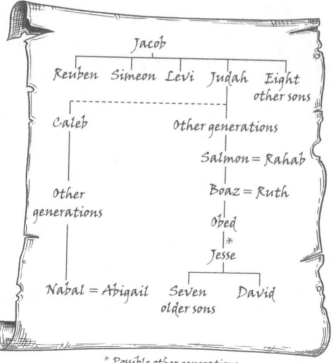

Jacob

Reuben   Simeon   Levi   Judah   Eight
                                       other sons

Caleb   Other generations

                         Salmon = Rahab

                         Boaz = Ruth

                         Obed
                          *
                         Jesse

Other
generations

Nabal = Abigail   Seven   David
                    older sons

* Possible other generations

GESHUR

Jezreel

Mt Gilboa

The
Great
Sea

Mahanaim

Shiloh

River
Jordan

Gibeon • Gibeah Jericho
Kiriath Jearim • • Nob
Jerusalem

Gath • Adullam Bethlehem
Ashkelon

The
Salt
Sea

Keilah

• Hebron
Ziph • En
Gedi
Ziklag • Carmel

• Beersheba

0   10   20
miles

I

Then the word of the LORD came to Samuel: 'I regret that I have made Saul king, because he has turned away from me and has not carried out my instructions.'... Early in the morning Samuel got up and went to meet Saul, but he was told, 'Saul has gone to Carmel. There he has set up a monument in his own honour.' (1 Samuel 15:10-12)

'Will you come to worship?' Abigail knew what her husband's answer would be, but it was still right to ask.

Nabal paused momentarily, the bread in his hand poised over the large dish of stew. She'd cooked the lamb, onions and cumin slowly until the meat was tender and falling off the bone, its pleasing aroma pervading the air. Nabal plunged the bread into it. 'No—' He scooped up a generous portion, and seemed unconcerned when some dripped from the bread to the table on its way to his mouth. He didn't bother waiting until it was finished before speaking again. '—too much to do.' He took a large swig of wine to wash the remains down. Nabal sated all of his appetites with the same vigour. He turned his attention back to the stew.

Abigail wasn't so sure what his next answer would be, but as always, she chose her moment wisely. *Nabal would always be in a better mood with meat and wine inside him, and could interrupt less easily when his mouth was full—as it was now.* 'It would be best, then, if Eliam comes with me. We will only be away for five days at most, and it will give Joel the chance to rise on his own wings. He is perfectly capable of running the house whilst we are away—Eliam has prepared him well.' She waited as Nabal swallowed and then drained his cup. *If he was going to refuse he would have done so already.*

'No more than five days. I can't spare Eliam longer than that.' He

285

wiped the back of his hand across his mouth and belched. 'He needs to get the iron tools sharpened with another trip to those Philistine dogs!' He spat on the floor in contempt. 'How is it no Israelite has the wits to forge iron? And do you know how much those accursed cheats charge?' He did not wait for an answer. 'A third of a shekel of silver for sharpening every axe and the same to repoint a goad.' Nabal uttered a curse under his breath. 'It is madness!' He paused whilst he pushed his empty cup towards his wife. 'When do you intend to leave?'

'The day after tomorrow—so we can worship at Nob on the Sabbath.' Abigail knew he would view the time it would take them to travel to the sanctuary and back as an indulgence, a waste of time. She picked up the jug and refilled Nabal's vessel. She had learned quickly in their four years of marriage that he was, as a rule, niggardly in all things save one—his own cravings.

When the meal was over, she left Nabal with what was left of the jug of wine and went in search of Eliam, their most trusted servant. The house was far more extensive than the one she had grown up in. Being the youngest of the family, she had only ever known a crowded home—though one filled with love. Her parents had brought her up in the ways of Yahweh, and, if they had still been living when she came of age, she was sure they would not have chosen Nabal for her. However, as the head of the family after their father's death, her eldest brother cared less about a man's standing than his wealth. It mattered little to him that Nabal had already dismissed one wife with a certificate of divorce after she'd failed to please him, most notably in bearing him an heir. And so, after the passing of her fifteenth winter, she found herself being sent from her home to Carmel to marry her father's cousin. She was yet to conceive a child, but assumed that Nabal was happy enough in the meantime to lie with a wife young enough to be his daughter until that time came—though it was always a prospect that made her shudder.

As Abigail emerged into the cool of the spacious courtyard, a smile graced her lips. 'Eliam—I have found you at last.'

The older man, who was seated on a bench against one of the walls, lowered his eyes which had been lifted to the heavens. He returned her smile, and then raised his gaze once more. 'Look, Abigail! Yahweh has given the first star of the evening a glorious brilliance tonight.'

Ever since coming into the household, Abigail had insisted that he call her by her name, rather than *mistress*. He was more than twice her age, and more like a father to her than a servant. She followed his gaze towards the western sky, darkening as dusk slipped towards night. Against the deep blue, a tiny jewel sparkled. 'It is beautiful.'

'Yahweh's wonders make my heart soar like an eagle.'

Eliam fell silent again, his expression one of child-like awe and his mind seemingly in some faraway place. *He never seemed to grow tired of life, despite his years.* Then the moment passed, and she had his attention once more.

'How may I help you tonight?' He lifted the cup of beer in his hand to his mouth and drank. Wine was a rich man's drink, unless it was a special time of celebration.

She sat down on the bench beside him. It was always far easier talking to him than her husband. Eliam and his family were the beating heart of Nabal's household and land. His wife, Rebekah, had lips that were quick to scold but a heart that was generous and kind. His eldest, Joel, seemed to be able to turn his hand to any problem, as long as it involved an animal, metal or wood. The twins, Mered and Mahlah, were more opposites than like, Mered rarely being serious about anything, much to his elder brother's frustration, whilst Mahlah seemed to have more sense than most girls of fourteen years. Her sister, Hephzibah, born two years after them, brought sunshine into all of their lives.

'Nabal has given me permission to travel to Nob to worship,' she began, 'and for you to accompany me. Joel can be at Nabal's right hand whilst we are away. He has learned much from you.'

Eliam nodded and seemed deep in thought for a few moments. 'There are three or four of the older herders who can advise him, if needed.' He immediately named them—there were none of Nabal's servants or hired hands who weren't known to him. 'Who else would you have journey with us?'

'Mered should come, and Mahlah if Rebekah can spare her. I would wish for Hephzibah's company, but I would not deprive a mother of both of her daughters. Zillah can come in her stead. She was too young last time I made the journey to the sanctuary, and she will benefit from Mahlah's example.'

Eliam chuckled. 'If she doesn't drive my daughter mad with her chattering! Sometimes she is as unceasing as a stream swollen by snow in spring!'

Abigail laughed. She enjoyed Eliam's good-natured observations, which often carried much wisdom but never malice. 'True. But it will do her good, and—who knows?—seeing the beauty of both the land and the sanctuary may yet still her tongue.'

'When do you wish to leave?'

'We will begin our preparations in the morning, and leave the day after.'

Abigail delighted in gathering together the necessary provisions. Although she had Mahlah, Zillah and a number of other girls to attend to her, she did not believe in being idle. Her mother had taught her well, and so despite Nabal's wealth, she still wove and dyed both linen and wool by her own hand, sewing and mending clothes when needed. With the help of Rebekah, she kept a garden close to the house sown with vegetables and herbs, but left the olive grove and vines in the care of Eliam. She also showed a keen interest in the household, and made sure she knew all that was in the storehouse—where she was at that moment.

She sang quietly to herself as she packed raisin cakes into a cloth bag.

> 'The mountains quaked before Yahweh, the One of Sinai,
> before Yahweh, the God of Israel.'

It was a song her father had taught her, a song which told of the victory of God's people over a Canaanite army some two hundred years earlier and wrought, in part, through women. *Deborah and Jael had been tools in the hand of Yahweh.* The thought lifted her heart. *If those women had been helped by Yahweh to defeat an army, then she would also find strength through Him to face her own trials.* She carried on singing as she selected two skins for milk, but it was not only the deeds of Yahweh that put a song in her heart. It was also the prospect of five days away.

Later, as the other servants continued the preparations, there was one final task that she knew was hers alone, although she took Mahlah with her. Both were carrying ropes. She found Nabal with one of the flocks of sheep.

'Is something wrong?' he asked sharply.

Abigail shook her head, 'No, my lord, but I need two animals to take to Nob to sacrifice, one as a sin offering and one as a fellowship offering.'

He grunted—but didn't refuse. He cast his eyes over the sheep nearby. 'How about that one?'

The word *scrawny* came to Abigail's mind. But she knew that Nabal only understood one language, and she was ready to speak it. 'That would do, my lord, for certain. But I will be standing in your stead at the sanctuary. Surely if you seek the blessing of Yahweh on all you have, and desire Him to bless your flocks with healthy and numerous offspring, would it not be better to offer the best that you have? Two lambs are only, after all, a tiny drop in the river of what Yahweh has already given.' The truth was, Nabal had three thousand sheep and a thousand goats. She paused to let the words sink in as she cast her eyes over the flock. She found what she was looking for—two plump, healthy females. She pointed at them. 'Would not Yahweh be delighted by those two there?'

Nabal was silent for a moment. 'Take them, then.' There was no pleasure in his voice.

As she and Mahlah were putting nooses over the animals' heads, Mahlah whispered with a little smile, 'You chose well, Mistress!'

Abigail returned the smile, but held her peace. *She would not have Yahweh dishonoured by offering Him anything other than the best.*

As the cart trundled away from the house the following morning, Abigail's spirit was lighter than it had been for some months. She drew in a deep breath and let it out slowly as they began the journey north. An embroidered light blue shawl covered her head, with her darker blue tunic now covering her sandalled feet, as she perched next to Eliam who was driving the oxen harnessed to the cart. The two girls sat cross-legged on cushions in the back next to the provisions for the journey, whilst Mered—for the time being at least—chose to walk alongside. The two lambs, tethered to the back of the cart, had no choice but to trot along behind. Zillah had started chattering already, though Abigail let her words fade into the distance, as she savoured every sight.

As they neared the main settlement of Carmel, Abigail's eyes were far away, following an eagle soaring in the clear blue sky.

'What's that?'

Zillah's change of tone suddenly drew Abigail's gaze earthward. Zillah was pointing ahead to a tall stone edifice.

Mered looked up at the cart. 'It's a monument that King Saul set up last year after he had a great victory over the Amalekites.' He thrust his arm forward, as if he bore a sword. 'He smashed them, and even caught their king!'

'Where was the battle?' asked Zillah, wide-eyed.

'Oh, near here,' said Mered, waving his hand around vaguely. 'The clouds were dark and the heavens thundered! It was truly terrifying.'

'Mered,' said Eliam drily, looking down at his son, 'do not just make up a story when you do not know the answer.' Mered grinned. 'The battle, Zillah, was further to the south.'

'So why did King Saul set up a monument here?' asked Mahlah.

Eliam shrugged. 'Maybe it reminds the tribe of Judah the debt we owe him. We are nearest to the Amalek cities, and so benefit most from their defeat, now there is no danger of an attack or raid by them.'

Mered turned towards Eliam, his eyes bright. 'Tell us the stories about King Saul and Jonathan, Father!'

'You've heard them all before!'

'Yes, but Zillah hasn't.' He looked behind. 'Have you, Zillah?'

Abigail looked behind once more, her eyebrows raised, inviting the girl to answer.

Zillah flushed at Mered's sudden attention, and answered almost breathlessly, 'No!'

Mahlah rolled her eyes, but Abigail's sparkled with amusement. 'Well, Eliam,' said Abigail, facing forward once more, 'it seems that you will be entertaining us with your stories on our journey. It will certainly help pass the time.' She also thought it would give them some respite from Zillah's tongue.

'Hmm…' Eliam seemed to be in deep thought for a moment, but then he began. 'You cannot understand the story of Saul unless you understand the rest of our story in this land. It is almost four hundred years since Joshua led the people of Israel across the Jordan and into Canaan, the land promised by Yahweh to our forefather Abraham, yet Saul is our first king. For it was not kings who came after Joshua, but men who were raised up by Yahweh to judge the land—'

'And a woman!' interrupted Abigail with a laugh.

'You are right to correct me,' replied Eliam, smiling. 'We must not forget Deborah.' And starting with Othniel, he told the stories of the judges—of Ehud and Gideon, of Jephthah and Samson, of Barak and Deborah, and of how they had time and again defeated the enemies of Israel and turned the hearts of the people back to Yahweh.

While the rugged hills of southern Judah, more suited to pasturing animals than growing crops, slipped by, Abigail drank in the stories, as if they were sweetest water and her throat parched. Nabal rarely thought it worth telling her anything, unless it was somehow in his own interest. Some of the tales were new to her, others she'd heard before. She took them all in, vowing to herself that she would never forget the deeds of Yahweh.

They stopped as noon approached and sheltered from the hottest sun of the day under some oak trees north of Hebron. Their simple meal consisted of bread cooked earlier that morning, which they dipped in a bowl of curds, and a cake of raisins shared between them afterwards, though it was Mered who enjoyed the largest portion.

Abigail had insisted that they allow Eliam a break from story-telling and let him rest, and for a while they all dozed quietly in the shade, their heads on cushions from the cart.

Abigail, with her eyes closed, listened as the breeze gently rustled the leaves of the oak tree. A dove was cooing somewhere nearby, but aside from those sounds and the heavier breathing of Eliam, all was quiet. A prayer formed in her head. *Praise to you, Yahweh, for your faithfulness. You did not abandon your people when we strayed from you. Keep my heart close to you, and may I always honour you both with my lips and with my life.*

'We should be moving again, Abigail.'

Eliam's voice suddenly roused her. *She had drifted off.* She pulled herself into a sitting position.

'There is still some distance to go,' he continued, 'if we are to reach your cousin at Etam by nightfall.'

Abigail nodded. 'It would be good to lodge at his house.'

'It will mean a shorter journey tomorrow.'

'And a safer and more comfortable night for each one of us. I am sure it will please Mahlah and Zillah more than one spent under the stars.'

'Is the story of King Saul and Jonathan next?' asked Zillah. She and Mahlah were already returning the cushions to the cart.

Abigail adjusted her shawl. 'Let Eliam finish tending to the animals first!'

Eliam smiled. 'The answer to your question, Zillah, is *no*. You must hear first of one of our darkest times, several years before I was born, in the days of my father and the youth of the prophet Samuel.' His face clouded. 'It is the reason why we are travelling now to Nob, and not further north to Shiloh.'

When they were all seated in the cart again, with Mered also in the back, Eliam resumed his tales. 'Israel went out to meet the Philistines in battle, gathering at Ebenezer...' He then told of how their own army had mistakenly thought that taking the ark of the covenant into battle with them would ensure their victory. Instead, they had met with a terrible defeat, and even worse, the ark had been captured by the Philistines. The destruction of the sanctuary at Shiloh had followed, though not before the tent—and everything else that could be moved—had been swiftly taken elsewhere. Even Zillah held her peace when Eliam fell silent. But the sadness soon passed.

'I was a young man—Mered's age—when the people asked Samuel for a king as other nations had. I am told it grieved Samuel's heart, for he believed in doing so the people were rejecting Yahweh as their ruler. But he gathered the people at Mizpah, to the north of Gibeah, where King Saul now reigns. My father went, and watched as a tribe was taken by lot.' He turned his head slightly, and said over his shoulder. 'Which tribe?'

'The tribe of Benjamin,' said Mahlah and Mered together.

'That's right. And then a family was taken by lot, and then Saul was chosen.' He smiled. 'My father said that when he was finally found, the man of Yahweh's choice stood taller than any other man there!'

Abigail was puzzled. 'But if Yahweh was truly being rejected, surely he would not have chosen a king for them.'

Eliam shrugged. 'Maybe the people *were* wrong to ask, but surely a leader who submits to Yahweh as the true King does not replace His rule, but merely helps the people to follow it.'

Abigail smiled. *Nabal would never have spoken with such wisdom.* 'Then tell us how Yahweh still rules through Saul.' And so began the story of Israel's king, and with it, the story of his firstborn son, Jonathan, through whom the God of Israel brought about great victories against the Ammonites and the Philistines.

When Eliam finally brought his tale to a close, Mered called from behind, 'Jonathan will be a great king one day, won't he, Father?'

'You are right, my son. He is a brave warrior who trusts Yahweh.' Eliam then sighed. 'But I fear we will yet see the Philistines take up arms against us again. They still hold the plains that run down to the Great Sea in the west, and we have nothing that can match their iron chariots.'

'You are wrong, Father!' Mered's voice had a note of triumph. 'We have the hills of Judah!'

Eliam put his head back and laughed, and then looked around at the slopes that were speckled with sheep and goats. 'You are right again, Mered. The flocks fare better on these hills than Philistine chariots!'

Suddenly, the line of a song drifted into Abigail's mind—a line that she had sung the day before: *The mountains quaked before Yahweh.* 'Ah, but there is One who is greater than the hills and the mountains because He created them. And He is the God of Israel, not the god of the Philistines.'

Eliam nodded. 'Yes, and maybe Yahweh will yet strengthen the hands of Saul and Jonathan to defeat them again.'

There was a pause. 'Jonathan's wife must be very fortunate. He is married, isn't he?' Abigail caught the wistful tone in Mahlah's voice.

'Yes, my daughter, I believe he is.'

But it was Zillah who sighed the loudest.

It was late on the second day of their travel that they passed the city of the Jebusites, though from a distance. 'Is that Jerusalem, Father?' asked Mered, as it came into view.

'It is indeed. It is only one of the trials that our king faces. The city stands between Judah and Benjamin, and divides our nation. It does not make it any easier for him to rule this land.'

'And the other trials?' asked Mahlah.

'The lands of Moab and Edom to the east could still be a threat, and I am told that to the north, in the Jezreel valley, there are city strongholds that the Canaanites still hold. They further divide the land by cutting off the tribes to the north. We are not yet one land... but one day we will be, if Yahweh wills.'

'But at least the presence of Jerusalem reminds us of something else,' added Abigail. 'It surely means that we are almost at Nob.'

The sanctuary was not much farther north than the city of Jerusalem, and neither was it very far south of where Saul ruled. Early on the third day, the Sabbath, they walked together from the town where they had found lodging to the tent which housed all the sacred items, save the ark. That still resided at Kiriath Jearim, where it had come to rest after being sent back by the Philistines to whom it had only brought death.

A thrill coursed through Abigail, as it had done before when she had visited the sanctuary. *This was the same tabernacle that had been made at Mount Sinai hundreds of years earlier! It was the same bronze altar, and within, hidden from her view, was the same golden lampstand.* Despite the absence of the ark, being in such a sacred place made Yahweh feel closer. *This was where He commanded His people to worship and bring their offerings. Surely here they were in the centre of Yahweh's will!*

The five stood watching, with a crowd of others, as the morning sacrifice was made. An older priest, aided by two others, placed a burnt offering of a ram, skinned and divided, upon the altar. As the aroma of the roasting meat drifted across the gathering, two younger priests took twelve fresh loaves made from purest wheat flour into the tent, to be set on the golden table, bringing out the ones set there a week earlier. Then began the offerings of the worshippers. They were not the only ones who had brought animals. Some had wicker cages with pigeons or doves. A few, like them, had brought goats or sheep. The priests were kept busy.

A cheerful priest, dressed in his white linen tunic and cap, approached them. Abigail guessed he was only a few years older than her. He smiled at them. 'Which of Yahweh's offerings are these fine animals for?'

Whilst one of their animals was offered whole as a sacrifice for sin, Yahweh had ordained that the meat of the peace offering was to be shared between the altar, the priests and the worshippers. It was a rare pleasure for many. The portion of lamb they were to enjoy in the presence of their God was far more than the five of them could eat, and, after it was boiled in a pot they had brought, Abigail shared it generously with others eating meals like themselves. She felt, as she had done on other occasions, the lifting of her heart as she did so.

As their meal drew to an end, Abigail rose and left the others, drawing as close to the tent of the sanctuary as she was allowed. She bowed her head reverently. Nabal may have cared little for the nation beyond its safety and wealth, but she had been taught better. Her lips moved, but the words were spoken only in her heart. *Yahweh, God of your people Israel and Lord of all the earth, graciously hear the prayers of Your handmaid.* She thanked Him for His goodness, and she prayed for the land and for its king. She asked that He would grant Saul and Jonathan victory in battle, that other nations would know that their God was the true God. And finally she prayed for herself. *Please look on the trials of your servant, and give me strength to endure. Grant me, I pray, the courage to do what is pleasing in your sight, even when it may not be pleasing in the sight of Nabal. Hear my prayer, O Yahweh.* That she might be delivered from Nabal completely was more than she could either hope or pray.

Notes

1. *There are challenges in determining the chronology of these times, particularly given what appears to be incomplete manuscript evidence in 1 Samuel 13:1, regarding both Saul's age when he became king and the length of his reign. The apostle Paul, however, states that Saul ruled for forty years (Acts 13:41), although this may be a rounded or symbolic figure. Another difficulty in dating is not knowing how long Samuel lived.*

2. *Scripture does not seem to give a complete history of either the movements of the ark or the sanctuary. (See note 10 at the end of Ruth (1) above.) In 1 Samuel 1-3, it is clear that 'the house of God' and the ark are both at Shiloh (3:3), about 18 miles north of Jerusalem, and on the main north-south route through the hill country of Israel. Shiloh therefore seems to be the first fulfilment of Moses' words concerning that place 'the* LORD *your God will choose as a dwelling for his Name' (Deuteronomy 12:11). Regular sacrifice at Shiloh is referred to in 1 Samuel 2:14, but it is not spoken of as the sanctuary after 1 Samuel 4, when the ark was captured by the Philistines. Psalm 78:59-61 and Jeremiah 7:12 suggest the destruction of Shiloh, and in what are thought to be its Iron Age ruins, there is evidence of devastation by fire—presumably by the Philistines pressing home their victory. A reasonable explanation of the movements of the sanctuary can be found in*

Jewish Bible Quarterly, which seems to accord well with Scripture, i.e. the sanctuary being at Shiloh, then at Nob, and then at Gibeon. (See http://jbqnew.jewishbible.org/jbq-past-issues/2016/441-january-march-2016/reconstructing-destruction-tabernacle-shiloh.) When the Philistines sent the ark back several months after its capture, it is recorded as spending twenty years in Kiriath Jearim (1 Samuel 7:2). However, this seems far too few years to cover the period until the ark is brought to Jerusalem in 2 Samuel 6. It may be that the twenty years only refers to the period until the assembly at Mizpah in 1 Samuel 7, unless it also spent time elsewhere.

3. There is a good example of family worship at Shiloh in 1 Samuel 1, maybe 60-70 years before the story in this chapter. It is not clear whether this worship was part of one of the annual Jewish festivals, or a yearly family tradition that was an expression of personal piety. The example has been used as the basis for the trip to Nob in this chapter. Other family or local sacrifices are recorded in 1 Samuel 9:12 (in Ramah) and in 20:6 (in Bethlehem).

4. Nabal's name means 'fool' in Hebrew. Some scholars think his original name has been replaced by a symbolic one in the text (given that it would be a strange choice of name for a son!), or that the name may originally have had a less pejorative meaning, although that isn't implied in the text (1 Samuel 25:25).

5. Although Nabal is described as living at Carmel (1 Samuel 25:2), it has been assumed that, because of his extensive flocks and wealth and the descriptions in chapter 25, they were not in the town as such, but maybe on something akin to a farm outside it.

6. Neither Abigail's age nor that of Nabal is known. However, given the fact that Nabal is a wealthy landowner and the possibility that he was struck down by a stroke, it has been assumed that there is an age gap between him and Abigail, as Abigail still needs to be young enough to bear a child several years later (2 Samuel 3:3). Nabal divorcing a first wife is simply a plot device to both paint a picture of Nabal's character and account for an age difference between them.

7. It seems that by this time, at least in the houses of the wealthy, meals were now eaten at tables that were sufficiently raised to require seating—presumably chairs, stools or benches. (See, for example, Judges 1:7 and 1 Samuel 20:24-29.)

8. It has been assumed that many would know the stories of the judges, and that an oral history would have existed alongside or before a written one.

9. It is unclear how widely Saul's disobedience and his rejection as king by God (in 1 Samuel 15) would have been known to others beside Samuel. It is assumed here that it would not be widely known, at least initially.

2

David asked the men standing near him, 'What will be done for the man who kills this Philistine and removes this disgrace from Israel? Who is this uncircumcised Philistine that he should defy the armies of the living God?' (1 Samuel 17:26)

Abigail was choosing some fresh herbs for that evening's meal when she heard Rebekah hailing her. 'I am here—in the garden.'

Rebekah looked slightly flustered when she appeared. 'The master is calling for you. Ira has returned from the war. They're in the courtyard.'

Abigail straightened up, a bunch of coriander in her hand. 'Did he say how the war goes?' As Eliam had foretold two years before, the Philistines were once more a thorn in Israel's side. Ira, Nabal's younger brother, had passed through over two months earlier on the way to join Saul's army. It had been disturbing to learn shortly afterwards that battle lines had been drawn up not much more than two days' march away from Carmel, though they were yet to hear of any fighting. Abigail began walking towards the house.

Rebekah shook her head as she drew alongside. 'I wasn't long enough in his presence to hear, but his mood seemed cheerful enough.'

Relief coursed through Abigail. 'Is he well, then?'

'I saw no injury. He is intending to stay here tonight before going on.'

Abigail raised an eyebrow. 'More likely a week than a night! Ask Eliam to slaughter a fattened goat. It should be meat enough for Ira's stay.'

'I will ask Mahlah to mill some more wheat.'

'Good. And has Ira been given a cup of beer yet?'

'Mered is bringing a jug.'

'And a bowl of water and a towel?'

'I was just about to fetch them when Nabal sent me to find you.'

'Thank you.' As they reached one of the doors, Rebekah hurried off. Abigail made her way through the house, her long silver earrings bumping gently against her neck, just above where tresses of her dark hair cascaded out from under the bright orange shawl. Her leather sandals slapped against the cool stone floor. She was cheered to hear that Ira's mood had been good, and was all the more eager to hear any news about the fortunes of Saul and his army. She soon emerged into the light of the large paved courtyard. Two small fig trees stood in earthenware pots towards the centre. A stocky man of around thirty years was sitting on a bench in the shade, cradling a cup of beer, his back against the wall and his legs crossed and stretched out in front of him. He was taller than Nabal and dressed in a dusty tunic, and had the grime of a long journey upon him. Near his feet lay a bronze helmet, a sheathed sword attached to a belt, and what Abigail took to be a discarded coat of scale armour heaped on the ground. A jug was next to the pile. His gaze shifted, and he looked her up and down.

'Ah! How fares my fine-looking cousin?' Ira did not stand, but raised his cup with a large grin. His eyes lingered on her.

Abigail crossed over to him and kissed him on both cheeks. 'Why ask after my wellbeing, my brother? You are the one who has been fighting in the war!' She stepped back and studied him. 'It seems you have returned unscathed—I hope my eyes do not deceive me. Did all go well against the Philistines?'

Before he could answer, Rebekah appeared with a bowl of water drawn from the cistern and a towel draped over her arm. She set the bowl on the floor by Ira's feet, and placed the towel on the bench beside him.

'Get us another jug of beer,' said Nabal, who was also clasping a cup. 'This one's almost empty.'

Rebekah nodded, 'Yes, my lord.'

It always fell to Abigail to supply the manners that Nabal lacked. 'Thank you, Rebekah.'

Ira was already pulling off his boots. Abigail tried not to wince as the powerful odour rose up from his unclad feet. She was grateful when he plunged them into the water, almost immediately turning it a dirty brown. 'You asked of the war, Abigail,' he began. 'Well, I have a story to tell that may sound fanciful to your ears. But I will tell it better when I have had a bath and washed the battle off me, and when I have a belly full of good food.'

Abigail smiled. 'Then I will instruct Mered to fill a tub with water, and he will tell you when it is ready. I will return to preparing your meal.' With that she bowed to him, and turned to leave.

'My brother married a capable woman as well as a comely one!' Ira called after her. It was a compliment she never heard on her husband's lips.

Ira ate like a man who had been fasting for a week—the dish of spicy goat stew was wiped clean by the time he had finished, though Nabal had also eaten freely. Just a few torn pieces of bread were left in the basket, and it was only when Ira had then devoured almost half the figs soaked in honey syrup that he seemed ready to tell his story.

Abigail had requested and Nabal had granted Eliam's presence at the meal. It was not unknown for him to share their table, and Abigail knew that he would dearly love to hear news of Saul and the army of Israel. She also arranged for both Joel and Mered to wait on the table—not that there was much requirement for their services, but it gave them the opportunity to listen too. They were both standing attentively at the side of the room where Abigail could see them and motion to them if the jug of wine needed refilling—as it had done twice already.

Ira was wearing one of Nabal's deep green tunics whilst his own clothes were being washed. Despite Ira's broad shoulders, there was room to spare in the tunic. Ira loosened his belt as he sat back in his chair, took another swig of wine, and ran his tongue around his lips. 'It was a good meal, Brother.'

Nabal crossed his arms and rested them on his belly as he leaned back. 'You have kept us waiting long enough. Tell us this unbelievable tale of yours. We heard you were to the north-west in the Valley of Elah, facing the Philistine dogs, but no more than that.'

'He who holds Elah,' commented Eliam, 'holds the pass between the plains to the west and the hills of Judah.'

Ira nodded. 'It is no surprise the Philistines wanted to take it and gathered there for battle. We were on one hill, they were on another, with the valley between us.'

'Were the armies evenly matched?' asked Eliam.

'In most respects, save one,' replied Ira, raising an eyebrow. 'They had a champion, and one the like of which none of us had ever seen before. I am not a small man, but he was a monster—easily half my height again.' The eyes of both Joel and Mered widened. 'The shaft of his spear was like weaver's rod, and it was said that its point was six hundred shekels weight of iron.'

'Gideon's fleece!' exclaimed Nabal. 'You are making a cubit out of a span, surely.'

'I only speak of what I saw, as truly as the sun rises in the east. You can ask any man who was there.'

'And did this Philistine monster have a name?'

'Goliath...of Gath.' Ira shook his head slowly in wonder, as if the giant was before him once more. 'Every day when the armies went out to take up their battle positions, he would come out from the Philistine lines, his armour bearer before him, a javelin slung over his back, and sheathed from toe to head in bronze. Then he would taunt us, as we stood lined up for battle. He challenged us to find a man who would fight him. He claimed that if our champion overcame him, the Philistines would become our subjects, but if he killed our man, we would be theirs.' He spat on the ground to show what he thought of the truth of those words.

'And no one would fight him?' offered Eliam.

Ira shook his head. 'Not one.'

'Not even Jonathan?' asked Abigail. She had always treasured the stories of his victories, won through his courage and his faith in Yahweh.

'Jonathan is brave but he is no fool. Saul was even offering great wealth and his daughter's hand in marriage to the man who could kill the Philistine giant—and freedom from taxes for his father's whole family.'

'And you did not take up the challenge?' asked Nabal, with a hint of annoyance.

Abigail could not let it pass. 'Surely, my lord, you would not have wanted your brother to be so reckless with his life?' The rest of her words, *just so that you could grow richer,* remained unspoken. Though Nabal had nothing to say against Saul, especially since the army brought some protection to all he owned, he often had much to say about the livestock, olives and wine that were required from him to help support the royal household.

Ira brushed off Nabal's question. 'Not even for all the treasures in Egypt would I have faced that brute—and neither would any other man. It would have been a lamb against a lion. Utter madness!' He then smiled slyly at Abigail. 'Or so we thought.'

Joel and Mered exchanged glances, though their eyes were soon fixed on Nabal's brother once more, bright with anticipation.

'For forty days,' continued Ira, 'he came out shouting the same words: *This day I defy the ranks of Israel! Give me a man and let us fight each other*—and worse. Things I will not repeat in the hearing of a woman.'

'So what happened?' asked Nabal.

'About five days ago, shortly after the Philistine shouted out his usual challenge, there was a disturbance near Saul's tent—something had clearly happened, and there was murmuring amongst those nearby. I went over to find out more, and found a small group gathered around three brothers. I knew them by sight, if not by name, as they were also from the tribe of Judah—from Bethlehem. They had a much younger brother who had arrived with supplies from the town that morning, and he was the cause of the commotion. Apparently, when he heard the Philistine's taunts he called it a disgrace. And not only that.' Ira paused, shook his head and gave a little laugh. '*Who is this uncircumcised Philistine that he should defy the armies of the living God?* Those were his words, according to those who heard him.'

Abigail's spirit soared. *Here surely was a man in whose heart burned the honour of Yahweh and His people!*

'He was also asking how the man who killed the giant would be rewarded, and this was reported to Saul who then summoned him.'

Nabal emptied the jug of wine into his cup. 'Did this warrior intend to fight the Philistine then?' Ira laughed.

'Why do you laugh?' asked Abigail, even as her eyes reassured Joel and Mered they could leave the jug empty. Neither would want to miss anything.

'He was no warrior—far from it!'

Nabal put his cup down and leaned forward slightly. 'What do you mean?'

'*Just a shepherd boy*—that's what his eldest brother called him, and he was clearly furious at what the boy had said. He thought he should have stayed back in Bethlehem with the sheep, and wasn't slow in saying so. But then he swiftly shut his mouth. I followed his gaze and there was Saul, walking forward with a young man at his side. I doubt he was more than twenty years, if that.'

'Are you saying the king was sending this boy to fight the Philistine monster?' asked Nabal, incredulous.

'And not only that. He was going to fight him with neither helmet nor armour, sword nor spear.' Nabal spluttered. 'I told you you would not believe my story!' said Ira, an eyebrow raised. Abigail stared at him more in wonder than disbelief.

Nabal shook his head, clearly perplexed. 'But what on earth possessed Saul to agree to such madness?'

Ira's mood became sombre. He swilled the wine around in his cup for a few moments, staring at it, and then cast his gaze around the table. 'There are rumours,' he began. 'You hear whispers in the camp that there is a spirit that torments the king at times; that he is scarcely in his right mind when it comes upon him.' He paused. 'Whether this seeming madness was that, I do not know.' He shrugged. 'Maybe there was just something about this young man—' He smiled wryly. '—because there was.'

Eliam broke his silence. 'In what way?'

Ira sucked in a deep breath and shrugged again. 'How to describe it? It is true that he was little more than a boy, though a fine-looking one at that, and that Saul stood a head taller than him. But even dressed only in a tunic with a shepherd's bag over his shoulder, he carried himself well. As if...' Ira paused again, seemingly searching for the right words. 'As if he knew the outcome already.' The room was absolutely still. 'If he was terrified, he certainly did not show it.'

A question burned within Abigail. 'But you said he was going to fight the Philistine without a weapon...'

'Ah, no. I said he had neither sword nor spear, but he did not go unarmed. He had a sling and his shepherd's staff, and before he went to fight, he went in a search of a stream.'

'Why?' asked Abigail, mystified.

'It is stones washed smooth by water that will leave the sling most cleanly. He clearly knew that. And it would not have been a pebble!' Ira reached across and took Abigail's much smaller hand in his own. He studied it for a moment. 'The stone may have been as wide as your palm. The sling is not just a shepherd's weapon—there are those within armies who wield them too.' He paused again, a sly smile coming to his face once more. 'He was brave, yes—not a man standing there would have questioned that—but he was not stupid. Oh, he knew what he was doing!'

'Why do you say that?' asked Abigail.

Ira leaned forward, his dark eyes bright. 'What do you *not* do if you are facing an enemy who is more than six cubits tall with a sword and a huge spear?' Silence. Ira swept his gaze around the table, but the answer, when it was finally offered, came from the youngest in the room.

'You do not let him get anywhere near you!' exclaimed Mered, clearly unable to contain his excitement any longer. Abigail's face lit up with delight.

Ira slapped the table. 'Exactly, my young friend! And that is why he chose a sling—though you still need to be able to handle it well.'

'And did he?' asked Nabal.

'You must wait for my answer, for I must tell you of the words that were exchanged first—for I will remember them until the day I draw my last breath.'

The room fell silent once more. Abigail was rapt, her eyes fixed on Ira and scarcely breathing.

He went on. 'The Philistine called out as he approached, *Am I a dog that you come against me with sticks?* He clearly saw only the lad's staff. Then he cursed him by Dagon and the other Philistine gods, and said he would feed his flesh to the birds of the air and the beasts of the field. But the youth shouted out an answer that surely stirred every Israelite: *You come against me with sword and spear and javelin, but I come against you in the name of Yahweh Almighty, the God of the armies of Israel, whom you have defied. This day Yahweh will hand you over to me, and I'll strike you down and cut off your head.*' Ira paused and laughed. 'He did not even have a sword at that moment! Then he said that *he* would be the one feeding the birds and the beasts—and not just with the dead Philistine, but with the carcasses of their whole army! He said the whole world would know that there is a God in Israel, and all there that day would know that it is not by sword or spear that Yahweh saves. Then he ended with these words: *for the battle is Yahweh's, and He will give all of you into our hands.*'

Although Abigail was not standing on the battle lines, the words stirred her heart nevertheless. She now had no doubt as to how the story would end, but still hung on Ira's words as if they were sweetest honey.

'They both moved toward the battle line, but the boy ran—not away from the Philistine, but towards him. He threw his staff down and drew a stone from his bag. Whether the Philistine grasped what was happening or not, I do not know, but within a few heartbeats, the shepherd boy was whirling the sling around. When he released the stone, it flew fast as a lightning bolt and just as deadly. It found its mark in the centre of Goliath's forehead, just below the rim of his helmet. Whether he was dead before he fell face first to the ground, again I do not know. But I tell you this: the shepherd boy made sure of it. He ran over to the fallen giant, drew out the Philistine's own sword from its scabbard, and cut off his head.'

Abigail's eyes finally left her brother-in-law. She looked towards Joel and Mered. Their faces were alight with some joyous muddle of excitement, triumph and elation.

'What happened then?' asked Nabal.

'So much for the Philistine's words that they would become our servants. Pah!' He spat on the ground for a second time. 'They turned and ran! And so for the rest of the day we pursued them and struck them down, even as far as the gates of Gath and Ekron. Their bodies were strewn along the road. Then all that remained was to plunder all that they'd abandoned in their camp.' He tapped a small leather bag hanging from his belt. 'And now we are all richer men, and there is one fortunate family in Israel that no longer has taxes to pay!'

But there was one final question on Abigail's lips. 'The young man—what was his name?'

'David,' replied Ira. 'His name is David son of Jesse.'

As the seasons slipped by, news from the north trickled southward, like water in a wadi at the start of the autumn rains. Scarcely a month went by without some new tale of how David, now a commander in Saul's army, had led his troops to victory. And with the stories, a new song.

An unfamiliar tune drew Abigail out of the storehouse and into the sunshine, where Mahlah and Zillah were crouched over tubs of washing. 'What is it you're singing?'

'Just a song we learned from some girls in Carmel,' said Mahlah, as both she and Zillah paused from rubbing the cloth tunics together.

'And will you sing it for me?' Zillah giggled whilst Mahlah smiled coyly. The girls then looked at each other and Mahlah drew in a breath, giving both of them their cue.

'Saul has slain his thousands,' they intoned together in a cheerful melody, 'and David his tens of thousands.' The words were repeated several times, their voices rising higher and skipping about, like hinds on a crag, until they reached their triumphant peak. Zillah then giggled again.

Abigail smiled, but silently wondered what their king would make of it, if it ever reached his ears.

'It's true, isn't is, Mistress?' said Mahlah. 'Every time we hear of battles, it is David who is winning them and defeating the Philistines!'

'He is not winning them single-handedly!' replied Abigail with a little laugh. 'But, yes, it does seem to be true that our God grants him success whenever he leads his men into battle.' She paused, her heart gladdened. 'Yahweh is with him!'

Zillah stared into the distance, and then asked slightly breathlessly. 'Do you think he's married?'

To Abigail's amusement, Mahlah raised her eyes, tutted and shook her head. 'He is not going to wed a serving girl!' *She was becoming more like her mother every day.*

Zillah turned towards Abigail, the hope in her eyes not entirely quenched. 'But *is* he married?'

'I have not heard, but I do know Saul was offering his daughter in marriage to the man who killed Goliath.' As Zillah's face fell, a moment's desolation swept over Abigail. *It was not hard for the heart to be disappointed when it came to love. But neither was it wise to linger on ways in which her life could have been different.* She shook it off. 'How would it be,' began Abigail, 'if I found both of you a pomegranate when you have finished the washing?' She was rewarded with two broad smiles. *It never took much to divert Zillah's mind.*

It seemed that the name of David was never far from the lips of any who passed by. The story that David had presented Saul with two hundred Philistine foreskins, a bride price for the king's daughter Michal, was told and retold around Nabal's household until not a single person remained who did not know it. Abigail's heart continued to be stirred by any reports of David's exploits against the enemies of Israel—and by the triumphs that Yahweh granted him. Only one response seemed fitting.

'Will you come to worship?' The same question that Abigail had asked Nabal more than four years earlier received the same answer. It didn't deter her. 'The Philistines will not be a danger now if I travel to Nob to make our offerings.'

Nabal grunted. 'Go if you must, but not with Eliam. Take Joel this time.'

Abigail decided then and there she would take Rebekah instead of Zillah. Her story-telling was almost as rich as that of her husband, and when they departed two days later, Abigail's heart danced like a carefree swallow in flight above the hills of Judah.

They were about to recommence their journey, after breaking it at midday for food and a rest, when a man travelling south on foot rounded a bend on the road ahead. The supplies in their own cart were generous. As the man approached, Abigail bowed her head briefly and then smiled. 'Yahweh be with you, friend! Do you require food or water to refresh you on your travels? We have plenty.'

He returned her smile and accepted her offer.

'Have you travelled far?' she asked, as the stranger ate some bread Rebekah had baked that morning.

'From Shechem. I am journeying to Beersheba.'

'That is some distance to walk! We are blessed with a cart and are only going as far as the sanctuary at Nob.'

Her words had an immediate effect. He stopped eating, clearly taken aback. He looked round at each one of them. 'You haven't heard yet?'

The tone of the stranger's question and his clouded face filled Abigail's heart with dread. 'Heard what?' Her voice sounded very far away.

'The sanctuary at Nob is no more. Its priests were slaughtered.'

Abigail staggered and reached for Rebekah to steady herself. The older woman swiftly put a supporting arm around her. An image rose clearly in Abigail's mind: the cheerful face of the young priest who had made their offerings for them. She felt sick.

'All of them?' asked Rebekah, her voice strained.

'That is what I have heard…'

Mahlah began sobbing and Abigail let out a wail. 'Who would do such a terrible thing?'

'The Philistines!' interjected Joel angrily before the stranger had a chance to reply.

'No, worse than that.'

Abigail's mind was reeling. She could not possibly imagine how it could be worse—until she heard his answer.

He glanced around, as if to check that no others were near, and then leaned in. 'It was on the orders of King Saul.'

Joel and Rebekah gasped, but Abigail knew only horror. Suddenly she was falling, falling, down into darkness, with nothing to grasp hold of. *How could Yahweh's king slaughter Yahweh's priests?* It made no sense. She was too stunned to speak, too numb even to weep.

After a moment, Rebekah shook her head as if in utter incomprehension, and asked, 'Has he no fear of Yahweh? What madness possessed him to commit such evil?'

The man glanced around again and lowered his voice, though no one else was in sight. 'It is said that the priests there aided David.'

'Why should that matter to Saul?' asked Joel, utterly bewildered.

'Because it is also said that David was fleeing from the king, and that Saul wants him dead.'

Abigail finally found her voice again. 'But why?' she asked, in little more than a whisper. 'David fights Israel's battles. Everyone knows that Yahweh is with him…'

The stranger paused. 'Maybe there is your answer. Saul no longer sees a warrior but a rival.'

And Abigail remembered the song.

Notes

1. *Although David is popularly shown as young boy in artwork depicting his fight with Goliath, and is referred to twice in the passage as a 'boy' (1 Samuel 17:33,42), he is also described three times as a 'young man' (17:55-58) and has previously been referred to as a 'brave man and a warrior' (16:18). He is also seemingly old enough to immediately form a strong friendship with Jonathan (who may have been around forty at this time) and very soon was given a high rank in the army, with command over a significant number of soldiers (18:5,13). Consideration also needs*

to be given to chronology, and to the period David would have been on the run before becoming king at thirty. It may be best, therefore, to see David being around twenty when he killed Goliath.

2. Slingshots were used by armies and could be used with great accuracy: 'Among all these soldiers there were seven hundred select troops who were left-handed, each of whom could sling a stone at a hair and not miss' (Judges 20:16). See also 1 Chronicles 12:2 and 2 Chronicles 26:14. It seems they were the marksmen of the ancient world, and David was clearly one of them.

3. The introduction of taxes (and the corresponding economic changes) would have accompanied kingship. A king would require a supporting administration, which would also need to be fed and housed, as would the king's family and army. Samuel, in his speech about kingship to the people in 1 Samuel 8:11-18, mentions not only taxes and the need for an army, but also the need for labourers to farm the king's land and make weapons of war, and women to be cooks, bakers and perfumers—presumably to keep the king and his family regularly fed, his garments regularly perfumed, and spices burning around the palace to maintain a pleasing fragrance.

3

While David was in the wilderness, he heard that Nabal was shearing sheep. (1 Samuel 25:4)

Abigail's mind often flitted northwards to Nob in the months that followed the slaughter there, but each flight of her thoughts only ended in perplexity. *Even if Saul was jealous of David, how had that become a murderous rampage against the priests of Yahweh? Or, if the rumours were to be believed, maybe his mind had been in torment when he'd issued the order. Whatever his reasons, he had surely cut himself off from the Almighty by the act.* She wondered how Samuel—the prophet who had anointed Saul king over Israel—had reacted to the bloodshed. *Had he felt the same horror as she had done?* Nabal had shrugged it all off, muttering something about priests failing to honour their king. She had seen little point in reasoning with him. He remained loyal to a king who had protected his interests but his lips never spoke the name of the God of Israel—the true King that the priests had served. Abigail was sure of one thing, however: she could never again think of Saul as Yahweh's anointed.

They no longer heard tales of David fighting Saul's wars, but rather of the king's pursuit of his former champion. But even in that, Abigail found a strange hope. *Surely Yahweh would now be with David, the one whose faith in Him had already been rewarded with so many triumphs. After all, there were other rumours—rumours that David had been anointed king over Israel by Samuel. So would not Yahweh keep safe the one who honoured Him—not despite what had happened at Nob but also because of it?* Her daily prayers for the leader of Israel were no longer for Saul, and it was clear to her, at least, that by the hand of the Almighty, David continued to evade his pursuer.

'Is Eliam's foot sound again?' Despite her enquiry, Abigail's eyes stayed fixed on her labours. She let the spindle drop, flicking the stone whorl half way down the wooden rod to spin it round, so that it twisted the strands of wool from which it was hanging.

Rebekah tutted. 'He will not be told! He seems to think that walking into Carmel and back will aid its healing.'

Abigail laughed. The two women were perched on wooden stools in the shade on the north side of the house, both of them spinning wool. It was an art Abigail had learned from her mother, who had also taught her all the necessary preparations: how to wash the wool until it was free from mud, hay and seeds; then how to comb it back and forth, until the strands lay in the same direction and could be wrapped around the distaff, ready for spinning. The women chatted easily, almost oblivious of the steady rhythm of their fingers: teasing out more strands from the long, thin distaff tucked in the crook of their left arm, to feed into the long thread that was being twisted as the spindle spun round. When the yarn was long enough, they would stop the spindle, wind the thread around it until the free length was much shorter, securing it on the notch at the top of the spindle before continuing the teasing out and the spinning.

The wool was from the shearing that spring. Most was sold in exchange for silver, or bartered for grain or linen cloth or whatever else the household needed, and it was chiefly the wool that sustained or added to Nabal's wealth. But the spring was now over, and the days were becoming ever hotter as the barley harvest neared its end. Abigail suddenly looked up when she heard the sound of running. Mered slid on the dirt as he stopped himself, scattering stones. Both women grasped their spindles. 'The Philistines are raiding Keilah!' he exclaimed, before either could speak.

The town was not much more than a day's journey away. Abigail's brow furrowed. 'What do you mean?'

'A man from Hebron arrived in Carmel. He said that each time the men of Keilah finish threshing barley, the Philistines swoop down on the threshing floor in numbers and take the grain.'

'Do they not fight to protect it?' asked Rebekah, resting her spindle against the distaff.

Mered shook his head. 'They have not the numbers, so they abandon the grain and flee back to the town, where they can at least close and bar the gates against the Philistines.'

'They will starve, next year if not this, if it does not stop,' said Rebekah gravely.

Abigail nodded. 'Yes, and if they are raiding the barley with ease, they will do the same with the wheat.'

'It is as well that we are more than twice the distance from Gath as Keilah,' added Mered, 'and with the highest hills between us and the Philistines.'

'What of Saul and his army?' asked Abigail. 'Have they not come to defend the town?'

Mered shrugged. 'He did not say.'

All were silent for a moment, but then Rebekah's lips tightened. 'Please tell me, Mered, that you have not abandoned your sheep to run and tell us that.'

'I told one of the others to watch them until I returned. I thought the mistress would want to hear the news.'

Rebekah tutted. 'Get back at once, before your master hears that one of his new shepherds has little more sense than his sheep!' Her son grinned.

Abigail smiled. 'Thank you, Mered. Nabal would want to know of it.' But as Mered ran off as swiftly as he had arrived, Abigail's thoughts returned to the plight of Keilah. *At least the men had not been slaughtered. But would that continue to be the case?*

When, not many days later, further news came, it was, however, of the deliverance of the town—though not by Saul. Salvation had come by the hand of his former captain, David.

'They are like a lion and a gazelle in a chase,' said Eliam one day, as he and Abigail sat together in the courtyard. 'Our king seems as relentless as a beast with the smell of blood in its nostrils.'

Now and then, a new report would reach them of Saul's pursuit of David. They had heard how David had fled from Keilah before the king had mustered his troops to march south to besiege the town.

Saul's search then continued much closer, in the empty wilds of the hills nearby. Until, that is, the report of a Philistine raid drew Saul and his troops to the west, whilst David and the men gathered round him headed eastwards, towards the oasis and caves of En Gedi, on the shores of the Salt Sea.

Abigail laid her embroidery down in her lap, and turned to face her most trusted servant. 'The lion's paws may be deadly, but they are futile if the gazelle stays out of reach.'

'Then we must pray that its swift feet do not tire.'

The seasons slipped by, but the next news that reached Carmel was of neither David nor Saul. Samuel was dead. The prophet had been the voice of Yahweh to the people through the whole of Abigail's life and the lives of her parents before her, and Abigail mourned with the whole of Israel. *It was as if the land had lost its elderly father.*

Then winter turned to spring once more and to the season for shearing sheep—and with it came rumours that David and his men were once more nearby.

Abigail surveyed the scene. It seemed that every household servant was busy with preparations for the feast. Shearing was always marked with festivities and with rewards for the shepherds who safely returned the sheep under their care. Nabal's recompenses were never the most generous, given the ever-swelling mountain of fleeces near the house, but each year he did expect a lavish banquet when the shearing was completed. Abigail smiled to herself. *At least by eating at Nabal's table, the hired men received something more than just his niggardly payments.*

The smell of sheep roasting slowly over the extra fire pits that had been dug for the feast pervaded the air, both inside and out. Abigail drew alongside Eliam, who was overseeing the spits. 'Have the other five sheep been dressed?'

Eliam craned his head, peering between the horde of servants and through the smoke rising from the fires. 'It looks as though Joel has almost finished the final sheep. I will begin roasting them when these ten are nearly ready, so freshly cooked meat can be brought out later, as you suggest.'

'Good.' She held up a handful of herbs she had picked herself. 'I must return to the pots of stew.'

The rich aroma of the cooking meat was soon mingling with that of fresh bread, as scores upon scores of flat loaves were swiftly baked on the surfaces of the bronze domed ovens.

As the shadows began to lengthen and Nabal's hired men started gathering for the feast, Abigail allowed herself both a moment to pause and a small measure of satisfaction. *Aside from the broken jug of oil, everything was going according to the plan she had drawn up with Rebekah.* But almost as soon as she had joined Joel to oversee the mounting of the remaining sheep onto spits, he suddenly paused and looked beyond Abigail. His expression changed in an instant.

'What is it, Joel?' But the moment Abigail turned, she had her answer, at least in part. Eliam was hurrying towards them with Mered at his side. Neither countenance matched the festive mood. For a moment, their faces reminded her of the man who had brought them the news of the slaughter at Nob, and Abigail suddenly felt as if a weight of iron had dropped into her stomach. She had not seen Mered for the best part of a month, as he had been in the fields with the sheep.

'Something's happened,' murmured Joel.

Mered's face was red and damp, as though he had run some distance at speed, and there were no greetings when the two arrived moments later. 'Mered,' began Eliam, his voice urgent, 'tell Abigail what you told me.'

'I was with my sheep as they were being shorn,' he began breathlessly. 'Nabal was nearby, overseeing the shearers. A group of ten men came up the hill towards us. They asked one of the men nearby to point Nabal out, and then approached him. They were messengers sent by David from the desert to give our master his greeting. I heard them wishing him long life and good health. They then asked Nabal if he would be generous to them, since it was a festive time and they had always treated his shepherds well.'

Abigail's stomach tightened, almost fearing to ask her question. 'And what was Nabal's reply?'

Mered glanced at Eliam, who nodded to him. 'He hurled insults at them. He spoke as if he'd never heard of David, and then as if he was some sort of worthless servant rebelling against Saul. He asked why he should take what he had prepared for his shearers and give it to men coming from who knows where, and he sent them away.'

Despite the spring sunshine, Abigail felt a sudden chill.

But Mered hadn't finished. 'The messengers had spoken truly. David's men were very good to us when we were out in the fields. They never ill-treated us and never took anything from us. In fact, night and day they were a wall around us, protecting us all the time we were tending our sheep.' Mered paused and then stared at Abigail, wide-eyed. 'Do something quickly, Mistress!' he implored. 'Disaster is hanging over all of us—not just Nabal. But he's so stubborn—he won't listen to anyone. He never does!'

'Mered!' exclaimed Joel sharply. 'Put a guard on your mouth!'

'No, do not chide him, Joel,' interjected Abigail. She glanced at both him and his father. 'You both know, as I do, that Mered speaks the truth.'

'If we do not act soon,' said Eliam grimly, 'we may face the wrath of David. And he and his men know how to handle a sword.'

But even as he spoke, Abigail's mind was running ahead. She turned to Mered. 'How many men does David have with him? Do you know?'

Mered nodded. 'Yes, six hundred. That's what one of his men told us.'

She thought for a moment. 'Fetch ten donkeys—the pack animals—and my donkey with them. Bring them here as quickly as you can. Get help if you need it. Go now—delay may bring our doom!' Mered turned and ran. 'Joel—I want to you load the five sheep you've prepared onto donkeys when Mered returns. While you are waiting for him, find five others in the flock to replace these. You will then have to dress them again for the feast.'

Joel nodded, 'Yes, Mistress.' He left immediately.

'Eliam, find some other servants to help you and go to the storehouse. Tell them to load a hundred cakes of raisins and two hundred cakes of pressed figs into the wide-mouthed jars with handles, and then bring them here with some rope to tie them to the donkeys. Leave them to the task, and return to me with two wineskins and some empty sacks. I will be with Rebekah. Go now—and may Yahweh grant us both speed and success in our time of peril.'

As Eliam hurried off in one direction, Abigail picked up her skirts and ran in the other.

Rebekah looked up as Abigail approached. Her face fell. 'Whatever is the matter?'

'Quick, Rebekah. There is no time to lose. Gather together as many loaves as you and the others have baked so far. You will have to grind more barley and wheat to replace them.'

'What on earth has happened?' she asked, perplexed. 'And what if the new bread isn't ready when Nabal returns?'

'Our lives—and Nabal's too—may depend upon these loaves. If the replacements are not ready, he will just have to wait. Ply Nabal with wine and meat and he will be happy enough. Come now, we must hurry—and I will explain as we are gathering the bread.'

When Eliam returned with the wine and sacks, the women began loading the bread into them. 'Please, Eliam,' said Abigail as she picked up a loaf, 'take one of the empty sacks and find Hephzibah. She is roasting grain. Tell her to measure five seahs of roasted wheat or barley into it and then have one of the men bring the sack here. Again, she will need to fetch more grain from the storehouse to replace it. Then I will need you to make sure that everything is securely loaded onto the donkeys when Mered returns.'

As her urgent commands were being carried out, Abigail stopped for a moment and closed her eyes. The commotion faded as she stilled her heart. *Yahweh, hear the voice of Your handmaid,* she prayed silently. *Have mercy on Your servants around whom the cords of death are coiled through my husband's folly. Grant me wisdom in the words I speak and favour with Your servant David. Come quickly to save us, Lord Almighty, or we are lost.'* Then a tap on her shoulder, and all was noise again. She turned and found Joel.

'The donkeys are here.'

'Already? Are you sure?'

'Mered rounded up some of the lads and they raced them over here.'

Despite their peril, Abigail laughed with incredulity. 'Yahweh be praised for the rashness of your brother!' Her eyes then darted about her until they found the person she was looking for. 'Mahlah!' When the young woman looked up, Abigail beckoned. 'Come! Follow me.' She turned to Joel. 'Now let us go and make sure all is ready.'

When the animals were loaded, aided by the skill of Eliam, Abigail again spoke urgently. 'Joel—you and Mered lead the donkeys with some of the other lads. Your brother will show you the way towards David's camp.' She turned to Eliam. 'You must stay here so that nothing seems amiss. Nabal must know nothing of what is being done.'

'I will make sure no servant utters a single word of it.'

Abigail was grateful that he was a man of his word. 'Thank you. And ask Rebekah to ready my donkey.' Her eyes shifted to the brothers. 'Go on ahead, Joel. I will follow.' He acknowledged her with a nod, and she then turned to Mahlah. 'Come to the house with me—we must be quick.'

Once she was in her own room, with a bowl of cool water brought by Mahlah, she swiftly cast aside both the shawl covering her head and her grubby tunic, soiled with flour and dust. She quickly washed away the dirt and sweat of the day, and slipped on the fresh, clean garments that Mahlah had picked out for her. The muted greens and yellows of the embroidered clothes blended well. 'You have chosen wisely,' said Abigail, as her maid adjusted her shawl so that it fell evenly on both sides. She then slipped on her best sandals, before they both hurried out to where Rebekah was holding her donkey in readiness.

As she mounted the beast, her eyes met those of the older woman. 'Pray for me, please, Rebekah, that Yahweh will grant me success.'

She smiled. 'I will not stop until He returns you safely.'

'Thank you.' With that, Abigail urged the donkey forward and into a trot, her mind now on one matter and one matter only. *Help me, Yahweh. The words I speak must be as seed upon fertile ground.* As the house receded into the distance, one thought more than any other impressed itself on her mind: *Yahweh's future leader must not sully his hands with the blood of revenge. Carmel must not become another Nob.* And words began to flow into her mind.

Before too long, the path descended a hill and went into a wide ravine. She rounded a bend at the bottom, and the other donkeys came into view ahead of her. She nudged her own animal on, until she had passed them and was at the head of the line with Joel. She slowed her donkey to the walking pace of the others. She had reached them none too soon.

As they rounded another bend, Joel suddenly drew in a deep breath. 'Look!'

Abigail's breast tightened. A stone's throw ahead of them, just where the ground began to rise again, a cascade of men was pouring into the ravine. Hundreds of them—and they were armed.

She dismounted quickly and turned swiftly to those behind her. Every face was filled with fear and there was nowhere to run. 'Yahweh is with us—do not be afraid.' But she knew her words were as much to herself as them. She turned back to face the small army that now confronted her. There was one young man of roughly her age leading them, sword unsheathed and with a face as dark as a thundercloud. She had no doubt it was David. She hurried forward and fell before him, bowing her head low to the dirt at his feet. She raised her head slightly, but kept it bowed. A hush seemed to fall over the men with David, but she did not wait for him to speak.

'My lord,' she began, 'let the blame fall on me alone. Please let your servant speak to you, and listen to the words of your servant.' Her heart was thundering within her chest. 'May my lord pay no regard to this worthless man, Nabal, for his name describes him well. Folly is his name and folly goes with him. But as for me, your servant did not see the young men that my lord sent to my husband. Now, my lord, as surely as Yahweh lives and as you live, Yahweh has kept you from shedding blood, and from avenging yourself by your own hand. So now let your enemies and those who seek evil against my lord, become as Nabal.' She paused for the briefest of moments. *Help, me Yahweh!* 'Now let this gift, which your servant has brought to my lord, be given to the men with you. Please forgive your servant's offence; for Yahweh will certainly make for my lord an enduring house, because my lord is fighting Yahweh's battles. Let no wrongdoing be found in you all your days.'

She paused again, and suddenly—unbidden—a picture rose in her mind of David standing facing a giant with only a sling in his hand. Then words that she had not planned flowed freely, as if they had come from beyond her own heart and mind. 'Even though someone is pursuing you to seek your life, the life of my lord will be bound securely in the bundle of the living by Yahweh your God. But the lives of your enemies He will hurl out as from the pocket of a sling. And when Yahweh does for my lord all the good that He has promised you, and appoints you ruler over Israel, my lord will not be grieved or burdened with a troubled mind, either by needless bloodshed or by having avenged himself.' She drew a breath. Still David did not speak. 'And when Yahweh brings success to my lord, then remember your servant.' *She had said all that she could.* Abigail stared at the dirt, her chest heaving.

For a few moments there was silence. Then Abigail felt a finger under her chin, lifting her head. She looked up into David's face— and she knew her prayers had been heard. All anger had drained from it, and instead she saw only a youthful smile and found herself staring into deep brown eyes that radiated joy. He offered her a hand, which she took, and he raised her to her feet. For a moment he simply stared at her in wonder. He then lifted his eyes to heaven.

'Blessed be Yahweh, the God of Israel, who has this day sent you to meet me.' His gaze returned to her. 'And blessed be you and your good judgment, which has indeed kept me this day from bloodshed and from avenging myself by my own hand.' His smile faded into solemnity. 'As surely as Yahweh, the God of Israel, lives, who has kept me from harming you, if you had not hurried to meet me, not one male belonging to Nabal's household would have been left alive by daybreak.'

For a moment, it was as if spring had been overtaken by winter, as the truth of how close disaster had come to them swept over Abigail. She thought of Eliam, of Joel and of Mered, and her heart offered a silent prayer of thanks to the unseen God. Nabal did not enter her mind, save as the one who had almost brought ruin down upon his own foolish head—and the heads of all around him. She bowed low once again, and then turned and beckoned her companions forward. 'There is meat and bread, my lord, as well as roasted grain, raisins and figs. And may my lord's heart be gladdened by the skins of wine. Take all the donkeys also, and may Yahweh bless your feasting tonight at this festive season.'

David smiled broadly, and then with a hint of mirth. 'I will gladly receive all from your hand, save the donkey on which you rode. I would not deprive such a wise woman of her mount.' He bowed his head slightly to her, as if in deference.

Abigail felt herself flushing, and swiftly lowered her eyes. She was relieved when his attention left her.

David turned slightly and called over his shoulder: 'Benaiah—come and bring men to take this generous offering.' His gaze returned to her. 'Go up in peace to your house. I have heard your words and granted your petition.'

Before taking her leave, she bowed low one final time.

Eliam was watching for their return and hurried to meet them. 'Yahweh be praised for your safe return,' he breathed as he embraced Abigail like a father would his daughter. He stepped back, clearly also relieved to see his sons at her side. Rebekah ran out and threw her arms around Mered and then Joel. 'All went well?' asked Eliam. 'I see no loaded donkeys.'

'All went well,' echoed Abigail. 'David gladly took what we offered and the sword has been turned away.' She glanced at the house. The sound of tables being banged mingled with rowdy laughter. 'Nabal knows nothing of this?'

'He is in high spirits and feasting like a king. The servants have all been true to their word. He knows nothing.'

'As ever,' quipped Mered with a mischievous smile.

Abigail's laughter saved him from another reprimand, and the others joined her, relieved as much as amused. When the laughter subsided Eliam became serious again. He looked Abigail in the eye. 'Will you tell Nabal?'

She drew in a deep breath and then released it. 'I must. I will not deceive my husband.' She then added quietly, 'He has no idea how close he has come to death.'

Eliam nodded. 'But you will not do it alone. I will stand by your side.'

But when they entered the house, it was clear to Abigail that the news would have to wait. She shook her head. 'He is already so drunk that he will barely know what I am saying. I will wait until daybreak when he is sober.' And with that, she left the room. She didn't see him that night—and was grateful.

Eliam was true to his word, and accompanied her the following morning back into the room, bearing bread, water and curds between them. Nabal was slumped at the table snoring. Abigail cleared a space on the table still littered with the remnants of the banquet, and they set what they were carrying before him. They looked at each other, and Abigail then shook Nabal gently. 'My lord.' The words sounded hollow. *It had been different with David.* She shook him once more and repeated the words. Nabal grunted and opened his eyes blearily. He winced at the light. 'My lord, we have brought you bread, and water to quench your thirst.'

Without a word, Nabal pushed the bread and curds away from him, and drank straight from the jug, ignoring the cup beside it. Water ran down his beard. As he set the jug down and wiped his hand across his mouth, Abigail began. 'My lord, I must tell you some news.'

He listened wide-eyed as she began her story, but against all expectation failed to utter a single word. He suddenly jolted as she finished.

'My lord?' When Nabal failed to respond, staring blankly ahead, Abigail turned towards Eliam, confused. 'What has happened to him?'

'I do not know.' But however much Eliam tried to rouse him, Nabal neither spoke nor moved. 'It is as if he has been turned to stone,' whispered Eliam eventually, after all his efforts had failed.

'We must move him to his bed,' said Abigail. 'Fetch some others—you will need at least three or four strong men.' As Eliam left them, Abigail remembered her words to David the previous day. *Let your enemies become as Nabal. Had she somehow known that doom still dangled over him? Was this Yahweh fulfilling her words?* She couldn't be sure. Neither could she know if his strange state had come upon him in rage at her gifts to David or maybe terror at knowing how narrowly he had missed the sword. Either way, something deep within told her that Yahweh's hand was at work.

When Nabal died ten days later, and after his swift burial, Abigail sent a simple message to David by the mouth of Joel: *Yahweh has avenged his servant David, striking down his enemy Nabal by His own mighty hand.* There was nothing more that needed to be said.

Eliam sat beside her on a bench in the courtyard. 'What will you do?'

She understood his meaning, despite the brevity of the question. She was now a widow, and all that was Nabal's would pass to Ira. But she had no desire to be given to him simply to raise up a line for Nabal, and Ira would not want to lose any or all of the inheritance to a child. *Besides, Nabal's name was best forgotten.*

'I do not yet know, but whatever I do or wherever I go, you must stay. No one knows how to run this household and the servants as you do.'

'Except you!'

Abigail laughed. Her heart felt free for the first time for many years. But before either of them could say another word, Abigail heard her name being called by Joel. 'I'm in the courtyard.' She heard his approach. *He was not alone.* She rose as Joel entered with two unfamiliar men. He was grinning as if he were his younger brother. Abigail bowed her head to the men, and then looked from one to the other. 'How may I help you?'

'David has sent us,' began one of the men, 'to take you to become his wife.'

For a moment she stared at them. *Had she heard them rightly?* But then her heart suddenly flooded with childhood dreams that had been strangled and then buried, she'd thought, forever. Dreams of being taken into the home of a godly man—like her father. Dreams of a husband she would deeply respect and then grow to love. Even dreams of a man to whom she would be naturally drawn. Her heart soared. She bowed down with her face to the ground, as she had done ten days earlier before David. 'Here is your maidservant,' she said simply, 'ready to serve you and wash the feet of my master's servants.'

A flurry of hasty preparations had followed the pronouncement of David's servants, and when Abigail mounted her donkey once more, after embracing every member of Eliam's family, she was not clothed in muted colours as she had been before, but in vibrant orange and a deep red, perfumed and ready for her new husband. Zillah and four younger girls accompanied her as her maids. Much as she would have loved Hephzibah or Mahlah, both were now married, but thankfully, some of the latter's sense had finally rubbed off on Zillah.

Abigail knew there would be no lavish feast to follow her marriage, as there had been when she had wed Nabal. But she cared little for that. She was marrying a man whom she was finally happy to call *my lord*. That he was still an outlaw in the eyes of the king was, for the moment at least, all but forgotten.

Notes

1. *It is not clear how widely others knew of David's anointing by Samuel, though it had been done in the presence of his family, and quite likely also the townspeople of Bethlehem (see 1 Samuel 16:4-5). As the story of David unfolds, it certainly seems that others know of God's promises to David—as Abigail does here (1 Samuel 25:30).*
2. *Scripture gives little description of Nabal's demise, other than to say that*

when Abigail told him what had happened, 'his heart failed him and he became like a stone. About ten days later, the LORD struck Nabal and he died.' (1 Samuel 25:37-38). The above story has tried to stay faithful to these scant details.

4

'Abigail…went with David's messengers and became his wife.'
(1 Samuel 25:42)

As Abigail gradually slipped out of sleep, the first thing of which she became aware was the sweet sound of a lyre. Nimble fingers were plucking the strings, sometimes playing single notes, at other times, two together. A melody was being picked out as the pitch rose and fell, and woven into it was a soft but rich voice. *It was beautiful.* She opened her eyes. David was wearing only a simple tunic as he sat on a small wooden stool. The lyre, with its two curved arms rising to meet the crossbar at the top, rested on one knee as he played it. His fingers danced across the ten strings that stretched from the base to the top of the instrument, like yarn on a loom. His eyes appeared to be closed, and his words were as sweet as the music

> *'Taste and see that Yahweh is good;*
> *blessed is the one who takes refuge in Him.'*

Her heart drank in all that her senses gifted her. She had forgotten what it felt like to be overwhelmed with such joy and contentment that she wondered she didn't shatter. It mattered little that she was lying on a mat not a bed, and was in a small, simple tent rather than a large house marked by the trappings of wealth. *She had a husband whose heart sought Yahweh's.* And as if that were not enough, it was almost impossible not to feel drawn towards him like a child towards honey. Even in the dim light of the tent, she could make out the reddish tinge to his hair and his features that seemed without flaw. There was only one word that seemed capable of carrying the weight of what she was feeling: *blessed.*

They had lain together the previous evening to seal their marriage, though David had swiftly succumbed to sleep after their union. Abigail had seen the exhaustion in his eyes. *Running from Saul clearly bore a cost.* She had fallen asleep with her head on his chest and his arm flung over her—and David did not snore. Rather, his steady, deep breathing lulled her to sleep. In all her years with Nabal, she had never felt such intimacy or security.

The plucking of the strings slowed.

'Yahweh will rescue His servants;
no one who takes refuge in Him will be condemned.'

After a few more notes and a final strum, the instrument fell silent. David suddenly seemed to become aware of her and turned his head. 'Did I wake you?'

'If you did, it was the sweetest awakening I have ever had.' She smiled but suddenly felt shy. *Here was a man who would be king!* When David returned her smile, her heart quietened. She suddenly went to move. 'Are you hungry, my lord?'

David held up his hand. 'For one day at least, this is not a morning for you to be baking bread. Ahinoam will take care of it.' That David was married to Saul's daughter Michal had been known to all Israel for some years, but that he had taken a second wife from the city of Jezreel in the hills of Judah was something Abigail had only discovered the previous night. Her reason told her that it was in David's interest to form alliances that might yield refuge or support or friends amongst the elders of Israel—but her heart still felt a pang.

David rose, pulled back the tent flap and disappeared outside. It was only then that Abigail began to properly notice the sounds outside: men calling out, animals bleating, laughter, women chattering. The sounds of a small town. She marvelled at how David had managed to evade Saul's grasp for so long with such a following.

Zillah's head suddenly appeared at the door of the tent. 'Shall I bring you water to wash, Mistress?'

'Only if there is plenty here.' Abigail was suddenly conscious of her new station and of the privations that might accompany it. 'I would not deplete precious supplies for the sake of a wash.'

'There is a stream nearby. I will fill a bowl.'

'Tell one of the others to bring the dark green dress.'

'Yes, Mistress.' And then she was gone.

By the time David reappeared bearing bread, a skin of milk and raisin cakes, Abigail was both washed and dressed, and was busy tidying the covers and pillows that had been their bed for the night. David paused as the tent flap fell back behind him and studied her. She straightened up and saw what she took to be approval in his eyes—and blushed.

'Yahweh has blessed me with a wife who has both wisdom *and* beauty.'

She smiled coyly, lowering her gaze. She was not used to such compliments. 'I only wish to be pleasing in my lord's eyes.'

He placed all that was in his hands on the patterned rug and approached her. He ran a hand through her newly-brushed hair and kissed her, before stepping back and studying her again, a questioning look in his eyes. He glanced at the bed covers. 'Most would leave a maid to do that, if they had one.'

Abigail laughed. 'I see little sense in asking another to do a task that will take but a moment or two. Besides, it is better to be diligent than idle.'

David smiled wryly as he indicated for her to join him on the rug. 'It is as well that you think that, for life is often hard in the camp.'

Abigail sat down opposite David, her legs tucked under her, and voiced the matter she had pondered earlier. 'It cannot be easy staying beyond Saul's reach with so many following you.'

David tore a piece from a round of bread. 'There is a constant need for scouts out in the hills, watching for any sign of the king. But it is by the goodness of Yahweh more than anything else that we are delivered from the hand of Saul.' He paused, the bread still in his hand. 'We have Abiathar son of Ahimelek, one of the priests of Nob, with us—and with him, the ephod. Yahweh directs us through it.'

Abigail stared at him, dumbfounded. 'Praise be to Yahweh! I had thought all the priests dead!'

David's brow furrowed, however, and he looked troubled. 'It was by the mouth of Abiathar that I learned the news of the slaughter. He alone escaped the sword of Doeg the Edomite.'

'Was it not at Saul's behest though?'

'It was, but the hand that wielded the weapon was Doeg's alone. But the blood of the priests is on my hands.'

Abigail's wonder turned to confusion. 'How so, my lord?'

'I knew that Doeg was there when I sought help at Nob from Ahimelek. I knew he was a servant of Saul and would surely tell him.'

'But you could not know that the king would command such an unimaginably wicked act!'

David shrugged. 'I know Saul better than many, and yet I did nothing.'

Abigail leant over and rested a hand on David's arm. 'But it was Saul who commanded the deed—surely it is he alone who bears the guilt before Yahweh.'

A moment passed and the cloud lifted from David. 'It is not only the goodness of Yahweh that follows me wherever I go, but also His mercy.'

Abigail thought again of her recent deliverance from Nabal. 'Yahweh is merciful indeed.'

David ate the bread and then took the skin and drank from it. He passed it to Abigail as he drew a finger across his lips to wipe away the remnants of the milk. After she too had drunk and passed the skin back to him to stopper, he paused, his deep brown eyes sparkling as he held her gaze. 'Few women I have met speak of Yahweh as you do.'

'My mother spoke freely of Him from my earliest days. It is her and my father I have to thank for the greatest gift they could ever have given me—the knowledge of the God of Israel.'

'Do they live still?'

'I lost them some years ago. It was my eldest brother who arranged my marriage to Nabal. But from what I hear, you also have elder brothers who may not see as you do. My brother-in-law spoke of seeing the three of them in Saul's camp at Elam.'

David chuckled as he took a bite from a raisin cake.

There was something delightfully boyish about him. 'Why do you laugh?'

When David had swallowed, he grinned. 'If it were only three elder brothers, my life might have been easier! I am the youngest of the eight sons of Jesse.' For a while, as they continued to eat, both spoke of their families and homes. As Abigail consumed the last of her raisin cake, he described learning the skills of a shepherd. 'And that is why,' he added as he finished, 'my father had to send for me when Samuel came to Bethlehem—being the youngest, I was left tending the sheep.'

'We heard rumours that Samuel had anointed you king over Israel...'

'It was eight years ago,' said David quietly. 'I was only eighteen. I am not sure anyone but Samuel would have chosen me among my brothers—the youngest and the least impressive.'

'And yet are not those the ones that Yahweh so often calls, as He has done you?' Abigail suddenly realised what she had said. 'Not that I am saying that you are unimpressive, my lord! What I mean is...' She hesitated, flustered.

David laughed and laid his hand on her arm. 'Do not worry, Abigail. The words were my own before they were yours, and I have been called much worse, particularly by my brothers!'

Abigail had collected her thoughts, however. 'But is it not true, my lord, that it is not the first time Yahweh has chosen the younger over the older? Did he not also choose Shem over Japheth, Jacob over Esau, and Judah over Reuben?'

'You know our people's story well...'

'I have learned it from men who love not only our people but our God—as you do. And maybe that is why Yahweh has anointed *you* over His people.'

David was silent for a few moments, his thoughts seemingly far away. 'I felt His Spirit come upon me as the oil ran down my face.' He paused and Abigail waited. His eyes were fixed beyond the walls of the tent. 'I knew on the day I faced Goliath that the fervour that stirred in my heart was not mine alone. The God of Israel had never seemed so great nor the enemy so puny, and the zeal for Yahweh's honour burned so powerfully in my soul that it was as if I would find no rest unless I acted. And I had never been so sure that the stone from my sling would find its mark.' His attention was suddenly back in the tent. He rolled over and reached for a leather bag and pulled it towards him. He resumed his cross-legged position and drew an item from the bag. He set it before Abigail. A piece of leather, pointed at both ends and wider in the middle, was fastened between two lengths of braided cord, each maybe a cubit or more in length. One cord had a small loop at its end, the other a large knot. It looked worn.

Abigail looked at it in wonder. 'Is that the sling you used to defeat the Philistine giant?'

David nodded. 'It is the one I have used since I was a boy in the fields with the sheep. My father made it for me and he made it well.' He glanced up at her. 'Have you ever seen one wielded?'

'No, though my husband's brother spoke of their use.'

David returned the sling to the bag and threw it over his shoulder. 'Come!' He rose and held a hand out to Abigail, pulling her to her feet.

Moments later they were walking through the camp. David acknowledged most, as they passed men tending animals or weapons or fires and women watching over bread or babies. They seemed a strange assembly and as far from what she imagined an army to be as east was from west. 'How is it that these men have joined themselves to you?' It seemed the most prudent way to voice her curiosity.

David shrugged. 'Distress or debt or discontent have driven most of them to me—or I could say that Yahweh has brought them. Hardship and a purpose has made keen fighters of many of them, and I am grateful for each one.' He paused and grinned. 'Well, mostly...'

When a man hailed David across the company, he called back, 'Later, Joab, later...' He turned to Abigail with a wry smile. 'That is the eldest son of my sister Zeruiah. As she was old enough to be my mother—and married—by the time I was born, I am more like a cousin to them than an uncle. Those two with him—they are his brothers, Abishai and Asahel. Joab is cunning as a fox, and I have never seen a spear as deft and so deadly as that of Abishai. Although I would better Asahel any day in wielding a sling, none here could outrun him. He is fleet-footed and could match the pace of a gazelle.' But then he shook his head and said in a low voice, 'There are few better fighters, and each as valiant as a lioness defending her cubs—yet all untameable as the Jordan in flood.'

Abigail's heart delighted in David's trust in her. Though they had been wed for less than a day, he spoke to her as Nabal had never done. She was at ease with him as if he had been Eliam or Joel. They continued walking to the edge of the company, Abigail watching closely as David greeted others or stopped to talk. In addition to Abiathar the priest, there were two others to whom David seemed particularly close. Gad was one, whom David described as a prophet, though he had not said whether he had been among the prophets under Samuel. The other was a man named Benaiah, who had a javelin slung across his back and who spoke freely and easily with her husband. Abigail recognised him as the man in the ravine to whom David had entrusted the supplies she had brought from Nabal's store. He was taller and stockier than David—a bear of a man—and brave would be the warrior who would face him on the battle field. There was something about him that Abigail instinctively liked and David clearly trusted him. They spoke and laughed together as if they were kin.

As they left Benaiah, Abigail suddenly asked, 'Your brothers—do they still fight with Saul?'

He glanced about him, his eyes searching. 'No, they are here somewhere. They came to me with my mother and father when I was taking refuge in the cave of Adullam. My parents are old—too old for the life of a fugitive, so I have sent them beyond the Salt Sea. They are with the king of Moab.' David clearly saw Abigail's surprise. 'You wonder why Moab? The answer is simple: I have Moabite bone and flesh within me. One of my ancestors, Boaz, married a Moabitess.' He turned his face towards Abigail as they walked along. 'I will tell you her story one day—it is a fine story and one that I treasure. Her name was Ruth, and she was a woman of noble character who placed her trust in Yahweh. And now Yahweh has blessed me with my own Ruth.'

Abigail blushed. 'I will look forward to hearing her tale.'

David slowed his pace and then stopped. They had reached the edge of the settlement. The familiar hill country of Judah lay in every direction, with trees, rocks and bushes scattered over the slopes nearby. David's eyes roamed the stony ground near his feet until he found what he wanted. He leaned down and picked up a stone. 'It is not perfect, but it is the smoothest I will find here and it will suffice.' He glanced at her and grinned. 'After all, I learned how to use this out in the fields with the sheep and there was not always a stream nearby. The passing of countless days was helped not only by my lyre but also by a game I could play by myself.' He drew the sling from his bag. 'See—I put the loop at this end of the sling over my tallest finger.'

She watched as he slipped it on. 'So it holds the sling fast to your hand?'

'You are a quick learner. I then hold the knot at the end of the other cord between my thumb and first finger—' He did so. '—and put the stone in the pouch of the sling.' He paused when the stone was in place as his gaze returned to the land around them. 'When I swing it and then let go of the knot, releasing one end of the sling, the stone will fly out. Now, name your mark.'

Abigail glanced around her, her eyes coming to rest on a tree which she judged to be thirty or forty paces away. 'That tree,' she said, pointing.

He raised an eyebrow. 'Then I will ask, which part of the tree?'

'The middle of the trunk.'

'As you wish.' He took two steps away from her, and in barely the blink of an eye and before she had time to move her gaze from him, he had whipped the sling around in the air and let go of the knot. She didn't see the stone fly—only the freed end of the cord leaping into the air. There was a sharp thud at the same moment.

'Did it hit the tree?' she asked, looking towards it.

'You were meant to be watching the trunk not the slinger!' laughed David.

'You were too swift for me—I wasn't ready.'

'And that is also why the giant fell.' David looked around him. 'The uncircumcised Philistine received his due for mocking the God of Israel. Yahweh had been with me when I had fought lions and bears in the field protecting the sheep—and I knew it would be no different with the Philistine.' Suddenly he put his head back and laughed again. 'My father had only sent me to the battle line to deliver bread to my brothers and cheese to their commander!'

'But Yahweh had other ideas.'

'He chose a shepherd boy whom He had put out in the fields years earlier, to learn there not only how to shepherd sheep and but also how to master the sling, so he could hit a knot in a tree at a hundred paces.' He searched the ground again and picked up a small, roundish rock, the size of her clenched fist. He tossed it in the air and caught it, feeling its weight. He looked around once more and then pointed. 'There—see the rock that is set apart on yonder slope, to the left of the oak?'

Abigail shaded her eyes and squinted at the far point. 'I see it.'

'Now watch it—not me.'

Abigail saw only the briefest flash of movement, but heard the thunderous *crack* that echoed off the hills around. A barely visible wisp of dust rose from the rock—and Abigail thought of the Philistine's head. *No wonder he had toppled like a felled cedar.* 'Yahweh chose you to be a shepherd of His people,' she murmured, her eyes still on the rock, '*and* a mighty warrior,'

'Hmm. But the day the Spirit of Yahweh came upon me was also the day that set me on the path that has brought me here. I have been hunted and betrayed, and driven into exile, into caves and to the edge of God's people.' He sighed. 'Yahweh may have anointed me after rejecting Saul as king, but I know not what hardships still lie ahead or how long it will be until His promises are fulfilled.'

Both stood in silence for a few moments. 'But you are not alone,' said Abigail softly. 'Yahweh is with you, and has given you men and women who love you and who will follow you anywhere!'

He turned to her. 'And you are among them?'

'My heart loved you before I ever met you.' He smiled and kissed her. She went on. 'You were singing of Yahweh's deliverance as I woke this morning. He will surely be faithful in continuing to deliver you from the hand of Saul.'

'He has delivered me from my own folly too. I wrote that psalm after I had to feign madness to escape from Abimilek, the king of Gath. Though I cannot have been in my right mind to flee from the reach of Saul into Philistine territory! Thankfully none there had set eyes on me before—they had only heard of a fighter named David. So to the king, I was just another madman claiming to be someone of renown. But I know it is from Yahweh that salvation truly comes.'

'Maybe Yahweh will strike Saul down as He did Nabal…'

'Then once again, it will not be by my hand.'

Abigail turned to face David. 'But Nabal did not seek your life as Saul does…'

'I know that well, but I have already had Saul within my grasp, when he was as close to me as you are now and I the one with the drawn sword. I did not kill him then and will never do so, nor command it of another. He is still Yahweh's anointed and I will not be the one to strike him down.'

Abigail soon became familiar with her new life. There was little of the comfort she had known before, but plenty to keep her hand occupied, with six hundred men and their families to be kept fed and clothed. None dared leave their kin behind and at the mercy of Saul. She built a friendship—of sorts—with Ahinoam. Both seemed to realise there was nothing to be gained and much to be lost by hostility with the other wife who shared both David's affections and his bed, though the latter was rare as David kept himself consecrated for battle. But as the months slipped by and the seasons began to repeat themselves, Abigail could see the growing weariness in David's eyes—and he no longer seemed to pick up his lyre as he had done before. *It could not be easy to live with the sword of Saul constantly dangling over him.* But his decision to flee once more to the land of the Philistines disturbed her heart. She had not directly questioned the wisdom of the move, but when she had asked if prophet or priest had spoken to him about it, his only answer had been, *Saul will not seek for me there.*

The words brought her no comfort—though comfort was found in another psalm she had learned from David. The words he had sung to her became her prayer for them all:

> *Have mercy on me, my God, have mercy on me,*
> *for in You I take refuge.*
> *I will take refuge in the shadow of Your wings*
> *until the disaster has passed.*

When Achish, the Philistine king, clearly believing that Saul's enemy must be his friend, granted David the city of Ziklag to dwell in, she hoped that the disaster of which the psalm spoke had indeed passed them. But she continued praying—in case it hadn't.

Notes

1. *Although ancient lyres could have varying numbers of strings, Scripture, when it specifies a number of strings, always refers to ten (e.g. Psalm 92:3).*

2. *In the narrative that tells of David on the run from Saul, very little detail is given as to how David, his men and their families (1 Samuel 27:3) lived, although reference is made at times to him being at the cave of Adullam (e.g. 22:1) or in 'strongholds' (e.g. 22:5, 23:14) or in the town of Keilah (23:7). Given that there are points in 1 Samuel 17 (vs 1-2, 54) that suggest that armies used tents when they moved around (see also 2 Samuel 11:11), it seems reasonable to assume that for part of the time, at least, David and his men also followed this practice.*

3. *1 Samuel 23:6 states: 'Now Abiathar son of Ahimelek had brought the ephod down with him when he fled to David at Keilah.' It is not clear exactly what is meant by the 'ephod', as it seems to be used in Scripture both of a linen garment of some sort (e.g. 1 Samuel 2:18) and of a device for seeking guidance from God (1 Samuel 30:7-8). It may be that it is a reference to the Urim and Thummin of the high priest's breastpiece (Exodus 28:30), which the high priest was to use for guidance, such as for Joshua (Numbers 27:21). It seems that David sought specific guidance from Yahweh through Abiathar and the ephod – see 1 Samuel 23:9-12. This example does, however, illustrate that Urim and Thummin were used with yes-no questions. See also notes on Ithamar (7).*

4. *Both David's age when anointed and his age when he married Abigail are 'best guesses' here, as Scripture does not give details of either.*

5. *It seems likely that David's brothers were with him when he was on the run, given the details in 1 Samuel 22:1-4.*

6. *It seems that sexual abstinence whilst on military service may have been a habit of Israelite soldiers (see 1 Samuel 21:4-5 and maybe also 2 Samuel 11:11). This may have been because the law of Moses commanded them, 'When you are encamped against your enemies, keep away from everything impure…For the LORD your God moves about in your camp to protect you and to deliver your enemies to you. Your camp must be holy' (Deuteronomy 23:9, 14). Abstaining from sexual relations seems to have been a part of consecration and ritual cleanliness (see Exodus 19:10, 14-15), as temporary ritual uncleanliness seems to have accompanied the sexual act because of bodily emissions (Leviticus 15:16-18) rather than because of the act of sex, per se. This may also explain why children were only born to David when he was secure in Hebron.*

7. *Scripture does not give any moral commentary on David's decision to move to Gath, merely describing his decision and the thinking behind it (1 Samuel 27:1). However, the absence of any reference to God or His guidance (through the prophet Gad or Abiathar the priest), coupled with David's belief that unless he acts in this way he will be destroyed by Saul (with the associated assumption that Yahweh can't protect him in Israel), seem to point both towards a lack of trust in God at this point and the constant pressure he was under.*

8. *The psalms referenced in this chapter are 34 and 57.*

5

David lived in Philistine territory for a year and four months.
(1 Samuel 27:7)

'David returns!' Zillah's words rarely lacked fervour. For her, life in David's camp offered excitement that Carmel never had. Her eyes were shining and her breath rapid, having hurried or run through Ziklag to the house shared by David, his wives and their maids. 'There are camels this time!'

Whenever David and his men returned from a raid among the people to the south, it seemed that most of the town went out to meet them: wives anxious to learn of their husband's safe return, children eager to see their fathers, and all wanting know how well they would be eating for the days to come.

While Abigail put down her mending, Ahinoam picked up the bowl beneath the goat she had been milking and took it inside, out of the reach of unwelcome mouths. The two wives of David then walked together, followed by the maids, through the narrow passages between Ziklag's crowded dwellings. They were soon part of a living torrent flowing towards the town gate, the excited chatter as unceasing as that of a river running over rocks. Most faces were, by now, familiar to Abigail.

'Let us hope they have finally returned with some finery,' began Ahinoam, as she walked half a step ahead of Abigail. 'There was precious little that a woman might delight in last time!'

Abigail smiled to herself. *Ahinoam already liked to think of herself as the wife of a future king.* 'I would be satisfied with onions and garlic.' There were always hungry mouths to feed, if not of their own household, then of those where women or children

339

were sick. They were not a community that had grown up over many generations in one town; they had been drawn together in adversity and through necessity, their bonds of loyalty not to one place but to one man.

As Ahinoam continued sharing her opinions on what things were most needful, Abigail kept looking ahead, craning her neck this way and that to see better. Once through the town gates, Philistine hills and sunshine replaced bricks and shadows. Abigail drew in a deep breath of the fresher, sweeter air. Beyond the women and children, who were spreading out to the left and right, a sizeable horde of men and animals was making its way up the broad path towards the hilltop town. Abigail could see the camels of which Zillah had spoken, but also sheep, cattle and loaded donkeys. There were no captives in sight. *There never were.*

Abigail was perfectly aware of David's reasoning: if he left alive any from the settlements they raided, they might tell Achish that David had not been where the Philistine king believed him to be— and was not the loyal subject that he supposed. *But although David might be attacking the enemies of Israel (rather than the subjects of Saul, as Achish thought), not even the Amalekites wiped out those they raided. David's methods were brutal.* But, for the moment at least, disquieting thoughts could be put aside. *He had returned safely.*

'Yahweh be praised!' said a familiar voice nearby.

Abigail smiled at Benaiah's wife, clad in a garment of bright green that fell gracefully to her ankles. She had clearly just caught sight of her husband, a short distance behind David who was leading the men. 'He is, indeed, to be praised, Rachel.' Her eyes returned to David. *Weariness seemed to have been, for the moment at least, banished by either by the success of the raid or the mood of his men.* She murmured a prayer of thanks.

When the feasting that night was over and they all returned to the house, David's eyes lingered on Abigail. 'Come.' They left the other women, and went to David's small room, where rugs and cushions were scattered over the floor. Abigail lit the two small clay lamps, whose newly-kindled flames threw flickering shadows on the mud brick walls. 'That was a fine meal that you made for us.'

'It is easier to prepare a feast,' replied Abigail, setting the second lamp down, 'when there is more than lentils to hand.' The Amalekite raid had yielded not only meat for the pot but also garlic and spices.

David laughed and patted the rug. She joined him, removing the covering from her head. He ran a hand through her silky hair. 'It is good to be back.'

'Will you go to Achish tomorrow?'

David drew in a deep breath as he lay back against a cushion, making himself comfortable. He closed his eyes and exhaled slowly. 'I would rather I did not have to, but I must.'

'Where will you tell him you have been raiding this time?'

He opened his eyes and fixed them on the wooden beams above them. 'Against the Negev of Judah.'

'And Achish still suspects nothing?' She wondered how long his lies could remain undiscovered.

David rolled over onto his side to face her. 'Being in Ziklag puts us beyond his scrutiny and his trust seems only to grow. Not only does he know my enmity with Saul but he now believes I am also making myself a stench in the nostrils of the Israelites. I will take him sheep and goats and grain tomorrow and gain more of his favour.' He grinned. 'The animals of Amalek look exactly like those of Judah. They will not betray me!'

'But it is a dangerous game you play, David…'

His smile faded. 'Do I have any choice? I liberated Keilah—people from my own tribe—from the Philistines and yet even they were ready to betray me to Saul! If I cannot trust my own kin, where else can I go?' He didn't wait for an answer. 'It is far easier to find food to fill our bellies here, and plunder is the only reward I have for these men. And we are free from the reach of Saul. Not one of the scouts has seen any of his men in the time since we have been here. He has given up the search. We grow richer in Ziklag and, in time, I can use that wealth to win the loyalty of the elders of Judah, especially as our raids also weaken the true enemies of Israel. In every way, it is better we are here—trust me.' And with that he gently drew her towards him, putting an end to any further questions.

As she lay listening to David's slow, steady breathing later, Abigail pondered his earlier words. *Trust me. She would rather he had asked her to trust Yahweh.* But she knew the responsibility to provide both safety and sustenance for his men and their families weighed heavily upon his shoulders. *Yet David had been anointed to be king of Israel, and one day he would have to break from Achish, revealing where his allegiance truly lay.* Only one thought brought real comfort that night: Yahweh would hear her prayers as easily in Philistia as in Judah.

'What is it, Abigail?' The smile had faded from Rachel's face when her eyes met those of Abigail at the well. All around them, men were streaming to a meeting place on a slope just outside Ziklag, having been summoned by David. Among them were new faces—men from the tribe of Benjamin who had recently gone over to David from Saul's army.

Abigail set her water jar down, glanced around at the other women by the well, and then whispered to Benaiah's wife, 'Come aside with me.' Without speaking, they removed themselves twenty paces from those nearby, until they were standing in the shade of a small tree and out of earshot. Abigail had slept little the previous night after David's latest return from Achish. 'This is no raid they are planning. Achish has commanded that David and his men march with the Philistine army.'

'What?' exclaimed Rachel, shocked. Both glanced around. Although the eyes of some at the well had been upon them, they quickly looked away. 'Against whom?' asked Rachel, lowering her voice.

Abigail shook her head. 'Against Saul and the army of Israel.'

Rachel was silent for moment. 'There are few here who would not support David if he marched only against Saul and his men. Saul has made an enemy of most families here. But to march with the Philistines against the army of Israel…?' She met Abigail's eyes. 'That is a different matter. David would make enemies of those he has been anointed to rule.' She clicked her tongue. 'Benaiah would follow David to the ends of the earth, but he would surely question the wisdom of such a course of action. But then again, to refuse Achish…' Her anguished voice trailed off.

It was left to Abigail to voice the predicament. 'We are as flies caught in a web. If David refuses, he will be discovered as playing false whilst we are yet within Philistine lands, and they would not wait a heartbeat to slaughter each and every man.' The words hung in the air like dark thunderclouds threatening a storm. 'I feared this might happen one day. The king of Gath sees David and his men as swords he can wield. David has played the loyal ally, and now that loyalty is to be tested.'

'But what is he going to do? He cannot cradle fire in his hands and remain unburnt, surely?'

Abigail glanced around once more before she spoke, this time in a whisper. 'I believe it may be in his mind to march with the Philistines but to a different end…'

Rachel stared at her for a few moments before the light dawned in her eyes. 'You mean he would then fight with the Israelites when it came to battle and not against them?'

Abigail nodded. 'He has not voiced it to me, but he said to Achish, *You will see for yourself what your servant can do.* You are right, though—he is cradling fire.' Her eyes returned to the growing mass of men nearby. *It was indeed a dangerous game to play.*

When David and his six hundred men marched north at the rear of the Philistine lines two days later, the two wives of David stood together watching them go. 'I hope he knows what he's doing,' murmured Ahinoam.

Abigail feared he did not.

The attack on Ziklag came without warning. Abigail's prayers had persistently been directed to the north but disaster, when it fell, came from the south. Suddenly all was noise and fire and confusion, as women and children, young and old, fled from burning houses and into the arms of the Amalekites. The small force of men guarding

Ziklag, left by David three days earlier, had been utterly overrun by the vast numbers that had swarmed into the town, taking anything of value and everything that breathed. The raid was swift and thorough. As fire filled the sky behind them, Abigail found herself being herded like an animal away from Ziklag with the rest of the women and children, by men whose faces bore triumph as unmistakably as their hands bore swords and spears.

'What are they going to do to us?' asked Zillah, hugging a shawl tightly around her, her eyes darting in every direction.

Ahinoam did not turn to face her, but kept her gaze fixed steadfastly ahead. 'You are worth more to them alive than dead. They may take you and keep you if they find you pleasing to their eye, otherwise they will sell you to whoever will pay silver for a slave. Either way, they will seek to profit from you.'

Zillah began to whimper and fixed her eyes on the ground, as if that would somehow make her invisible. Abigail was not sure of the wisdom of Ahinoam's words though their truth was not in doubt—*that was, indeed, why raiders took captives.* 'We must all put our trust in Yahweh.' Abigail spoke as much to her own heart as to the others. She suddenly felt someone at her side—and was comforted to see Rachel.

'They must have known that our men had gone—and the men of the Philistines too.'

'David may have kept his raids on Amalek from the eyes of Achish,' said Ahinoam, 'but maybe not completely from the eyes of those in the south. Is this not the Amalekites avenging their brothers?'

'Whether it is vengeance or easy plunder, the outcome is the same,' replied Rachel. She turned towards Abigail. 'What can we do?'

Abigail was silent for a few moments. *Was there any truthful answer she could give that didn't counsel despair?* Then, as if borne by the wind, she heard within the sound of a lyre and with it, the rich voice of her husband singing. She murmured the words to herself.

Rachel turned to her. 'What's that?'

'It is one of David's songs. He wrote it when he was trapped in Gath and fearing the hand of the Philistines. *The angel of Yahweh encamps around those who fear Him, and He delivers them.*' Even as she repeated the words, she resolved to believe them. 'What if it is not the Amalekites that are surrounding us, but the angel of Yahweh? Is He not able to deliver us?' No one answered. Abigail had seen Yahweh's deliverance more than once, but her own question was not whether Yahweh was able to deliver them—*but would He? And would He also deliver David?*

'We would surely move more swiftly if we crawled,' announced Ahinoam, glancing about her, on their fourth day of travelling south, 'though I have no complaint.'

'They doubtless see no need for haste,' replied Abigail. 'After all, there are seemingly none left in the land to challenge them. Besides, they almost have more plunder than they can carry and flocks than they can drive.' They had soon learned after leaving Ziklag that they were not the only captives and their goods not the only plunder. The Amalekites had raided both Judah and Philistine territory before them, and Ziklag had been a final prize as they returned south again.

'Maybe they reason,' said Ahinoam with contempt, 'that their load will be lighter if they carry the food in their bellies rather than on their backs and if they empty all the wineskins down their throats.'

'You speak truly—and they will, without doubt, feast tonight as they have done the last three nights.' They fell silent again, and Abigail wondered, not for the first time, how David and the six hundred were faring. *Was their plight any less desperate than theirs? Had the battle commenced, and, if so, had David triumphed over the Philistines or fallen at their hands?* She wrenched her thoughts away from images of battlefields strewn with the dead. *She must keep trusting Yahweh! Had He not struck down Nabal when her fate with him had seemed inescapable? If they were to escape now, it would have to be by His hand once more.* Although whispered conversations about the possibility of fleeing had taken place as the Amalekites ate and drank freely each night, as Rachel had observed, even if they did manage to escape, they had babies and children among them. They would not be able to go far in the dark, even if they had somewhere to flee, and the Amalekites had camels that would soon overtake them, whichever direction they went.

As the afternoon lengthened, the Amalekites once more stopped for the night. It wasn't long before the songs, the laughter and the other sounds of revelling began to fill the open ground over which the Amalekites, their plunder and their captives were scattered. Fires were lit as the light began to fade and the wine began to flow freely. The women drew together around fires of their own, making the most of the meagre supplies that had been tossed in their direction by their captors.

They had barely begun to eat when Rachel's eyes suddenly widened, the light in them burning bright. 'Look!' The word was barely out of her mouth before everything changed. Even as Abigail turned her head in the direction of Rachel's gaze, the cries in the camp turned from triumph to terror. There was the blur of swift movement all around them. Abigail leapt to her feet, her eyes swiftly sweeping across the landscape. Then her eyes brightened as Rachel's had done. *Wonder of wonders!* 'It is David!' Although she could not see her husband, she recognised his men as they surged across the camp like the Jordan overflowing its banks in spring. Drunken Amalekites tried to stumble to their feet, only to be cut down by Israelite swords.

As twilight slipped into night, the noises of fighting persisted, though there was little doubt who prevailed. Few slept. First light brought a scene of devastation, with lifeless Amalekite bodies strewn across the land as far as the eye could see. Some of David's men remained while most continued the chase. Abigail did not sit idle. She and the other women began to gather the plunder that had been abandoned by the Amalekites as they fled. They brought back animals that had scattered, piled sacks of grain, made heaps of weapons, and—most importantly—began searching out each and every woman and child who had been with them in Ziklag. Not one was missing.

As the sun passed its zenith and neared the land far to the west, David's army gradually returned in small waves to what had been the Amalekites' camp. When Abigail finally caught sight of her husband, he was striding confidently forward, Benaiah at his side. She ran to him and embraced him, with Ahinoam and Rachel not far behind.

When he finally released her from his embrace, their eyes met. There was a light in them that she hadn't seen in months. Both weariness and wariness had been banished, and no hint of the hunted look remained. He smiled. *She had David back!*

When the men had greeted the other two women, they began walking back to the centre of the camp where the plunder was piled. 'We are all here!' began Abigail. 'Every man, woman and child that you left in Ziklag!'

'Yahweh be praised!' shouted David to the heavens in joyful triumph. 'He has delivered us all as He said He would!' His eyes returned to the women. 'Abiathar enquired of Yahweh for us when we found Ziklag burned and the Lord told us to pursue the Amalekites and that we would overtake them and rescue you.'

Abigail silently voiced a prayer of thanksgiving. *David was seeking Yahweh again!*

'But what happened with the Philistines?' asked Ahinoam. 'All we have heard so far is that they sent you back.'

'Achish was happy enough for us to march with him, but the rest of the Philistine commanders were not,' replied David. 'They feared we would turn on them in battle to regain the favour of Saul.'

Abigail glanced sideways at David. 'And they would have been right, would they not?'

Benaiah's laughter suddenly split the air. 'You should have heard our leader remonstrating to Achish. *Why can't I go and fight against the enemies of my lord the king?* He failed to mention the particular king he had in mind!' He chuckled and shook his head and a little smile played across David's lips.

Abigail's heart brimmed with joy. 'How great are the mercies and deliverance of Yahweh!'

'And we will celebrate His victory with a feast. There are more mouths to feed now, too—warriors from the tribe of Manasseh joined us as we were marching with the Philistines. But we will not feast before we have returned to the rest of my men. Two hundred were left at the Besor Ravine, too exhausted to continue the pursuit. This plunder will be theirs as much as ours.'

'But what of the battle to the north?' asked Rachel suddenly. 'How went it?'

David's mood suddenly became sombre and he slowed to a halt. He turned his face northward and stood in silence for a moment. 'We heard that Israel were camped by the spring in Jezreel. As we marched south at first light, the Philistine ranks were heading up towards them. No news of battle has reached us. We do not even know if the armies have engaged yet.' Then he spoke more softly. 'Yahweh will yet deliver me from Saul, but I would not see it done by the hand of the Philistines. And I fear for Jonathan.' He fell silent again for several moments, but then suddenly drew in a breath. 'But Yahweh is God and He will do what is right.' With that, he turned and continued walking.

The first two days back in Ziklag were spent making as much of the town as possible habitable. David, for his part, was busy sending gifts from the plunder to the elders and towns of Judah that had supported him as he fled from Saul. The third day was different. Abigail was busy sweeping ash from the tiny courtyard of their house when a strange noise began to make itself heard above the bustle of the town. Abigail stopped and listened.

Ahinoam drew alongside her. 'What is it?'

'I do not know—but something is amiss.' Their eyes met and suddenly both of them were running, the broom clattering to the ground behind them. They were joined by others, all hurrying towards the charred gate of the town. Beyond it, the strange noise became discernible; it was the sound of weeping and wailing. Abigail's chest tightened. She touched the shoulder of a man at the edge of the crowd whom she recognised. 'Joash! What's happened?' It was only as he turned that she realised that his garment had been torn. 'Why do you mourn?'

'A messenger has come from Mount Gilboa. King Saul is dead. The army of Israel fell before the Philistines.'

It took a moment to sink in. The man who had tried again and again to kill David was finally vanquished. But the news brought neither joy nor relief. She shared her husband's heart for the honour of Yahweh. Her mind suddenly flitted back to the defeat of Goliath. David had called his defiance of the Israelite army a disgrace. *A Philistine insulting Israel and her God was shame enough. That the name of Yahweh should be dishonoured by the slaughtering of His anointed king and His army was too dreadful to contemplate.* 'What of Jonathan?' she said suddenly. 'Is there news of him?' Even as she voiced the question, she remembered that Joash was one of those who had come to them in Ziklag from the tribe of Benjamin. *Saul and Jonathan were his kin.*

He shook his head slowly. 'Saul's sons died with him.'

And among the wailing, Abigail heard her husband's pain.

Before the day was out, David had picked up his lyre once more. It had evaded the hands of the Amalekites and escaped their fires, but the first tune to grace its strings was a lament, crafted and picked out by the fingers of David and woven together with words that tore the soul:

How the mighty have fallen!
Tell it not in Gath,
   proclaim it not in the streets of Ashkelon,
lest the daughters of the Philistines be glad,
   lest the daughters of the uncircumcised rejoice.

It grieved Abigail's heart to know that, despite David's words, they would indeed be telling it in Gath and proclaiming it Ashkelon. While the daughters of Israel mourned, those of the Philistines would indeed be rejoicing. David's lament was kinder to Saul than he deserved, honouring him still as Yahweh's anointed. But it was his words for Jonathan that truly reflected his heart.

I grieve for you, Jonathan my brother;
   you were very dear to me.
Your love for me was wonderful,
   more wonderful than that of women.

They had been close as brothers, both their hearts beating for the honour of Yahweh. Abigail knew it was that zeal that had drawn them into friendship and into a brotherhood sealed with a covenant.

When David sought solace later in the arms of Abigail, all that was required of her was to listen as he spoke of his friend. 'When Saul could not find me, Jonathan did. In the months before I came to Carmel, I was hiding in the Desert of Ziph. Saul sought me day after day, but Yahweh kept him from me.' He smiled wryly. 'But somehow our God guided Jonathan to me when I needed him most. The men of Keilah were ready to betray me and I was losing heart, but Jonathan helped me to find strength in God.' For a moment, he fell silent, as if savouring the memory. 'He told me not to be afraid, and assured me that Saul would not lay a hand on me. Even though he was Saul's heir, he told me that I would one day be king.' He paused. 'It was the last time I saw him.' When he spoke again his voice wavered. 'He said that he would be second to me. But now that will never be.' David wept once more.

As Abigail held him, she wondered if the hand of Yahweh had deliberately sent David back from the battle lines, not only to rescue the women and children from the Amalekites but also so that David's hand would not save Saul from the judgment that had finally come upon him. *But Jonathan had been caught up in that judgment. Disobeying Yahweh came at a high price—not only for the king but also for his family.*

Zillah giggled. 'Mistress!'

Abigail looked up from the kneading trough, her hands covered in dough. She drew her forearm across her face to remove the hair that had fallen over her eyes. Zillah was grinning and her eyes flitted to one side. Abigail followed her gaze and saw David leaning casually against the doorway of the small of the courtyard. He was watching her with a broad smile on his face. Abigail chuckled. 'How long have you been standing there, my lord?'

'Long enough to grow impatient to tell you the news!'

Abigail quickly rubbed her hands together to remove as much of the dough as she could before rising to her feet. 'What news?'

'We are leaving!'

'Where for, Master?' asked Zillah eagerly. She would never have dared to ask such a question of Nabal, but, despite his position—and hers—David rarely chided her. When he did, it was usually for her excess of words.

He drew himself upright, away from the doorway, and approached Abigail. 'We are returning to Judah—to Hebron. I enquired of Yahweh, and He has answered clearly that that is where I should go.'

Abigail beheld him with wonder in her eyes. 'To become king?'

'That will be up to the men of Judah.'

'But you *are* Yahweh's anointed…'

'And Yahweh will therefore be the One to direct how and when I become king.'

'Will you have a palace?' Ahinoam's youngest maid, Huldah, had appeared at the door to the house.

David raised an eyebrow to her playfully. 'Do you tire of living in a house much smaller than your mistress's house back in Jezreel, Huldah?' He didn't wait for an answer, however. 'Being a king is not about wearing fine clothes or living in fine houses. Yahweh's people have been scattered like sheep and they need a shepherd, and that is what I will try to be to them. My task is to serve the Lord's people for their good, not to be made rich at their expense.'

Abigail loved him all the more for his answer.

The young girl, however, appeared crest-fallen, but David laughed. 'Fear not, Huldah. It will not be without its own rewards!'

It did not take the men of Judah long to know their minds. David's gifts from the plunder had, indeed, won him friends. As Abiathar poured the fragranced oil over David's head, anointing him king over the house of Judah, Abigail's heart danced. It was not because she was now the wife of a king; it was witnessing the faithfulness of Yahweh once more. *The Almighty had fulfilled His promise to David despite all the adversity, danger and desperate decisions on the long journey from Bethlehem to Hebron. The path he had travelled had brought him close to a murderous* adversary, taken him into the cities of the Philistines, and led him to the brink of disaster. And yet Yahweh's hand had been upon him the whole time. A thunderous cheer rose from David's men, and from those who now stood with them, as the crown that had once belonged to Saul and which had been brought back to David from Mount Gilboa, was lowered onto David's head. Then a cry was taken up by every person in the crowd, both old and young, man and woman, with Abigail's voice amongst them—*Long live the king! Long live the king! Long live the king!*

Abigail caught sight of Huldah and Zillah nearby. Both were waving and cheering, with Huldah's face a picture of delight and excitement. Abigail smiled to herself. *There was a big house, after all.*

Notes

1. *There is much debate concerning the locations of both Gath and Ziklag. Although an announcement in July 2019 by a team of researchers, led by the Israel Antiquities Authority, suggested that they had uncovered the location of Ziklag at a hilltop site, not all archaeologists are convinced.*

2. *It is not clear exactly how David's time in Philistine territory was split between Gath and Ziklag—only that he was there for one year and four months in total (1 Samuel 27:7).*

3. *No details are given in the text as to what the town of Ziklag was like. It is assumed here that it was a walled city with some form of gate, and that maybe the gates were burned when it was overrun by the Amalekites.*

4. *Although the text speaks of David having six hundred men with him when he goes over to Achish (1 Samuel 27:2) and that number being with him when he returns to Ziklag after marching north (1 Samuel 30:9), it would seem reasonable to suppose that David left at least a few men at the town. Although adult male captives are not mentioned explicitly, the text may allow for them: 'Now the Amalekites had…attacked Ziklag and burned it, and had taken captive the women and everyone else in it, both young and old. They killed none of them, but carried them off as they went on their way' (1 Samuel 30:1-2).*

5. *Translations differ as to whether the twilight in 1 Samuel 30:17 (when David attacks the Amalekites) refers to the period around sunrise or sunset. The latter has been assumed, as the previous verse refers to eating, drinking and revelling.*

6. *It is not clear how soon after David's return to Ziklag (and Israel's defeat at Mount Gilboa) he goes to Hebron and is made king. The text simply says, 'In the course of time' (2 Samuel 2:1).*

7. *It has been assumed (although it is not specifically stated in the text) that David was anointed by Abiathar the priest. A later (and longer) description of a coronation (in 2 Kings 11:12) includes the priest crowning Joash as king, presenting him with a copy of the covenant and proclaiming him as king, as well as Joash being anointed, the applause of the people, and a cry of 'Long live the king!' The brevity of the text describing David being made king (in 2 Samuel 2:4) need not preclude these other elements.*

6

David grew stronger and stronger, while the house of Saul grew weaker and weaker. (2 Samuel 3:1)

Abigail gazed across the hills of Judah. Hebron, sitting as it did on the top of a north-south ridge and being blessed with the honour of being the highest city in the land, afforded views of the surrounding countryside that could not be matched elsewhere. The deep green of olive trees coloured the slopes nearby. Other bushes and patches of grass were scattered across the rugged terrain, some of them amply watered by one or more of Hebron's numerous springs. Sheep and goats wandered between the greenery, watched over (or ignored) by local boys wielding staffs or sticks. It was Abigail's favourite spot, and the bustle of life in the city could be, at least for a while, forgotten. It was a place to remember the stories she had learned in her childhood: of Abraham and Sarah, of Isaac and Rebekah, of Jacob and Leah—for all had been buried at Hebron. *Here Yahweh had touched the lives of each of these ancestors, and she had come forth from them. Her life was also now wonderfully woven into the story of His people and of the Promised Land.* She smiled to herself.

The moment was broken when a small hand tugged on hers. She looked down to find her three-year-old son peering up at her, his brow furrowed. 'Go now...' She had named him Daniel, but it was not the name he was used to.

'Yes, Kileab, we will go now.' She was instantly rewarded by a broad smile as the frown disappeared and he started singing to himself, though it could scarcely be called a tune. This habit—and the red tinge to his hair—had led David laughingly to give him another name: *Kileab: like his father.* It had stuck.

The youngster had been born two years after David was made king. He had an elder brother, Amnon, born a year earlier to Ahinoam, but David had also taken four more wives since they had been in Hebron. Two had already given Kileab younger brothers named Absalom and Adonijah. One of the other two wives was also with child. Abigail had never seen a new-born with such a shock of dark hair as Absalom. Even now, Kileab had less hair than his younger brother had when he was born. His mother, Maacah, was blessed with a similar abundance of black hair, and striking features with it, though those had not been the reason that David had wed her. She was the daughter of the king of Geshur, a small kingdom beyond the Jordan. The marriage was, more than anything else, an alliance to strengthen David's hand in that area—not least because Saul's one surviving son, Ish-Bosheth, had fled across the Jordan after the Philistine victory. It was there that, more recently, Abner—who had been Saul's cousin and commander—had pronounced Ish-Bosheth king over all Israel.

Although she never voiced it, Abigail doubted that the Almighty needed such unions to make His Anointed secure. *Other nations might measure the power of a king by the number of his wives and sons and alliances, but was not the power of David Yahweh Himself?*

Abigail cast her eyes around the hillside. She caught sight of the one she was looking for. 'Mahlah!' The other woman suddenly turned and Abigail beckoned her, calling out, 'We are returning now.' It had been Eliam and Rebekah's joy to allow their eldest daughter and her husband to leave the household at Carmel and journey the short distance north-west to Hebron, to serve both Abigail and the king. Although now over thirty and married for well over ten years, Mahlah had shown no sign of being able to bear children. To share the care of Kileab with her was a blessing to both women, and to Abigail she was more of a friend than a servant. She was also Abigail's eyes in a house where it was servants who watched the doors and who served the men wine as they talked. Abigail made it her aim to understand as much as she could of any matter that affected David and his rule. *It might not be her place to influence her husband or the affairs of the land—but she could always seek Yahweh for both.*

Mahlah began making her way back up the slope, her hands grasping a mass of green and white. 'Look! I have found myrtle.'

When she reached them, Mahlah lowered the stems taken from the shrub to Kileab's nose for him to smell. Fragrant white flowers nestled among the larger, almond-shaped leaves. He pulled a face.

It was Mahlah who brought the news early next morning of Asahel's death. Abigail stared at her, aghast, as she tried to dress Kileab. 'Asahel? Are you sure?' David's fleet-footed nephew was by now well-known to her, as were his two brothers, Joab and Abishai.

'The news has come from Joab's own mouth. It was at the hand of Abner.'

'All I had heard was that Joab had taken men north…'

'They met Abner and his army near Gibeon. Well over three hundred of Abner's men fell in the fighting, but only twenty of David's, though Asahel was among them. He was pursuing Abner who could not outrun him, so he directed his spear towards Asahel when he was almost upon him.' She did not have to complete the details for Abigail to guess the gruesome outcome. 'Joab laid Asahel in their father's tomb at Bethlehem, and then marched through the night, returning here at daybreak.'

Abigail was quiet for a few moments, oblivious of Kileab as he tried to take off the tunic that had just been put over his head. She drew in a breath. 'Joab will not bear that easily. Asahel's death will grieve David's heart as much as Abishai's, but Joab…?' She shook her head. 'If I know him, grieving will not be enough.'

Michal's arrival at David's spacious, many-roomed house in Hebron did not go unnoticed—not least because she was accompanied by more than twenty men. Not that any knew David's first wife by sight, but none were left in ignorance for long.

'She has demanded a room of her own,' whispered Mahlah, as other servants hurried to attend to her.

As she swept past, Abigail judged her to be slightly younger than herself. Once out of earshot, she whispered with a wry smile, 'She and Maacah will get on well...'

Mahlah chuckled. 'Or be at each other's throats!'

As the men who had accompanied Michal were being ushered into the large paved courtyard to meet David, Abigail caught sight of Benaiah. She hurried over to him, tapping his arm lightly to get his attention. He turned, and although he towered over Abigail, he smiled when he saw her. 'What is happening, Benaiah?' she whispered. 'And how is it that Michal has returned to David?'

He glanced around and with a little motion of his head and eyes, directed them away from any others. Then, with a small nod towards the courtyard he said in a lowered voice, 'Do you see the tall man with the yellow and green scarf?'

Abigail's eyes quickly found the imposing man whose mere stance marked him out as the leader of the men. 'I see him.'

'That is Abner.'

'Abner!' exclaimed Abigail, wide-eyed. 'What is he doing here?'

'He secretly sent messengers to David recently. He said he would help David bring all Israel over to him.'

'Why on earth would he do that? It was he who made Ish-Bosheth king!'

Benaiah shrugged. 'It is rumoured that the son of Saul has angered him in some way.'

'But is it within Abner's power to change the hearts of the men of Israel?'

'I have seen Abner in battle and commanding an army. There is little doubt in my mind that it is he who wields the true power. I imagine Ish-Bosheth has little control over him.'

Benaiah's words reminded Abigail of what David had said of Joab: *untameable as the Jordan in flood*. But she held her peace.

'Abner is blowing with the wind,' continued Benaiah. 'His changed loyalties probably have more to do with his own fortunes than any belief that David is Yahweh's anointed.'

'But why is Michal here?'

'David sent word to Abner that he could only come if he brought Michal with him. That he has done so is measure of his influence.' Benaiah looked towards the courtyard as the last man disappeared outside. 'I must go, but it would be as well not speak of this to others—at least not yet.' He smiled. 'I know I can trust you.'

Despite Benaiah's words, David's household all knew of the presence of not only Michal but also Abner before the sun had climbed to its highest point. The feast that David had the servants prepare for the commander of the army of Israel was lavish. He had summoned Abigail to oversee the work in the kitchen. *She was, after all, used to it, as Nabal himself had feasted like a king at the end of the sheep shearing season.* She had smiled when he had unknowingly echoed Benaiah's words, *I know I can trust you.* But she had also smiled because of David's demeanour. *He was elated.*

As Abigail checked on pots bubbling with meat, onions and spices and made sure the maids only used flour for bread that had been finely milled, she could not help beginning to hope that the strife between the two royal houses of Saul and David might finally be coming to an end. *Maybe soon there would be an end to Israelite bearing sword against Israelite. Maybe now they would be able to come together against their true enemies, including the Philistines. They still controlled the plain of Jezreel, and other land in the north and to the west of the Jordan, following their victory at Mount Gilboa.* It did not surprise her that David had sought the return of Saul's daughter. *It would unite the two houses and maybe win over some who had been loyal to her father. And maybe it was in his mind to sire a child with her who could one day take the throne.* She suddenly chuckled to herself. Although she would meet Michal soon enough, she had already seen enough of her to know that their meeting was unlikely to be in the kitchen.

The mood of hope was short-lived. 'By whose hand?' asked Abigail quietly—though she feared she knew how Mahlah would answer.

'Joab.'

Abigail sighed. 'I heard him arguing with David when he found out Abner had been here. He almost called David a fool to his face, telling him that Abner's only reason for coming was to spy on him.' She paused only to shake her head in disbelief. 'How did he kill him?'

'It is said that he sent Abner a message to bring him back to Hebron, and then lured him to one side in the gate and thrust a knife into his belly.'

'Does Joab not know what he has done?' murmured Abigail. 'He may have avenged Asahel's death but at what cost to David and at what cost to the land?' She feared the answer. She suddenly shook herself out of her shock, and reached for a richly embroidered veil that was carefully folded on her bed. 'I must go to David.' She knew where she would find him.

The narrow streets of Hebron were completely in shadow. In the twilight sky, barely visible between the houses and buildings of the city, the colours of sunset still lingered. The gates of Hebron had already been shut for the night as she approached them.

A guard at the bottom of a flight of stone steps beside the gates nodded to her as she neared him, guessing the reason for her presence. 'He is on the wall.'

Abigail drew up her long linen tunic above her ankles as she carefully made her way up the steps. There was nothing that would save her from falling if she missed her footing. Once at the top, the watchman stepped aside to let her pass. A lone figure was standing on the ramparts, motionless as a statue, his arms outstretched against the parapet and looking out into the evening sky. A solitary star was now visible. If he saw her approach out of the corner of his eye, he did not show it. 'My lord?' He finally turned his head, his eyes full of a weariness that Abigail had not seen for more than six years. She laid a hand gently on his right arm. 'I have just heard about Abner.'

David turned back to face the west. 'It is murder but Joab will call it justice.' He paused, glanced down and gave the stone wall a kick. 'Abner killed Asahel in battle, but Joab wielded his blade in treachery, and I have little doubt it was in rivalry as much as revenge. There can only be one commander of an army and Joab has made sure it will not be Abner.'

'What will you do with Joab, my lord?' Abigail's voice was as gentle as her touch upon on David's arm.

'*Do?*' laughed David bitterly. 'What can any man do with Joab? It makes no difference to him that I am king over Judah. Most of the time Joab does what pleases Joab.' He shook his head and sighed. 'I do not know what I should do with him, Abigail. He has spilled the innocent blood of Abner, and by doing so may have made peace a distant hope. But is it prudent to punish my kinsman when he leads men into battle for me and they trust him? I cursed him openly when I heard of his treachery, calling down retribution upon his head, but should I leave it only to the hand of Yahweh?' He shook his head once more. 'These sons of Zeruaiah are too strong for me.'

He did not look to her for an answer, but she spoke anyway. 'You must do only what you believe to be right before Yahweh.' She only hoped that he would—if he knew what that was.

He suddenly turned to face her, eyes ablaze. 'I will tell you one thing that *will* happen with Joab, though. I have already told him that he will clothe himself with sackcloth, and walk in mourning before the body of Abner when we bury him in Hebron tomorrow morning. And I will sing a lament for a great man and weep over him, and men will know that I had no part in his murder.'

There was uncertainty in Abigail's mind as to whether David's final decision—leaving any punishment of Joab to Yahweh—had been the right one. She kept those doubts to herself, however, and simply continued to pray for wisdom and success for David. Within a year, Ish-Bosheth had also been killed by treachery and without pity, but this time by his own men. Unlike Abner's murder, David brought down a swift reckoning upon the two servants of Saul's son, who had supposed their actions would bring reward—not retribution—when they presented the head of Ish-Bosheth to him. It was not long after that that all the elders of Israel came to David at Hebron—and not only them.

Abigail had never seen anything like it. The hillsides around the city were covered with men, with tents and with joyful celebration.

Thousands upon thousands of warriors and chiefs had arrived from every tribe in Israel, including those across the Jordan, and all had arrived with one aim only—to make David king of all Israel. It was as if the eyes of every descendant of Jacob—including those from Saul's own tribe of Benjamin—suddenly beheld the shepherd from Bethlehem as the one truly destined to wear the crown. There seemed to be no doubt in any mind that he was Yahweh's anointed. For the first time in many years, the nation was united in heart and mind, and from that truth, now evident to all, sprang joy like almond blossom bursting forth in the warmth of early spring.

Hebron was overwhelmed. 'There is not room even for one more donkey within the walls,' observed Abigail in wonder, as she and Mahlah surveyed the scene from the ramparts.

'And yet they continue to come!' laughed Mahlah.

For two or three days, camels, oxen, donkeys and mules had been streaming towards Hebron loaded with flour and fig-cakes, wine and oil. Cattle and sheep accompanied them, fated to be boiled or roasted over fires—in the houses of Hebron or out on the surrounding countryside.

'We will be busy tomorrow,' continued Mahlah.

'We must be busy today! We still have a five-and-a-half-year-old to bath who baulks at the sight of water—and let us hope he has not picked up any more bruises from rolling around the floor with his brother Amnon.'

On a day marked by glorious sunshine, the wives of David stood together with their sons, with the women clad in their finest clothes and jewellery, and every boy bathed and clean, from the eldest, Amnon, to the youngest, Ithream. Maacah also held in her arms a daughter, Tamar, who already seemed destined to be blessed with the beauty of both mother and brother.

Abigail did her best to keep Kileab both quiet and still as, for the third time in his life, sacred oil was poured upon the head of David, and for the second time, a crown was set upon it. As David and the elders of every tribe entered into a solemn covenant, Kileab began to fidget and whine. Out of a small, draw-string bag, Abigail produced a round, honey-flavoured wafer. Not only was the whining assuaged, but she was rewarded with cheerful humming when his mouth was finally emptied. Her foresight was also rewarded by a grateful smile from Ahinoam, as further wafers pacified each of David's offspring. Michal, the only wife yet to bear a child, remained aloof.

While the elders surrounded David and vows were taken, Abigail's heart whispered prayers of gratitude. *David had been anointed as the Shepherd of God's people by Samuel when he was only eighteen years old. Although Hebron was barely a day's walk from Bethlehem, the journey to the fulfilment of Yahweh's promise and purposes had taken almost twenty years, and both tears and blood had been shed along the tortuous path. But Yahweh had never left David's side, even if at times his trust had wavered.*

Into Abigail's thoughts drifted an awareness that a tune was being softly hummed, though somewhat imperfectly. Kileab, seemingly oblivious of the momentous events before him, had (to Abigail's amazement and joy) clearly remembered at least part of the melody composed on David's lyre only two days before. But it was the psalm's words that lifted her heart once more in praise:

> *Yahweh is faithful to all His promises,*
> *and loving towards all He has made.*

The truths of those words, evident in her own life as well as David's, filled her with wonder. With joy in her heart, she echoed the words with which David had begun the psalm, humbly acknowledging Israel's true ruler:

> *I will exalt you, my God the King.*

Abigail doubted that the feasting that followed the ceremony would ever find its equal in Israel. Although she had allowed others to labour on the day of David's anointing, in the two days of celebration that followed, she preferred to ensure that all who ate at David's table were amply supplied with the finest of dishes. But the eating and drinking filled the entire city and the land around, with stews bubbling in pots and lambs roasting over fires. There was no place where the rich aromas of cooking meat did not fill the air and gladden the heart—as did the wine that flowed as freely as water.

'I wonder,' began Abigail on the final day of feasting, her face as red as Mahlah's from the ovens, 'if the loaves being baked in Hebron are the equal of the abundance of manna that Yahweh rained down in the desert...'

'Do you mean the bread He sent for one night,' replied Mahlah playfully, 'or for the whole forty years?'

Abigail threw back her head and laughed so that her gold earrings jangled. 'It feels as if it is the latter!' And she slept that night as if it was.

When David and Abigail stood together once more on the walls of Hebron looking out over the hill country of Judah, their moods were as different from the occasion of Abner's murder as noon from midnight. David was jubilant, having returned that day from a successful campaign against the city of the Jebusites to the north.

Abigail exulted in the precious time with her husband—she was not often alone with him, and supposed she had been chosen by him that evening for a reason. 'Was it a hard battle to take Jerusalem, my lord?'

David chuckled. 'The Jebusites thought their city unassailable, with its ramparts as thick as the height of two men and with deep valleys to the east and west of it. Do you know what they shouted at us from the walls? *You will not get in here—even the blind and lame could ward you off!* They believed even the weakest could hold the city, with its strong defences—and strong they were.'

Abigail was intrigued. She turned towards him. 'So how did you take it?'

David's eyes stayed fixed on the hills, now dark against the deepening blue of the evening sky. 'I said that whoever led the attack on Jerusalem would become chief and commander of the army.' He smiled wryly to himself. 'Joab would not let any other man take that honour! Still, it was not easy. Even when Joab and I were in Bethlehem, we knew that the Jebusites had a shaft to bring water into the city from the spring of Gihon. A siege would have been lengthy, given that they had fresh water without having to go out through the city gates. I told Joab that if we could not take the city by scaling its walls, maybe we could take it by subtlety.' He turned to face her. 'And Joab did! By torch at night he crawled and waded from Gihon through the water-shaft, leading men behind him, and climbed the shaft into the city itself. They overcame the night watch and opened the gate for us!' He laughed. 'We had taken the city before they knew of it, and they could do nothing but surrender. Most are probably still wondering how we did it!' He looked out again over the Judean countryside. 'I love these hills and this city, but we will be moving to Jerusalem. That is where I will rule over Israel and I will call it *the City of David*.'

Abigail studied him for a few moments as he fell silent, and then she smiled. 'It is a wise move, my lord!'

David turned to face her, folded his arms and leant back against the parapet, looking pleased. It was Abigail's turn to be studied. 'And why is that?'

Abigail smiled coyly. 'Is my lord testing me, to see if I know what is in his mind?'

'You have shown me more than once that wisdom is not imparted by Yahweh to men alone…'

She drew in a deep breath and let it out. 'Then I will tell you. Since the time our people entered the land, Jerusalem has belonged to none of the tribes. It is not counted as either part of Judah or part of Benjamin, but lies between them. Hebron is a fine city, but it is a city of Judah. It was the natural place from which to rule your tribe, but now you must be seen, not as the king of Judah but the king of all Israel. No tribe can claim you for themselves if you make Jerusalem your city.' She then fell silent and waited for David's judgment.

He straightened up, smiling. 'Such an answer deserves to be rewarded!' He took her in his arms, and gave her a long and lingering kiss. He eyes twinkled though as he released her. 'You have spoken truly, but there is more. The city also lies on the road that runs west from where the Jordan is forded near Jericho, all the way to the plains that slope down to the shores of the Great Sea. But it is also on the road running through the hill country, from Beersheba in the south to Beth-Shan in the north. There are few places within Israel like it, and no longer will a Canaanite city divide Judah from the rest of the tribes. Now we can more easily stand together, and begin to drive the Philistines out from the rest of the land that the Almighty gave to our father Abraham.'

At the mention of their ancestor, a question rose in Abigail's mind. 'In one matter, my lord, Jerusalem cannot match Hebron. The tombs of Abraham, Isaac and Jacob are here, and stories of Hebron are woven into the history of our people. Jerusalem has no such heritage.'

'Then we will make the City of David famous! We will give it such a name that every nation on earth will hear of it!' David's eyes suddenly seemed fixed on a distant point, as if he were seeing wonders beyond the hills of Judah to the west. He spoke in hushed tones. 'By the hand of Yahweh, Jerusalem will become greater and more glorious than any other city, and for one reason only—the greatness and glory of our God.' And then he suddenly turned to her, and it was as if the sun rose in David's eyes. He stared at her in wonder. 'And I know now how that will be. I will bring the ark of Yahweh to Jerusalem! The city will not only be the centre of this land's power—it will be the heart of our people's worship!' There was exhilaration in his voice. 'Yahweh chose to put His name at Shiloh when we entered the land, but the Philistines overran the sanctuary there and the ark was lost to them until they sent it back. It has languished too long on the hill at Kiriath Jearim. After I have prepared Jerusalem, I will leave the ark abandoned no more.'

Abigail suddenly remembered a story from her childhood. 'My lord, was there not trouble in Beth Shemesh before the ark reached Kiriath Jearim? We heard tales told of men being struck down. Was not the hand of Yahweh against them there?'

'Those tales reached Bethlehem too. It was said the wrath of the Almighty fell upon them because they dared to look into the ark of God. I will not repeat their mistake.'

The ark did not get far. David's error was not that of Beth Shemesh, but the hand of Yahweh had struck all the same. When the oxen pulling the cart on which the ark rested stumbled, the hand of Uzzah had reached out to steady it. He did not live to draw another breath, and the ark was abandoned once more, this time at the house of Obed-Edom, whose dwelling was closest to where Uzzah had fallen.

Abigail had seen both anger and fear in David's eyes when he had returned to his new seat of rule that night: anger that his plan had failed in the sight of the thousands he had called out to accompany the ark; fear that he could never be worthy to bring it within the walls of Jerusalem. But that had been three months earlier.

When news came one morning, Abigail—for once—did not hear it first from the mouth of Mahlah. The sons of David had been brought into the king, and their mothers with them, and David was trying in vain to teach his eldest sons to master the lyre. Only Kileab—now aged seven—showed any aptitude for it. For Absalom, a wooden sword was of more interest.

Two young men entered the room. Abigail immediately recognised them. One was the son of a priest and the other a young prophet who had entered David's service. Abigail touched David's arm. 'My lord, Zadok and Nathan are here.'

He looked up and passed the lyre to Kileab. 'Try again.' He then rose to his feet and beckoned the men to him. 'What brings you both here?'

Although Abigail's eyes were on Kileab, her ears heeded every word of the conversation.

'We have brought news of the house of Obed-Edom, my lord,' began Nathan.

'Go on…'

'Yahweh has blessed his household and everything he has. It is because of the ark of God.'

There was a long pause and Abigail glanced up. David was looking steadily at the men. 'And you believe I should take that as a sign that I should repeat my endeavour?'

'My lord, we have been to the sanctuary at Gibeon,' replied Zadok. 'But not to the altar of Moses. The Law of Yahweh is also kept there. We have been reading it, and Yahweh's instructions. The Philistines may have sent the ark back to Israel on a cart, but that is not how we are to carry it. It must be borne on its poles by the sons of Levi. That is the way we must bring the ark up, and that is why the wrath of Yahweh fell before. If it is carried by priests, all will be well!'

'Not only that, my lord,' continued Nathan. 'Yahweh also commanded through Moses that the king should read the Law. When you bring the ark here, I believe the Law of Yahweh, His covenant with His people, should be reunited with it also—as it was in the time of Moses. You will then be able to study it yourself.'

In the moments of silence that followed, Abigail's gaze returned to David. There was wonder in his eyes—and his voice brimmed with excitement when he spoke. 'You have served me well, my friends! We will do all that you say. Tomorrow we will begin preparations to bring the ark to Jerusalem, and we will do so with even greater celebration than before, with ram's horns and trumpets, and harps and lyres.' He paused and laughed. 'Though it grieves me to say that it will not be my sons playing them!'

Abigail, with Mahlah at her side and Kileab's hand in hers, joined the joyful throng making its way westwards, down from Jerusalem and towards the house of Obed-Edom. They had started out as the sun rose and it was only midway to its zenith by the time they were assembling for the momentous journey back. 'Look, Kileab,' said Abigail pointing to the west. 'Can you see the Great Sea?' The blue of the water was only slightly darker than that of the sky.'

'He would see better if he were taller,' said a familiar voice behind him.

'Mered!' exclaimed Abigail, overjoyed. 'You have come!' She had sent a message to Carmel inviting Mahlah's family to join them, but had no certainty that any of them would be able to join the procession.

'Father and Mother could not make the journey,' he began after freeing himself from his twin sister's embrace, 'so they sent Joel and me in their stead.' He glanced around and laughed. 'Though where my brother is now in this crowd, the Almighty alone knows!'

'It is a wonder you found us at all!'

Mered crouched down to be on the level of the seven-year-old. 'I knew David's household would not be far from the ark.' Kileab grinned. 'Shall we now make this young noble grow taller?' Moments later, Kileab was being lifted high on the shoulders of Mered.

Mahlah looked aghast. 'Mered! He is the son of the king! It is hardly dignified.'

'Hush, Mahlah,' laughed Abigail. 'It is not a day for dignity but for joy.' She turned her gaze upwards to her son. '*Now* do you see the Great Sea?'

'I see it,' he cried.

Mered turned him around. 'And what is that?' he asked, pointing to an outline in the distance on the eastern ridge, the sun behind it.

'Jerusalem,' he beamed. 'I live there.'

'And can you see your father?' asked Abigail.

All looked towards the middle of the joyful throng. Many from the city had joined the elders of every tribe of Israel who were there, as were commanders from the army. But at the heart of the assembly were a large number clothed in robes of fine white linen: singers, musicians, priests and those whose duty and joy it would be to carry the ark—but they were not the only ones dressed thus.

'I see him,' said Kileab. 'He's wearing white.' Gone were the royal robes and any vestiges of kingship. He was dressed simply like the other servants of Yahweh. Kileab waved to him, but David's attention was elsewhere.

Gradually a hush fell over the huge crowd, each sensing that something momentous was about to happen. If there was any doubt that the procession was about to begin, it was dispelled as the blast of trumpets split the air. A shiver of anticipation coursed through Abigail, and she craned her neck to try to see better. Between the heads, she caught sight of Zadok and three others raising poles to their shoulders. He looked nervous, and Abigail wondered if he was thinking of Uzzah and praying desperately that they would find favour with Yahweh. She then saw a flash of gold and blue among the white, and realised that they had raised the ark, shrouded with a blue cloth of fine linen. A great shout of joy rose from the assembly and the ark, borne on its gold-covered poles, began to move forward, accompanied by further blasts from ram's horns as well as trumpets. Cymbals clashed.

Several moments later, a puzzled voice came from above her. 'Why have they stopped?' Abigail had no answer. It fell to Mered a short while later to provide the answer.

'The king is offering sacrifices to honour Yahweh.' And Abigail knew that this time all was well.

When the procession began moving again, it was to the sound of men's voices joining together to sing the praises of Yahweh in a new psalm. The words, written by David, rose majestically, lifted by the playing of harps and lyres, and Abigail's heart soared with them:

> *Give thanks to Yahweh, call on His name;*
> *make known among the nations what He has done.*

Whilst the Levites sang, David danced as if God's honour depended upon it. Although he was almost forty, Abigail had never seen him leap and spin around to the beat of the cymbal and sistrum with such abandon. As the effort began to darken his tunic and redden his face, Abigail knew that it was only One he sought to please with his dance. 'Praise Yahweh!' she cried out, waving her arms in the air with joy. A young voice from above shouted the same words in reply. Her son was flinging his arms in wide arcs and bouncing around wildly on Mered's shoulders. *Kileab: like his father.* Abigail laughed out loud with joy.

If there was one small cloud in the sky that day, bringing shadow rather than sunlight and chill rather than warmth, that cloud had a name: *Michal.* Abigail spotted her looking down from a window as the procession entered Jerusalem. Despite the shouts and songs of joy, her lips were tight. The sour image was soon forgotten, however, as the ark was finally set down in its resting place—the tent prepared for it within the city walls. David then sacrificed offerings to Yahweh and gave gifts of food to all the people.

But Michal did not stay forgotten.

'Hush, Kileab!'

David's sudden, firm words drew Abigail's attention away from Mahlah. Kileab's excited chatter stopped.

Michal was standing just outside the doorway in the courtyard of David's house, arms folded. She didn't bother greeting them. 'How the king of Israel distinguished himself today!' she began contemptuously. 'He uncovered himself before the eyes of his servants' maids as if he were a shameless fool!'

David's voice was as cold as a mountain stream bearing melted snows in spring. 'It was before Yahweh that I danced and celebrated—Yahweh, who chose me above your father and his house and who appointed me to rule over His people in Israel. I will become yet more undignified and low in my own eyes, but in the eyes of those maids of whom you have spoken, I will be held in honour.' Without a further word, he passed her by and entered his house.

Abigail wondered if he would ever take her into his room and into his arms again.

Whether Abigail was right concerning Michal or not, the daughter of Saul continued to remain without child. David's household, however, grew by other means. He took further wives and also concubines, and these began to bear him more sons and daughters.

But as Kileab approached the age of eight, Abigail began to notice a difference among David's first wives—*a wariness, a distance*—and she suspected she knew from whence it came. *One day, one of David's sons would be king, and there were mothers who seemed to believe already that it should be their offspring, whether it was Ahinoam, whose son was David's firstborn, or Maacah, who was the daughter of a king, or Haggith, who simply believed her son was the equal of any of his elders.*

David had not spoken yet of any successor, and seemed to indulge all his sons equally. *Maybe David would simply leave it to Yahweh to anoint the one who would follow him, and was making no assumptions that it would be a son of his own.* Abigail did not know what was in his mind, and would not be the one to ask him. She determined, however, that Kileab's head would never be filled with any ideas of kingship. *Only one son of David—if it was to be one of them—could be king. It would be wise to keep Kileab from any struggle there might be between them.* She thought of Saul and David. *Such struggles only brought grief.*

It was not only by wives and sons that David's household grew though. The new palace, built with the help and skills of the ally that David had found in the king of Tyre, was situated in the north-west of the small city where the greater height and fresher breezes favoured the king's household. Sweet-smelling cedar panels adorned each room of the two-storey stone building. There were large halls and rooms where David could meet those who sought an audience with the king. The gracious courtyard had small trees upon which sparrows would often sit, and steps led up to further rooms in which David's household lived and where those administering his kingdom could work. The roof of the palace, from which both the city and the hills around could be viewed, was often visited by Abigail. It was there that she came across David one evening.

She bowed her head, 'My lord,' and made to return down the steps to leave him in the peace and solitude he clearly desired.

'No, come join me, Abigail.'

To her surprise, he seemed excited. 'Does this evening find you well, my lord?'

Instead of answering her question, he asked another. 'Do you remember that I spoke of making Jerusalem great by bringing the footstool of Yahweh's throne, the ark itself, within these walls?'

'Of course, my lord, and such you have done.'

'But it is not all I will do to honour Yahweh!' His eyes were bright. 'I went to Nathan earlier, and spoke to him of what is on my heart. Here I live in a palace of cedar…' He swept his arm across the rooftop, and then took Abigail by the hand and led her to the parapet on the south side of the roof. He extended his arm towards the tent he had pitched within the city. 'And yet the ark remains in the most humble of dwellings.'

'And what is it that is on your heart, my lord?'

'To build a temple fit for the God of all the earth, here in Jerusalem!'

Abigail surveyed the crowded city. 'Where, my lord?'

David put his head back and laughed. 'That I do not yet know!' He looked around him, mirth in his eyes. 'Maybe we will have to enlarge the city and build new walls. Anything could be possible with Yahweh's help. All I know now is that Nathan has told me to do whatever is in my mind, for Yahweh is with me!' He took her hand again. 'I came up onto the roof to look upon the city, but come with me and see what I have planned already.'

She followed him down the steps and into his room. He reminded her of Kileab when excitement had gripped him on seeing a horse for the first time. David led her over to a table on which scrolls were scattered. He picked up one and opened it out flat. It had a design on it that could have come from the hand of a child.

'There,' he said proudly.

'It is a fine beginning, my lord.' She hesitated. 'Though, forgive me for saying so, but my lord plays the lyre better than he draws.'

David laughed and nodded his head. Nothing it seemed could dampen his spirits. 'It is true that my hand is more used to wielding a sword than a pen!' He paused for a moment, staring intently, as if the temple itself were before him. 'I see it so clearly in my mind...' he said, awed.

'But you can weave words into beautiful patterns to glorify Yahweh, my lord. Let your temple be as a psalm, and show me in words all that your heart imagines for the glory of our God!'

As he spoke, his hands and fingers did not remain still, however, as they painted in the air his glorious vision. Abigail watched every shape they traced out. She had not been into David's bedroom for some months, but that night his only passion was for the honour of the name of Yahweh.

A knock on the door stopped David. All was suddenly quiet. Abigail had no idea how much of the night had slipped by, but she knew it was very late.

'Come!' said David loudly, clearly puzzled by the interruption. The door opened and Nathan entered. His eyes flitted to Abigail, sitting next to David, and then back to the king. He bowed. 'What brings you here, Nathan? Is there trouble?'

'Not trouble, my lord. But it is about the matter of which you spoke to me earlier.' His eyes flitted to Abigail again.

David smiled. 'You may speak freely, Nathan. I have been telling Abigail about my plans for the temple.'

Nathan stiffened slightly, as if drawing himself up to deliver his words. 'The word of Yahweh has come to me this night,' he announced.

David stood slowly and turned himself to face Nathan fully, his eyes fixed on the prophet. 'Speak—the servant of Yahweh is listening.'

'This is what Yahweh says,' began Nathan solemnly, '*Are you the one to build me a house to dwell in?*'

Abigail listened, rapt, as Nathan repeated the words he had heard from the Almighty. She soon realised that what she was hearing was not a rebuke but a promise—a promise as rich and beautiful and immeasurable as the night sky in all its glory. *It was a promise of a name for David as great as any upon earth. A promise of peace and security for God's people. A promise that although David would not build a house for Yahweh, Yahweh Himself would establish David's throne, David's kingdom and David's own house—and a son from his own body would succeed him and build a house for the Name of Yahweh, for the God who would be as a father to him.* Tears of wonder and joy began to roll down Abigail's face. David eyes were also brimming with unspilt tears.

But Nathan went on. '*Your house and your kingdom shall endure for ever before Me; your throne shall be established for ever.*' He fell silent. He had delivered the final words.

David stood motionless and quiet for several moments. Then he whispered, 'Who am I...?' But he could go no further, and could only shake his head in wonder. When he was able to speak again, it was more to himself than to Abigail or Nathan. 'I must go to sit before Him...' He did not wait for either to respond.

'It is the middle of the night,' said Abigail, with a shake of her head and a little laugh of wonder as David disappeared through the door.

Nathan nodded. 'But David himself appointed Asaph and other Levites to serve before the ark. It is never left unattended. After all—' He turned to her and smiled. '—Yahweh never sleeps...'

Notes

1. *After David becomes king in Hebron, Abigail is only referred to once more and that is as the mother of David's second son. It is assumed here that she remains with David for the rest of his life, with ongoing (though possibly limited) contact with her husband as he takes more wives. Apart from Bathsheba, she is the only one of David's wives about whom any details are given beyond where she came from and to whom she gave birth.*

2. *There are few (if any!) details in Scripture about the life of a king's wife or how David's house or family life were arranged. Although sons, for example, would probably have eaten at the table of the king, it is not clear if this would have been the case for wives. How much time they spent with the king and their sons and how they occupied their time is not spoken of in Scripture. For these reasons, much in these chapters is conjecture, although Abigail is assumed (given the description of the wife of noble character in Proverbs 31) not to remain idle.*

3. *Abigail's son is called Kileab in 2 Samuel 3:3 and Daniel in 1 Chronicles 3:1. At least one commentator suggests that Kileab is a 'nickname', meaning 'the father prevails' (or similar), though the idea that it was given him by David is speculation.*

4. *Seventeen sons of David are named altogether, and although it is possible that each wife had only one son, it may be more likely that the list names only the firstborn son of each wife. David is also recorded as having a number of daughters, although only one (Tamar) is named, and only then because of her role in the story. There is also no indication of the timings*

of David's marriages or the births of sons—only the order of the latter (2 Samuel 3:2-5).

5. Although the text states that David reigned in Hebron for seven years and six months before being made king over all Israel (2 Samuel 2:11), it is not clear where Ish-Bosheth's reign of two years (2 Samuel 2:10) falls within that period, i.e. at the beginning, middle or end of it. Different commentators suggest different things. Here is it assumed that there is a lengthy period of disarray after the defeat and scattering at Mount Gilboa, with Ish-Bosheth only being crowned approximately five years into David's reign. (Ish-Bosheth is also called Ishvi or Eshbaal.)

6. Commentators suggest that the various parts of 2 Samuel 5 (following David's anointing over the whole kingdom) might not follow a strict chronological order. For ease of the narrative here, his battles with the Philistines have largely been left out.

7. The first time the Law of Moses is explicitly mentioned in the account of David is in his commission to Solomon at the end of his life in 1 Kings 2:3. His psalm at the end of 2 Samuel, sung 'when the LORD delivered him from the hand of all his enemies and from the hand of Saul', does speak, however, of all God's laws being before him (2 Samuel 22:23) and Psalm 19, written by David, speaks of his love for God's law. The bringing of the Book of the Law to Jerusalem, as described in this chapter, is one way in which it might have happened, but is speculation.

8. Although Judges 1:8 refers to the men of Judah taking the city of Jerusalem much earlier in Israel's history, it seems that this was not a permanent capture. Also, different translations of 2 Samuel 5:8 suggest either scaling hooks or the water-shaft as being the means of capturing Jerusalem. The latter has been assumed in this story, and archaeologists certainly discovered a water-shaft in 1867 (Warren's Shaft) in Jerusalem. Some think, however, that the text simply refers to the water supply being cut off to conquer the city.

9. That Abigail was in the crowd accompanying the ark to Jerusalem is conjecture. However, women were at the very least present when the crowd reached Jerusalem (2 Samuel 6:19). It certainly seems reasonable to assume that David's sons would have been in the gathering.

10. The sistrum is a form of percussion instrument that is shaken or rattled.

11. The implied punishment of childlessness upon Michal for her despising David's dancing to honour God could simply have come about by David not lying with her again after she rebuked him.

12. There are problems concerning the dating of the building of David's palace and the dating of Hiram, king of Tyre, who is mentioned in the account, as some date the beginning of his reign to the last ten years of David's life. However, Yahweh's promise to David in 2 Samuel 7 seems to be before the incident with Bathsheba (and is certainly placed there in Scripture), and therefore earlier in his reign, but it is where David speaks of living in a palace of cedar (2 Samuel 7:2). Therefore, whatever the problems with dating, the building of the palace is assumed here to be shortly after the taking of Jerusalem.

7

In the spring, at the time when kings go off to war, David sent Joab out with the king's men and the whole Israelite army... But David remained in Jerusalem. (2 Samuel 11:1)

Abigail was watching her step as she ascended the stone stairs, but suddenly became aware of someone hurrying down. She stopped and looked up, and bowed her head to David—but not before she'd caught a strange look in his eyes. 'My lord.' He barely seemed to notice her as he brushed past, as if something far more important or pressing was on his mind. He reached the bottom and quickly disappeared from sight. Abigail stared after him for a few moments. The encounter had done nothing to dispel the unease in her mind— it had only increased it. She turned back and continued her climb to the roof of the palace. *If she was fortunate, she could find solitude there*—a rare gift in the busy household where the wives, children, servants and officials of the king were all difficult to avoid. David alone had the privilege and privacy of a room to himself.

She mounted the top step. *She had her wish*—the roof was empty. She had no desire to look out over the city where the streets and roofs and their occupants would be a distraction. *Though many of the men were now away at war.* She made her way to the north side and looked out. A few sheep and goats were scattered over the hillside nearby, which was blessed with greenery from the winter rains. To her left, the sun was just visible in the western sky, and the evening breeze was as refreshing as water drawn from a deep well. *It was little wonder that many in Jerusalem favoured their rooftops after the heat of a day.*

The roof had become her refuge some eight years earlier when she had lost Kileab. Neither her desperate pleas before the ark nor David's physicians had resulted in a lessening of his fever, and towards the end of Kileab's ninth autumn, his short life came to an end. David had wept with her and comforted her the best he could, but it had only been in the more recent years that the sunshine had begun to return to her days. A cloud had arisen once more, however, and she again sought solitude on the palace roof. *Here she could bring before Yahweh her troubled thoughts concerning the man she had just met on the stairs.*

It had started in the winter months when David's lyre fell silent. She had rarely known him without a new song in his heart—and when she had, he had not been himself. He began to seem restless and dissatisfied, though he had no reason to be so. When spring had approached, she told herself it would be different. With the passing of the heavy rains, which made battles too difficult, several months lay ahead when men could be called upon to fight before they were needed for the harvests. *David would lead his men out as he always did, and all would be as before.* But he didn't. She told herself that maybe there was some urgent matter to deal with in Jerusalem—but she knew of none. In the fourteen years since David had been made king over the whole nation, he had regained the territories of Israel, defeating the Philistines and even taking more land from them; he had made Moab and Edom, together with the Arameans and Ammonites, subject to him, and had even extended his power as far as the Euphrates. *Yahweh had granted him victory wherever he went.* The only matter that concerned the kingdom that year was the rebellion of Ammon. But David remained in Jerusalem, and had just sent the army with Joab to engage the Ammonites. *It was not like him.*

Abigail turned her troubled thoughts into prayer, entreating the God of Israel for the land, for the army, but chiefly for her husband. She did not see David again that evening.

She rose early after a night in which sleep largely eluded her. In the cool of the courtyard, she ate a simple meal of bread, curds and figs with honey, as the sky above her turned from pink to blue. She tarried, pondering the tasks intended for the day, including visiting some of the wives of David's warriors whilst they were away in battle. *David might not know the families of his officers, but she did.* By the time she made her way back inside, the rest of the household was beginning to stir, but the first person she encountered was not one she had expected to see.

The young and beautiful woman stopped, bowed her head briefly to acknowledge a wife of the king, and then continued on her way. Abigail caught both her inscrutable expression and the scent of perfume as Bathsheba passed her. She paused and turned to watch her as she made her way towards and then through the palace door, the sash around the waist of her deep red dress showing the curves of her body. Abigail was perplexed. *What had brought her to the palace?* She walked upstairs slowly to the women's quarters. *Had she been there to see one of the officials? Her husband, well-known as one of David's Thirty, was after all away fighting with Joab—had she come to the palace in his stead on some household matter?* Her instincts told her otherwise.

'Mahlah,' began Abigail as she'd found her, 'I have a task for you.' She drew her aside and away from the ears of the other wives of David.

'What is it you wish?'

'I have seen something that puzzles me. I came across Bathsheba, the wife of Uriah the Hittite, in the palace earlier this morning.' She glanced around. *None of the other women were paying them any attention.* 'What brought her here? Someone will know.'

When Mahlah returned as noon approached, she appeared troubled. 'We should go up to the roof.'

The words did nothing to dispel Abigail's disquiet. *The roof was likely to be empty in the middle of the day. Even in spring, noon could be hot.* They were soon out in the open, with only drying clothes for company. 'What have you discovered, Mahlah?'

Her maid seemed hesitant. 'It is only the word of another servant…'

Abigail's chest tightened. 'Do you have any reason to doubt them?'

'Only because of the answer they have given.'

The last time she had felt such dread had been when Mahlah had brought her the news of Abner's murder. 'Tell me.'

Mahlah looked her in the eye. 'They said that the king sent for her last night and that she spent the night alone with him in his room.'

Abigail suddenly recalled David's demeanour when he had passed her the previous evening coming down from the roof. Her dread became horror. For several moments it was as if she had been struck dumb, unable to find either a voice or words to adequately describe her turmoil and shock. 'David cannot do that,' she whispered eventually. She had seen David lose his way before, but had never seen him deliberately leave Yahweh's path—and it scared her. 'He is the king, but that does not put him above God's laws. The kings of other nations may do as they wish and make their own laws, but we are the people of Yahweh and He is our judge.' After a moment she added, 'Do many know?'

'You know what the servants are like. They talk...'

Abigail shook her head slowly. 'There is one who will certainly know—Yahweh. Has David lost his mind?' Her own words threw up a memory of Saul, and the thought that followed was too terrible to voice, even to Mahlah. *Saul had disobeyed God and had been rejected as king. Could the unthinkable happen to Yahweh's anointed once again?* She turned her eyes upwards. 'O Yahweh, have mercy!'

'I thought you would want to know,' said Mahlah meekly.

Abigail nodded. 'You are right, although I cannot guess what is in the king's mind.' She lowered her voice. 'Why would David lie with Uriah's wife, and then only weeks later invite him to the palace to feast with him?'

'The king asked him how the war was going—'

'But why Uriah? Why not send for Helez or Abiezer or any other man among the Thirty? Any of them would have the ear of Joab and would know the true course of the conflict.' She shook her head and then added bitterly, 'How could he look Uriah in the eye and treat his trusted warrior as if nothing has happened?' *David certainly never looked her in the eye anymore.* The greater question in her mind, however, continued to be whether David would yet face Yahweh's wrath. It was the question that kept her from sleeping soundly at night.

The news of Uriah's death in battle perplexed Abigail further, though she was not surprised when David took Bathsheba as his wife seven days later, after her period of mourning was over. She herself had come under David's protection as his wife only days after God had struck Nabal down. *But she knew this was different. Why would Yahweh let Uriah fall by an Ammonite sword, allowing David to enjoy lawfully the fruit previously forbidden and yet which he had reached out, taken and tasted?*

That the fruit of the womb should begin growing so swiftly within Bathsheba after marrying the king seemed another mystery in the purposes of Yahweh. *Why bless their union further with a child?* Abigail had no answer. No answer, that is, until the child was born.

'The boy is healthy and strong for one born so early,' commented Ahinoam, her voice heavy with scorn. Abigail was not the only one to know either the rumours or the truth of the king's adultery. That the child was David's rather than Uriah's seemed the inescapable truth. But Ahinoam had not finished. 'How sad that Uriah died so tragically,' she sneered.

'Why do you speak in such a tone?' asked Abigail. 'He died in battle.' Her voice sounded distant.

Ahinoam raised her eyebrows. 'I do not dispute that, but my son was with David when the messenger brought the report from Joab. The king was furious that they had been fighting so close to the city where the soldiers were exposed—until he was told that Uriah was among them. Then he simply told Joab not to let it trouble him.'

Abigail suddenly felt sick. 'That does not make David the cause of Uriah's death.'

Ahinoam shrugged. 'I am not saying he is,' though Abigail knew she was at least suggesting it.

She walked away slowly. *It was as if a rotting, fetid carcass had been slung into the spring of Gihon, polluting the water on which the city depended. She had known for some years that David was capable of deceit. Now she knew he was also capable of adultery. But deliberately causing the death of another? He was a better man than Joab.* Abigail stopped. *He had been.* She went up onto the roof and wept.

Abigail sometimes watched as the people brought their petitions to the king. It helped her to know the struggles of the people, whether they were disputes among neighbours or the plight of widows or any other grievance. It laid bare the mood of the nation and Abigail judged that prudent to know. David required his sons to be present, that they might know how justice should be properly administered, though his younger sons often looked bored. Abigail could no longer, however, view David's judgments as she had done before. *He was holding others to the standards of Yahweh's laws—laws he had discarded so readily himself, despite having brought the Book of the Law to the city.* Sometimes she could not even bring herself to look at David. At other times, grief for the man she had known threatened to overwhelm her.

She was surprised when Nathan the prophet presented himself before the king one morning.

David seemed to share at least a measure of her curiosity. 'Speak, Nathan—what troubles you?'

Part way through Nathan's petition, Abigail stiffened. She leant forward slightly on the bench on which she was sitting, her heart beginning to race. *Were the prophet's words—concerning a rich man with many sheep and a poor man with a single ewe lamb—really about that?* She listened intently. When Nathan told how the rich man had taken the lamb that wasn't his own, she stared wide-eyed at him in both astonishment and dread. Her eyes darted to David. *Did he not realise what the prophet had just done?*

David was leaning forward, his hands gripping the arms of the throne and his eyes fierce with indignation. 'As surely as Yahweh lives, the man who did this deserves to die! He must pay for the lamb four times over because he did such a thing and had no pity.'

Nathan looked straight at David. 'You are the man!'

There were gasps and then utter silence. Every man, woman and child was as still as the cedar pillars which graced the audience room, each staring at the two men who faced each other. Even David's younger sons, who had seemed disinterested a short while before, were now sitting up and alert, regardless of whether they understood what was happening or not.

Nathan had not finished. 'Thus says Yahweh, the God of Israel: *It is I who anointed you king over Israel and it is I who have delivered you from the hand of Saul. I gave your master's house to you and your master's wives into your care, and I gave you the house of Israel and Judah. And if all that had been too little, I would have added to these even more. Why did you despise the word of Yahweh by doing evil in His eyes? You have struck down Uriah the Hittite with the sword, taken his wife to be your own, and killed him with the sword of the sons of Ammon. Now, therefore, the sword shall never depart from your own house, because you have despised Me and have taken the wife of Uriah the Hittite to be your own.'*

Abigail was reeling, but there was still more judgment to be delivered by the mouth of Nathan.

'Thus says Yahweh: *Behold, out of your own household I am going to bring calamity upon you. Before your very eyes I will take your wives and give them to one who is close to you, and he will lie with your wives in broad daylight. You did it in secret, but I will do this thing before all Israel and under the sun.'*

The final words filled Abigail with horror, but still her eyes did not leave David. His face was ashen. *Would he defy the prophet or lash out in rage?* He suddenly slumped, as if all life had left him, his shoulders and head drooping as his shame was laid bare for all to see. He lowered his eyes. 'I have sinned against Yahweh.' There was no excuse, no attempt at vindication—and no denial of any of it.

For the first time, Abigail saw a single blessing in Kileab's death. *His eyes had been saved from seeing the utter humiliation and disgrace of his beloved father.*

Nathan stood quietly for several moments, as if listening, though all was silent. David lifted his face towards the prophet—and within it was an honesty that Abigail had not seen for more than nine months. He suddenly seemed oblivious of all else, and Abigail knew there was only one whose judgment mattered to him at that moment. Nathan finally spoke, his tone softer: 'Yahweh has taken away your sin—you will not die. But because your deed has given the enemies of Yahweh cause to show Him utter contempt, the son born to you will die.' For a moment the two men beheld each other, but David did not protest.

Instead, he dropped his eyes once more, and the prophet, his work done, turned and left.

As David continued staring at the floor, those around the room began to look at one another awkwardly, wondering what to do. Eventually, without uttering another word, David rose and left the room. And Abigail knew she had witnessed once more the holy and faithful love of Yahweh—not in a gentle breeze but in a furious storm.

Abigail did not see David for the rest of the day. She suspected he had gone to the one place he had avoided in recent months: the tent of Yahweh's ark. She stayed away from the other wives that day—*there would only be one matter upon their lips.* But as she mounted the steps to return to the women's quarters that evening, she heard the faint sound of a lyre. It had been a long time since she had heard the sound, and there was only one person who could play it with such ease and skill. She looked around, picked up the skirt of her tunic, and hurried to the top of the steps before making her way towards David's room. Even though the door was closed, the notes were clear. She stood quietly outside listening to the haunting melody. *She had not heard it before.* But then David began to sing, not hesitantly or softly, but as if he were pouring out the very depths of his being in song. She didn't have to strain to catch the words.

Have mercy upon me, O God,
> *according to Your unfailing love;*
according to Your great compassion
> *blot out my transgressions.*
Wash away all my iniquity
> *and cleanse me from my sin.*

Abigail's eyes filled with tears and her heart with gratitude. *Yahweh had granted the one thing she had desired more than any other—that her husband's sin would be rooted out like an ugly weed from among golden wheat.* She continued to listen, amazed by the mercy and kindness of the God of Israel. She had heard the words of judgment to come, but they mattered little to her at that moment. *As long as David's heart was right before Yahweh, anything could be borne—even the judgment of the Almighty.* Abigail continued to listen.

*Create in me a pure heart, O God,
and renew a steadfast spirit within me.*

When David's voice fell silent again, his fingers continued to pick out the notes of the song. 'Hear his prayer, O Yahweh,' Abigail murmured over the music, 'and grant Your Anointed what he has asked of You.' She listened once again as he continued, but it was as he neared the end that her unspilt tears began to flow.

*The sacrifices of God are a broken spirit;
a broken and contrite heart
O God, You will not despise.*

Abigail marvelled. *The immensity of David's sin had been dwarfed by the mercy of God. The Almighty had removed David's sin in a heartbeat as soon as it had been acknowledged and owned. To live with Yahweh was to dwell in the presence of both a holy fire and yet an immeasurable love.* She bowed her head and her heart before the God of Israel. *To live apart from Yahweh was no life at all.*

'It shows the fullness of Yahweh's forgiveness, does it not, Mahlah?'

Mahlah nodded in answer to Abigail's question, as they both leant on the parapet of the roof, watching out over Jerusalem. 'That God should grant another son to David and Bathsheba, having taken their first, is wonder enough, but that Yahweh should send Nathan to tell them to call the child *Loved by Yahweh* is a marvel indeed.'

Abigail thought of the two names her own son had borne. Despite her having named him *Daniel, Kileab* was what he had been called. *Unless he had exasperated her to the limit of her patience.* The memory was bittersweet. 'Only the fullness of time will show whether it is *Solomon* that prevails or the name delivered by Nathan.' She fell silent for a few moments, musing. 'When Nathan delivered Yahweh's covenant promise to the king just over ten years ago, he spoke of a son who would come forth from David's own body to succeed him. Maybe that son is Solomon.' She thought of the sin that had wreaked such damage in David's life. 'If the Almighty were to choose a son of Bathsheba to sit on the throne after David, would that not show yet more of the glory of Yahweh's grace?'

'It would, but David has not yet spoken of who will succeed him, has he?'

Abigail shook her head. 'No.' Then she laughed, 'Though if it is to be Solomon, he is barely out of the womb!' She fell silent and then sighed.

'What is it, Abigail?'

'We may have seen the fullness of Yahweh's forgiveness, but His fidelity is as great as His mercy and the word of His judgment remains. I marvelled when David still sought God and fasted when the son of his adultery fell ill. He believed that God might yet be merciful despite the greatness of his sin, and yet accepted humbly Yahweh's judgment when the child died. I fear, then, that the rest of the Almighty's rulings that came by the mouth of Nathan will stand.'

Abigail paused as her eyes rested upon the roof of a nearby house, the gift that David had recently bestowed upon Amnon, his eldest son. '*Out of your own household I am going to bring calamity upon you.* Those were Nathan's words to David and I dread their meaning. It would not surprise me to see trouble among the king's sons, particularly as David has not spoken of his successor—'

Mahlah's brow furrowed. 'But David has only recently passed fifty. It may be many years yet before a new king needs to be crowned.'

'Even if David is waiting for Yahweh's word on who will be anointed, the desire to sit on the throne may already be in more than one heart.' Abigail fell silent. The rest of Nathan's words had not been forgotten—of David's wives being taken by one close to him who would lie with them in broad daylight. She shuddered.

Abigail always valued Rachel's company and her discretion—and the welcome at her house, particularly when both husbands were away. As captain of the king's own guard, Benaiah only left Jerusalem when David did and was never far from him.

Both women chatted easily and openly as they worked on garments destined for children—in Abigail's case, a child who had two years earlier been born to Mered's wife. Seven years had passed since Nathan's word of judgment, and the sword of which the prophet had spoken had already shed blood within David's house.

'Will the king still not see Absalom?' asked Rachel, as she inspected her latest seam. 'After all, *what is it now?* Almost a year since Absalom's return from Geshur?'

Abigail paused and laid her sewing in her lap. 'No, he won't. I suppose he imagines that allowing him to return to Jerusalem last year was restoration enough.' She sighed—and Rachel held her peace. 'David knows he has never really punished Absalom for murdering Amnon. He has the blood of Uriah on his own hands, and although Yahweh has forgiven him, I can only think that he believed he could not hold his son to account for a sin he himself had also committed. It was the same when Amnon defiled Tamar.'

The rape of Absalom's younger sister by David's firstborn, Amnon, had brought the king's fury, but little else. At the time, Abigail had suspected that David felt he couldn't condemn a sin so similar to the one he had committed the previous year. Yet none of the wives, save possibly Amnon's mother, Ahinoam, had though such inaction right, particularly when Tamar was left with only a life of desolation before her. Abigail couldn't imagine David offering to any man of standing a daughter who had been defiled and disgraced by her brother.

'Maybe Absalom will simply wait,' continued Rachel, re-threading her needle, 'and hope that David will change his mind. After all, he waited two whole years before meting out his own justice for Tamar.'

Although it had been four years earlier, Abigail still remembered keenly the horror that had gripped the household when they were told that Absalom had struck down all the king's sons—learning only later that it was the twenty-two-year-old Amnon alone who lay dead, struck down at his younger brother's behest. Ahinoam had been the only mother whose wails did not become tears of relief.

Abigail picked up her sewing again. 'It was not only Amnon that David wept for that day, believe me. He also mourned for Absalom after he fled to his grandfather. He was both angered and grieved by what he'd done—and yet loved him.' She thrust her needle into the linen. 'He still does.'

The whole of David's household knew the following year of Absalom's return to favour, after five years of not seeing the king's face. More than once, Abigail sighed in exasperation when servant girls giggled as the prince passed by or seemed suddenly to be struck dumb in his presence. That he was already married at the age of twenty-four seemed to make little difference.

'I do not dispute that he is probably the most handsome man in all Israel,' Mahlah said to her one day in a lowered voice. They were sitting together in the courtyard of the palace. 'But he knows it. I have never seen a man so concerned with his hair! He is like a bird preening its feathers.'

Abigail lifted her hand to stifle a laugh. 'You are not the only one to have noticed that truth.' Her mirth soon faded, however. She also knew what he was capable of.

Mahlah seemed to catch her change of mood. 'Is it true what they are saying, that Absalom ordered his servants to deliberately set Joab's fields on fire?'

Abigail nodded slowly. 'Yes. Joab had been refusing to see him, even though it was he who had persuaded the king to allow Absalom's return to Jerusalem.'

'So he sought Joab's attention by other means?'

'And succeeded. Joab then petitioned the king for him a second time, and Absalom is now back in the king's favour.' She paused. 'Yes, Absalom has his wish, but you should also know this, Mahlah.' She glanced around. 'The king is finally beginning to speak of the one Yahweh has chosen to follow him—and it is not Absalom.'

The door to the women's quarters flew open. Their shock at seeing Seraiah, David's secretary, in the area forbidden to men, was quickly overtaken by the shock of his message. 'We must all leave! Now!'

Abigail stepped forward. 'What are you talking about, Seraiah?'

'The king has ordered that all his household leave Jerusalem immediately.'

Abigail stared at him, aghast. 'But why?'

'A messenger has just arrived from Hebron. Absalom has been made king there and the hearts of the men of Israel are with him.'

Ahinoam drew alongside Abigail, her face drained of its usual colour. 'But surely we are safe here in Jerusalem? David has soldiers here to defend it.'

'The king is not willing to risk the city. He does not doubt that Absalom will destroy it and us with it if we remain. Absalom may also have men loyal to him within the walls already, waiting for his orders to strike. If we leave Jerusalem, the king will soon know who remains loyal to him by who goes with him. So be quick! Gather all the king's family and bring with you only what you need. Act now!'

'It will be done,' said Abigail, resolving to take charge. 'We will come down to the courtyard as soon as we are ready.'

Seraiah paused. 'It is said Ahithophel is with Absalom.' He then turned and hurried off.

She stared after him. That David's trusted counsellor had chosen to side with the king's son left her momentarily stunned. She shook herself out of it. *They were in Yahweh's hands.*

More than once Abigail had to tell one of David's younger wives or concubines to leave behind an item that they considered vital but which she did not. When one protested that she needed a cushion for her head, Abigail calmly took it from her. 'Use your arms to carry bread or raisin cakes. You will thank me when your daughter has food to eat in three days' time.' Ahinoam became her ally. Neither of them had offspring to chase and both remembered what it was like to be fugitives with David. Then, they had been fleeing from Saul and under thirty years of age. Now it was from David's own bone and flesh, and they had both passed their sixtieth year.

Between them, they soon had every woman and child gathered by the courtyard. Seraiah, however, immediately called ten of David's concubines to one side. 'The king has decreed that the ten of you should stay. Take care of the palace whilst we are away.'

It was a sign that David, at least, believed—or hoped—they would return.

After they made their way through the gates of Jerusalem and began their descent into the Kidron Valley to the east of the city, David sent them ahead. 'I will wait to see who is leaving the city with us. I will follow when all have left.' His head was covered and his feet bare, as if mourning. But David was not standing alone. Benaiah was at his side, as were Abiathar and Zadok, and with them, Levites bearing the ark. Abigail drew comfort from the sight. *The presence of Yahweh with them was more precious than ten thousand warriors—or indeed any number of men.*

As Abigail ascended the Mount of Olives on the other side of the valley, Rachel drew alongside her, the hand of her nine-year-old daughter in hers and a bulging bag slung over her shoulder. 'Take courage, Abigail. We are with you. Benaiah says that every man of the king's guard is with him, and even the six hundred Gittites who came with him from Gath have vowed to live or die with the king. I know there will be others too.'

Abigail glanced behind her. The end of the long line of those leaving Jerusalem had just reached the bottom of the Kidron Valley. David was there. 'I will wait here for the king.'

Rachel reached out her free hand and took Abigail's. She squeezed it. 'I will see you at the top.'

Abigail waited whilst others of the king's officials passed her, all of them with their heads covered like the king and many openly weeping. As David approached, flanked by large numbers of armed men on each side, he was weeping too. Abigail's heart stirred within her. *She, too, had watched Absalom grow from a baby, but he was David's son, not hers. David had longed to see his beloved son in the five years they were estranged. But now that same son had plunged a blade deep into David's soul—not a blade of Philistine iron, like the one that had been driven into*

Amnon at Absalom's command, but one of utter betrayal that was just as deadly. Abigail had no doubt that it was his intention to bring the king's life to an equally swift end. *After all, there could be only one king.* But as David neared her, Abigail wondered if his grief also sprang from the knowledge that it was his own sin that had brought the sword into his house.

Abigail bowed her head. 'My lord.' David raised his bowed head to acknowledge her. She then began walking alongside him, on the opposite side to Benaiah, who remained at the king's right hand. 'Are neither the ark nor Yahweh's priests to accompany you, my lord?'

'I have sent Zadok and Abiathar back to the city with the ark.'

'But why, my lord?'

'If I find favour in Yahweh's eyes, He will bring me back to see His dwelling-place again. But if not, then I am ready to bear the will of Yahweh. But Zadok and Abiathar will be my eyes in Jerusalem. I have told them to send any word of Absalom's plans to me by the mouth of their sons.' David then fell silent, clearly lost again in his own pain. She did not question him further but simply walked by his side, glad that his heart was both submitting to the God of Israel but also devising courses of action in the hope that Yahweh might yet restore him.

When they reached the top of the Mount of Olives, a man stepped forward to greet David, his outer garment rent in grief and dust upon his head. Abigail recognised him immediately as the one who had both David's trust and the title of *Friend of the King.* Hushai bowed low before him. 'I am with you, my king.'

David looked at him steadily, as if weighing a matter. He then spoke. 'You will be of more help to me in the city. Return there and tell Absalom that you will now serve him just as you have served his father in the past. Help me by frustrating any advice given by Ahithophel. Zadok and Abiathar are also in the city. They will send what they know to me by their sons. You do the same.'

Hushai bowed low before David again. 'I remain the faithful servant of Yahweh's anointed king.' As he stood to leave, a small, sly smile played on his lips. 'I will make sure I change my robe before I meet Absalom.'

For a few moments, David's mood seemed to lighten. Then he nodded and Hushai was gone.

Later, as the sun began to drop behind the hills to the west, they neared the fords of the Jordan River, and David gave the order for the hundreds with him to stop, so as to rest and be refreshed.

Ahinoam dropped her bag to the ground wearily and then sat down beside it. 'We are not as young as we were when last with David in the desert.'

Abigail joined her, grateful for some respite for her aching feet. Although they had been walking for most of the day, she had little appetite. She knew she must eat to keep up her strength, though, so nibbled on a cake of pressed figs. Their journey had not been made easier when a man named Shimei—clearly loyal to the house of Saul—had accompanied them for part of the way, pelting David and those near him with stones and dirt, and cursing them all. Although she had not been in earshot, she had seen Joab's brother, Abishai, approach David, one hand on the hilt of his sword and the other pointing at the man. *It had not been difficult to guess Abishai's intent.* David, however, removed Abishai's hand from his sword, and whatever words they exchanged, the man kept his head—and kept cursing. *Maybe she had been seeing once again the king's submission to Yahweh.*

Ahinoam's words suddenly wrenched her from her thoughts.

'Did you believe Ziba?'

It took a moment for Abigail to realise that she was being asked about the servant of Jonathan's son, Mephibosheth.

Ahinoam filled the pause with her own answer. 'I did not. For him to suggest that the lame grandson of Saul somehow thinks that he will now become king is absurd. It is many, many years since the throne passed to the house of David, and those who have rebelled against the king are with Absalom, not the house of Saul, whatever Shimei might say!'

Abigail had to agree. 'There are few more loyal than Mephibosheth.' It had been over ten years since David's kindness had brought the son of Jonathan to his table. All knew the king's act had been born of loyalty to the one who had been his closest friend. She held up the cake of figs. 'Still, Ziba brought this and much else beside.'

'And he has gained David's favour by doing so.'

The string of donkeys laden with provisions from Mephiboseth's estate had reminded Abigail of the day she had first met David. She suddenly felt weary and closed her eyes.

'Abigail!'

She opened her eyes again at the sound of Mahlah's voice. *If she had drifted into sleep, it could not have been for long.* A young serving girl from David's household was with her. 'What is it, Mahlah?'

The wrinkles beneath Mahlah's greying hair deepened. 'Azubah—tell your mistress what you have just told me.' The young girl fiddled with her hands nervously. 'Go on…'

'I saw it two years back, mistress. Just after harvest. I know it was harvest time, because my brother Kish had just had a baby. Well not Kish himself, but—'

'It doesn't matter about the baby,' interrupted Mahlah, exasperated. 'Just tell the wife of the king what you told me about Absalom.'

Looking chastened, Azubah began again. 'I was coming back to the city from seeing Kish—' Her eyes darted to Mahlah who nodded encouragingly. '—and I saw the son of the king.' She paused, as if suddenly awed.

Abigail met Mahlah's gaze. Mahlah shook her head slightly and rolled her eyes.

'He was by the side of the road standing by a chariot and horses. I stood and watched for a little while, well, it was quite a long time because he was so kind to everyone. He listened to their troubles and wanted to help them. He was so sad when he had to tell them that they wouldn't be able to see the king.'

Mahlah snorted and muttered scornfully under her breath, 'But the liar, of course, would be a faultless ruler…'

Azubah seemed not to notice. 'It was like he was their friend or their brother and not the son of a king, and he promised that if he was made judge of the land he would see that *everyone* was treated right.'

She lowered her voice slightly. 'Then they would go to bow down to him and do you know what he would do?'

Abigail tried to be patient. 'Go on…'

Her eyes widened. 'He would reach out to them and kiss them!'

It was clearly too much for Mahlah. 'And did you not think to mention this to anyone?'

Azubah looked crest-fallen. Abigail sighed. 'Do not be too hard on her, Mahlah.'

'I'm so sorry, mistress, if I've done wrong. He was just being so kind, him being the king's son too, and he seemed to be making everyone happy…or that's what I thought…' She dried up, and then her face crumpled. 'Have I done very bad?' A tear slipped down her cheek.

Abigail sighed again. She took her largely uneaten fig cake and gave it to her maid. 'Don't be afraid, Azubah. You were not to know. Thank you for telling me what you know. I will pass it on to the king.'

The girl's face brightened. 'May I go now?'

'Yes, thank you.' Azubah bowed her head to Abigail and left them. She turned to Mahlah. 'So Absalom has been planning this for two years at least.'

'He has not won the hearts of the people, he has stolen them!'

Abigail thought for a moment. 'It would not surprise me if he began scheming four years ago, as soon as he heard he would not be king. If he was not going to be given the crown as David's eldest son, he would take it instead.' She rose to her feet. 'It may yet be helpful for the king to know how his son has deceived everyone.'

She left her friend and began making her way towards where David was seated, surrounded by his guard. A sudden thought troubled her. *Had Absalom murdered Amnon only because of the rape of his sister, or had rivalry also been at work?* She couldn't be sure. She then felt a deeper chill in the evening air. *If Kileab had lived to become a man, would he by now have suffered a violent death at the hand of his younger brother?* The answer to that was more certain in her own mind. She shivered. But then, unbidden, a final question presented itself. *Had Yahweh mercifully taken Kileab when he had known only innocence and love?*

She would never know if that were so, but Abigail found a strange comfort in simply considering the idea.

As she approached David, however, she immediately recognised Ahimaaz and Jonathan, the two sons of the priests who were to be sent to David if there were news. Judging by the redness of their faces, their rapid breathing and the water they were being given, they had only just arrived. She listened as they handed their water jugs back and began to speak. They wasted no time.

'Hushai sends you a message, O King!' began Ahimaaz. '*Do not spend the night at the fords in the desert; cross over without fail, or the king and all the people with him will be swallowed up.*'

'What else can you tell me? Do you know why Hushai has counselled me so—is Absalom now in the palace?'

Jonathan continued. 'Yes, my lord. You had barely disappeared over the Mount of Olives when he entered the city. Ahithophel has now instructed Absalom to set out this night with twelve thousand men to strike you while you are still weary from the journey. He has counselled him to strike you alone down, O King, but to scatter those with you, so all will be unharmed and return to him as king. That is how Ahithopel advised him.'

The treachery sickened Abigail. *How could Absalom murder his own father to seize the crown?*

Murmuring broke out, and Benaiah was not the only man whose hand went to his sword. 'Absalom's men will have to kill every one of the guard first!' Cries of *Yes!* followed.

Ittai, the leader of those from Gath, stepped forward. 'And the six hundred Gittites too.' More voices called out in agreement.

'Hush, friends,' said David. 'I would hear if the Friend of the King has sought to frustrate the advice.' He turned back to the two young men. 'Have you more to say?'

'Yes, O King,' continued Ahimaaz. 'Hushai has won Absalom's trust. He told him that Ahitophel's advice was not good, and that you would be hiding by now and if he attacked with only twelve thousand men, he would likely lose troops against the experienced fighters of the king, and his men would lose heart.'

'That is good, but what did Hushai counsel instead?'

'He suggested, O King, that Absalom wait until the army of all Israel is gathered, so that Absalom himself can lead a whole army into battle and utterly overwhelm you and your men, wherever you are.'

'He gains time for us,' responded David, nodding.

'He does more than that, my lord,' said Benaiah. 'He appeals to your son's pride...'

'He appeals to the young man's vanity!' insisted Joab scornfully. 'How Absalom would love to see himself riding at the head of a vast and victorious army!'

'Enough, Joab!' said David sharply. He turned back to Ahimaaz. 'Do you know which course of action Absalom intends to take?'

'Hushai believes his own advice will be taken, but counsels you to act now in case Absalom follows Ahitophel's words after all.'

'There is much wisdom in his counsel, and we will do as he has said.'

David was about to speak again, but Jonathan spoke first. 'Forgive me, O King, but there is one more thing you should know. That was not Ahithophel's only advice.' He paused and glanced at Ahimaaz. Ahimaaz nodded. 'He told Absalom that he should lie with the ten concubines that you left to look after the palace. This afternoon Absalom pitched a tent on the roof where all in the city could see it and did exactly as Ahithophel told him.'

There was silence. David shook his head slowly, but then Joab spoke. 'He has let it be known that there is now no way back for him.'

David did not answer him. 'We must prepare to ford the Jordan. Make sure all the women and children are able to cross in safety.' And with that he began issuing further orders.

Abigail turned to go back. *Her news could wait.* She knew that Absalom's act of defiance on the palace roof—for all to see—was what conquering kings did to the wives of vanquished rulers. It asserted their power and ownership over all that had previously belonged to their foe. But she also knew there was more to this act. *Whether he knew it or not, Absalom had carried out that day the only part of Nathan's judgment that remained unfulfilled.* She still remembered every word, for she had long feared that it would fall upon her: *Before your very eyes I will take your wives and give them to one who is close to you, and he will lie with your wives in broad daylight. You did it in secret, but I will do this thing before all Israel and under the sun.*

As she approached Mahlah, she reminded herself of two truths she had carried for many years in her heart: *Yahweh was faithful, but Yahweh was also merciful.*

Abigail looked down from the window in the early light of day to where David was seated on a bench in the meeting place between the inner and outer gates of the town. The years had not robbed him of the fine features that had delighted her when she had first become his wife, but grey now streaked his hair and his beard, and any red that he had had in his youth had long since disappeared. Deep lines now etched his face, and sorrow clung to him like a beast to its prey. He was staring at the outer gates and Benaiah stood nearby. *All they could do now was wait and hope and pray to the God of Israel.*

They had reached Mahanaim the day before and David and his men had been welcomed and amply supplied with provisions. *Mahanaim had been where their father Jacob had met the angels of Yahweh as he had travelled back to the land of his birth, fearing to meet his brother, Esau. Maybe His angels would now be with the troops that David had just sent out to meet the army of Absalom.* The men had refused to let David march with them, and given the advice Ahithophel had given, Abigail knew it to be wise.

The door opened and Mahlah entered. She hurried to Abigail's side. 'There is not much to tell you—'

'Yet I will be glad of all you know.'

'David divided the men and sent them out, a third each under the command of Joab, Abishai and Ittai.'

'That much I saw...'

'He also gave a charge to the men,' added Mahlah, lowering her voice slightly. 'He told each of the three commanders to be gentle with Absalom for his sake.'

Abigail sighed, resigned to the uncertain outcome. 'Ittai will take the king's word to heart, but the sons of Zeruaiah…? When has gentleness ever marked their actions?'

Mahlah had no answer. 'I left Azubah down near the gate. She is eager to win your praise and will bring news to us, if there is any.'

'Then let us pray, for her sake and ours, that it will indeed be good when it comes.'

It was late in the afternoon when the door opened again. Abigail's heart immediately feared that all was lost when she saw the stricken look in David's eyes. She quickly rose to her feet. But then he seemed to crumple as if he were the walls of Jericho before Joshua, and began weeping.

'O my son Absalom!' He collapsed onto the nearest bench. 'My son, my son Absalom! If only I had died instead of you.' And then he wept—and not even Bathsheba attempted to console him.

Azubah appeared in the doorway a short while later, biting her lip as she looked inside. She glanced at the king before looking towards Abigail, her eyes reddened. She waited. When Mahlah silently beckoned her, she hurried across to them, her head bowed and avoiding looking at the king again.

'What can you tell us, Azubah?' began Abigail softly, although there was no doubt in her mind that the battle was now decided, if not entirely over.

'Two messengers came,' whispered Azubah. 'The first told the king all was well, and everyone seemed happy, and I was happy too. But when the king asked about Absalom, he said he didn't know.' She sniffed. 'Then a second arrived, just after, and he was also saying there was good news, so that was good. The king asked about Absalom again, but the man said something about the king's enemies being like the young man. I didn't know what he meant but that's when the king stood up and left. After he'd gone, they—I mean the men there—started talking to the messenger, the one who'd said the words that made the king leave. He was only about my age. I stood nearby so I could hear them.' She lowered her voice further so that Abigail could barely catch her words above the sound of David's grief. 'He said Absalom got his hair stuck in a tree but his mule kept going so he was left dangling there.' She gulped. 'He said Joab put a spear in his heart.' She could not stop her lip quivering.

Abigail sighed deeply. *There was no fig cake to comfort her this time.* She laid a hand lightly on the girl's shoulder. 'It is not easy news to bear, Azubah. You have done well to bring it to us.' The young maid smiled weakly and sniffed again. 'You may go now.'

A spear was piercing Abigail's own heart—not for the death of Absalom but for the grief of her husband. *He had won the battle but lost yet another son—and it was he himself who had brought into his household the sword that had slain them all.*

Notes

1. *Some commentators have suggested that Kileab died young because he is not mentioned (though David's second son) in the later events associated with the succession to the throne. Although there are other sons mentioned in 1 Samuel 3 who are also absent from the narrative, Kileab dying young does seem the most reasonable suggestion, given that, when Adonijah puts himself forward as king, the text states that 'He…was born next after Absalom' (1 Kings 1:6). The inference from this seems to be that he was 'next in line'. This would presumably only apply if Kileab (as well as Amnon) had already died. The timing of the death of Kileab (if that is a correct assumption) is, however, pure guesswork.*

2. *Nothing in the Biblical narrative indicates the extent to which Bathsheba was complicit in the act of adultery. There are no comments about her feelings or whether her bathing on the roof was a deliberate act to catch his attention. Scripture does, however, lay the blame clearly with David, and the emphasis of the text is solely on his actions and his guilt. Certainly, as king, it was he who wielded the power in the encounter and the main responsibility because of his position.*

3. *It is not clear how many knew of the adultery, but given the use of messengers and the presence of servants within the palace, it is difficult to*

imagine it going completely unnoticed, particularly given the likely general lack of privacy in those times. It has, therefore, been assumed that it was suspected and rumoured within the palace at least.

4. It is not clear if David's anger did actually flare up at news of his soldiers' deaths, as Joab had supposed it might (in 2 Samuel 11:19-21). Here it is assumed that it does, although that is not made explicit in the following verses (22-24).

5. The text gives no indication of how public Nathan's confrontation of David was. However, because of the public nature of the consequences of his sin (the death of Uriah and of other soldiers), it has been assumed that his sin was brought completely into the light and that he was not allowed to keep the façade of his righteousness intact. It is also not clear how long after the birth of the child Nathan confronts David. It has been assumed that it is soon after, given the nature of the judgment—that the child should die. Either way, it would still have been at least several months after David had married Bathsheba. It was decided to present Nathan's confrontation of David in the context of people's petitions, as this type of occasion is referenced in 2 Samuel 15:2 and described in 2 Samuel 14:4-22, where it is clear that others (in this case, Joab) are also present. There is no indication that David took the story as anything other than a true story, given the strength of his reaction: 'David burned with anger against the man' (2 Samuel 12:5).

6. It is surprising that, although it is God Himself who bestows the name 'Jedidah' (beloved of Yahweh) on Solomon, the name is only referred to once, and the text uses the name 'Solomon' everywhere else.

7. It is not clear how much time elapses after Nathan's word of judgment before Amnon rapes Tamar. Here it is assumed that it occurs roughly a year later.

8. The details in 2 Samuel 13:7-9 give a picture of women in the court who were able to cook, and who did not simply have a life of ease within the court.

8

David said, 'My son Solomon is young and inexperienced, and the house to be built for the LORD should be of great magnificence and fame and splendour in the sight of all nations. Therefore I will make preparations for it.' (1 Chronicles 22:5)

Abigail paused to catch her breath. *The steps to the roof were getting more taxing with each year that passed—and in only one year she would be three score and ten.* The heat of the day was not yet upon the city and spring was still to yield to the intensity of summer. She took a deep breath and continued her climb. David had slung a rope along the wall at her request and she held tight to it. The familiar sights of the palace rooftop eventually came into view. Here and there, servants were going about their tasks: washing garments or laying them out to dry in the sunlight; sitting mending clothes or sandals or bags where the light was good; rolling up bedding from where some had slept overnight under the stars. She nodded to some and spoke briefly to others, but was soon at her destination—the north side of the roof.

Beyond the northern wall of the City of David rose a small hill, its slightly flattened top clearly above the level of Jerusalem. Until the previous year, the site had belonged to a man named Araunah who had lived in the city before David took it. It was the perfect place for threshing grain, where nothing obstructed the breeze from the west and where the gentle evening winds could carry the chaff away from the grain. Looking at the hill then, it was hard for Abigail to quite believe that the angel of Yahweh Himself had been seen by David there—with the angel standing between heaven and earth, a drawn sword extended over the city. It had been Gad rather than Nathan who had brought the message of judgment for David's sin the year before. Gad had also, however, told him to build an altar on the threshing floor, and to offer sacrifices to stem the plague ravaging the land. Once more, it had been David's sin but others who had suffered—and yet David had felt the pain as if it were his own.

The same ink that had penned psalms of praise had once more been spilt across the papyrus scroll that was Israel, staining the sheet —and yet Yahweh had assimilated those stains, those blots, into His mysterious design. Out of David's sin with Bathsheba, Yahweh had blessed him with another son, Solomon—chosen by Yahweh to be not only his successor, but also the one who would build the temple. And now out of the census that even Joab had known to be wrong, Yahweh had led David—in the midst of the judgment that had followed—to the place where that temple would be built.

Abigail's gaze swept across the slope that rose before her—and soon found the man her eyes sought. David was unmistakable, surrounded by a number of masons, stonecutters and carpenters. Despite the increasing frailty that age had bestowed upon him, there was one matter that seemed to restore to him the vigour of his younger days. *He had once penned a psalm that spoke of Yahweh renewing one's strength to be like that of an eagle, soaring high above the earth.* It was that very thing that Abigail was witnessing, as David pointed, inspected and discussed, his frailties for the moment at least both forgotten and unseen.

She loved watching him making every preparation possible for the temple to be built by his son, whether that was preparing the site or gathering an abundance of materials—stone, cedar, gold, precious stones—or working on the designs for every aspect of the temple, inside and out. It was not uncommon for David to spend the greater part of a day in his room, poring over his plans. As he had told her with excitement one evening the previous year, Yahweh had only prohibited him from putting stone upon stone—He had not forbidden him from putting pen upon scroll.

Later that month, as the last of the sun's light was fading one day, Abigail made her way to David's room. She had caught sight of him earlier, and knew well the signs of the grief that he yet felt for the sons he had lost. She pushed open the door and went in. Abishag, the young woman who had been chosen to care for the king's daily needs, was removing a plate from before the king. The food appeared largely untouched. Abigail bowed low before the king. He smiled weakly. 'What is it you desire, Abigail?'

'My lord, I hear that your plans for the temple are soon to be completed. If you are not too weary, it would please me greatly if my lord the king could show them to your servant. But if you would rather, another day would be as good.'

He thought for a moment and then smiled more certainly. 'I will show you the plans.' Abishag hovered nearby as David rose to his feet. 'I would offer you a goblet of wine—' he began.

'And yet we both know it would be folly to do so, my lord, when spilt wine could so easily spoil that over which you have laboured so long.'

'Ah, Abigail! The years may have weakened both our bodies but they have not diminished your wisdom in any way.' As they approached a cedar wood table on which were piled numerous scrolls, he paused and turned to her. 'Do you know, you are my only wife who ever makes such requests.'

'Then the others are poorer for not doing so.'

He reached the table and cast his eyes over the scrolls, this way and that, as if he were surveying a banqueting table laden with choice delicacies and deciding which to savour first. He picked one up and opened it out until it was flat. Gone were the hasty drawings she had looked upon many years earlier. An elegant building graced the papyrus, its lines and proportions blending grandeur and beauty. Two columns with capitals like lilies rose majestically on either side of the imposing porch. As David began opening scroll after scroll, the weariness of grief seemed to lift, as mist dispersing in the warmth of a day. He suddenly seemed to brim with life. He showed her, with the zeal of a youth, pictures of decorative palm trees and open flowers to adorn the inner walls of the temple. 'And this,' he said, opening out another scroll, 'is for the priests to wash in.' It was an enormous bronze bath, supported on the backs of twelve oxen facing outwards to the north, west, south and east. He then showed her wheeled stands of bronze, with lions, oxen and cherubim decorating them.

'These are beautiful, my lord,' murmured Abigail.

'They should be,' replied David quietly. 'I believe they are from Yahweh Himself.'

'But you drew them, did you not, my lord?'

David was silent for a moment, as if searching for the right words, his eyes seemingly beholding some distant vista. 'It is as when a song comes to me. Sometimes I hear the melody in my head; sometimes it flows from my heart straight to the strings of my lyre. The words...' He broke off for a moment, deep in thought. 'They can be like a spring of water which can neither be stopped nor dammed. If you try, the water will soon burst forth with more urgency. At other times, it is an idea that bears down upon my heart and must be expressed, and I work to find the words that are sufficient to bear the truths that burn within me. Sometimes I return later and craft the words better; sometimes there is no need. So it is with these plans.'

His attention then returned to the table, and he cleared away all the scrolls save one. 'Here,' he said, his voice hushed as he unrolled the papyrus and placed weights at each corner, 'is where the ark will rest. No longer will it languish in a linen tent.'

Abigail stared down at the unfurled scroll. It was the design for the holy of holies at the heart of the temple. She had never gazed upon the ark of the covenant uncovered, and yet there it was before her, not in gold but in ink. Even a picture of the sacred chest, fashioned by craftsmen under Moses hundreds of years earlier, was enough to send a shiver through her. *The very presence of Yahweh Himself dwelt there!* The cherubim on the cover of the ark were themselves overshadowed by two further enormous cherubim in David's design, one standing either side of the ark. The wings of each of the strange creatures—part man, part beast—were stretched out on either side, one wing touching the wall of the room, the other wing touching that of the other cherub, over the centre of the ark.

'After the temple is dedicated,' murmured David, 'this will be a sight that none will see, save one. The Law of Moses tells us that it will be the high priest alone who enters the holy of holies, and only on the day that atonement is to be made for the people.'

'It is a sacred sight indeed, my lord, and I count myself fortunate to see it before me now.' She laid her hand upon his. 'Thank you.'

David's eyes did not leave the scroll, but their corners creased as a broad smile lit up his face.

Some days later, Abigail, accompanied by Mahlah, made her way from the palace down to Rachel's house. It had been some time since they had exchanged news, and they sat peacefully together in the courtyard, sharing stories from the royal household or the city, as they embroidered garments in the early afternoon sunshine. The good light was needed more than ever, with each woman's eyes not as keen as before.

'How is our lord the king, today?' asked Rachel, glancing up from her work.

'Ah, he is not so well,' said Abigail as she pulled her needle with its green thread through the neck of the tunic she was working on. 'He has taken to his bed again.'

'It saddens me to hear it—let us hope his strength will return soon. What of the rest of the royal household?'

Abigail tugged on the needle gently as the thread tangled itself. 'Eliada's wife has just borne him a fine son.'

'How she safely delivered a baby of such size I will never know,' laughed Mahlah. 'She is tiny!'

'What name has the child been given?' asked Rachel. But she never received her answer.

They all looked up when the door to the street outside was suddenly flung open. Rachel's husband stood framed in the doorway.

He did not enter the house, and others were clearly with him. 'You must all come to the palace—now!'

All three women rose to their feet. That something was wrong was not in any doubt. Both the urgency of Benaiah's words and his demeanour told them as much. 'What has happened?' asked Abigail as she reached the commander of David's guard.

He, like all of them, had aged and his dark hair and beard were amply streaked with grey, but his imposing figure and authority were unchanged. 'Adonijah is proclaiming himself king.'

Abigail glanced at her friends—both, like her, were aghast. It all felt sickeningly familiar.

'Is King David safe?'

Benaiah nodded, 'He is for the moment.' He gave no further explanation. 'Come now!' He then turned and began leading the women and the soldiers with him towards the palace.

Abigail had to hurry to keep up with his stride. 'Where is Adonijah then?'

He glanced back without slowing, his face grim. 'Just outside the city—at En Rogel. Joab and Abiathar and many of the king's household are with him.'

Abigail could scarcely believe what she had heard. 'Joab? Are you sure?'

Benaiah glanced back again. 'It is my job to know what happens in the city.'

'But does David know?'

'He should do by now. As soon as I heard, I sent a message ahead to Nathan. He will know what to do.' Benaiah fell silent and his stride seemed to lengthen. Abigail and the two other women were soon several paces behind him.

'Surely Adonijah knows that David intends to make Solomon king,' began Mahlah, her voice lowered.

'But Solomon is *not* king yet,' replied Abigail, somewhat breathlessly. 'Adonijah clearly believes, as Absalom did before him, that being David's eldest and being blessed with fine looks entitle him to be crowned king.'

Rachel shook her head. 'But while his father still lives? It is an outrage...'

Abigail thought for a moment. 'David is on his bed this day. Maybe Adonijah believes his father to be too frail to oppose him, particularly if he has persuaded Joab to support his cause.'

'My husband's loyalty and that of the guard will not waver, even if Joab's does!'

'I know that, Rachel.' But Abigail fell silent. Absalom's revolt had been six years earlier, but the memory of the battle was still fresh enough. A silent prayer rose within her. *O Yahweh, have mercy on us and on this city. Let not the sword be loosed once more within David's house and among Your people!*

'What of Solomon and Bathsheba?' asked Mahlah suddenly as the gates of the palace came into view. 'Surely their lives are in danger if Adonijah is seizing the throne!'

'Let us hope they are still safe within the palace walls,' answered Abigail between large gulps of air. 'And let us hope they have been warned.'

The palace felt eerily quiet. It soon became clear that all of the king's sons were with Adonijah—save Solomon—and that many of the men of Judah who served in the palace had also accompanied David's eldest. The women remained in the hall on the ground floor, seated on benches, both catching their breaths and waiting for the outcome of the meetings with David that they knew were occurring on the floor above. Abigail's lips moved as she silently voiced, again and again, her earlier prayer. She suddenly felt weary: weary of the seemingly never-ending struggle for power within David's household, and weary of the ways in which sin against the Almighty continually blighted their lives.

Eventually, the silence was broken by the sound of approaching feet. Abigail stood as Benaiah returned, accompanied this time by a number whose presence was noteworthy: Nathan and Zadok—prophet and priest of Yahweh—Bathsheba, and Solomon himself. Abigail bowed as the king's son approached and then swept passed.

Benaiah paused briefly. 'The king has commanded that Solomon be anointed king of Israel,' he said in a lowered voice, 'and that he should both ride on the king's own mule and sit on his throne this very day. Will you come with us, Abigail?'

Their flight back to the palace had already drained her, and her aching bones provided the answer. 'May the king's son excuse me, but I do not have the strength. I wish him Yahweh's blessing and will pray that no blood is shed this day.'

Benaiah glanced at the others, now some paces ahead of him. 'Very well. I will pass your good wishes to the king's son, and may your prayer be heard by the Almighty.' And with that, he was gone.

Mahlah and Rachel remained with Abigail. She sat down again on the bench and sighed. 'He will need more than my good wishes if the plans of Adonijah—and Joab—are to come to naught. May Yahweh be merciful to us, for my lord the king does not have the strength to flee another son rising against him.'

Abigail's prayers were unceasing, like the waters of the Jordan, her spirit far stronger than her aging body. When the palace remained quiet, save for the sounds of joy that had begun to drift in from the streets of Jerusalem, Abigail dared to hope that her petitions might have been answered. *Could it be that Yahweh had somehow thwarted Adonijah and those with him—as suddenly and completely as He had driven back the waters of the Sea of Reeds before Moses?*

By the end of the day, she knew her prayers had been heard, and that the sword of judgment, on this occasion at least, had remained sheathed.

Jerusalem had rejoiced in Solomon's anointing and Adonijah had fled to seek refuge at the altar of Yahweh in the tabernacle at Gibeon—only to be brought back to the city when Solomon swore he would be allowed to live. Abigail doubted that Adonijah, had he prevailed, would have offered the same clemency to his brother.

That night, in her area within the women's quarters, Abigail gave thanks to the God of Israel, but before finally yielding to sleep, she uttered one final prayer: *O Yahweh, great God of Israel, please now allow Your servant David to finish his remaining days in peace.*

Soon after, David charged Solomon with the sacred duty of building the temple, though that did not stop him making further preparations.

In a rare conversation with Bathsheba one evening, when they both found themselves enjoying the coolness of the roof after the heat of the day, Bathsheba shook her head, as if in disbelief. 'It is a wonder that King David still finds strength to do all he does.' All were slowly getting used to having to make clear which king was being referred to. Abigail gave a little laugh. 'Why do you smile?'

'It is the temple that puts new life into his bones. I have seen it before.' She paused. 'No, that is wrong. It is the power of Yahweh Himself that runs through him as he makes his plans.'

'It is as well that David is so thorough. Solomon is not yet twenty, but the day may soon come when he stands alone. I am grateful that he is being fully prepared for the task that will face him.'

Abigail's gaze drifted northwards, to the raised site on which the temple would stand. 'What has the king—King David—been labouring over in recent days?'

Bathsheba shook her head again. 'There is so much my son tells me of what his father is doing: appointing gatekeepers and singers for the temple and arranging them into groups; commanding new instruments to be made for giving praise; dividing the priests into twenty-four divisions for ministering before Yahweh.' She paused for a moment. 'In truth, there is more, but I cannot remember all the details, for they are many.'

'I cannot blame you for that. As the days left to me on this earth shorten, so does my memory.' They both laughed, but as silence fell again between them, Abigail was sure of one thing: *there was much in her life that would be etched deeply upon her memory until her dying day.*

The deep sigh made Abigail's whole body shudder. *She had known she would likely see this day, but that did not make it easy.* She repeated the words she had spoken so often. 'Thank you for letting me know, Mahlah.'

'I knew you would want to hear straight away. Abishag said that the king spoke with Solomon, and that Bathsheba was with them, and then he simply closed his eyes and breathed his last.' Mahlah paused. 'Is there anything I can do for you, dear friend?'

'I need nothing beyond your company.'

'Then I will sit with you…'

As they sat in silence together, with Abigail's hand in that of Mahlah, the muted sounds of mourning for King David began to fill the corridors of the palace beyond the closed door of the room. Further deep sighs racked Abigail's body and tears slipped silently down her cheeks as she began to grieve for the man who had been her husband for forty-five years. She cast her mind back over the journey she had shared with him since that first meeting in a narrow ravine when she had still been Nabal's wife. *Danger and triumph, joys and sorrows, blessing and judgment. They had all been part of her life with David. And yet through it all, Yahweh had been as a rock—the unmoving foundation beneath their lives. Yes, David had faced the stern judgment of the God of Israel more than once, and yet had not Yahweh been faithful to His promise of blessing despite that?* With her own eyes and not much more than a month earlier, Abigail had witnessed a ceremony not unlike the one when David himself had been crowned king over all Israel. Once again, it was to mark a new era, as the aging king—before a huge assembly—handed to his son the plans for the temple and charged him to walk faithfully before their God and complete the work that was being entrusted to him. Then, for a second and less-hasty time, Solomon had been anointed king over Yahweh's people. *It had been a glorious gathering, overflowing with praise and sacrifices to the God of Israel. Was that not indeed a fitting end to David's life?*

The tears ebbed and flowed throughout the day with the memories, and although she had no hunger, she did accept a cup of wine from Mahlah's hand. As the afternoon lengthened, she joined the procession that took the body of David to its resting place within Jerusalem, with flutes and harps playing laments as they walked the short distance to where his body was laid. The palace felt strangely empty when they returned, knowing that David was no longer there.

The light was beginning to fade as Abigail walked quietly through the hall, Mahlah at her side. A sudden urge welled up within her. She turned to her friend. 'Mahlah—there is yet one thing you can do for me.'

'Speak, Abigail, and it will be done.'

'Heman—see if you can find him and if he will come to me. Ask him to meet me in David's room. He cannot be far away—he was one of those singing the lament in the procession. Ask one of the Levites to find him if you can't.'

'I will be as quick as I can.' She hurried off.

Abigail made her way up the stairs and pushed open the carved cedar door to David's room. She asked one of the servants nearby to light the lamps in the room. The pink in the sky visible through the window was beginning to fade. She sat down and looked around her, taking in the familiar sights: the table and the chairs, the ornate carvings and the soft cushions, the silver jug and cups and the colourful hangings on the walls. The richly embroidered bedcover was neatly arranged over the place where David had lain so recently. *Abishag had tidied the room well. No signs of death remained.* She began praying quietly and with deep gratitude to the God she had known since she was a girl. She remembered the morning after she and David had been wed, and the words that David had been singing as she awoke: *Taste and see that Yahweh is good. She had done so. He was indeed good.*

She wasn't sure how long she had been waiting—only that the sky outside was dark by the time she heard a soft knock on the door. Mahlah entered with Heman. *No-one knew the psalms of David as he did—unless it was Asaph, his fellow Levite.*

Heman bowed to her. 'How can I serve you this night?'

Abigail smiled and rose. She did not answer immediately but crossed the room. *She knew where to look.* David's lyre was where it had always been—near his bed. She gently lifted the instrument, as if it were sacred, and held it out towards Heman. 'Play me one of David's psalms.'

A look of understanding dawned on the Levite's face and he smiled. 'Gladly.' All three sat down together on carved chairs near David's table. Heman ran his fingers over the ten strings, listening carefully, and tuning the instrument as he went. Eventually, when he seemed satisfied that it would play true, he looked up. 'Which psalm do you desire?'

Abigail did not hesitate. 'The Shepherd Song.'

Heman smiled again. 'You have chosen well. My voice has sung many laments this day, but we will find comfort in its words.'

'It flowed from his heart,' said Abigail simply. 'He knew the words to be true.'

Heman paused and then started to strum the lyre, his fingers soon picking out a beautiful melody that was a balm to Abigail's soul. He began to sing.

'Yahweh is my shepherd, therefore I lack nothing.
He makes me lie down in green pastures,
He leads me beside quiet waters,
He refreshes my soul.
He guides me along the right paths
for His name's sake.'

As Heman's voice fell silent to allow the lyre's sweet music to fill the room, Abigail marvelled afresh at the care and love of the Almighty—that He could be as a shepherd, caring for a single sheep and graciously meeting all of its needs. *He had done that not only for David but for her as well. It was her song as much as his.* She stilled her heart as familiar words began to flow from Heman's lips once more.

'Even though I walk through the darkest valley,
I will fear no evil, for You are with me;
Your rod and Your staff,
they comfort me.'

Once again, Heman's voice gave way to the lyre—and Abigail cast her mind back over the years. *Many swords had been drawn against David and he'd journeyed through many dark valleys, right from the time the oil from Samuel's horn had flowed down upon his head. And yet Yahweh had brought him through each vale, whether the darkness had been caused by Saul's heart or his own.* But her weary and bruised spirit also soared. *You are with me.* She knew she could again sing those words herself.

Tumbling notes of joy blended once more with the Levite's rich voice, as he sang the final words of the psalm:

'You prepare a table before me
in the presence of my enemies.
You anoint my head with oil;
my cup overflows.
Surely Your goodness and love will follow me
all the days of my life,
and I will dwell in the house of Yahweh
for ever.'

After a final flourish, the lyre at last fell silent. No-one spoke. Abigail's tears were flowing once more, springing not from grief this time, but from wonder at the tender mercy of the God who had caused her own cup to overflow. *'I will dwell in the house of Yahweh for ever,'* she suddenly whispered. 'David did not build the temple for Yahweh as he longed to—but what does that matter if he now dwells in Yahweh's own house?'

'The Creator's truths always bring light to our darkness,' said Heman softly, rising to his feet and then returning the lyre to its place. 'May His peace be upon you both this night.'

'Thank you, Heman—you have served us well. Yahweh bless you.'

As Heman left them, Abigail stood and made her way to the open window. *The steps to the roof were a mountain not to be attempted when her body was so drained.* Here and there, the light of lamps flickered in the dwellings of the city. *Jerusalem was now Solomon's to rule alone.* Her mind drifted from the past to the future, and she wondered how long it would be until the ark no longer dwelt in a tent of fine linen. 'Ah, Mahlah, I fear my eyes, like those of David, will not look upon the finished temple. But I have seen its plans and that is enough.' Her eyes drifted upwards. 'The Almighty granted David three score years and ten. He has already blessed me with one more than that. But whatever Yahweh in His wisdom grants me, I will thank Him.' Her mind returned to the words of David's psalm. 'I know His goodness and love will follow me until I draw my last breath.'

Mahlah laid her hand gently on Abigail's arm. 'I cannot bear to think of that day...'

Abigail turned her face towards her. 'Yahweh always gives us strength to bear whatever He sends.' She smiled. 'How well He has taught me that!' Her gaze returned to the night sky, and once more she murmured the final words that Heman had sung. *'I will dwell in the house of Yahweh forever.'* She had lived in the safety of her mother's home, in the dwelling of a wealthy but foolish man, in danger in caves and tents, in a foreign city and finally the palace of a king. A question rose unbidden in her mind. *Yahweh's anointed would surely be welcome in the courts of the Almighty, but would she be?* The thought troubled her for only a moment before peace filled her weary heart. *If a young shepherd boy who put His trust in Yahweh was welcome, then so was an elderly widow who did the same!* She smiled. 'Mahlah, I believe I could manage a little food.'

'Then let us find some sustenance for you.' Mahlah took Abigail's arm in hers as they made their way across the room.

Abigail paused as they reached the cedar doors. She turned, her gaze lingering on the king's chamber for one last time. *Tomorrow it would be Solomon's, but for tonight, it was still David's room.* Her heart whispered a simple prayer of thanks, and she closed the door behind her.

Notes

1. *The timings and order of the events in this chapter (David's census, Adonijah proclaiming himself king, David entrusting the plans to Solomon and Solomon being proclaimed king for a second time) cannot be easily determined. This is partly because of an absence of specific timings in Scripture, but also because of the somewhat different accounts in 1 Kings 1-2 and 1 Chronicles 22-29. The Chronicler states that he has used a number of accounts to write of the life of David (1 Chronicles 29:29-30). This re-telling has attempted to weave together details from both Biblical books.*

2. There are some intriguing questions concerning the census recorded in 2 Samuel 24 and 1 Chronicles 21. 2 Samuel 24:1 states: 'Again the anger of the LORD burned against Israel, and he incited David against them, saying, "Go and take a census of Israel and Judah."' It is not clear what the sin of Israel had been or why the census was such a heinous sin. The census does, however, explain the location of the temple. (Araunah, the owner of the site to the north of the city, has been identified by some as the former Jebusite governor of the city.)

3. It has been assumed, given the reference to a pen in psalm 45 (possibly written at the time of Solomon), that pen and ink were in use at this time.

4. In the surrounding culture of the day, there was a policy of new kings getting rid of rivals who might have a claim on the throne. Hence the danger that both Solomon and Bathsheba were in after Adonijah proclaimed himself king.

5. It is not clear how old Solomon was when he became king, but the chronology that has been used for this story assumes that David was around fifty when he committed adultery with Bathsheba, and hence Solomon would have still been under (although close to) twenty when David died, aged seventy, with the co-regency occurring for possibly anything from a few months to the last two years of David's life.

6. Scripture clearly states in 1 Chronicles 28:12,19 that the Spirit had put into David's mind the plans 'for the courts of the temple of the LORD and all the surrounding rooms, for the treasuries of the temple of God and for the treasuries for the dedicated things… "All this," David said, "I have in writing as a result of the LORD's hand on me, and he enabled me to understand all the details of the plan."' However, the process of inspiration, as for the psalms, is not clear. What is described in this chapter is a 'best guess'.

7. When it states that Adonijah fled to take hold of the horns of the altar (1 Kings 1:50), it is assumed that this is at Gibeon from the detail given in 1 Kings 3:4, when Solomon sacrifices on the altar there. Gibeon was around ten miles or less from Jerusalem, and it could be assumed that what remained of the tabernacle was moved from Nob to Gibeon (its location during David's reign, according to 1 Chronicles 16:39) after Saul's slaughter of the priests.

Bibliography

Books

A. A. Anderson, *Word Biblical Commentary – 2 Samuel*, (Word, 1989).

Clive Anderson, Brian Edwards, *Evidence for the Bible*, (Day One Publications, 2013).

John A. Beck, *Everyday Life in Bible Times*, (Baker Books, 2013).

Daniel I. Block, *Judges, Ruth (New American Commentary)*, (Holman Reference, 1999).

Daniel I. Block, *Ruth: The King is Coming*, (Zondervan, 2015).

R. E. Clements, *Deuteronomy* (JSOT Press, 1989).

R. Alan Cole, *Exodus* (IVP, 1973).

Arthur E. Cundall and Leon Morris, *Judges and Ruth* (IVP, 1968).

John D. Currid & David P. Barrett, *ESV Bible Atlas*, (Crossway, 2010).

Dave Ralph Davis, *1 Kings: The Wisdom and the Folly* (Christian Focus, 2008).

Dave Ralph Davis, *1 Samuel: Looking on the Heart* (Christian Focus, 2010).

Dave Ralph Davis, *2 Samuel: Out of Every Adversity* (Christian Focus, 2009).

Dave Ralph Davis, *Joshua: No Falling Words* (Christian Focus, 2010).

Dale Ralph Davis, *Judges: Such a Great Salvation* (Christian Focus, 2015).

J. D. Douglas (Ed.), *The Illustrated Bible Dictionary,* (IVP, 1988).

R. K. Harrison, *Leviticus* (IVP, 1980).

E. W. Heaton, *Everyday Life in Old Testament Times*, (Batsford, 1966).

Gordon J. Keddie, *According to Promise* (Evangelical Press, 2007).

K. A. Kitchen, *On the Reliability of the Old Testament*, (Eerdmans, 2006).

Ralph W. Klein, *Word Biblical Commentary – 1 Samuel*, (Word, 1983).

A. Boyd Luter & Barry C. Davis, *Ruth & Esther: God Behind the Seen*, (Christian Focus, 1995).

Lorna Oakes, Philip Steele, *Everyday Life in Ancient Egypt &*

Mesopotamia, (Southwater, 2005).

Nick Page, *The One-Stop Bible Atlas*, (Lion Hudson, 2010).

Nick Page, *Whatever Happened to the Ark of the Covenant?*, (Authentic Media, 2009).

Daniel C. Snell, *A Companion to the Ancient Near East*, (Wiley-Blackwell, 2007).

Chris Sinkinson, *Time Travel through the Old Testament*, (IVP, 2013).

J. A. Thompson, *Deuteronomy* (IVP, 1974).

J. A. Thompson, *Handbook of Life in Bible Times*, (IVP, 1986).

John H. Walton, Victor H. Matthews, Mark W. Chavalas, *The IVP Bible Background Commentary – Old Testament,* (IVP, 2000).

Gordon J. Wenham, *Numbers,* (IVP, 1990).

Various authors, *Explore Bible Notes,* The Good Book Company.

In addition to the above publications, numerous online articles have also been used, which are too many and varied to list. The subjects and titles have, for example, included: Amenhotep II and the historicity of the Exodus Pharaoh; the flooding of the Nile and the Egyptian calendar; Exodus routes and conquest theories; literacy in the ancient Near East; ancient grain stores; the agricultural cycle for barley; ancient brick-making in Egypt; the birth of the alphabet; archaeological discoveries at Perunefer; the use of papyrus and ink in ancient writing; clothing in Old Testament times; goat-keeping; chronologies for the judges, Saul and David—and how to use a sling.